Antioch

The Circle, Part One

William E. Harlan

ISBN 978-1482099973

For Carrie, thank you so much.

Contents

1 Paladin

Ares complained when Michael reined him in. The white stallion neighed and stamped, water bursting from the cobblestones at his hooves. He made a deafening clatter.

Michael steadied in the saddle, searching the cottages up ahead. He'd ridden through a terrible storm, hoping to arrive before the plague, but the old coastal town of Meroe was as still and quiet as a graveyard. Then, drawn out by the sound of Michael's mount, a shadow of life emerged from between the buildings.

The shade limped toward horse and rider in a slow, determined line. More of its kind followed out of the alleys, doorways and broken windows of the broken town. They lurched and crawled like injured soldiers. They smelled like rotten corpses on the wind. Michael stopped counting heads at twenty-four, with still more of them coming. He'd have to cut them all down before he could start looking for survivors.

He swung over to dismount, landing with a muffled clink of heavy chainmail and leather armor, and then from Ares' flank took his weapon, a huge sword sheathed in lacquered ash, his caligan. Its wide, double edge glinted as it slid from its scabbard's throat. In the ancient and sacred script of Michael's order, the Circle, four vows etched the caligan's fuller: Silence, Obedience, Chastity and Poverty. Five and a half feet from point to pommel, the handle almost as long as the blade, it weighed thirteen cleaving pounds of steel. It was a devil-slayer's weapon, built for slaughter more than swordsmanship.

Michael placed its polished case on the cobblestones and stepped away to wait for the coming of Meroe's dead. He would face them out there, on the road, to avoid attracting any more than his horse already had. Ares trotted off into the vast, coastal heath.

They came silently except for the brush of their decaying flesh and clothes. The nearest reached out for Michael, despite the distance, grasping for him desperately with its left hand. Its right arm had been torn out of the socket. Its skin was a pallid bag, swinging loose over the bones and muscles underneath. Smoke trailed gray out of its slack mouth, like it had a coal fire in its chest, and its eyes glittered like black glass.

Michael raised his weapon and waited. Then, concentrating… *he opened the way out of the world*. A power he knew as riin, something natural to all living things, blasted into his body in an unnatural amount, giving him unnatural strength - enough to send his heavy edge through a ten-inch pine in one stroke.

The ghoul came right at him. Michael struck and split it from collar to hip with the short sound of a butcher at the block - *whock*. Its head and shoulder spun away, spraying a strange, black ink from its spine. Gray clouds rolled out of its opened lungs. Its greater half was a stumbling fountain.

Michael held his breath. The ghoul's smoke seared into his eyes as it flowed over him. It was a contagion, the most rapacious by far he'd ever felt, and it took burning root in any opening of the skin. Even so, riin gave Michael more than strength; it healed and drove affliction from the body, glowing with a brilliant, aurous light wherever it did so. His eyes started to blaze like golden gateways to another realm.

Michael strode to the next ghoul and cut it in half with an upward stroke that mirrored his first. Again and again his caligan passed in swift, unbroken arcs through their fetid flesh and bone; again and again and again, until corpses littered the path in piles, spilling their disease into the air and their ink onto the stones.

The wind above the road became a river of smoke. Michael stepped out of it into the tall, wet heath to breathe. The ink marred his habit by then, having splashed across his high-collared, white tabard and the golden circle embroidered at his chest. It was dirty work. He noticed a ghoul harassing his horse nearby and turned to watch, concerned.

It was no more than a clumsy child to the mighty Ares, though. He scooted away with an irritated snort and a short burst of speed. It persisted, pawing once again at the horse's brawny haunches and causing another brief dash. Then, the third time it came up behind him, Ares lost patience and kicked it in the groin. The ghoul left its feet, rotating through the air, ejecting feculence.

Michael was reassured, but he'd also been distracted. A one-eyed, legless fiend had crawled on its belly through the mud, reached up its flayed hand from the weeds and grabbed him. He looked down just as it was lifting its mouth to his leg.

He blurted out, "God's Mercy!" and hopped away on one foot, trying to kick out of its grip. It was surprisingly strong. In that moment, in that brief lapse of awareness, Michael backed right into the full mass of the others. His strength was no match for their overwhelming numbers. They dragged him down, burying him in their writhing grasp.

Though protected by his thick, leather gauntlets, he yanked his fingers away from the crushing pressure of their teeth. He dropped his sword. Their bites could not break his mail, but still pinched and ripped his skin within the links. In the darkness of the squelching heap Michael's glowing eyes lit a crooked face that gnashed and snapped just inches from his own, held back only by the selfish effort of the others.

Out on the heath, a peaceful sea breeze flowed over the low, green leaves and tousled Ares' mane. He tossed his head and stamped the earth like a playful cloud that had left the wide, blue sky to take conquering form on the ground. He worried over nothing. The ghoul he'd kicked dragged its shattered hips through the bushes somewhere.

Under the weight of the pile, Michael's chest felt about to collapse. His lungs seized and threatened to breathe as blind, disintegrating fingers groped his head. He wasn't finished yet, though. He shoved and wormed, pushing with his elbows and heels into the mud until he could turn. Then he wrenched onto his stomach and scrambled out of the mound.

Michael ran until the light left his eyes - then he gasped for air. Though he could heal the infection, he still needed to breathe and he couldn't do that if the smoke clogged his lungs. The air was sweet. Any air was better than none, but he'd been in the ghouls' stink for so long he couldn't smell it anymore. Behind him, they crawled over each other in slow pursuit. He wanted to lead them away from there. He started jogging through the muddy grass.

Ares clopped up beside him, easily matching the man's speed, and, seeing the running as a game, gave him a little bump. That was how Ares liked to play. Michael didn't see it coming and got knocked flat on his face into the mud again. He jumped up furious, slinging filth and shouting, "No! Bad! That's a bad horse, Ares! Go away!" The animal obeyed, pitching up turf in a sprint.

Michael cast an angry glance back at the ghouls. They were far behind. He resumed his long, circular path, returning to where they'd brought him down. Once there, he searched the flattened plants for his sword and found it reflecting the sun.

With his caligan's weight in hand again, Michael met the gang of ghouls and gave ground, swinging like a reaper. Rotten limbs and pieces shot from his humming blade's path. He moved in a backward circle, keeping them in the sword's arc until none of them was capable of following him. Then he retraced his steps and destroyed the ones he'd merely crippled, making sure to bleed the ink out of their spines.

* * *

The road was a line of pebbled mortar in the wild, worn more by weather than use. Smoke still spilled sideways from the corpses farther south when Michael returned from the heath.

His scabbard's bright polish and steel were in stark contrast with the rest of him then. His once white tabard, with its high collar and golden embroidery, was a pair of torn and gore-soaked rat tails, dripping under the front and back of his belt. A jigsaw of cracking mud plates coated his mail and his caligan glistened with the ghouls' ink. He tried cleaning the blade with his filthy garment and then on the muddy grass beside the road, but merely traded muck for muck. Refusing to put the sword into its case that way, he left it unsheathed.

A rustling in the heath caught his attention. The one-eyed, legless fiend had found him again, that half of a ghoul that had caused him so much trouble. Slower than the others, it had survived the greater destruction and was scrabbling onto the road by itself. Michael narrowed his eyes on it and stepped forward. Then he raised his heavy boot and stomped the ghoul's head into the cobblestones. It splattered, like a black-gut walnut under a hammer, and the corpse went still.

Michael stood there, examining it, imagining that monster's final moments as a man; what horrors he must have gone through before the plague had claimed him. Out of respect for the dead, Michael put down his weapon and knelt. It had been more than thirty years since he'd last prayed. He didn't know if it would make a difference but there was something his father always said at funerals that seemed… *right* to say. He mouthed the words first, assembling them from his memory:

"Please, God, allow these souls peace and rest,"
"By your side, in your light,"
"Amen."

Ares snorted. Michael looked at him, thinking about the way forward. The town's narrow lanes would be filled with restless dead. Though unthreatened out in the open, his proud, white stallion could be cornered and overwhelmed in there. Michael went to him, unbuckled the saddle's girth and left Ares unbridled. The horse could find his way home. Then, picking up his caligan again, and almost sheathing it before he caught himself, Michael walked into Meroe.

2 Homestead

A storm gathered in the south as John rode up the farmhouse path. On his pinto filly, he sat head and shoulders over the rusty plants on either side. His hair waved long and iron-gray below his baldness. He was sixty-four years old, paunchy, and his white tabard's golden circle sparkled in the sun. Far before the house, the horse whined and slowed on its own.

John patted her neck. "Shh, there's a good girl. Don't run. Easy..." He noticed distinct movement in the crops' tops, about fifty yards out. Clucking at his nervous filly and scratching her mane, he reached down and lifted his caligan from the saddle.

"Alright, I'll walk." He landed with a solid thump on the dry dirt road. The horse pulled against the reins, already backing up. John let go and his eyebrows went up in surprise. She wrenched over backwards and bolted away in a cloud of dust. "Oh, well, that's fine. At least you let me get down first this time..."

The field towered over him in two walls of stalks to make a brown, windless corridor. Withering leaves hung from those lengths like dead tongues. John buckled his scabbard's belt around his waist and called out, "Horace?"

He heard something coming. Drawing the long-handled sword, he called out again, "Horace?" Then he raised it with a form almost identical to Michael's and opened the way, ready to strike. Horace would have answered him by then. Any person should have answered him by then. The plants opened and John was shocked.

A small girl, no more than five years old, hobbled from the field. Blood clotted in her clothes and hair as though she'd taken a swim in it days before. She trailed smoke like a breathless fire. One leg took her weight and wagging steps with its thigh-bone's

7

broken ends in the meat like climbing spikes. John just stood there as she came, watched her take hold of his leg and bite into the chain. Between his armor and her unnatural strength, her tiny teeth cracked.

He came to his senses, cursed, "Fwah!" and sheathed his weapon. He unfastened a gauntlet from his sleeve and put his naked hand on the little ghoul's forehead. His ring finger was missing. She ignored his touch and continued gnawing, the splinters of her teeth snapping in the pulp. The gruesome grinding and popping sounds made it difficult for John to concentrate. He was trying to open the way in her, but he couldn't find it. She was empty. "What is this? I don't understand."

His eyes began to water and then to burn. He reeled back, choking and coughing, having taken a full breath of the smoke that had collected around him without the wind to blow it away. Golden light burst from his eyes, nose and mouth and his throat glowed red from within. He stumbled out of the lingering haze with the monstrous child still clinging to his leg.

In the clean air, the light faded from his face. The decision was hard but quick. John drew his caligan again. With his bare hand on the grip and his armored hand on the blade, he placed an edge against the back of her small neck. She ignored what was coming just as she had ignored his healing touch. He pulled until the edge bit metal. She collapsed, decapitated.

John turned away and flung his caligan into the ground. He stood muttering and shaking his head as he refastened the gauntlet. He hadn't come home to the farm in more than eighteen years. He didn't know who the little girl had been, who she'd been to Horace... who she might have been to him. Without looking at the body, he snatched up his filthy cleaver, shoved it into the scabbard and started jogging toward the farmhouse.

The old building's thatched roof showed over the plants before the corridor opened into the front yard. The door was ajar. A tilted, wooden cart, piled with hay, blocked John's view of the adjacent barn. The wind in the yard, cool from the coming storm, had a savage stench. The boots of a man on his back stuck out from behind the cart.

John hurried around and found a slender corpse. A garden spade was driven into the earth just above the lower jaw. The rest of the head was gone. Bulbous, black flies boiled in the smoke between the blade and the throat. A wide, dark stain surrounded the wound on the ground and an intermittent pattern of ink led from there to the barn.

John didn't recognize the body. Trying to make sense of the scene, he thought, *Horace wouldn't have been so slight. No, he'd have been the one with the shovel.* He shouted, "Horace!" and waited, listening to the field and the flies. *If Horace did this, he'd have taken in the sickness.* John could only guess at how long a man could withstand the smoke without being able to open the way.

He followed the black trail through the barn's gate, where the wind died and dust hovered in slanted sunlight. There, a thirty yard toss from the body, on its cheeks and teeth beneath a bench, the severed head seethed with insects. Dull, gray eyes stared from the scuttle. John's mouth was dry when he tapped it with his fingers to chase the bugs away.

It wasn't Horace. He looked around. Dark little footprints nearby became more defined as they walked backwards into a broad pool of dried blood where a dead pig was tied by a rope around its neck to the slaughter post. The animal had been bled, but not by any method John knew. Its skin was torn open in sheets.

Flies lifted from the carcass when John approached. He found a funnel, a long knife and a pail on the shelf above. They were clean and sharp, ready for a blood-letting. He put them down and headed for the farmhouse.

The front door screeched under the weight of its planks. It was dim, cool and quiet inside. John shouted, "Horace!" over and over as he searched the old house, the house that had once belonged to him. He was afraid of what he'd find behind each door that he opened. There was a man's room with the mounted skull of a giant elk. Antlers spanned twelve feet from wall to wall. There was a boy's room with a bit of fishing tackle and then, saddest of all, a girl's room with a ragdoll and some little dresses. He went into the kitchen.

The back door's light cut the silent, windowless space in two. It was a disaster. Clay jugs and jars had been smashed everywhere. The table had been overturned against the fireplace. Clumsy tracks sketched through the flour, soot and blood that caked the floor. He saw little footprints again and also a much larger set made by a very large man. Those led outside, passed a raised, stone well and headed into the woods behind the house. John followed them, still calling his son's name.

3 Breahg and Bauran

His father struck him hard in the mouth and Daniel tumbled out of the kitchen into the night. From his hands and knees in the dirt Daniel screamed, "I hate you!" Tears, blood and spit trembled from his lips with the words. "I hate you!" He stood, wobbling like a frog on its hind legs, and then stumbled over to the well for protection, peering out from behind the winch.

Horace stepped into the doorway, six foot-three, three hundred and fifty pounds of muscle, fat and hair. His mass eclipsed the kitchen's light, returning the back yard to darkness. He paused there to put the small hole of his pot-jug deep in his beard and took a good swig of huckleberry whiskey. Then he started circling the well. Daniel scurried to keep it between them.

Horace spoke in a friendly tone but had murder in his eyes. "Come on, boy, don't stop there! If we're gonna get dirty, let's get filthy."

A small shadow appeared in the light of the doorway. "Papa, Papa, don't kill Danny!"

Horace slowed his menacing orbit to turn and offer a moment of drunken parental guidance. "Becca, I'm not about to kill him. Danny needs a spanky. Go to bed."

Rebecca immediately forgot about her brother's life. "Aaaw... but it's my biiirthdaaay... You said I don't have tooo..."

Horace threw his hands up into the air at her whining, spilling whiskey on himself and roaring all of his words into one. "*DannyneedsaspankyBeccagotobedAAAAAAH!*"

She vanished.

When Horace turned back, his son was sprinting away. Daniel disappeared into the woods at the end of the warm strip of firelight the kitchen cast across the yard. Horace stood there for a

11

long time, watching that spot in the trees and drinking from his jug.

Daniel's pace slowed after a hard minute. The cool air burned in his thumping chest. Glaring back through the moonlit trees, he realized his father wasn't following. He touched his throbbing mouth, tasted a split lip and clenched his fists. "Fwah!" Then he kicked the ground and shouted, "Fwaaah!" Before long he'd worked himself into a screaming, hopping and stomping fit.

Two, rugged miles into the woods from the farm was a very large, old oak. On one side of its gargantuan trunk, a rotten platform rested in the thick, chaotic branches. A rope wound around a bough above a hole in the platform's center and descended in a straight line to the forest floor. There the tree's huge, knuckled roots made seats for a dormant campfire's circle of stones.

Daniel moped through the gloom to the tree, inched up the rope and then climbed through the hole. The rope slithered up behind him. He lay down and frowned up at a starless blanket of leaves. "Fwah."

His fishing knife's handle was an annoying lump under his back. He snatched at it, nicking his fingers on the blade, cursed and jerked his hand away, smacking his fishing pole. He looked up with a bug-eyed scowl just in time for the toppling rod to thwack him in the face.

Daniel exploded. The poor pole bounced around in his flailing rage until it clattered from the platform. He sprang to his feet, quivering and screaming. Then he started punching the oak, slamming his fists bloody against the jagged bark.

* * *

Horace stepped into Daniel's room the next morning, sober, a huge man in a boy's empty space. Rebecca came up behind him, dragging her blanket and peeking around. She was no bigger than one of her father's arms.

"Papa, did you killed Danny?"

Horace had mixed regrets. "No. He's run off to the tree house again, I guess."

"Cause you give him a spanky?"

"Becca, stay inside today."

"Aw…"

"I don't want you outside without brother."

"Aaaw..."

"Keep it up. *You'll* get a spanky."

She vanished.

For two days Horace made Rebecca stay inside while he worked the farm. It was the longest Daniel had ever held out but Horace refused to go after him, feeling the boy should pay for his pride with hunger and loneliness. On the third morning, after much of her moaning, Horace let Rebecca out on her own, making her promise to stay close enough to hear him when he called.

Wind whipped through the tops of the plants but not where she sat in the dew at the base of the stalks. Rebecca loved playing in the field. She was frightened of the woods and never went there, but the field was safe. She had two animal-shaped carvings Daniel made for her. Trotting one through the air, she sang, "Cow, cow, cow, cow." Then the other reared back. "Hooorse! Hooorse!" It was a repetitive little song and she really belted it out on the horse's turn.

The barn shuddered and groaned in the wind. Horace led the pig into it on a rope. The garden spade rested on his meaty shoulder. At the back end of the building's eerie shelter, he looped the pig's noose over the slaughter post. He and the animal considered each other for a moment from where they stood.

Horace said, "I've a pigheaded boy, you know." It was a conversational observation.

The pig oinked.

Horace scratched it between the ears. "Can't put any more chores on hold waiting for him. I guess I just need a body to hold the funnel. Becca's old enough for a little blood."

Horace left the barn, his clothes fluttering in the wind outside. He frowned at the sun's position in the sky. He'd lost track of time. Dropping the spade next to the hay cart, he tied back his long, black hair. Then he put his fingers to his lips and let out a shrieking whistle. "Becca!" He released another piercing blast. "Becca! Come help Papa!"

The crops jostled across the way and he smiled, but a lanky man tore into view, not his daughter. The man was familiar, last summer's farmhand. "Oaky? What are you doing here?" Oaky didn't answer or slow his charge. It puzzled Horace. After the harvest, Oaky had gone home to Meroe on good terms and they'd made plans for his return, but not so soon.

Horace repeated himself. Then he reared up with an angry frown. As a younger man, he'd been an elk rider in Clan Breahg. Oaky was asking for a beating, charging at *him* like that. Horace stomped on the tip of his garden spade. It jumped into his hand.

Horace leapt aside at the last moment and rammed the spade's handle into Oaky's middle, folding him over the force of the blow. In the same deft motion, he swung one leg behind Oaky's knees, slammed him to the ground and stepped on his chest. The former farmhand heaved smoke into the wind like a wicked bellows. That, the unnatural strength, the eyes; Horace gawked at what he'd pinned. "What's happened to you?"

The ghoul pitched and kicked beneath the big man's weight like a beetle on its back, its skeleton lancing out of its flesh like talons. Horace drew back in a panic and flashed a look around, trying to decide between keeping Oaky down or just running away. Then he saw the spade. He'd forgotten it was in his hand.

Horace thrust the shovel into the monster's mouth, splitting its face from ear to ear. Then he stepped on the tread and drove it into the earth with a wet crunch. The head above the jaw fell away. Ink spilled out of the split. Horace shuddered and then regained his composure with an angry kick that sent Oaky's skull spiraling into the barn. The pig went berserk. As it squealed and tried to escape the slaughter post, Horace's face opened with horror.

"Becca... Oh my God, Becca! Becca!" He crashed through the plants around the house, shouting his daughter's name. "Please be in the house, oh please God be in the house!" He ran through the rooms, around the barn, down the road and back again with the pig shrieking its terror through every moment of the search. Horace looked everywhere. He called everywhere. He even shouted her name into the well with dread and hope.

Heartbroken and exhausted, Horace stumbled into his dark kitchen. He slumped into a chair at the table and prayed that Rebecca had disobeyed him, that she'd somehow gone to see Daniel at the tree house, though she didn't know the way. Horace prayed for his children's safety, turning to God out of despair.

He didn't know if he should go out there to find out. If she was somewhere on the farm, she might come back. He decided to wait just a little longer. Then he would go to the tree house.

The doorway was a brilliant rectangle of sunlight behind him. From the barn, the pig's voice was breaking. Horace cried, "Shut up," weeping into his hands. "You stupid animal, shut up." It did. Tears leaked from between his fingers and slid down his wrists for long minutes. Then a small shadow lurched into the light.

His head lifted with his heart. "Becca?" She came to him, silent, black-eyed and bathed in the pig's blood. Though a silhouette from where he sat, Horace knew by the way she moved that something was wrong. Something had happened to his little girl. He held out his arms, frightened again for her safety, and brought her in close. Her teeth sank into him like chisels.

He was slow to struggle, but the bite was a branding iron and he could not pull her off. Her smoke burned in the wound and then in his eyes and lungs. He thrashed around the kitchen, smashing his daughter into the wood and stone.

The infection sped on his desperate pulse. Paralysis crept behind it. Horace faltered and then fell, helpless and losing his senses, losing control until he couldn't even close his eyes or focus their stare. His daughter was somewhere out of sight, doing something to him. He didn't know what. What he could see shook, like the world in a looking glass, each time she pulled a piece away.

Rebecca stopped when Horace died. Her head lifted and swung from side to side. She was a bloody puppet, searching for something that had vanished. After struggling to her feet, she limped away with a peculiar, wagging step. Her father had snapped her leg in the thigh. She didn't feel any pain from the injury, or from anything else. The only thing left of her mind was a vague, instinctual memory of something important in the field.

Clouds of flour and soot settled on shattered glass. Hours passed. The sun turned slow shadows across the room. Black capillaries surfaced and burst in his deserted eyes. Gray smoke pushed itself out of his mouth and nostrils. Horace's huge corpse stirred and then staggered to its feet like a drunk. It stumbled outside with a vague, instinctual memory that something important was in the woods behind the house.

4 Lost Son

Daniel's feet dangled over the side of the tree house. An aging afternoon lengthened the shade. He whittled a figure with his fishing knife, pausing at times to blow the shavings away. When the figure took on a rough shape, he trotted it through the air and sang, "Puh-puh-puh piiig. Pih pih piiig."

His hands were swollen with infections from punching the tree three days before. His lip had a fat and nasty scab as well. Noticing the evening coming, he put the pig carving down and kicked the rope through the hole. He wanted a fire started before dark.

As he descended, he felt fluid trailing down his arms and thought his bloated fingers had cracked open like sausages. He dropped to the ground, relieved to find only the scabs had broken. Bloody pus flowed from his knuckles and cuts. He wiped them on his dirty shirt.

Gathering kindling was easy. It hadn't rained in days. A pile of sticks and pine cones soon waited in the stone circle for Daniel's tinderbox, a rusty canister, four inches long and a little slimmer than his wrist. It held a shard of chipped flint, a ring of firesteel and a hairy tuft of straw from their field. His father had given it to him and taught him how to use it.

He struck the steel with the flint, sending tiny sparks of molten metal to smolder in the straw. The glow passed from there to dry pine needles and then licked to twigs which lit the sticks within minutes. Daniel snuffed the tuft out and reloaded the box.

A warm, orange fire flickered in the pit. Pockets of sap snapped and hissed. Daniel propped a useless roasting spit against the oak. He hadn't managed to catch any fish. Sitting on one of those huge roots, thinking about food and his family, hands hurting so badly he hated the rope, Daniel quit. He'd just go home, apologize and *eat*. By then he'd forgotten why he'd run away in the first place.

That was when he heard footfalls in the forest. He searched and called out, "Pa? Is that you?" There was no answer except for an added urgency in the approach. Horace was coming to the oak. Daniel recognized him through the lowering gloom by the size of his shadow. "Pa!"

His father had never come to get him before. Horace always waited for Daniel to break. The boy smiled and thought, *not anymore. Now you're too old! You're too old and need help with the chores. Ha ha, Pa!* Daniel's smug grin narrowed into suspicion as he studied his father's stride, a staggering charge.

His eyes went wide. "Drunk on some!" He shimmied up the rope, regardless of his hands. "Oh no you don't, Pa!"

Horace grabbed the rope below, but it was too late; Daniel had reached the tree house and pulled himself through the opening. The boy tried to bring the rope up too but it stuck in his father's grip. Daniel scowled down at him. "Fwah! You can't get up it anyway. Even if you did you couldn't fit through the hole! You can go on home. I'm never coming back!"

Daniel plopped down, folded his arms and frowned at the rope. Horace's drunken slant showed in its tension and waver. Over a few silent minutes, the boy started to imagine fishing from a raft, an oak tree for a pole and a sea monster on the line. He narrowed his eyes and decided to wait him out, refusing to speak.

After half an hour, he started to think his father had fallen asleep. Daniel tugged on the rope. Horace still held it tight. The boy went back to frowning.

That night the campfire's glow came up from the hole and around the edges. The platform was like a lily pad on a pool of light, and Daniel was the toad. His wide, big-eyed frown watched the rope stay tight and wavering. He thought it was very strange. *What's he doing? Is he angry? Is he sorry?* He tugged the line again. "Pa?" His father had come and was down there waiting for him. It had to mean *something*.

Despite the things said in anger, Daniel always planned on going home. Every time he'd run off before, he'd been welcomed back. So, he spent much of his time away thinking about how to word his grievances upon return. Though the circumstances were odd, with his father having come to him rather than Daniel crawling home in defeat, it seemed like the right time. He gave Horace the prepared speech.

"Pa, if you've got to give me a wallop, you shouldn't call it a spanky. That's disrespectful to me. I'm grown up, or near there, and you shouldn't shame me like that in front of Becca. You always say to say sir and be respectful, but you should too. I don't mean calling me sir, but being respectful."

As Daniel waited for a response, guilt began to replace his draining frustration. He said things before he'd been knocked out of the kitchen that night. Part of him felt he deserved a wallop. "Pa, I'm sorry about what I said the other day, about Ma. I didn't mean it." He wanted to see his father's face. He needed something other than silence. But, descending the rope still felt like a bad idea. He lay down and waited for Horace to speak.

Daniel woke up in the morning, in the forest's dappled light. The rope was the same, tight and wavering. It wasn't just strange anymore. It was frightening. "Pa?" He crawled over to the hole and looked down at his father's blank, smoking stare. A cold weight settled in his stomach.

"What's wrong with you, Pa? Are you sick?" He bent lower to get a better look. His father pawed at him from yards below with the ignorant motion of an animal in a trap. Daniel was terrified. Over and over he cried, "What's wrong, Pa? What's going on?" That day passed and the sun set without an answer.

That night was a black lake around the oak. Sounds came out of everywhere to send Daniel scrambling. He was afraid any one of them might be the tell of his father climbing in the dark. His fear turned the autumn breeze into a freezing blast; it closed the platform in so that he always felt an inch from the edge, and that his every breath threatened his fall.

By sunrise Daniel was exhausted, dehydrated and shivering with fever. He crept over and peeked under the boards. His father was still there, holding the rope. The boy's face peeled into a silent, trembling scream that tore his lip open again. He backed up, buried his head in his knees and sobbed, "Please go away. Please, please go away…"

* * *

John had little trouble following Horace's trail. Trampled saplings and snapped branches made a hallway through the brush. He had an idea of where it was headed anyway. As the forest grew darker from the approaching storm, John kept calling out, "Horace!"

A strained voice answered him suddenly from up ahead. "Run! Run! He's coming! Run!" John stopped and searched. Lightning flashed across the sky, thunder rumbled in behind it and rain began to dot the path. The enormous zombie-Horace crashed forward with leaves and twigs in its hair.

"Horace..." John's face fell. He was too late. Drawing his sword, he stepped into a swing that clove a deep diagonal through his son's heart. That would have been enough to stop a man. Smoke and gore erupted from the gash but the spine remained intact.

The charging giant slammed into John and they hit the ground with a splatter, John's right arm and sword pinned across him. Horace drove forward. John locked his left hand against the nearly-severed shoulder. The wound yawned from their combined effort, tilting Horace's head and one thrashing arm away.

John's eyes glowed in the belching smoke and viscera. Riin coursed into him. He yanked his other hand free and pushed harder. Bones and tissue popped and ripped at the base of the cut. Then, with a loud, deep crack, like splintering lumber, Horace's spine broke. Ink puked out of the fissure. The monster went slack. John had folded its upper half onto its back.

He squirmed out from beneath the body, drenched blood, bile and black. John stood up, letting the rain wash it all away - water poured into the forest - and with a look of loss and sadness stared at what had once been Horace.

* * *

Daniel squeezed the platform's edge as he ducked and wove, trying to dodge trees with his gaze, swollen hands pale from his grip. Seconds before each thunderclap, lightning exploded for a stuttering, black and white heartbeat that let him see twice as far. He saw the golden circle first. Then John jogged into view.

Daniel recognized the dumpy, old man for what he was, a knight of the church from Antioch. He'd seen one once before, in Meroe, a big one named Gabriel. He was also related to one he'd never met, one he knew only as his father's uncle, John.

John called up to him, "Are you hurt, boy?" Daniel couldn't answer. Fever, deprivation and astonishment allowed him only to stare and tremble. John ran under the platform, dashed hand over hand up the rope and dropped to his boots on the boards. Removing his gauntlet quickly, he asked again, "Are you hurt?" He placed his gnarled old hand on the speechless boy's forehead.

John didn't "see" riin with his eyes. He felt it, like an emotion. When he touched Daniel's skin, he felt a picture of riin pooled around the boy's infections in small amounts and "saw" where it seeped into Daniel's body from somewhere outside of perception. It only seeped in because the way was dammed. With a physical sensation, like the decision to weep, John opened the way and riin blasted into Daniel.

The boy's eyes rolled back in his head and he fell unconscious, golden light flaring from his injuries. John lowered him and looked around. He found a cup among Daniel's things and filled it with rain water from one of the canopy's steadier leaks. Then he knelt next to Daniel and woke him up.

Daniel was muddled. "What... what happened? Who are you?"

John handed him the cup. "I'm from Antioch. My name is John. What's yours?"

Daniel's eyes bulged as he drank. He knew of John. That led to a cascade of more recent memories. He blinked as they came.

John waited, nodding. "It can take a bit to get your wits back." He took the empty cup and filled it again. "How long have you been up here? You're parched."

Daniel's recollection reached his father holding the rope. Of a dozen questions he wanted to ask, the first was, "Where's my pa?"

John's face opened - his grandson. He should have seen it. The boy was a scrawny, bug-eyed little Horace. "Do you know who I am?"

"Yes, sir, I think. You're Pa's uncle, aren't you? He told me you... he told me... where's my pa?"

John felt profound grief, the kind that builds in sudden stages as connections are made. He shoved his feelings aside to speak. "Do you know anything about a sickness in these parts, in Meroe?"

"No... Pa looked sick and drunk and, and stayed under the tree for a long time. I thought he had the whammy! I don't know what's happening at all! Where is he?"

John put a hand on Daniel's shoulder. "I'm sorry, son. Your father is dead. I'm..." Daniel's mouth fell open and he pulled away. John paused for a moment before he continued. "It's some kind of plague. People are getting sick and when they get sick, they... make other people sick too. The church is trying to help." He wanted to comfort Daniel but he didn't know what to say. "Tell me your name, son. We're family."

"Rebecca!" Daniel started to get up. "My sister, Becca's at the house! We have to go get her!"

John hung his head. "I've just come from the farm. I... found a little girl there. How old was your sister?"

"What do you mean *was*? She's five... she's only five years old!"

"Son, I'm so sorry."

Daniel's grief and anger rose up in him like a viper. He looked at the sword on John's hip. His tears and words squeezed out of a tightening scowl. "What did you do to them?"

John was firm. "The plague killed them. The last time you saw your father, he was already dead. I'm supposed to be in Meroe right now, but I came here instead, looking for him. I was too late. I couldn't help him and I couldn't help your sister but I can help you. And that's what I am going to do."

Daniel slumped.

John's face softened and he offered the cup again. "Please, tell me your name."

"Daniel." He accepted the cup, feeling thirst then more than anything else.

"Where is your mother, Daniel?"

"Ma died a long time ago, when Becca was born. It was just me, Pa and Becca."

"You've no other family?"

"Maybe, in Breahg. Ma was Breahg." He said it like a confession. The clan's history was barbaric.

John understood. He blew out a slow breath. "Alright, we'll wait out the storm here. Then you're coming with me."

"But, what about Becca and Pa? Don't they…"

"They're gone."

Daniel winced. "How come he moved around if he was…"

"I don't know. I've never seen anything like this before. The plague haunts the bodies like some kind of devil. It's atrocious."

Daniel was lost. "We've got animals. I've got Pa's chores to do for them now."

"No. You have to come with me. It isn't safe here. Your animals will just have to do their best. They aren't as important as you are." John waited, but the boy had no further arguments. "How old are you, Daniel?"

"Thirteen, sir."

"You're almost a man before we met." John sat down and put his legs over the edge. His chainmail grated against the planks. He waited in silence and then patted the wood, moist bits crumbling from his gauntlet. "I built this tree house." Daniel hadn't known. John nodded. "For your father when he was a boy. I grew up here too. A long time ago, all of this land was mine. It came to me because I was my father's oldest son. But, when I took my vows, I gave it all to my younger brother, Isaac."

"Grandpa Isaac?"

John nodded hesitantly. "A little more than eighteen years ago, when Isaac died, that was the last time I saw your father. We had an argument." He scratched his short, gray beard. "Fwah."

Daniel sniffed and looked up at him. The old man put his hand on the boy's shoulder again. The gauntlet was wet and horrible, but Daniel didn't pull away that time.

John said, "What did your father tell you about me?"

"He said you're busy and important and that's why you don't come to visit."

"Did he say why he never came to see me in Antioch?"

"He hardly ever left the farm. There's a lot of work to do. But… if we needed to trade, he said there's less bigots in Meroe."

John sighed. "We were both too stubborn to apologize."

Daniel couldn't remember his father ever having apologized for anything. Then his heart sank again. "The last thing I said to Pa was I hated him."

John nodded sadly. "We said things like that too, terrible things."

"Pa was drunk and I got mad at him. I told him he was stupid and he should've taken Ma to have Becca in the church. I told him Ma... I told him Ma died because of him!"

Death in childbirth was common outside of Antioch and the farm was days from there by wagon. John knew an unforeseen complication during delivery would have been impossible to help. Most people's injuries and illnesses were either too serious or too minor for a long journey to see the Circle.

John squeezed Daniel's shoulder. "Is that when you got the busted lip?" Daniel reached up to his mouth and felt smooth, painless flesh. His hands were lean and strong as well with tiny, white scars over the knuckles. His aches, fever and delirium were gone. He was still thirsty, though.

John said, "We all make mistakes, son. We all do things we regret. You never know if it will be the last time you see someone. Don't be too hard on yourself. Or others."

Daniel wiped his face with his shirt. The two of them sat there on that rotten platform, watching the storm rage through the wilderness.

5 The Grace

Aterrible storm had just passed, the *Grace* rested at sea and someone was knocking on Andalynn's door. She brought her head out of the basin between her knees, her short, blonde hair clumped from sweat and her face nearing green. She couldn't have said which was worse right then, seasickness or the rot. Her cabin smelled of sour milk.

She resolved to stop vomiting long enough to see who was knocking. The worst of it was over anyway. She'd been in dry heaves for a while by then and if someone was at *her* door, it could only mean trouble. Andalynn did not receive social calls.

She put on a pair of black, rubber goggles and tied a surgeon's cover over her nose and mouth. Then she opened the door to a fiery sunrise and a tall person wearing a gas mask that had the look of a startled walrus. The mask also muffled his speech. "Wung munnug!"

Andalynn hooded her eyes under the goggles. "Drake... take it off."

He did - *foomp* - a chipper nineteen-year-old with big teeth. "We found it!"

"Drake..." She wasn't in the mood for his garbledy-gook routine or his bad jokes.

"Is Biggs in there with you?" He tried to poke his head in to take a look.

She blocked him, clenched her teeth and barked, "Drake!"

He jumped back. "No, seriously, Captain sent me, everyone's on deck, *we found it!* We're there! Or, we're here. You know what I mean!"

She stepped out to empty her basin over the guardrail. The ship's lanes were compact, blocky and wood grain. One crewman and then another squeezed past. Drake bounced away with them, stuffing his head back into the mask. Andalynn's stomach jumped - *he is not joking*. She ducked inside, holstered on a pair of revolvers and then hurried to the front of the ship.

Fifty people, the entire crew, crowded the deck, wearing all kinds of goggles and respirators. They watched the horizon with telescopes, binoculars and unrestrained excitement. Captain looked out over the water through the big scope on his bolt action rifle, an M1903 Springstien BOSS (Bearing-Optimized Sniper System.) He wore a luxuriously purple calf-length coat. Wisps of wavy auburn hair trailed from the gauze cocooning his head.

Andalynn went to stand next to him at the rail. A sailor on her other side, not realizing who had just moved in, put his hand on her shoulder and said, "Can you believe it? We're finally…" Then he saw her face - the goggles and surgeon's cover - and took his hand away. "Oh… sorry." He left, wiping that hand on his shirt.

Andalynn watched him go. She said, "I am here, Captain." Her voice had the volume and confidence of a public speaker. Shielding her eyes from the sun, she followed the crowd's attention to a thin strip of land in the distance.

Captain spoke in a nautical drawl while concentrating on his aim. "I've heard you're bringin' up your guts again. Thought you're over that." Drake was on the other side of him, giving Andalynn the thumbs up.

She hooded her eyes at him again. "I did not do well during the storm."

Captain said, "Despicable tempest. We could've been here yesterday, to be true." He turned to face her, stray hair, goggles and gauze making his head look like a steaming, robotic egg. "If Zeke's points are right, port's around the bend." He sounded like he was smiling.

The crew buzzed with anticipation. They manned their stations to bring the ship around and, even as they worked the rigging, couldn't look away from the coast. Then, there it was - Meroe. Cheers erupted from the deck.

Captain balled his ebon fist triumphantly. "This is it! I know it!" He handed Andalynn his rifle. "Take a look at that! Those backward little shacks are beautiful!"

Shouldering the stock, she aimed at a cluster of cottages that dotted the steep incline of a small, natural harbor. Long piers branched out high over the water and blended into the town's wood plank pavement. They were slim strips meant for fishing, not for docking ships.

Andalynn said, "I do not see any people."

Captain said, "No, and it sits a bit shallow for the *Grace*, but that's not the first thing I'd say…" He opened a split in his mask to take his pipe's bit in his teeth. Then he drew a gnarly, homemade match out of a box from his coat pocket and struck it on the guardrail. It snapped, flared and spat brief, little fireballs and hissed like torn parchment. When it calmed to a flame, he lit the pipe and flicked the matchstick into the sea.

A murmur was spreading among the crew from another discovery. Andalynn said, "There is a ship farther east along the coast. It appears to have been beached."

Smoke curled from Captain's gauze. "Oh, aye? Hmm… We might should leave her out and drop the dinghy then."

Andalynn handed the rifle back and said to Drake, "Gather the others. Prepare to land."

Drake saluted. "Wung, mung!" They both hurried away.

Captain took aim at the distant shipwreck. With mixed feelings over what was on the horizon, he spoke to no one but himself. "No need to hurry now. We've nowhere else to be."

* * *

Andalynn sat at the dinghy's prow with her back to their destination, watching the *Grace* as they rowed away. Its three, tall masts were draped in ropes and pulleys like a spider web on blades of grass. A black-metal furnace hung on chains from the spars over one side instead of a lifeboat; the crew called it the Coffin. The glow from its grate gave it a lantern's quality. The Coffin, the *Grace* and the dinghy each rocked and swayed in their own rhythm. Andalynn's nausea returned and she closed her eyes.

Six others sat in the small boat with her. They served as the ship's marines. When it was necessary to go ashore, they were the ones who went. They were an improvised group that agreed to abide by a harsh code of law they called the System. They hadn't been ashore in a long time.

Drake pulled an oar, merrily honking nonsense through his mask. "Mung wunga gung. Gunga wumma munga mung!"

Ditch said, "Shut uuup, dummy..." He pulled the other oar. Under skimpy swimmer's goggles and a bi-valve respirator, Ditch was small, bald and tattooed. His stiff leather jacket and cargo pants jingled and chuffed as he rowed.

Biggs laid back with his legs crossed, an easy going country-boy. "Least you can't tell what he's on about in that thing." He wore a dangly strapped diver's mask and had a bandana pulled over his nose like an outlaw.

Ditch spoke rapidly. "Man, that's why it sucks, cause I get like, curious. I know whatever he's sayin's dooked - I know it - but then I start wantin' to know *how* dooked, you know?"

Biggs chuckled. "S'pose."

Drake pumped his fist. "Wum gum! Mung wumma gumma!"

Ditch said, "Alright, alright, shut up for real. We're gettin' close."

Welles watched Meroe through his binoculars all the way in. He said, "I keep hoping someone will just walk out and wave." He sounded like that hope was fading.

Ditch said, "Yeah, man, I used to do that too."

The wind followed them in from the sea. No one spoke above a whisper. They moored at the deep end of a long pier and, rifles and gear slung on their backs, took turns creeping up the creaking ladder. On the other side of the harbor, beneath the level of the boards and across a forest of pilings, a ghoul shuffled unnoticed into the water toward them.

Andalynn scanned inland with a spyglass. The doors and windows of the cottages closest to shore were open and broken. It was silent aside from the water lapping at their thumping boat.

Biggs looked up. "No gulls."

Ditch sighed. "This place is gone, man."

It discouraged them all. Meroe was supposed to be the end of the road, the end of their troubles. It was supposed to be safe.

Andalynn said, "We have the wind at our backs. This is an adequate position. We should take advantage of it and begin clearing immediately."

The other sailors mumbled and shifted.

Biggs backed her up. "Ever'thin' else is where Zeke said it'd be. Road north oughtta take us straight to Antioch, then, right?

Shoot, that's prob'ly where most a' these folks got to." He put his hand on Welles' shoulder. "Aint never gon' have to do this again, y'all."

They always responded better to him. Weapons clicked and clacked in their unanimous resolution.

Andalynn said, "Outstanding. Drake has the bag."

Drake slumped. "Wummaguh wahwah munguh mug?"

Ditch mocked him with a dopey whine, *"Why do I always have the bag,"* and then brushed by him with a little bit of a shove. "Cause you shot Biggs last time you were on the line, stupid."

Biggs said, "S'alright, Goober," and consoled him with a pat as he moved past.

The line, five riflemen kneeling in a row, leveled their weapons at the land's end of the pier. Drake crouched behind them and unzipped the bag, a hefty, olive-green cylinder filled with a nest of cartridges, each one as long and as thick as a man's finger, pointed and brass. Drake set out five-shot stripper clips to reduce the line's loading time. They only had six of those clips and he put the extra next to Biggs.

Andalynn stood beside Drake, looking out over their heads. When he gave her the thumbs up, she pulled down her surgeon's cover, cupped her hands to her mouth and called out, "Ahoy!" The message was loud, clear and saved a bullet.

Silence had been broken. They didn't need to whisper anymore. Welles shook out his nerves and said, "Not us." Each of them said it - *not us* - and they waited.

Two figures staggered into view, two hundred yards away. Andalynn inspected them with her spyglass and was surprised. "These are young..." Somewhat encouraging, the young were slower and easier to hit. She called out the target order, "Twelve, eleven!" Twelve o'clock was dead ahead.

Five violent reports stuttered from their ready weapons. The ghoul at twelve o'clock jerked and twitched in the whizzing bullets, lost balance and dropped to its hands and knees. Then it brought up one foot and tried to stand.

The riflemen lifted and pulled their bolts with fluid clicks. Empty cases spun smoking from the chambers to make way for new rounds. The bolts slid home again and then - more roaring blasts. Debris exploded out of the distant monster. It crumpled, motionless. The line was dialing in.

Biggs cried, "Down!" the signal to switch targets to the eleven o'clock zombie. They focused on one at a time and couldn't settle for flesh wounds. They had to hit the head.

All of them were accurate shooters with a Springstien BOSS, it was an accurate weapon, but they strove for speed in addition to that. Ditch was pretty good. He could hit a six inch target at one hundred yards every seven seconds. Biggs could put five rounds through an apple at that range in under fifteen. Before Ditch chambered his third round, the eleven o'clock zombie's head detonated.

"Down!"

The others whistled and hooted in appreciation of the shot.

"The boss with a BOSS."
"I'm just gonna put mine down."
"Biggs is the man, man."

Biggs said, "Listen up! Lynn's callin' em."

"One, twelve, eleven!"

They tore the ghouls apart. The last to the left hadn't taken ten steps before it fell and Biggs called, "Down!" for the fifth time. The sailors reloaded, staying tense. They'd only begun to clear. If large groups appeared, or a small group of older ones, the odds could quickly force them to retreat.

Drake fumbled with the spent stripper clips. Once the line was firing at full speed and every shot started in the bag it would become a challenge just to keep Biggs in bullets. The bag was a chaotic position under pressure with desperate hands grasping at the slick cartridges. Drake dropped them even under ideal conditions, such as right then. One hit the wood and rolled behind him. When he turned around to get it, he saw a rotten arm jutting up from where the ladder met the pier.

"Wungamung! GUM!" He slapped at Andalynn's rear. She shot a frown at him and then her face twisted at the wet, quivering thing that was pulling itself onto the boards, coming out of its skin like a molting insect. Its smoke bled into their company on the wind from the sea.

Andalynn raced toward it, shouting, "Hold your breath! Hold your breath! Six! Six!" She stomped on its arm to hold it in place, pulled her right hip's revolver and emptied it into the ghoul's face. The blasts splattered rancid flesh and ink. She fired until she felt the thing relax and then took her weight away. It fell as a limp corpse, careening off the ladder before splashing into the water below.

She was trembling, reloading and still holding her breath when she heard someone cough. Andalynn turned and her eyes went wide under the gore-speckled goggles. It was Biggs. She said, "Biggs? Biggs?" She couldn't believe it. Everyone stared at him.

Ditch became so upset he almost threw his rifle off the pier. "Aaah, *come on!* Swimmin? Climbin' ladders? Aaah! Whatever, man!"

The smoke burrowed into Biggs' mouth and throat like tiny cactus spines. He sighed and shook his head. It made sense to him that he'd catch it then, just when he'd started wanting to live again. It was fine. If he stayed calm, he'd have an hour, maybe two. He'd use it to do what he could for his friends.

Biggs looked back at Andalynn - the goggles and surgeon's cover - the face of death. When one of them caught the rot, that mask tended to be the last thing they saw. He said, "It's in deep. Gon' ride it out, alright?" She nodded in a strange way, like she'd lost her balance. He turned and pumped his index finger at Meroe. "Stay on it."

Grim, they leveled their rifles again. Andalynn remained at the ladder to look out over their heads. Her strong voice broke when she said, "Twelve, one…"

6 Devil's Mark

A dried mixture of mud and ink crumbled from Michael as he walked through Meroe's sunlit silence. It should have been a bustling, happy town. The cobbled path passed deserted homes and businesses before branching from the main road and expanding into a circular courtyard, the marketplace. A stone well stood in the center, its small, wooden roof angled and shingled in the fashion of the surrounding storefronts. And next to that stood a ghoul.

Michael paused in plain sight, watching. Unaware of him, it stooped and picked up something small and shiny from near the base of the well. Then it teetered back and forth until the object fell from its senseless fingers. The ghoul bent to retrieve it and resumed teetering only to drop it once more.

Michael set down his scabbard. He shouted, "Here, devil!" It turned and lurched toward him. He lopped off its upper right half, strode through the smoke and arcing fluid and started looking for what it had been playing with.

It was a copper coin. Michael picked it up, wondering what sort of fascination it could have held for that mindless monster. Then he heard shuffling sounds from the narrow lanes all around. More were coming. Stepping out of the shadows and into the day, the ghouls were a rotten mockery of the old marketplace. Michael charged.

The courtyard became a slaughterhouse and the former residents of Meroe herded themselves into it like bloodthirsty cattle. Michael met them, shouting, "Come, devils!" And they came - in dense, tripping crowds - to be cut down two at a time in the alley's mouths by that unstoppable sledgehammer of a sword. Michael shouted and swung for what felt like hours and kept shouting long after the last had fallen.

***

Smoke swept north from log jams of carnage in the courtyard, the bodies of hundreds. Ink lined the awnings, posts and walls and diffused with the rainwater in the cobblestones' grooves. A lonely screaking came from the well's winch as Michael cranked up the bucket.

He lifted it to his mouth and drank brackish water from it. Traces of the ghouls' rot fizzled in his throat and stomach, cleansed by riin. Michael poured the water over himself, bathing as much of the encrusted mud and remains from his habit as he could.

The ghoul's coin sparkled in the water at his feet. He picked it up again, the majestic impression of Gabriel's profile on it in low relief. That was how Meroe had honored their favorite son's ordination. Michael remembered Gabriel saying, *it might be the least of our currency, but it's good enough for a squad of herring or a bag of taffy.* Gabriel wouldn't have preferred to be on one of the more valuable coins, he just liked to point out that he wasn't. Michael didn't want to think about telling him. He set the coin on the well's stone lip and left.

The cobblestones ended there. Wood planks paved the ways through town to the coast. Following one in, Michael was about to start shouting again when he heard strange noises coming from the harbor, like small thunder calls. He broke into a run.

As he neared the source of the mysterious sounds, he found corpses where the cottages stopped. Rounding the corner of a dead bait shop, he discovered a field of fallen ghouls between the buildings and the piers. Smoke drifted up out of curious holes in their backs and chests. Michael went out to investigate...

Bullets punched through his mail, broken ringlets, chunks of flesh and blood following them out. A shot grazed his left cheek, shattering his jaw near the ear. His vision went dark. Then he was on his hands and knees with a powerful urge to let go and to sleep, his life falling out of him.

Michael had to concentrate to open the way. At that moment, he couldn't have recalled his own name. He would have bled to death then if not for a strange bit of luck. A bullet hit short into the boards, ate through the ground and shot back out at a quarter of its speed. It struck Michael above the knee, burrowed the length of his thigh and lodged itself next to the bone. The painful jolt woke him up like a slap to the face. He remembered what to do. Light beaming from his wounds, he brought up one foot and tried to stand.

Biggs coughed and missed again, hitting Michael in a low rib and flooring him. Biggs' aim was off without steady breath and he was frustrated. It was bad enough he was about to die, he didn't want to die a bad shot. He kicked out the case, locked the bolt and aligned his sights, a hair's breadth up and to the left; the bullet would drift from there to the head. He knew the wind and the distance, if he could just keep from coughing during his squeeze...

Andalynn shouted, "Down, down, down, down!" Biggs took his finger off the trigger. The others complained.

"What're you do'n?"
"That turkey isn't down, man!"
"Yeah, *Biggs* is on point!"

Andalynn had moved her spyglass back to Michael because there were no other targets and she wanted to watch one die. But, she saw something different in the way he moved, something other than blind determination - self-preservation. She said, "That is not a bauran!"

They watched through their scopes. Michael regained his feet and ran for cover in the bait shop. The sailor's jaws dropped.

"We shot a guy, man!"
"There's no way to cross the smoke..."
"That guy's gonna die."

Andalynn said, "No! You do not see? He came through town. Only someone like Zeke could have done that!" She pushed out in front of them and fanned her arms, shouting verbose apologies across the killing field, "It was not our intention to fire upon you! Please disregard that act of aggression!" The rest of them dropped their rifles and started waving and shouting as well.

Michael peeked out of the broken window. On the end of a pier, about two hundred yards away, there were people waving and shouting - *living people*. He couldn't make out what they were saying. He knelt, contemplating the holes in the corpses outside and the damage in his body. They'd done it… He didn't know how or who they were, but he was sure they'd mistaken him for a devil.

He leaned halfway out of the bait shop's doorway and waved back. They responded with more enthusiastic waves and shouts. It was a friendly standoff that lasted for a tense minute. Then Michael went out to them, jogging right through the smoke. The sailors were astonished.

"Man, look at this guy…"
"Cap was tellin' the truth."
"Unprecedented!"

As Michael approached, the sailors saw evidence of their accuracy. Finger-width holes riddled his armor and an evil scar carved a trench from his mustache to the back of his neck. But, there were no open wounds.

Andalynn uncovered her face. Captain had told them the people of Meroe spoke Continental, the language of the Great Nations, so she'd written and practiced a formal introduction for their arrival. She could deliver it impressively but right then had no time for diplomacy. She dragged Biggs forward and shouted in long, loud syllables, hoping the native would understand, "WE - HAVE - AN - INJURED - MAN!"

Michael was taken aback; they were outlandish! Despite the masks, he'd never seen such color in hair and skin… and that woman's accent! Also, it may have been an accident, but after what they'd done to him he'd expected to hear quite a few apologies. Putting all of that aside, he gave Andalynn a courteous nod and said, "Excuse me then, young lady." He lifted his left hand, unfastening the gauntlet from the sleeve, and said to Biggs, "May I offer you hospital, sir?"

The way Michael spoke surprised them. Oversea, it would have been described as quaint.

Biggs said, "Uh… alright," but he didn't think Michael was quaint. Michael looked like a diabolically polite proctologist. And Biggs had just put him in a pickle with a Springstien BOSS. He had to guess what Michael meant by hospital.

Michael said, "Here, you'll want to lie down," and helped him to the ground. The rest of them gathered around, removing their masks. Michael laid his hand on Biggs' forehead and then, before opening the way, took some extra time to examine riin's natural reflection in him.

It radiated from the smoke's infections, surrounded a lump of metal in his hip, like the one in Michael's leg, and showed an extensive cancer branching through his body in ghostly veins. Michael had seen cancer many times before, but never one like that in someone so young; Biggs seemed to be in his early twenties but would have died from it within a month. Despite the curious ailment, Biggs was only a man. Michael flooded him with riin.

Biggs' eyes rolled back and his body went stiff. A brief, red glow pulsed once under the skin where the cancer had been. The sailors had never seen anything like it.

"Oh no, Biggs is dead!"
"Nah, man, that's like, a knock-out or somethin."
"Unreal…"

Biggs regained consciousness about a minute later and found his friends surrounding him and staring. He said, "What… what's go'n on?" Andalynn was kneeling beside him, holding his hand.

Drake said, "Now he's got amnesia!"

Michael wasn't familiar with the term. He was familiar with that sort of reaction, though, and tried to reassure them all. "This is normal, don't worry."

Amazed, Ditch tapped Drake's chest with the back of his hand. "See, pinhead, I told you. He got knocked out! I seen guys go out like that a hundred times, just, you know, not from gettin' hospital'd."

Andalynn helped him sit up. "Everything is under control, Biggs. We are safe. How do you feel?"

Biggs was dazed but he said, "I'm alright." Then he tensed, noticing his mask was off. So were theirs - *naked air*. He was scared but at the same time felt strong and healthy, like an oppressive weight had been lifted off of him. He couldn't remember past being a part of the line on the pier. The others had to tell him what had happened. Biggs turned a huge smile on Michael and said, "Thanks, mister!" The sailors cheered and patted Biggs and Michael on the back.

Michael smiled too. "You're welcome." He didn't share any of what he'd discovered in Biggs, the bullet or the cancer, because he didn't want to discourage any of the others from cooperating with his examinations. "Is anyone else hurt?"

Drake raised his hand. "Ooh me, do me!"

Michael motioned him over. Ditch pointed and cackled when Drake passed out. Michael recommended they all receive hospital, saying it was healthy... and customary. They submitted to him with introductions, apologies and gratitude.

None of them looked older than their early twenties, no more than children to Michael, but inside they showed peculiar signs of age. The first had been Biggs' cancer but then Ditch, though shaven, had John's horseshoe patterned baldness in his scalp. Andalynn was somewhat menopausal. Individually they would have been no more than intriguing abnormalities but across a group like that Michael found them especially curious.

The sailors whooped and congratulated one another as they regained consciousness. They discussed their next move and waved at their friends on the *Grace*, who they knew were watching from afar.

"This is astounding!"
"We can sleep on land again!"
"We're finally here!"

Michael couldn't believe what he was hearing. "Are you all mad? You can't stay in Meroe! Hundreds of people have died here! It isn't safe! You have to go back where you came from!" Confounded by them, he said, "Where *did* you come from?" and thought, *and why are you waving at the sea?* Michael looked out over the water. When he saw their distantly anchored ship, his mouth fell open; he'd seen the impossible.

The sailors exchanged ominous glances. Andalynn took a folded note out of her pocket and handed it to him. "Michael, we are the crew of the refugee vessel, *Grace*, sailing out of the Great Nations. This is a message from Zeke."

Michael accepted it mid-stun. "Zeke?"

Andalynn said, "We do not know what that letter contains. None of us can read those symbols. We have been instructed to present it to the Circle. You are a member of the Circle, are you not?"

Michael nodded, surprised she'd named his order. That wasn't even common knowledge in Antioch. Then, upon unfolding the note, he was shocked to find three short lines and a signature in sacred script:

Armageddon is arrived.
Break your silence.
Open the library.

Ezekiel

Only those ordained in the church knew the script, and he'd never heard of Ezekiel. Michael sat down on a pier post and studied the note. He rubbed it in his fingers, put his hand through his hair, looked around and then read it again. "I… I don't understand. I don't understand any of this. You've honestly come from oversea?"

Ditch said, "Yeah, man..." The sailors had crossed the third meridian. It had never been done before, as far as they knew, but it certainly wasn't considered impossible - not like what Zeke and Michael could do. For Michael's people, sailors and pirates from oversea were very much like wizards and pixies; it was generally accepted those things didn't exist and seeing them was the mark of a loon or a rube. And for a man of the church, the contents of the note were just as challenging.

Michael didn't know where to begin. He gestured out at the smoking corpses. "What… What have you seen of this devilry… where you're from?"

Andalynn said, "We have been at sea for eleven months. This is what became of the world we left behind."

7 Ghost Ship

Biggs motioned at the note. "Well, what's it say?" They were all curious. They were a miserable year's worth of curious.

Michael weighed the note in his hand. "It says you must all come with me to Antioch." The instructions and the circumstances were difficult for him to accept. "I never believed in people oversea. Now you're telling me they're all gone because of this plague. I'm afraid no one has escaped Meroe."

The sailors had been living in spite of the bauran for months but Michael was just beginning to comprehend the devastation. Andalynn remembered that moment of realization. She spoke, believing if they were to be welcome they had to help. "You said hundreds of people have died. That cannot account for this entire town. Where are the others?"

"I don't know. I don't know where they are." Michael put his head in his hands, trying to think of the right thing to do. "And while I sit here the smoke carries on the wind."

Biggs said, "Might be some over at the other boat."

Michael looked up at him. "What other boat?"

"We aint the first ones to get here. There's another boat over yonder up the coast. Zeke sent more'n us."

Michael stood up. "The survivors could be there!"

* * *

The high, rocky coast overlooked an endless, crashing ocean to the south. The cliffs appeared to thrust out of the water. Michael and the sailors traveled the ridge, searching for a safe way down. The second ship was still farther east and a long swim out as well.

Climbing back up from another dead end, Michael said, "What is that name you call them, bauran?"

Andalynn said, "It means *deaf ones.*"

He paused. "But they're not deaf."

"No, they are not. It is morbid humor."

Michael frowned and moved on to the next possible descent. "Tell me about this Zeke."

Andalynn said, "We know very little about him, actually. Our memories of him, collectively, are muddled. I did not understand why that was until having just now experienced the effect of your ability."

Drake said, "Whoa, you're right. That's why!"

Ditch said, "Good job, man. Way to keep up."

Michael said, "What *can* you tell me about him?"

Biggs said, "Cap's only one remembers talkin' to him. Said he's in a big hurry, worry'n 'bout the others gon' die."

Michael did his best to understand the sailors without constantly interrupting them, but the way they spoke Meroan was very strange, and they all spoke it in different ways. Ditch's rapid slang baffled him the most. "Yeah, we all got pretty much the same story, man. It goes, *oh crap zombies, oh crap, oh crap, oh crap* and then maybe somethin' about Zeke. We just woke up on a boat. Nobody saw him before we saw him, you know? Then he's gone."

"Ah... I see. Well, what does he look like?"

Drake said, "He's a white guy, like Ditch."

"Man, I'm not white! What's wrong with you?"

Andalynn said, "Personally, I do not remember him at all, but everyone has described him as very much like you, Michael, black hair and light skin, although... younger. He was young, was he not?"

Biggs said, "Yup, lil'squirt. Just a kid."

Andalynn said, "Michael, forgive me for asking this, but, why are you so... mature?" At forty-five years old and with much gray in the black of his tidy cut and thick mustache, Michael looked like a chaperone among the sailors.

He pretended to be paying more attention to the path than her odd question but he suspected she was about to reveal something about the curious senescence he'd noticed in them earlier. "Don't people grow old oversea?"

Andalynn said, "We did, until we met Zeke. I am fifty-two. But after waking up on the *Grace* I appeared to be thirty years younger than that."

Biggs said, "Maybe twenty." Andalynn glanced at him sideways and let a smile slip.

Drake laughed and then blurted out, "Ditch is so old, he's bald!"

Ditch frowned. "I'm thirty-seven, man. I'm not old. But, yeah, my tats look older'n me now. Look at 'em. Ink's all faded."

Drake persisted. "It's really funny when Ditch's stubble comes in. He looks like a little bald kid."

"Man, you *are* a kid. And you're gettin' on my nerves."

Andalynn redirected the conversation. "Does your ability not restore youth, Michael?"

Michael had stopped trying to find a way down. He was just standing there, thinking about what the sailors were saying. They were describing *athanasy*, deathlessness, another thing that didn't exist. "No… it doesn't."

Ditch whistled. "I guess Zeke's hospital's a beast!" Michael frowned, not convinced that any of them were telling him the truth. Ditch said, "Oh, sorry, man. Yours is good too."

Michael said, "Did any of you witness him give hospital, as I did?"

Andalynn had always been suspicious of Zeke. "I did not. What Ditch said is true. Most of us simply woke up on a boat."

Ditch said, "We been talkin' about Zeke, man." He said it like it was the only thing they'd been talking about for the last eleven months. "It doesn't look like nothin' anyway, right? Like, when you put the hospital on Biggs, he just, kind a' went out for a sec. Isn't that what Zeke did to us?"

Michael couldn't say.

Andalynn said, "My first assumption was that he had administered some sort of an injection, a medical antidote for the infection, but that did not explain the change in my appearance or how I had escaped the situation I last remember."

Michael said, "What do you mean?"

"I had been traveling with a small group of survivors for twelve days. The last thing I am able to recall is being trapped against a locked door, burning from the infection and surrounded by the bauran that were killing my companions. I cannot imagine Zeke trotting in to save me from that with a hypodermic needle."

Michael started looking for the way down again, thinking about everything they'd said. It was all so unbelievable, but they told it like the truth. He said, "What do you know about my order?"

Andalynn said, "Only the impossible. That you are capable of curing the infection by some sort of putative energy manipulation." The look on Michael's face prompted her to clarify, "That you are psychic healers?"

Ditch said, "Yeah, that was real weird for us. Cap got us all together after Zeke split and said there's these guys with magic powers that are gonna help us. At first I was like, *whatever, man*, but then I was like, *whatever, man!* You know? There's already zombies. Wizards? Pfft. Sure!"

Andalynn said, "Not long before that day, I would have considered Captain's story laughable. Since then I have only hoped it was true."

Michael took out the note. "Did anyone see who wrote this?"

Ditch said, "Cap said Zeke did. At first I thought it was just like, illegible. Turns out it's this whole other language."

Michael realized he was going to have to speak to their captain if he wanted to learn anything about Ezekiel. Then he paused. "Another language... How is it all of you speak Meroan? Wherever did you learn it?" Meroan was one of the oldest languages in the kingdom, but there were towns only a few days away that didn't use it at all. He didn't know how it could exist oversea.

Andalynn wanted to ask the same question. "Where we are from, what we are speaking is known as Continental. It is the most generally accepted form of communication in all of the Great Nations."

Michael's confusion only deepened with every question he asked. He went back to scrutinizing the note.

Andalynn said, "I had not expected you to be completely unfamiliar with Zeke."

Michael shook his head helplessly. "I've no knowledge of this man."

They were all puzzled.

Andalynn said, "Michael, his primary concern was in guiding us to Meroe. He told Captain it was the shortest path by land to Antioch."

Michael nodded. "It's a three day walk, but that's right. The coast is high and wild for miles in either direction. Any other way would take much longer."

"More ships are coming. What are your plans? Are you going to stay to meet them? I do not know if they can survive three days of travel by land now that the bauran have a foothold."

Michael went blank for a moment, so tremendous were his responsibilities. Then he shook his head. "I can't. People are going to die no matter what I do, but I think the best thing is to return to Antioch as soon as possible, to inform the rest of my order. I'm only here by chance. The others sit there useless, ignorant of what is happening."

Andalynn nodded. "May I suggest then that, before we leave, we burn Meroe along with the bodies? We should at least clear a path for any others." She assumed he would have a problem with burning the town, so she had arguments ready to support the suggestion.

Michael drew back. "We can't do that... It's blasphemy to burn a body. They'll be damned..." It was a lesson from his childhood that he had never challenged. Repeating it, in the wake of everything that had happened, he didn't know if he believed it or not, or if it mattered.

Andalynn found herself in an awkward and unexpected position, arguing against religion. Not wanting to offend Michael, she spoke cautiously. "Bauran continue to spore after they are put down. The smallest particle of their haze is deadly and reproductive. We know of no other way than burning them to stop that process."

Michael couldn't respond. After years of distance from the faith in which he'd been raised, he had difficulty remembering even the shortest of its prayers. He didn't feel qualified to argue against life on behalf of the soul.

* * *

They found a worn trail leading down to the waves. From there, the shipwreck leaned among jagged rocks a hundred yards out to sea. Its vast, square sails fluttered in a perpetual death spasm. Even from that distance, Michael knew it was the largest structure he'd ever seen. The hull loomed out of the water, taller than his father's inn.

He started working toward it through the spray. "We don't have much daylight left. I suggest you all come with me. The shore is certainly dangerous." The sailors left everything but their rifles behind and followed him in.

They half-swam and half-scrambled over the rocks to reach the ship. Scaling its quaking height onto the angled deck was a wet hazard as well. It smelled of mold and decay. Its name, engraved on rusted plates, was *Vesper*.

As the others quietly helped each other over the rail, Michael stood with his caligan drawn before the dark openings to the hold and the deckhouse. No one needed to say the ship was deserted. They all knew it. With the last of them aboard, Michael raised his sword and shouted, "Come, devils!"

The sailors readied their weapons behind him and craned their necks to see. Nothing came. After too much of Michael's unproductive shouting, Drake suggested, "Maybe you should try something else?" He pulled his chin into his throat, imitating Michael's voice and manner. "*Come devils.*" Michael raised an eyebrow at him. The others covered embarrassed faces. Then Drake said, "Andalynn likes, *ahoy!*" copying her clear-call with a man's screeching impersonation of a woman and a limp-wristed wave.

Ditch swatted him and hissed, "Don't piss him off, dookus!"

Michael frowned at Drake's impropriety. "I don't believe any are coming either." Then he marveled for a moment at what he stood upon. "I've never seen anything so huge. Do you recognize it?" They did not, but suggested they could find out more by searching the deckhouse. Michael walked it through, making sure they were safe to search its scattered documents. He decided to explore below. "Perhaps one of us will discover something illuminating."

Andalynn said, "I will accompany you. Since you have never been aboard a ship, I might be useful." Michael nodded and they left the deckhouse together. The door locked behind them.

She followed him into the stairwell's tilted darkness. In the divided light, they hadn't been able to see that the ship was filled with smoke. Halfway down, he stopped and turned to face her. His eyes were glowing gold. Andalynn's face opened and she backed away from him.

Michael said, "Go back to the others."

She went on her heels up the awkward stairs, moving faster and faster as she approached the relative safety of the deckhouse. Michael's eyes had come as a shock and now she was alone, exposed. Her body stiffened with fear. As she pounded on the locked door, that last memory before the *Grace* overcame her. She pounded harder and shouted, watching over her shoulder for the *Vesper's* dead hands, knowing they were on their way.

Michael took a deep breath and plunged into the hold, his eyes like candles in the billowing darkness. Shadows leapt and shrank as he turned his head. The ship rocked in the wind and tide like a chair with a short leg. Every time it set down, thin, hovering clouds lifted from the walls and the floor.

He tried a door near the base of the stairs. It resisted but with a shrug he broke the wood around the handle. He went inside and closed it behind him. A starved corpse in the corner of the small room disappeared with the dimming of Michael's light. He breathed.

Using cabins as pockets of air, Michael explored the vessel into its belly, where he heard the clinking and rattling of chains inside the rooms, an idle, metallic shuffling. The sounds stopped when he drew near. What was bound within had noticed him. The chains suddenly wrenched and caught, like they held ferocious, mute beasts.

Michael kicked a door in. Smoke surged out of the room. In the curling shadows of its cell, a skinless, human body struggled against shackles on its wrists and ankles. Naked muscle stretched tight and spare over its frame and made a sound like twisting leather as it lunged and strained. Its black eyes sparkled in the light from Michael's.

Gunshots came from overhead. The bauran pulled forward, baring its chest on its restraints. Michael swung his sword. The chains went slack and the halves hit the floor.

He ran back through the smoky gloom, skipping the air pockets, lungs bursting before the orange light of the stairwell. Then he raced up the steps and onto the deck to gasp in the clean air. Hands on his knees, breathing, Michael looked over and saw the deckhouse door hanging open. The frame around the latch was splintered.

He hurried over, but stopped right before going through. He didn't want to get shot again. "Sailors?"

"We're in here! We're ok!" Their weapons clicked and clacked as they stood down.

Michael peeked through the doorway, cleaning his blade with the lower front of his tabard. "What happened?"

Drake said, "I couldn't figure out the lock fast enough for Andalynn, so she told me to shoot it off. She was freaking out."

Andalynn's eyes and lips were slits. "You could not open a door!"

A little burst of laughter escaped from Drake as he defended himself. "It's not like I did it on purpose! It's a foreign door!"

Ditch said, "Hey, shut up, man. It's not funny..." but couldn't look up from the ship's log. He was discovering the tale of the hold.

Biggs said, "Michael, look here," and handed him a crumpled, bloody sheet of parchment. Michael darkened - three lines and a signature in sacred script.

Ditch lowered the ship's log with wide eyes and gooseflesh. "There's a mess a' bauran locked up down there, isn't there, man?"

Michael nodded.

The sailors froze, suddenly feeling like juicy crickets on an ant bed. Welles said, "Um... are they coming?" Michael shook his head no.

Sunset was an hour off.

Biggs said, "Come stay with us on the *Grace* tonight. We'll come back tomorrow with Cap, burn this thing to the water."

It was a difficult decision for Michael. Every moment he spent purging the smoke, more people were going to die. But, he couldn't leave those tasks behind or do them by himself in the dark.

* * *

Fifty sailors gathered around a bonfire near the shore, watching the *Vesper* burn through the next evening's sunset. The blaze made an immense, roiling column of smoke. To the west, similar dark spires rose from the burning of Meroe. As the shipwreck collapsed, some swore they saw its demon crew dancing in the inferno.

8 Wizards

Daniel squinted up at him. "Uncle John, are you gonna be in trouble when we get to town?"

"What are you talking about?" John said. The two of them walked through wet, knee-high grass on a bright afternoon. John's gauntlets hung from his belt and the fastenings swung loose with the mail on his forearms.

"You said you were supposed to be in Meroe, but came out to the farm instead."

"Oh! No. Michael commanded me to go to the farm. I've been thinking about that quite a bit, actually. We were at the crossroads when we first discovered the plague." John stared out across the field. "Michael officially commanded me to go home... He went on alone."

"How come he can tell you what to do?"

"Well, it wasn't... he didn't..." John frowned at Daniel. "He knows a little bit about my relationship with your father. He knew I was worried and that I wanted to go to the farm but he also knew I wouldn't go if I had the choice, out of duty I suppose. I was moved by Michael's compassion and his courage, and I was proud of him. I was concerned for his safety but also thankful and somewhat ashamed of myself for that. I should have been someone he could rely on, not someone he felt the need to sacrifice for." John scratched his beard, thinking about it even more.

Daniel hadn't listened to any of that. "But how come he can tell you what to do?"

John's face went flat. "Michael will be the next templar after Abraham. He's already been consecrated. That's why he can tell me what to do."

"How come you're not gonna be the templar?"

"Oh, no, I'd have been a bad choice. I'm almost as old as Abraham." It was an old man's exaggeration; John was twenty-three years younger. "I'd be consecrating the next templar *during my consecration!*" He laughed but Daniel just squinted up at him. "I've known I would never command the Circle since the day that Abraham was chosen, many, many years ago. And, honestly, I've never wanted the responsibility."

"What's Abraham gonna do when Michael's the templar?"

"Well, Michael will take over when Abraham passes on. Abraham is very old. No one lives forever."

"How old is he?"

"Eighty-seven."

Daniel frowned with thought. "How come you're so old, Uncle John?"

"What are you talking about?"

"Pa told me you can't get sick or anything and you fixed my lip and stuff. Can't you fix, um, how old you are?"

"Oh! No, I can't do that. No one can do that."

"How come?"

"People are simply meant to age."

"But isn't getting old just like getting sicker and sicker for a really long time? How come you can't just…"

John interrupted him. "No, aging is not like being sick! What a thing to say!"

Daniel withdrew. "I'm sorry."

"Yes, well…" John sniffed the air. "Stop." Daniel's eyes bulged and his ears pulled back. John stalked away from him, searching the grass. Then he stooped and started rummaging in it. Pulling up several bulbous plants from the moist soil, John said, "We can eat these! Here, hold them for me. I'll get some more."

Daniel held up the filthy vegetables and frowned at them. "How come we didn't go back to the farm to pack some food yesterday? I don't wanna eat these."

"Oh, no, the farm is far too dangerous right now. And besides, I needed to secure these fields!" John gestured to the vast, innocuous fields of grass around them as he rooted in the ground. Daniel frowned at the fields and then frowned at John. The old man said, "Nothing can be done about it, son. We'll just have to do our best."

That evening they reached a tree line and a creek and stopped for the night. Though tired, Daniel left John by the water and went off on his own to find dry sticks. When John climbed back up the bank, Daniel had a campfire started and was sitting next to it, hugging his knees.

John said, "That's a beautiful fire! How did you make it?"

Daniel showed him the tinderbox. "Pa gave it to me." He didn't look up. The pig carving was in his other hand.

"I found some good mushrooms by the creek, see?" John displayed the fungi. "Now we can roast them on your fire with the wild onions we found earlier!"

"I don't like mushrooms or onions, Uncle John."

John stayed positive. "Well, sometimes something you don't like is better than nothing at all." Daniel dropped his forehead onto his knees.

The onions and mushrooms roasted fragrantly on makeshift hickory skewers John broke and soaked in the river. They soon became irresistible to the hungry boy. He devoured a stomach-full and fell asleep not long after. John crept over and placed his hand on Daniel's forehead, making sure that he was asleep and that he was well.

Then he stepped away and drew his sword. He removed his stained belt and tabard and placed them on the campfire along with his gauntlets and scabbard. John cleansed his blade over the flames of his burning habit. He couldn't carry his family's blood any farther. He'd taken a longer way back, avoiding the farm, so the boy wouldn't see the bodies.

Daniel woke up the next morning with the sun. John was kneeling next to the campfire's smoking ashes. His chainmail glittered, uncovered, and his sword was bare on the ground in front of him.

"You look different, Uncle John."

John stood. "I took a bath in the creek. You should too. You smell like a stinkhorn!"

Daniel frowned. "Are any of those mushrooms and onions left?"

"You ate them all last night! Don't worry, though, apples are ripe ahead and you'll have the best meal of your life tomorrow at Fergus' place."

They reached Antioch near four o'clock in the next day's afternoon. Chimneys jutted up from the steep, shingled rooftops and narrow, cobbled streets ran between the wood and stone walls. Pale, black-haired people bustled about, practically uniformed in humble brown wool and white linen. They recognized John and met him, asking what he knew. He stopped and offered hospital, according to the custom of the church, and advised them to stay inside and be careful, but he didn't mention the plague.

John led Daniel through a circular courtyard with a well, similar to the marketplace in Meroe, before reaching the northern edge of town and a two story building with multiple smokestacks. The smell of burning apple wood and good food hung in the cool autumn air all around it. A sign on an iron arm over the door read "Cauldron" with a painting of a steaming stew pot.

A bell on a coiled metal strip at the doorjamb rang as they entered and a man called, "Sarah!" from out of sight, down the cramped hallway to the kitchen. John smiled at the sound of that voice; it was all kindness, business and mischief.

The dark wood common room had a low ceiling and a warm hearth. It was filled with the rich, smoky scent of roasting meat, the fragrant bouquet of stewing vegetables and the thick, pillowy aroma of baked bread. Four big bowls of apples lined the lone, long table in the center of the room. At the far end, a man wearing crude, deer-hide clothing waved from his seat in the shadows. Short and stocky, he had a shaggy, black and brown mane of hair and beard, and the amber eyes of a wolf.

John lifted a hand to return the greeting and told Daniel, "Go sit next to Marabbas over there. Be friendly. I'll get us some *real* food."

Daniel scrutinized the stranger. "Yes, sir, but…" He leaned close to John and whispered, *"He looks like a gunder."*

John nodded, impressed, and did not whisper. "That's very good! Marabbas is a gunder!" He gave the boy a gentle push.

John felt the kitchen's heat from the hallway and walked into a torrid, stone dungeon of hanging pans and cooking tools. A plump, sweaty man in a bloody apron darted between the bubbling pots on the stovetop and an open grill that sizzled with steaks. A heavy butcher's table crowded the center of the room and on the other side of it an oven and fireplace radiated hotter than an average man could stand. A big, black cauldron hung simmering from a hook in that fireplace.

The door to the kitchen from outside burst open and Margot, a plump woman with her hair tied up under a scarf, stomped in yelling, "Fergus! You'll cook yourself again! Leave the door open! Oh, hi John! Cider?"

Fergus turned around with a big smile on his dripping face. "Oh, hi John! I'll be a few minutes here. Steak?"

John said, "Yes please, to both. I have a boy with me as well and I need your help." John told them Daniel's story. They promised a room upstairs for him as long as he needed it.

John grinned when he returned to the common room. Daniel was sitting where he'd been told, but leaned away from Marabbas, whose muffled snorts echoed in his upturned mug. John sat with them and Margot came in with a heaping tray of cider mugs, dark loaves of bread and soft butter. The bread was very different from the unleavened griddle cakes Daniel was accustomed to.

Margot said, "Eat up, dear. You've been on a long road." After a careful taste, he attacked the crusty, fluffy loaves.

Fergus brought in steaming bowls of vegetable stew and then plates of thick, fatty steaks. Marabbas' steak was bigger than anyone's. His eyes widened on it as Fergus set it down. If Marabbas had a tail, it would have wagged.

The doorbell rang and rang again. By the time the five of them finished eating, the common room was filled with noisy people. Many of them went to John requesting news. The men of the church usually had interesting stories to tell. John gave them repetitive, vague advice to stay indoors and be careful.

A girl came from upstairs to help serve. She refilled Daniel's mug with a pitcher and a quick smile. After she passed, Daniel asked, "Who was that?"

Fergus grinned. "My youngest, Sarah." Then he winked. "She's sixteen!"

Margot swatted him. "Fergus!"

Daniel was embarrassed. He thought the girl was pretty, but he didn't want anyone to *know* he thought that. He'd simply never been in a restaurant before.

John put his hand on Daniel's shoulder. "You'll be alright here, son. Remember what we talked about. Do what Fergus and Margot say. If I'm not back tomorrow, I'll be about a week."

Daniel knew John was leaving, they'd talked about it, but he was overcome by uncertainty anyway and missing John already. "Yes, sir."

John left the table, bid goodbyes and took his sword from where it leaned against the wall.

Fergus met him at the door. "If you're off to Meroe, let me pack you some."

John looked over at Daniel, sharing the boy's anxiety, and turned back, eyes dark and circled. Rubbing his face, he said, "I haven't slept in days. My chest hurts. I'll lie down at the church for now, but unless Gabriel or Sam can go in my place, I'll have to leave tomorrow. Michael might need me."

Fergus nodded. "If you do, I'll have you ready twenty pounds of good, smoked jerky, some tack and a skin of Margot's firejack." He smiled and winked. "So you won't get too cold."

John couldn't help smiling back. "You're a good friend, Gus. Thank you. Keep this plague business quiet if you can. I don't think it would be good to have people heading out there trying to help. I don't know what's happened yet."

Fergus nodded again.

* * *

Cold, morning air came into the kitchen. The door was propped open with a log. Sarah held up one end of a big, raw bone on the butcher table for her father. The two of them were discussing Daniel, Sarah being unreceptive to her father's suggestion of a marriage.

"He's a little boy, Daddy."

Fergus stripped the flesh and the tendons from the bone. "A little boy that owns a farm and has kin in the church."

Sarah thought about it for a moment. "That's true."

Fergus grinned. "Good girl. If you get to work on it, in a few years you'll be better matched than Beth!" Sarah crinkled her nose and grinned just like her father, mostly at the thought of besting her older sister.

Daniel came in with his arms full of firewood. Sarah gave him a sweet smile and a wave. Her hand was slick with gristle and little blood clots. Daniel would have waved back, but he was holding the wood, so he just stared. Then Margot called for Sarah to come along to the market and the girl flitted away.

Fergus put a greasy arm around Daniel's shoulders and said, "We've our *mise en place*, boy!"

"Meez and what?"

Fergus enunciated. "*Meez - En - Plahss*. Everything is ready! How'd you like to learn some *wizardry*?"

The boy paused. *Wizard* was a dark word, surprising to hear in the morning, in a kitchen. He'd been raised on the brutal fables of Clan Breahg, tales told by the fire at night. They warned of witches and wizards who never drink water, preferring instead the virgin blood of children put to sleep by the awful spell, *the whammy*. Fergus didn't seem like someone who'd drink a sleeping child's blood, but Daniel had never heard the word wizard associated with anything other than a calamitous moral lesson. The boy was on his guard.

Fergus lifted a large, jagged saw from the rack of tools overhead. "They've a ham-fisted gunder over at Betheford's," he said, shoving the saw through the bone, "that'll toss some flesh and *maybe* a veg in a pot and boil it - in water - then call it a soup or a stew. That's neither soup nor stew. It's not even food. There's no *magic* in it. Real food has magic in it and you need *bones* to make magic, boy." Daniel watched the saw's teeth notch an inch of the bone's width per stroke. *Zzz, Vvv, Zzz, Vvv.* It was the length of his leg.

Fergus arranged the segments and joints on a metal tray. "Listen, boy, water is like air and air is nothing. The only thing you get from swallowing air is a belch. Real food has *flavor* and *texture* and since air is nothing, just like water, we can see that water is nothing! It's just air… that's wet. Never add *nothing* when you can add flavor!" He shoved the tray of bones into the blazing oven.

Daniel was confused and nervous. "Yes, sir, but you… drink water, don't you?"

"Fwah, water. I wouldn't drink water if they shunned me. Why drink water when you can drink cider?"

"I… I don't know…"

"No, water's only good for sucking the magic out of other things, like bones and this!" Fergus chopped vegetables into rough chunks for another tray. "The bones by themselves are powerful, but they're wickedly powerful with *this!* Hoo-hoo! Do you know the name of one part carrot, one part celery and two parts onion?"

"No, sir..."

Fergus swept up his hands, holding his big knife in one, and posed like that in his bloody apron, dramatically chanting the words, "*ASSORDEDICUS, AROMATICUS, VEGITABIDILOUS!*"

Daniel let out a shout, "uuhooOOAAAH!" and backed away to the other side of the butcher table, nearly falling over a sack of potatoes. Sure that an evil spell was about to sizzle from the wizard's lips, he picked up a potato and threw it at him.

It hit Fergus in the elbow. "Ow! Bedevil you, Daniel! What was that for?"

"Don't put the whammy on me!" Daniel had another spud cocked and ready.

Fergus gaped. Then he started laughing. He laughed for a long time, hooting, wheezing, wiping his eyes and holding his knees to brace himself. "I promise I won't... *put the whammy on you,*" he struggled to say, then laughed some more. "But, Daniel, listen to me, you're only safe as long as you've a potato! The moment you put it down..." Fergus became serious, raised his eyebrows and squinted.

Daniel frowned at Fergus and then frowned at his potato.

Fergus started laughing again and had to fight the giggles to keep working. Glancing smiles at Daniel, Fergus put his tray of chopped vegetables into the oven under the bones, wiped the butcher block with a dirty rag and then brought down some jars and a few big bowls. Daniel sat on the sack of potatoes, watching him.

Fergus poured steaming water from his kettle into the bowls. He stuck his finger in one and then yanked it out, wagging. "Ouch! Too hot. I don't want to kill them..." He looked sly and sideways. "*Yet.*"

Daniel squatted like a toad on the potatoes, a wide, low frown under his bulging eyes.

Fergus patted one of his jars. "The pixies I have in here, you see. Do you want to see?" Daniel shook his head and stayed where he was. Fergus chuckled, tested the water again and said, "Perfect! Just hot enough to make them scream. It's their screaming that makes the bread rise." He opened the jar and started spooning thick, muddy yeast into the water.

"That's not pixies."

"Pfft, what do you know?"

"That's just mud or something."

"Fwah! Mud. These are my screaming pixies."

Daniel came over to look. "What is it, really? What makes the bread like that?"

Fergus looked around conspicuously, as if to make sure no one was listening, and then whispered the mysteries of leavening to Daniel while the yeast bloomed in the water. The boy was fascinated. Fergus gave him some molasses to taste and then, tossing flour like fairy dust on the blood-stained table, taught Daniel how to mix and knead bread dough. They set their dough balls aside, to let the pixies scream, and went with buckets to the well.

Daniel sloshed his water trying to keep up. "Is the cook at Betheford's really a gunder?"

Fergus smiled. "No." Then he winked, said, "He's *dumber than a gunder!*" and laughed. Daniel didn't laugh, so Fergus said, "Don't they say *dumber than a gunder* over in Breahg? It's funny!"

"No. I mean, no sir, they don't say that. They say to stay away from thieving gunders. If a gunder'd come round the farm, Pa'd call him a rascal and run him off."

"Oh, well, that's…"

Daniel interrupted unintentionally, opening up to Fergus. "I've been to Meroe."

"Oh! Well…"

"Oaky's from there. He works for Pa… or, I guess he used to work for Pa in the summer. Oaky took me a couple times but they didn't say dumb as gunders either and he got me some chewy candy there."

"Ah, I…"

"I'm sure sorry I chucked that baker at you, sir." It had taken him a while to get to it, but Daniel wanted to apologize. "Thank you, for keeping me while my uncle's away."

Fergus smiled. "You're welcome, boy. Let's get back to our mise en place. Who knows what villain may have fouled our *mise* while we've been bothering with these wretched buckets? Never touch another man's mise. It's the most important rule in the kitchen!"

The bones roasted to a golden brown in the oven. Fergus placed them in the bottom of the cauldron with the carrots, celery and onions and then waved his hands over his work, chanting again, but a little less dramatically. "From the mists of *thyme*," he said, giving Daniel a cheesy wink, "come forth, spirits! Oo-de-lally!" and tossed in a small, cloth bag of mixed herbs.

They poured cold well water in up to the pot's rim, lit a fire under it with a taper - there were plenty of tapers and always a fire in Fergus' house - and then turned back to the business of the bread. By twelve o'clock, stock and bread had filled the building with powerful, wholesome aromas. Daniel followed Fergus around, assisting him and getting quizzed.

Fergus waved his wooden spoon like a wand and tapped the stove. "What is the single most important spell component at a wizard's disposal, boy?"

"Huh?"

Fergus folded his arms. "What is the most important thing in the kitchen?"

"Uh... never let another man touch me?"

Fergus shook his head. "No!" He waved his hand around. "What's the best thing in here?" Behind his grin, Fergus was preparing a lecture on the magical qualities of butter, which, in his opinion, was by far the best and most important thing in the kitchen. Fergus had recipes, techniques and taste buds devoted to butter and enjoyed arguing butter's superiority over all other culinary devices.

Daniel said, "Oh, Pa'd say it's bacon, I guess."

Fergus paused. "Your pa's right." He didn't want to argue with the memory of the boy's father. Besides, Fergus knew a few tasty things about bacon. It wasn't the worst thing the boy could have said.

9 The Golden Rule

John rode his pinto south toward Meroe, leading Ares on a rope. An hour after the crossroads to the farm he saw a group trudging up ahead. Worried they were a mass of devils, he brought the horses to a stop. As the group approached, John noticed they had goats, small carts with chicken coops and other supplies. At the front, waving and carrying his saddle over one shoulder, was Michael. John went to them, dismounted and embraced his filthy, scarred and tattered friend. The sailors gathered around them.

* * *

The group's pace was slow. John walked next to Captain, who told some of what he knew while impressing with his matches and his pipe. To John, he was a mysterious, black-skinned pirate, conjuring fire and breathing smoke.

Captain said, "Zeke didn't tell us much about them, the bauran. He'd no time for questions. That might've been why it happened the way it did for the *Vesper*. She didn't have our crew of course, but, had Zeke told them more..." Captain shrugged and paused for a smoke. "Mmm, no. He'd only time to tell us where to go. And now, after leagues of water and heartbreaking impossibilities, we've come, and found you, the strangest of all. I've wondered if you're even men."

Drake spoke up from behind, "Well they're not women, Captain. Look at the mustache on Michael."

John brightened and clapped Michael on the back. "Hah, Michael! You're not a woman!" Michael shook his head with a weak smile. He'd had quite enough of Drake by then.

Drake went on, "Even Andalynn can't grow one like that."

Andalynn hooded her eyes. She *didn't* have a mustache. Biggs grinned. There was a smile hiding in her face. For her, friendly teasing was a comfort. She didn't have many friends among the crew. Most of them avoided her or referred to her in secret by derogatory names, like *Armymom* and *Shooty McShoot-shoot*.

Michael scolded Drake. "Be careful, young man. That's an off thing to say to a woman. Show some courtesy."

Drake smirked.

John smirked too.

Captain tried to redirect the conversation. "They've burned down the world and you just walk through them. How do you do it?"

John didn't respond. He behaved as though Captain had said nothing. It was the same with Michael any time he didn't want to answer a question about the church. They answered such questions with silence.

Captain said, "Not ones to share your secrets, are you?"

John pointed at Captain's pipe and changed the subject. "Why do you do that? Does it protect you from those devils?"

Captain said, "Mmm, no," letting go of the other matter. "This is an herbal remedy that eases my condition. Land sickness, you see." He cleared his throat. Michael and John shared a dubious expression.

Ditch adjusted his pack. "Whatever, man."

The sailors stayed close to Michael and John during the long walk north, secrets or not. A sparse forest began to frame the road. The trees were long before their leaves and white, like lonely bones. None grew close enough to touch another. The nights in those woods terrified the sailors. At sea, their ship's height and cabin doors protected them, but on open land they were vulnerable. Their campfires made long, flickering shadows in the trees that looked like silent bauran lurching from every direction. Michael and John took turns to rest. No sailor slept.

Weeds penetrated cracks in the weathered path's mortar. Three fires glowed by the roadside but almost everyone huddled around the one near Michael. He sat on his saddle, hunched over a book with a quill pen, taking notes from the sailors' stories. They spoke in whispers, trying to avoid attracting any attention from what might be wandering in the woods. John lay sleeping with his back to a deserted fire twenty feet away.

Captain said, "Let's talk about another thing or other. Being out here is one thing. Being out here and talking about them has me crawling out of my skin."

Drake said, "Uh oh, Captain, a bauran's gonna get you!" and broke the quiet with a dopey, "Oowoooh", raising his arms and wiggling his fingers. Everyone stared at him in stark disbelief. Drake slapped his hands over his mouth, realizing he'd been too loud.

Ditch splayed and hissed, "Shut up you dumb stupid!" Other angry sailors shushed Drake and threw things at him. Then, as the group's shushing grew louder than the offense it punished, John started to snore. It was a phlegm-toothed snarl that gnawed on the edge of the sibilant din, drawing silence and worried glances. Michael got up and stopped it with a swat to John's boots.

When Michael came back, he pointed at Drake and gave him a hard stare. "Inappropriate." Drake shied away.

Biggs said, "Yeah, never heard one go *oowoooh*."

Ditch apologized for Drake, "He's a dookus, man."

Biggs chuckled. "The lot of us seen more'n people oughtta, Michael. Oughtta be nuttier'n a case a' fruit cakes."

As usual, Michael had to rely on context for meaning. He picked up his book and tapped his quill in its little ink jar. "You said they eventually stop smoking. How long does that take?"

Biggs poked at the fire. "Not sure, just seen some that don't, or smoke less I guess. Might be they run out. Been thinkin' they make it out the parts they don't need, like little factories." Michael's pen scratched the page as Biggs spoke. "Never watched one for longer'n it takes to put a bullet in 'em, but it's always the old ones that don't smoke. The ones that're real lean and settled down to muscle and bone. The fast ones."

Captain covered his face and mouthed an ancient nursery rhyme to himself, "*A llama, a llama, a llama lying down...*" He hoped it would get stuck in his head and leave no room for thoughts about the developmental stages of bauran.

Ditch said, "I hate the fast ones, man. They're like, spiders, or somethin, you know? Hard to hit."

Michael said, "I've not seen one I'd call fast. I'd say they barely move along."

Andalynn said, "You have encountered the young. They are uncoordinated and struggle in their own flesh like a straightjacket.

We have seen bauran that would be impossible to outrun. It is unsettling."

Michael thought of the lean horror chained in the *Vesper's* hold. "The one in the ship must have been old."

A twig snapped in the darkness, more alarming than a rifle going off. Michael stood up, dropped his book and pulled his sword. The sailors held their breath. Everyone listened, trying to pick the sound of an approach out of the campfires' crackle. A bauran wouldn't wait or be cautious; it would come right at them.

A creature was out there, but it wasn't what they thought, or anything the sailors had ever heard of. Firelight shined in her eyes, amber, like those of a wolf. She paused after stepping on the twig, realizing it would alert the men by the fire. They smelled of sour milk. She stared at John without blinking and started coiling her strength. He was the most removed from the group. She could drag him out of the light before the others could react.

Then, like a bear in a cave, John's snore returned. The creature's face flared and she shot straight up into the air. She landed scrabbling and bounded away. The sailors exhaled, imagining she'd been a curious deer or some such. Michael kept his sword drawn, though. He gave John's boots a swat strong enough to wake him up. John yawned and looked around with his eyes closed.

Captain lit a match and held it to his pipe with trembling hands. "Just an animal. That means there're no bauran about then... right?" He looked to Andalynn.

She said, "Sometimes."

Captain said, "A puff or two, to give me some ease..."

Ditch said, "Man, grow up. That stuff's for kids. And it stinks."

Captain dismissed Ditch with the usual defense, "Mmm, it's medicinal. I've a condition." He held the smoke in his lungs and passed his pipe to an eager Welles.

Welles said, "I'm sick too."

Michael took longer to relax, thinking about what was out there, stalking them. At least three books in the church bestiary applied to the woods between Antioch and Meroe. At the sailors' claims of being sick, however, Michael sheathed his caligan and returned to the conversation. "You're not ill." They were in exceptional health. He'd made sure of it.

Sailors snickered and smiled. Captain's eyes shifted while he waited for the pipe to make its rounds. He didn't need to explain himself to Michael.

* * *

Neither hospital nor pipe-smoking could replace sleep. Restless nights made the sailors grumble and drag their feet. They felt like they would never arrive. Then, as one morning's fog lifted and the forest's scent was heavy and moist, John and Michael pointed out hazy buildings in the inclining miles ahead where the forest thinned into a field. The sailors were revived.

"Look, everybody!"
"Yeah, man, look out! There it is!"
"At last, Antioch!"

They celebrated, hugging and cheering. Their pace doubled. As they got closer, however, their jubilance gave way to concern and their conversation focused on a glaring hole in the town's defense.

"No wall? There's no wall."
"Not even, like, a fence, man."
"It is de-*fence*-less."

Ditch frowned at Drake. "Man…"

Biggs went to Michael. "Never even thought to ask! We'll help y'all put up a wall. We all wanna help." Others supported him on that.

Michael said, "I don't know what the fellowship is going to do about all this. It's their city."

Biggs was surprised. "But, they'll listen to you, right? I know we're on our own and all when we get there, but they gotta listen to you guys 'bout sump'n like this."

Michael answered the question carefully. "Our influence is… limited. They're more like our neighbors than anything else."

Biggs didn't think Michael was taking the threat seriously enough. "Those things are comin' here. They find people. And when they do, they aint gon' wait for you guys to show up."

Michael nodded, not wanting to appear indifferent. "Of course, I'll help however I can. A wall seems like a good idea to me."

Captain tapped himself on the nose. "First, the incinerator."

Ditch added, "A big one."

Michael and John looked at each other, sharing unspoken concern over how the fellowship would respond to the blasphemy of corpse burning, especially on a scale requiring an incinerator larger than the one on the *Grace*. What such a machine meant for the surrounding population sobered the two healers.

Michael said, "John, I want you to ride ahead and get my father. I'll walk the sailors in from here."

John said, "Of course. Here, I'll bring Ares in too."

* * *

A sign beside the road read "Antioch" above a painted bull's-eye of spiraling rings that represented the town's streets. The word "Church" labeled a mark in the wide center. Northeast of that, on one of the inner rings, another mark read, "Betheford's Inn." On the sign, the inn was slightly more prominent than the church, it was Betheford's sign after all, but the governing principle of Antioch's construction was that every building fought for a spot closest to the Circle's house. The inner rings were the oldest streets.

Townsfolk called out to each other and collected by the hundreds, whispering about the approaching group. They met with cautious curiosity. A human circle of sailors and citizens formed around Michael as he prepared to speak.

The man standing next to Ditch stared at the tattoos. Ditch looked up at him, held out a hand and said, "What's up, man? I'm Ditch."

Surprised by the mean-looking little stranger's friendliness, the citizen shook hands with him and interpreted the unfamiliar greeting. "Oh my, excuse me! How do you do?"

Michael shouted, "Everyone, listen to me!" The crowd shushed each other to hear. Michael waited for their attention and then said, "These people are from oversea!" He had to shout over gasps and murmurs after that. "By the grace of God, they've found you! You are their sanctuary! They've traveled very far.

They're tired and hungry! Please, do for them as you would have them do for you!"

Questions swelled from all around about the sailors and Meroe. Guesses and rumors had stemmed from John's brief visit two weeks before, when he'd left Daniel at the Cauldron, but neither any news of the tragedy nor any bauran had yet come to Antioch. Michael's repetitive response, trying to add incentive to housing the sailors, was that they could tell the whole story.

As he redirected attention to the sailors, Michael searched the milling crowd for his father. There was John. Next to him stood an older, bearded version of Michael in Antioch's brown and white, Deacon Betheford. They pushed toward each other for a close conversation. Betheford listened and nodded.

Michael felt some relief then, for the sailors at least. He left. John followed him. The citizens discussed the announcement with astonishment and the sailors held their breath.

The crew of the *Grace* had known that moment would come. There was no room for fifty people at the church. Having been at the mercy of the smoke, the sea and the Circle, they were finally at the mercy of the fellowship.

They had little time for worry, though. Betheford took the crowd's attention and made a show of offering rooms at his inn to ten sailors, including Drake, Ditch and Biggs. Others followed his example and came forward, offering places in their homes. Captain chose then to light his pipe, receiving appreciative *oohs* and *aahs* and a prompt invitation from the candle maker, Bing. Margot, a basket of vegetables on her hip, asked Andalynn to take the extra bed in Sarah's room.

As sailors waved goodbye to one another and followed their hosts into the city, Biggs and Andalynn made plans to meet the following morning.

* * *

Andalynn chose a seat at the far end of the table from Marabbas in the Cauldron's otherwise empty common room. Margot went into the kitchen. When Margot returned, with cider, bread, cheese and stew, Marabbas had moved down. Andalynn was rigid and tight lipped, suspecting that he'd sniffed her.

Margot set out the food and drinks gently. "It's a good life here, dear." She sat and started slicing apples onto a plate. "We'll do right by you and your friends. You'll see."

Andalynn gave her a mechanical smile.

Margot said, "You know, people have been arguing forever over whether anyone was really oversea. I've heard stories about pirates coming to shore at night and mollygoddling folk out to the water for wicked revelries, but that's always sounded to me like they'd too much to drink and passed out on the beach."

Andalynn took a careful bite of the stew. She melted. The dish was an enchantment of hearty, tender meat, potatoes and carrots in a rich, beefy broth - homemade food. That bite ended a year of death and flight. She said, "Delicious."

Margot beamed. "Oh yes, Fergus is a wizard. That's my husband. His food's the only part of him I can get out of the kitchen! You should take a pull of that cider, dear. That's mine. Fergus says my brewing's why he married me."

Andalynn drank the cider and dipped the bread in the stew. The cheese was firm and tangy with a pan-seared crust. She ate chunks of it on sweet, crisp apple wedges. Andalynn abandoned her guard with Margot and even smiled at that hairy sniffer, Marabbas. Sarah, Fergus and Daniel came in gawking. Andalynn's blonde hair and copper skin were unlike anything they'd ever seen. They ate together before business picked up at five o'clock.

Guests gathered around and exchanged stories with Andalynn for hours. She had already learned much about them from Michael and John and heard those tales again. The fellowship was a religious community that had fled from persecution in the north a hundred years before. Despite a sad and bloody history, they'd made a peaceful and happy home in the south when they'd found the church.

They marveled at her tales of fallen civilizations and of encounters with the living dead on the high sea. It was of continual surprise to Andalynn how they handled it all. They believed no harm would come to them, she assumed because of the church.

The bell rang and greeting shouts of, "Davies!" vaulted from the room.

Davies, the milkman, was twenty-eight years old and had arms like corded steel from squeezing teats. "Ha, ha, yes! I heard you've got a sailor over here! Everywhere that does is packed!"

"You won't believe it!"
"They're just like us oversea!"
"But look! She wears pants!"

Davies smiled like he'd heard an interesting joke. "*She?*" Then he saw Andalynn's hair and, "Yellow!" burst out of his mouth.

She raised an eyebrow at him. That simple, common expression told Davies everything he needed to know about sailors. He boomed laughter and shouted, "Well, that's Fergus! First contact and he grabs a dishwasher!" The room laughed with him. Then he told her, "No offense."

Andalynn was puzzled. The man seemed to be taunting her.

The room treated Davies like a hero, offering him seats and information. Someone put a mug in his hand. He sat down opposite Andalynn, who was no longer in conversation with anyone. The milkman drank cider and tried to respond to his peers' flooding, excited explanations. "No, I didn't know that. I've been at work all day, not gossiping! What's that about Meroe? Oh, well, they'll be in our prayers. Breahg? Pfft, who cares about them?"

Jacob, a blacksmith as burly as the milkman, had been in the Cauldron for an hour by then and had met with Michael and John at the church before that. He raised an informed yet friendly challenge to Davies' quick dismissal of Breahg. "Meroe'd make for Breahg to get away from these bauran devils, wouldn't they? That's probably where they all are. Breahg's close to Meroe and always ready for a fight." He held up a meaty fist.

Davies grimaced. "Breahg. Fwah. Better Meroe made for the woods! The clan's worse than a few booyah devils. Savages and thieves. Everybody knows there's gunder in their blood."

Andalynn saw the makings of an altercation and flashed a look at Marabbas, who still sat next to her. She'd discovered earlier he was known as a gunder. Marabbas, however, didn't mind the insult that Davies had made no attempt to hide.

Daniel glared from the kitchen. "I hate Davies."

Fergus laughed. "I know you do!"

"He's out there right now saying Breahg's got gunder blood!"

Fergus held out a potato to him. "Here, see if you can hit him in the mouth." Daniel reached for it and Fergus pulled it away, amused to have been taken seriously. "Daniel! Don't waste a good potato on Davies!" Fergus tossed the spud back in the sack and went to tend his coals.

Daniel swiped his hand through the air at Davies as if to say *forget you!* Then he picked up a rag and twisted it. "Where's Uncle John? How come he didn't come over here before some sailor?"

"I'm sure he's in that church, boy, kneeling." Fergus stepped on a clever pedal beneath his grill's basin and the rack rose up on a pole in the center, exposing the coals - Jacob's work.

Fergus said, "Trouble in Meroe, devils, sailors, this is all going to require hours and hours of kneeling." He pulled his chin into his throat, trying to look stuffy. *"Hmm, something's happened, old boy. We'd better kneel and give that some thought. Ah."* He turned the coals with his poker and tossed in a piece of apple wood. "Don't worry, he'll come," then, grinning, added, "at the very least to eat." Daniel frowned at him.

Davies smirked at Andalynn. "So, you'll be staying here then?"

She kept a polite tone. "I will, as long as they choose to extend their hospitality to me."

He set his mug in front of her and leaned back in his chair, hands behind his head. "Well, get us a drink then, dearie, I'm dry!" Jacob chuckled at his friend's mischief and watched Andalynn for a reaction. A few men in the room did some chortling and some *ooh-woo*'ing.

She was speechless. Here was this milkman, relaxing and smirking, hoping she would do something rash, like throwing the mug at him. She saw it. Davies enjoyed causing people to lose their tempers, especially women, and considered it a great victory when he did so. Andalynn stood, picked up his mug… and took it toward the kitchen.

Sarah scooted after her. "Wow, I thought you were going to throw it at him!"

Andalynn said, "Would that have been the appropriate response? What you would have done?"

"I guess. I don't know. No, not really, but I would have liked to see someone else do it. I'd have at least cussed him and I for d sister, Beth, was married to him.

Andalynn smiled. "It is comforting to know that my initial impulses were not out of the ordinary here."

Daniel had been watching from the kitchen and kept a frown on Andalynn as she entered. When she picked up the cider pitcher to refill the mug, Daniel's mouth fell open in disgust. "Don't get Davies a drink! He's a rascal! All he does is talk mess! You should've shot him with your pisser!" The kitchen went silent. Those things on her hips had been the subject of conversation earlier.

Andalynn corrected him. "Pistol."

Fergus grinned from the grill. "Davies sent you to wait on him? That's rich. Why are you doing it?"

Andalynn looked into the empty pitcher. "Unsure of the possible consequences to a visceral response, I chose one that I thought, cross-culturally, could not be considered offensive."

Fergus paused. "Oh, well..." His smile returned. "Let's put a beetle in it!"

Andalynn laughed. "I am still considering amendments to my position." She held up the pitcher. "Fergus, where may I refill this container?"

Fergus said, "Margot's out back, tapping a cask. Come on, I'll show you!" Andalynn followed him out, trailed by Sarah and Daniel.

The Cauldron marked north on Antioch's outer ring and was one of the newest buildings in the city. A hundred yards of apple trees separated it from the deeper forest. A small, open yard connected it to a little cottage and a shed. The cottage was Margot's cider house and Fergus used the shed for smoking meats. Evening was lowering into night.

As they crossed the yard, Fergus sent Daniel to check the wood pile for a beetle or a spider. "A big, wriggly one!" Daniel obeyed like a grim soldier.

The rest of them entered the cider house. The spicy scent of apples and alcohol sat in the stone and boards. One wall was a deep rack of casks in the candlelight. Margot looked up at them from where she worked. "Fergus! What's happened?"

Fergus was amused. "Davies sent our sailor to get him a drink. And she's doing it."

"*What?*" Margot stood up and put her fists on her hips. "Davies! The spleen on him! I'll tell *him* where to go to get a drink!" She clucked her tongue at Andalynn. "Ooh, dear, you shouldn't let a man treat you like that."

Andalynn was amused too. "I am educating myself in local custom by way of this adventure."

The five of them returned to the common room as a pack, Andalynn at their lead, holding the mug. She put it in front of Davies and sat. The others stood behind her, waiting. Davies was in conversation and hadn't noticed them yet.

Jacob tapped his arm and pointed them out. "It's the end for you, brother." Davies looked up, surprised.

Margot put her fists on her hips. "You should be ashamed of yourself - *Davies!*" She declared his name, accusing of him of being who he was. "You should be *ashamed*, sending her to get your drink!" Margot had the whole room's attention then. Davies was in trouble.

Davies laughed. "I didn't think she'd do it! I was just... ruffling her feathers a little."

Margot said, "Oh, I know exactly what you were doing. Where's Beth?"

"She's at home with our five, fine sons, of course. She thinks we're being invaded! I'm here to get the lay of the land and to protect my family." At the look of indignation on Margot's face, Davies laughed again and slapped the table.

"With your mug in a mug? Pouring sauce on our guests? Well, you've got your drink now, so drink it!" Margot pointed her finger at it like it was a fitting punishment for him.

Davies shrewdly looked the five of them over: Margot's indignation, Daniel's hate, Sarah's confusion and Fergus' anticipation. Andalynn's face was a wall. Davies said, "Fergie, what'd you put in this?" Fergus raised his hands innocently. Davies declined the suspicious beverage. "No, thank you. I've had enough for the evening." Then he feigned injury at Andalynn. "You tattled on me?"

Andalynn raised the eyebrow again. "I apologize." Had he been flirting with her? She couldn't tell. She wondered if Davies would treat her differently if he knew she was old enough to be his mother. Probably not.

Davies held out his hand and said, "Welcome to Antioch." She took it. Then he said, "It's alright, I've got a mean woman at home as well." He looked to Margot. "Isn't that right, *Gran-gran?*" Margot was only thirty-eight, but Davies had made her a grandmother five times. They were some of his greatest victories.

Margot said, "Cheeky devil. I'd better not catch you with an odd lip to these sailors, Davies. They've been through too much to be sassed by the likes of *you!*" She narrowed her eyes on him before going back through the kitchen. Sarah, Fergus and Daniel followed her.

Sarah said, "I don't understand why Andalynn didn't stick up for herself. Are the women cowards oversea?"

Fergus said, "That's rude, Sarah. Besides, I think she did, didn't she?"

Daniel said, "Huh? Davies told her what to do and she did it. That was awful!"

After Margot was gone, Davies taunted Andalynn again. "You, yellow-crested tattletale! I guess pants don't make you a man, do they, sailor?"

Andalynn said, "They do not." Then she picked up the suspicious mug, the one Davies had ordered and had then refused, and she drank.

Jacob smiled. "Fwah! I like sailors!" With strength that hammered steel for the Circle, Jacob gave Davies a playful shove. It almost tipped the milkman out of his chair. Davies laughed and kept his balance.

* * *

Near eleven o'clock that night, the Cauldron cleared down to family and the doorbell finally stopped ringing. Andalynn was already asleep upstairs. Margot had instructed her to bring some friends, especially "that handsome Biggs," to dinner the next day. Daniel sulked at the long table by himself. John never came.

Fergus entered from the narrow hall, wiping his hands with a rag. "I'm sorry, Daniel. I'm sure he'll come tomorrow. He's got very important things to do right now."

Daniel didn't want to hear it. After listening to Andalynn's stories, he knew John wasn't coming back. He knew because he'd seen the bauran in their terrible truth. John would have to abandon him to face them.

Fergus patted the boy's shoulder. "Poor devil."

The end of a conversation followed Sarah out of the kitchen as she swept through the common room. She said, "Betheford's, eew!" and bounced up the stairs without looking twice at Daniel.

Margot called after her, "Andalynn's bringing them to dinner tomorrow, dear, so get some clean clothes ready for her! Ooh, I hope she doesn't bring too many friends. *Fergus!* Don't forget to lock the door! Those sailor-stories are giving me the heebs and jeebs!"

Fergus sighed and pulled the latch. "We never used to lock the door."

10 The Circle

Antioch's buildings and streets spiraled around a broad clearing of earth and grass, sown in rows with tombstones. It was the Circle's graveyard, where their dead lay buried as saints. In the center stood the old, single-story, stone church, its thatched roof extended over one side to cover a forge. From there Jacob's hammer rang.

Michael leaned his caligan against a post under the thatch. "Hello, Jacob."

The blacksmith came out to meet him, smiling. "Michael! Welcome back, sir!" Then Jacob's smile fell away. "Fwah... you've been in it with a devil, hey?"

Michael nodded, removing his tattered habit.

John said, "Jacob."

Jacob said, "John."

Michael dropped his gauntlets, belt and boots on the ground. "I don't know if anything can be done with those." He pulled off his tabard. "This is for the fire."

Jacob collected everything. "Phew, what a stench! These'll never do any good again."

Michael unlaced his one-piece, chainmail sleeve. He stepped out of it and then shed the dingy shreds of his longhandles, a formerly white, full body-stocking of padded underwear. Bullet scars mapped his skin. Whole chunks of him had been blasted away. He gave his armor to Jacob, pointing out the damage.

Jacob stared at Michael's wounds. "You're all... chewed up..."

Michael motioned at the mail.

Jacob focused and poked his fingers through the holes. "The metal's shattered, no ripping. Wasn't claws or teeth... I'd almost guess arrows. What did this to you?"

"If you've something with a point, I'll show you."

Michael sat on the rough tree-stump outside. Jacob went to rummage in his tools and came back with a rusty, six-inch awl, wiping it on his apron before handing it over. John linked his hands behind his back to watch.

Michael exhaled and relaxed, trying to avoid opening the way reflexively; if his flesh healed around the tool, it would leave a permanent hole in his leg. He pushed the awl into his thigh until the point touched bone. Blood spurted from the puncture. Jacob cringed. Michael dug in with his finger, keeping his breath deep and even, and then pulled out a lead slug. Light beamed from the wound and the bleeding stopped.

John said, "Your control is remarkable, Michael. You'll want some food before you do much more of that, though. Why'd you walk all the way back with that thing in your leg?"

Michael held up the bloody slug, remembering how it had jolted him awake when he'd been so close to death. He handed it to Jacob. "That one saved my life. I'll need your help digging out some smaller bits later, John." He felt the riin around a peppering of metal in his body - the metal dragged through his body by the bullets. "I think they're pieces of my sleeve, actually."

John scratched his beard, worried. "I see."

Michael ran his finger along the ugly scar from his cheek to his neck. "This one almost killed me. They struck me down from a hundred and fifty, maybe two hundred yards away," he pointed at the bullet in Jacob's hand, "with those little things."

Jacob said, "Who did?"

"Sailors."

Jacob paused. "Sailors... really?" It was as though he'd heard pixies did the shooting.

Michael nodded. "It's true. There are a few headed for my father's place right now, if you want to meet them and hear some stories. I'm sure it's all over town."

Jacob gaped. "Just like that? There are *sailors* in Antioch?"

Michael nodded again but his attention drifted. The sailors were the best of his news, a small group of curious lives saved. Michael would rather talk about them than what dominated his mind: Meroe, bauran and Armageddon.

John said, "Jacob, could we have a moment?"

"Oh, sure. I… I think I'll stop by Fergus' place, first, hey. I'll need a cider if I'm going to see sailors." He wandered into the forge with Michael's sleeve.

John turned to Michael. "I've wanted to talk to you about what happened in Meroe. It must have been very difficult." Michael had been knee-deep in death for too long and had mentioned God more in the last week than he had in thirty years. It was a growing source of concern for John.

Michael said, "It had to be done. The bodies were smoking. The buildings were filled with it. We had to make a safe path. More ships may come."

John's sympathy showed. "Were there many… bodies?"

"Four hundred and thirty-three. It was an awful day's work. Dreadful." Michael went to the well, cranked up the bucket and took a long drink of good, clean water. Then he poured it over himself, rinsing away the road and the blood. "No one could help me, because of the smoke. I carried them in pieces, from the northern edge of town and from the coast. Then I burned them. They'll haunt me forever, whether or not they haunt Meroe."

John wanted to comfort Michael, to embrace him and to reassure him, but Michael wasn't his acolyte anymore. Michael was a grown man and the templar's consecrate. He was also nude. John stayed where he was. "It's horrible. You've been through too much. Come to the Cauldron with me. Sit and eat with friends before we advise Abraham."

Michael shook his head. "No. I know you're worried, but I need you to help me act. We can't rest now, there's no time."

John nodded. "I'll gather them in the library for you."

* * *

Michael left the forge in full white with a touch of gold, wearing a new tabard and longhandles. His head, hands and feet were bare. Three teenage boys knelt in silence on the grass near the church's front door.

Michael passed them but then hesitated and stopped. "I've just returned from Meroe. Did any of you have family there?" He winced right after he said it.

Edward lifted his head. "*Did?* What do you mean *did?*" Then he realized what had just happened; his resolve had been tested and he'd failed. His hands went to his face. Those were the first words he'd spoken in three months.

Michael's face was an apology. "Edward, I... I'll be your advocate next year. I promise." *If there is a next year. How could I have tested them with that? How could I have been so callous?*

Edward gritted his teeth. "That's... you... what a dirty trick! Did something happen in Meroe? My cousin lives there."

Michael refused to say. The other boys bowed their heads when he looked at them. Edward shouted, "Fwah!" more than once as he stomped away, "FWAAAH!" Michael sighed and went in.

The church was a windowless hall lit by a single hearth. Ten straw mats lined the cold stone floor. Two men knelt inside, both wearing blank acolyte's tabards over their clothes. Joseph wore a kind of yellow plaid under his, dyed from the flowers around his home town of Summerset. Thomas had been wearing the fellowship's brown and white for years.

They stood and saluted. Michael returned their respect but made it clear he was bound for the oak and iron door at the other end of the room. After he passed, Thomas and Joseph whispered to one another.

"John was just as grim."
"I say, what do you think has happened?"
"Something bad."

Michael knocked. Abraham opened the door from the other side as if he'd been waiting there. The mail sagged on his scrawny frame. Hair and beard flowed like white willow from his head and four scars clawed through the right side of his deep and withered face. An iron key hung from a chain around his neck. He stepped aside for Michael.

Books, papers and scrolls crammed the small library's shelves on every wall, shadowy from the candles on the round table in the center. Michael took a seat with John, Samuel and Gabriel while Abraham locked the door with his key. Other than Michael, all wore the full habit of the Circle.

Samuel touched his own rugged face, indicating Michael's scar. "That's a good one, Michael!" Samuel was missing his two front teeth. It gave him a boyish look when he smiled, despite his beef and wrinkles.

Gabriel was a huge man, tall, even in his chair, and broad. Burn scars webbed his jaw and throat and descended into his collar, as though he'd been splashed with acid. His voice was rich bass and sarcastic. "Where is your sleeve, Michael? Are you going to advise the templar in your longhandles? Outrageous."

Sudden pity crossed Michael's face. He knew by Gabriel's manner that no rumor had reached him. Gabriel, who had come from generations of Meroans, who was that town's pride and champion, had no idea what Michael was about to reveal.

John passed Michael a book. The cover and spine read *Bauran* in sacred script. It was Michael's full account of those monsters, taken from his, John's and the sailors' experiences. The ships' notes stuck out from its pages. John passed the *Vesper's* logbook as well.

Michael took out the bloody, crumpled parchment Biggs had found, passed it to Gabriel and addressed the table. "That letter, in our script, was on a ship that ran aground near Meroe, undoubtedly the source of... what happened. A ship from oversea."

Gabriel, Samuel and Abraham paused and looked at John, who nodded.

Michael held up the note Andalynn had given him. "This one came by the sailors of another ship, who are here, now, in the..."

Abraham interrupted. "You've examined them?"

Michael said, "Of course," and resumed, dreading Gabriel's imminent reaction. "The notes are nearly identical..."

Abraham interrupted again. "No, no, Michael, not the notes! I meant these *sailors*. You've laid hands on them?"

Michael breathed like he was pulling a bullet out of his thigh. "Of course, sir, that is what I meant as well. Human. Men and women. Fifty altogether." He waited for another interruption. Abraham motioned impatiently for him to continue.

Michael read the note aloud:

"Armageddon is arrived."
"Break your silence."
"Open the library."

"Ezekiel."

He handed it to Gabriel, who still held the other and didn't know what to think of either. Samuel's mouth fell open. Abraham put his elbows on the table and covered his face, hair spouting from behind his gauntlets.

Comparing the two notes, Gabriel spluttered, "Outrageous!"

Abraham brought down his hands and pushed himself up from his chair. He pulled a dusty ledger from one of the shelves and opened it close to his face, squinting at the text and grumbling. "Mmrnmhrn... Armageddon... prophecy... idiocy..." Michael tried to wait for Abraham's attention but Gabriel demanded to know what had happened. So, with the templar flipping pages in the background, Michael reported the story of Meroe.

Gabriel's face emptied. "You burned the bodies and you burned the town..." His heart broke as he began to understand. Abraham still flipped through the book.

Michael said, "Sir, did you hear what I said?"

Abraham looked up. "Some sort of devil-fever destroyed Meroe. I'm going blind, Michael, not deaf." He put the ledger on the table and his finger on a name. "Here he is, Ezekiel, ordained as paladin on September tenth..." He mumbled and counted on his hand for a moment. "This *Zeke* is a liar or he's two hundred and eighty-seven years old." His discovery and his lack of compassion struck the table. Gabriel looked about to vomit.

Michael said, "The sailors described him as a young man and told of him restoring them to youth."

Abraham scoffed. "I can't imagine a two hundred and eighty-seven year old man looking very young, can you?"

Michael tried to clarify. "Perhaps Ezekiel's path allows athanasy." It was a fabled ability, curing age, near-immortality.

Abraham scoffed again. "Oh! And not only that, he's discovered life oversea! And a way to get there, without leaving any record or inkling of it here. But despite those great accomplishments, he sends us *sailors* to protect. Why is he bothering us to break our silence? Why doesn't he break his own silence and mind his own business?"

"I... I don't know. What are you saying?"

"You've got some paper instructing us to break the most sacred vow and the word of a handful of strangers to authorize it." Abraham slid the old ledger toward Michael. "Our record says Ezekiel died over two hundred years ago. He's buried in the churchyard." Michael studied the book. Abraham continued, "How do you know these *sailors* are who they say they are? How do you know any of this is what it appears to be?"

Michael said, "I believe them. I've been with them. They aren't lying to me." Abraham shook his head at what he saw as the younger man's foolishness. Michael tried to provide an example on the sailors' behalf. "If the writer is a liar, how does he know so much? Look at how practiced he is with the script. His hand is better than mine." Samuel offered Abraham one of the notes.

Abraham glanced at it. "Yes, he has beautiful penmanship." He gave it back. "Has it occurred to you that it might be easier to *burn down the world* than to infiltrate the Circle?"

The idea disgusted Michael. "No, it hasn't."

"It's easier to learn the script than it is to learn the way."

John said, "You'll have to meet them, Abraham. They're like no people I've ever seen. I believe them too."

Abraham stroked his beard.

Samuel compared the notes. "Well, he could have written a little more than this. *Open the library…* What's that supposed to mean?" He looked around the small room. Sure, they kept it locked most of the time, the books were old and valuable, but only to them. Why would opening the library accompany such heavy matters as breaking silence and Armageddon?

Abraham raised a sage finger. "The deceiver hides in brevity."

Gabriel glared. "You didn't tell me where John and Michael were! I could have helped!"

Abraham ignored him.

Gabriel slammed the table. "There's enough truth in those notes to place the blame where it belongs! We kept our secrets while everyone died!"

Abraham said, "Careful…"

Their eyes met for a tense moment. Gabriel looked away.

John tried to comfort him. "There was nothing you could have done. It was over before any of us knew."

In the following quiet, Samuel studied Ezekiel's signature in the ledger. A similar hand wrote the notes. Something occurred to him. "Two hundred years ago... that's before the Reformation." They considered his observation. The Reformation referred to a dispute over the abuse of power within the church. It fathered many of the Circle's traditions. Little history remained of the ages before it.

Samuel pushed the notes and the ledger away. "If there are any lies, or even a conspiracy in all of this, I really don't think it matters. These bauran devils are the same problem either way. What are we going to do about them?"

Michael agreed and turned to Abraham. "Sir?"

Abraham hurried him up. "Your advice, consecrate, then I'll decide."

Michael stood, took a scroll from the shelf and unrolled it on the table, revealing a map of the kingdom. "We can't stay here, not all of us. If these things find people, like the sailors said, we should be assigned to the larger towns, east and west." He slid his finger in an arc over the southern coast, through Golgotha, Calvary, Mt. Tabor and Salem. Antioch marked the center of that imaginary line. "Then we hope they come to us... and pray they don't wander north."

Abraham harrumphed. "Hopes and prayers, is it? These places are days and weeks apart. How long of an assignment are you suggesting for each?"

Michael said, "No one returns." Abraham questioned him with a look. Michael continued, "Five towns, five churches." He'd been thinking of the plan for days. He held up the book of bauran like an executioner before the cut. "I know them. Anyone more than a few hours from one of us is a life at risk. If the worst happens, these are the last five towns in the world."

John had been involved in that conclusion. Samuel was speechless. The worst had already happened for Gabriel.

Abraham reached out for Michael's book. "Shocking news and advice. I'll study this now. We may all need to copy it tonight." He opened it close to his face, squinting and frowning at Michael's script. Then he picked up one of the notes. Ezekiel's hand was much better than Michael's.

Samuel cleared his throat. "Ahem, ah, Must *those* be the five?" He pointed out a town on the map, closer to Meroe. "What about, Breahg? They'll hold out."

Michael said, "It's too late for them. And traveling that far would risk breaking the line." Samuel looked to John, whose somber nod confirmed that assessment.

Michael continued, "Also, the sailors suggested building a wall to protect against the smoke and wandering bauran. That should be our first goal in each place. Support the idea and help."

Gabriel's sarcasm returned with a hard edge. "A *wall*. What about the people outside of the walls, *Michael*. What about them?"

"What do you suggest?"

Gabriel didn't really want to attack Michael, so he calmed himself and explained, "It's not enough, to preserve a few patches of men. Our responsibility is greater than that. The Circle kept its secrets for too long." He touched the bloody note. "This is the result of our effort." His grief surged and he snatched the note from the table. "Meroe was the result of our effort!"

Abraham's eyes narrowed.

Gabriel said, "We must atone for those sins. We must make every man a *wall*. We must abandon crucibles and the order of trust and begin training acolytes openly and immediately."

Abraham stabbed a finger at him. "That's dishonest! We're sworn to protect the way, not the world. You can't break the sacred vow!"

"Silence isn't sacred. It's evil. We've been hiding a gift from God. If we don't share it now, we'll be keeping secrets from the dead."

Abraham trembled with frustration. "Aaah! It's that cult! You've been preaching *God* like that dirty deacon! In Tabor and now *here*! I doubt you'd have been so cavalier before your ordination, Gabriel! Where is your honor? The church trusts you!"

Gabriel stood up, almost to the ceiling. "I can no longer be faithful to both. I choose God. Damn the church."

Unseen energies began to boil out of Abraham. "You'll force me to…"

Michael cut between them. "Gabriel! Abraham is not interested in your advice on religion. Each of us is trusted and will be so where we go. Our honor goes with us." Gabriel considered the implications of those words.

Abraham flashed reproach at Michael. "How dare you tell him that? And right in front of me no less. You just told him to go off on his own if he wants to commit heresy." Samuel and John stayed quietly out of that argument.

"Gabriel is upset. He isn't thinking clearly right now." Michael stared a warning at the large man, who yielded and sat down. "Regardless, we can't break any vows in here." He scanned the table. "Should Abraham take my advice, none of us will ever meet again. You would all leave with the trust you've earned."

Abraham stared at him, momentarily shocked. None of what Michael had said broke the law, but he was no less the herald of the order's end. *And Gabriel...* Abraham sat, exasperated. The others stayed quiet. "Anything else, consecrate? Or are you done destroying everything?"

Michael said, "Yes, I have a request, actually."

Abraham was incredulous. "You have a... What could you possibly have the nerve to request right now?"

"Assign me to Antioch."

11 Crusade

John and Michael waited outside of the stable. The sun rose. Gabriel, Samuel, Thomas and Joseph were inside, preparing to leave. Abraham was alone in the church across a field of fog and graves.

Michael said, "You know, before Gabriel said it, I planned on doing everything the hard way. I expected to fail. Honestly, I did. Gabriel opened my eyes."

John said, "He certainly was the quickest to *damn the church*. Fwah!"

Michael shook his head, remembering a time when Abraham and Gabriel were close friends. "There's nothing left between them. Tell me, what happened with Gabriel in Tabor? What was Abraham talking about?"

"Oh! Abraham's had him in the hairshirt for weeks over that." The men of the Circle sometimes wore an uncomfortable horse-hair shirt under their longhandles as punishment for ill-minded behavior. Gabriel wore the hairshirt often since his conversion to the fellowship's religion. Secretly, he'd come to see it as a symbol of the suffering righteous men bore for God.

"What happened?"

"I don't know the whole of it, but some poor fellow came in from there begging for help from what he called *The Carter-Miller Gang*. Seems they've taken the law into their own hands around the mountain. The poor fellow's wife was… well, nasty business. The king isn't doing anything about it."

"So, Abraham sent *Gabriel* to kill a band of outlaws?"

John nodded.

"He knows Gabriel won't do anything like that."

John said, "I'm pretty sure that's why he did it, to try Gabriel."

"Well, what happened in Tabor then?"

"Gabriel went and stood in the street for three days talking about God from what I understand. He described the people there as *unreceptive* when he got back."

Michael restated that in his own terms, trying to understand. "Abraham sent the wrong man on purpose, who disobeyed outright, and no one did anything about the outlaws?"

John nodded again. It was a fair account.

In a rumble of hooves and leather, Gabriel came forth from the stable. Everything about him was big and menacing, especially his black horse, Gooseberry. Thomas followed him out, saddled on a swollen-uddered cow that had the brand "DB" for Davies' Barn.

Gabriel's face was as dark as his mount. "I envy you, Michael. I would give anything for the chance you have."

They'd known each other for more than thirty years, all of that time in the church, and had never been friends or enemies. Michael and Gabriel simply viewed the world in different ways.

Michael said, "I cannot tell you how sorry I am."

"Yes, well, goodbye."

"Wait, Gabriel… A great many are depending on us. These bauran are soulless devils, not men. The time will come for you to raise your sword in Calvary. What will you do?"

Gabriel looked down on him from Gooseberry's high back. "Do you believe in the soul now?"

Michael didn't answer. He had a terrible feeling that in Gabriel they were sending Calvary an empty scabbard.

Gabriel said, "This is the wrath of God. If He does not wish it, Calvary will not fall."

Michael didn't know what else to say, so he said, "God be with you then."

"And also with you."

John shook hands with Thomas. "Fifteen years! You'd have earned your trust the old way, Tom."

Thomas said, "I should say so. It's too bad it had to be like this…" He looked around cautiously before continuing in a lower voice, "However, we've God's work to do now and that's quite a lot more important, I'd say."

John scratched his beard. "Oh, well, I suppose it would be. Good luck, Thomas. Good luck, Gabriel."

Luck indeed was on Gabriel's face. "John. Thomas, come." Then he shouted, "Heya, Gooseberry!" His powerful mare surged, pitching divots with her stride.

Michael waved as they left. "God be with you, Thomas!"

Thomas waved back, trotting after his master. "And also with you!" The cow's udder waved as well. Her baggage clanked and rattled.

John linked his hands behind his back and watched them go. "Peas in a pod."

Samuel came out of the stable saying, "That's the truth. Can you imagine if I'd been saddled with Thomas? I'd go mad in a month." He led his red roan, Rascal. Joseph followed, that yellow plaid shirt under his tabard. He had a DB cow as well, packed for travel.

Joseph was twenty-one years old, eight of those spent in the church. He'd been working through an extra year for failing the crucible of loyalty. Samuel had just told him they were abandoning the crucibles and that his training would begin on their arrival in Tabor. Joseph was immodestly pleased.

The four men clasped hands in fond farewell. Samuel swung into his saddle, smiling. "Since we're breaking vows, I think I'll take a wife in Tabor." John and Michael raised eyebrows at one another. Samuel added, "If you're going to get dirty, go ahead and get filthy."

Joseph laughed. "If you take a wife, I'll gloat over both of your misfortunes!" They all laughed.

Samuel said, "Mount thy steed, acolyte!"

"Why *am* I riding a cow?"

Samuel gave him a toothless, boyish grin. "You can have Rascal if you like."

Joseph leapt up. "No, thank you. I've a better chance of keeping my seat on this one." Samuel's horse was unpredictable. "We shouldn't forget that thief from Breahg..."

They all laughed at his reference to the false, local legend about how Rascal had come home after throwing a Breahg horse thief. Really, the clan didn't steal horses, preferring their *great-war-moose*, and Rascal had only escaped from the stable again. A boy had found him in the meadow and embellished a bit among friends. The men of the church said nothing to dispute the tale and enjoyed hearing it around town. It was better than the truth - Rascal had been throwing all of them.

They could have traded stories for hours but they were responsible men. They said goodbye again and waved more goodbyes as Samuel and Joseph rode away. Michael was truly saddened to see them go. Both had been good company through trouble in the past. It was difficult that then, when he needed his friends the most, they were forced to part forever.

That thought in his mind, his eyes threatened to water when he looked at John. The old man had been his closest friend and mentor for most of his life. Michael said, "Let's go to the Cauldron now. I'm starving."

John said, "It's a little early for that," and started walking with Michael anyway.

"You know Fergus is up. I've heard his breakfast is the best kept secret in Antioch."

John laughed. "I suppose it is, now!" Michael was a different man, throwing himself wholeheartedly into the disintegration of the Circle, even able to make light of it with a joke about secrets. It relieved some of John's previous worry. "God-god-god-god-god-god-god. I've never heard so much about God! When did God sneak into the church?"

"They say He's everywhere."

"I've felt lately like I'd stumbled into one of your father's sermons."

"How would you know what one of his sermons is like?"

"I walked by the inn once when one was happening."

Michael laughed. "I can't imagine why you didn't go in. You've been afraid for my sanity, haven't you?"

"Oh, obviously! But, *sanity*..." John waved his hand in the air like there wasn't much he could say about the benefits of such a quality.

Michael sighed. "I've always felt we aren't supposed to know what happens after we die. That it gives more weight, more meaning, to what we do with our lives if we're uncertain of some reward or punishment. But there, in Meroe, nothing I could do mattered. They were already dead. More are going to die, much more, and there's nothing I can do to stop it. I remembered my father's lessons, from my childhood, and I found comfort and hope in the idea that there's something better after this. It felt like a revelation."

"I'm sorry you had to do that alone."

Michael smiled. "I wasn't alone." He felt then he'd come too close to preaching and so reserved the rest of his thoughts on the matter.

John said, "I can't thank you enough for sending me home. Daniel would be dead if you hadn't."

"Tell me about him."

"He looks just like Horace did at that age. It's stirring to look at him. I can't even describe it. It's a feeling only blood could have..." *It's a second chance...* John paused. "Oh, there, I had my own revelation."

"I can't say I *feel my blood* when I look at my nephews, but I think I understand. You're taking him with you then?"

"Of course."

"And you'll teach him?"

"Absolutely. I wasn't there for Horace but I'll be there for his son. I can do that much for him. Nothing is more important to me than Daniel now."

Michael smiled. "He's lucky."

"No, he's not. I chose to give up my family. His was taken from him. I'm a poor substitute for what he has lost."

"Don't be so hard on yourself. We've all made choices."

John smiled, remembering having given similar advice to Daniel. "You must take a student too. Gabriel's right."

"I know."

"Do you have someone in mind?"

"That I don't know. With Joseph and Thomas gone, there's no one to recognize. I failed Edward on resolve yesterday. I think he hates me for it. I could start with him as an apology."

"Not that I object to the choice, but I don't see why you'd feel the need to apologize. The other boys were upset too when we sent them home, and they hadn't failed! We've all lost years to the crucibles. This next generation is having the way handed to them like taffy."

"Considering the circumstances, I wouldn't say it like that. Either way, I'm not proud of how I did it."

"How'd you get him?"

Michael grimaced. "I asked if any of them had family in Meroe, and I said *did*. *Did any of you have family in Meroe*."

John gasped. "Michael!"

Michael cringed.

"Fwah! What's wrong with you?"

"I wished I hadn't said it the moment I did. It's hard to think of something every time you walk into the church. It was on my mind and it just... came out."

"Fwah!"

John frowned at Michael and shook his head. The younger man endured much harrumphing and headshaking before the older one finally settled down. John was quiet for a while. Then he whistled and scratched. "You know, I failed that crucible twice. Both times to the same man and the same question."

Michael said, "I know," and smiled because the story was coming anyway.

"It was David. Oh, *he* enjoyed tormenting the resolved. My first time, he'd a smoked turkey leg with him. He said, '*Want some?*' and I said, '*Yes, sir!*' like an idiot. I even saluted him. I was only thirteen. To me, David was a hero! It was even more embarrassing because it took me so long to realize what I'd done. The next year, here he comes with a pork chop, cheerful as the sun. *Want some?* I believe I groaned or something."

"He failed you for a groan?"

"David was ruthless. I've seen that pork chop in my nightmares."

"This was Edward's third time to fail. He's sixteen."

"Oh, you're right. That boy hates you."

"I know."

"Can't keep his mouth shut, can he?" John burst into hearty laughter. "Do you remember when Gabriel failed tolerance?" Michael laughed too and John gripped his shoulder. "Oh, I enjoyed teaching you. I'm looking forward to teaching Daniel. It's a very special thing to share with someone, the way."

Michael's smile faded into worry. "John, what do you think Abraham is going to do?"

"Oh, you'll have Antioch. He hates it here. He told me once he would have aged better somewhere else. Or, no, I believe he said *anywhere* else."

"No, I meant, what do you think he'll do about the rest of us."

"Ah. Without evidence or a confession? Nothing. I'm sure he suspects what we intend to do, but intentions aren't broken vows. Some crusade to find out for sure would only compromise his assignment. No, Abraham has taken your advice. He'll keep his word to death. The Circle is going to die with him."

Michael nodded. "Those are my thoughts as well. I felt that, in his own way, he accommodated us."

"It's possible, but still, be careful with him before he leaves. You can trust him, but don't bet your life on him trusting you. I've never seen him so upset. And I wouldn't go anywhere near Salem for at least, oh, what do you think, a decade?"

Michael agreed.

They reached the Cauldron and John looked up in dismay when he tried the door. "It's locked! They never lock the door. Hmm, I suppose I did advise them to…" He banged on it. "Fergus! Help! I'm hungry!"

The latch clicked, the bell rang and Daniel stood in the doorway, a scowl on his face and a towel on his shoulder. "We aren't open until… Uncle John!" Daniel flung himself at John and embraced him. John's face melted. Daniel said, "I didn't think you were ever coming back!"

John wanted to hug his grandson for longer than he did. "We were making important plans, son. I couldn't get away until now." He ruffled the boy's hair. "Daniel, this is Michael."

Daniel had heard many stories about Michael by then, first from John, then at the Cauldron, from Fergus' family and guests, and finally from Andalynn. The tales had turned Michael into a hero. "Pleased to meet you, sir!"

Michael smiled and held out his hand. "I am honored."

Daniel took it and his arm flopped around in the handshake. He was star-struck.

John laughed. "Daniel, feed us!"

"Huh? Oh! Yes, sir!" He took off.

John added, "Oh, and, if you haven't eaten, please join us as well."

"Yes, sir!" The boy disappeared into the kitchen.

Michael said, "Look at him go. Breahg's first acolyte." John nodded, considering that. The Circle had a joke about Breahg acolytes. In the privacy of the library it was said: *Before Breahg, woman* - meaning neither.

Margot came out to greet them, hugged Michael and touched his scar. "Ooh, Michael, what's happened to you?" He blushed and shied away.

John sat at the table. "Some sailors shot him in the face." Her mouth fell open. "Why'd they do that?"

Michael took a seat as well. "I was rather dirty at the time."

Daniel came in then with bread and cider, speaking rapidly in his excitement as he laid them out. He said they had a sailor staying with them and that she was bringing her friends to dinner that night. He took a giant bite of bread and his muffled words came out with crumbs. "One of them has pictures on his skin!"

Michael said, "Ah, that's Ditch. So, the woman staying here is Andalynn?"

Daniel said, "Uh huh," then he frowned. "She's still asleep." He'd been raised to believe that sleeping past sunup was a sin. He didn't know how difficult it was for a person to go without sleep for three days, or that John had done that for him.

Michael said, "That's interesting. She's an important member of their crew, you know. Something of a commander."

Margot said, "No, I didn't know that. She never said a word."

Michael said, "Fierce woman." Then he cringed. "Especially that smell..." Margot chided him.

Fergus came in with bowls of stew and pointed at Michael like he'd been thinking the same thing. "Yes!" He lowered his voice. "*She smells like sour milk!*"

Michael said, "They all do! They think rubbing themselves with milk protects them from these devils. Honestly, I thought it would be rude to ask, so I had to wait quite a while before one of them explained it to me." John, Fergus and Margot all agreed that it was a bad smell and a touchy matter to investigate.

Daniel said, "Davies called it her *dairy air*," and narrowed his eyes. "Because he's a milkman."

Margot raised an eyebrow suspiciously. "And just what did my son-in-law have to say about Andalynn's derrière?"

Daniel tried to share his hatred of Davies with the table. "That she'd need to get it off her chair before she could get him another drink!" But instead of agreeing with him, they laughed.

Fergus said, "I think he meant her backside, boy! I couldn't believe him last night! Hoo-hoo, he was in prime condition."

Daniel frowned, not understanding how anyone could tolerate Davies, much less enjoy his company.

Looking at Daniel, John said, "You know, I don't care for that Davies. He rubs me the wrong way." The boy nodded, validated.

Michael said, "He's playing with fire, Fergus. He wouldn't be so saucy if he knew some of what that woman's done."

Fergus laughed. "I seriously doubt anything could put a cork in Davies' sauce!"

Everyone, other than Daniel, laughed again. Michael untied a drawstring pouch from his belt and placed it on the table next to his meal. Fergus deflated at the sight of it.

John said to Michael, "You don't need that anymore, do you?"

Michael stopped, thinking about all that was changing, and then smiled. "No, perhaps I don't."

Fergus raised his hands, proclaiming, "Hallelujah!"

Michael laughed. "Oh Fergus, I'm sorry, I really am. I know it's been hard for you to watch us with our wretched pouches at your good table for all these years."

Fergus said, "It has been!" not mentioning that John never brought one to the table.

Michael weighed the pouch in his hand. "We're supposed to do it in secret, to avoid offending our hosts, but that's worse than the truth among friends."

Fergus smiled. "I understand. Oh, this is exciting! I want to see your first unadulterated bite." He rubbed his hands together vigorously.

Daniel was baffled. "What's in the pouch?"

The others allowed Michael the opportunity to explain. He said, "Ashes from the hearth of the church. We're sworn to put them in our food, to prevent us from enjoying it too much. Pleasure corrupts." The words were bitter in his mouth.

Daniel frowned. "You don't do that, Uncle John."

John's eyes shifted. "Ahem, shh, this is a solemn moment for Michael. Don't ruin it."

Michael put his hand over his face and laughed. "John!" Everyone laughed, except Daniel. Michael took a decisive bite of the stew. "Mmff, so good, Fergus." His jaw popped in the bullet-scar as he chewed. Pain shot up into his ear. It was still better than the ashes.

Fergus beamed. "It's at its best too! It's the second day. The flavors have had a night for a *how-do-you-do-oh-fine-how-are-you*. There's never enough of it left over to serve twice and that's really too bad, well, for the guests. It's good for our breakfast!" Everyone ate then, enjoying each other's company.

Daniel said, "Uncle John, Fergus told me you think the most important thing in the kitchen is salt."

John chuckled. "The old debate! That's right, son, salt. Humble, yet powerful, it improves every dish and leaves an empty space when forgotten. Don't let Fergus' fancy tricks confuse you. Butter is a lie!"

Daniel's mouth was full again. "Fergus says it's bacon."

John paused. "You mean butter."

Daniel turned to Fergus. "No, he said bacon, just like Pa."

Fergus looked caught in a trap. "Daniel, I... I said that to be kind, but... it's butter. It really is. It's always been butter! Hoo, I feel better getting that off my chest." Fergus fanned himself as though he'd overcome a great obstacle. Daniel frowned at him.

John took a sly bite of the stew. "Oh? Did you put butter in this?" He knew.

Fergus said, "No, that is beside the point, and come to think of it I sweat the onions in butter, so there."

Margot raised her tankard and said, "It's apples!" as though they all should have known that. John laughed, clanked tankards with her and drank.

Daniel asked Michael, "What do you think it is, sir?"

Michael sat back, chewing and thinking. Then he said, "Hunger."

John and Fergus shared a look.

Fergus said, "Fwah."

John said, "You've always some queer thing to say." Michael laughed and went back to enjoying his meal. Daniel thought Michael's answer was the smartest thing he'd ever heard.

Fergus grinned at John and said, "I thought he'd say coffee..." Then they both watched Michael for a reaction.

Michael knew he was being baited. A frown snuck onto his face anyway. *Coffee.*

Fergus laughed, "You're a good sport, Michael. You know I'd never serve the evil stuff in here. So, no more pouch! What's brought that on?"

Michael put down his spoon, wiped his mouth and shared a look with John. Then he said, "Andalynn's told you what's happened?"

Margot said, "Ooh, it's dreadful. I didn't even know anyone from Meroe. To find out there've been people oversea this whole time and that now they're all... well I don't know how to feel about it."

Michael said, "I think *dreadful* is the right word."

Margot smiled at him and at John. "I'm so glad nothing like that could ever happen here."

Michael wasn't as sure as she was. "I've forgotten what day it is. Service is tomorrow, isn't it?"

Fergus raised an eyebrow. "Yes..." He looked over at John.

John said, "Michael's found religion."

Michael said, "God's mercy, John. Listen, service will be a good time to discuss what needs to be done here in Antioch. We'll be able to get the word out to almost everyone at once that way. Ask Andalynn to get the other sailors to attend, especially the one named Biggs. Also, tell everyone that I will be there." Michael paused for a moment and then came out with it. "The church is separating. Gabriel and Samuel left this morning."

Fergus said, "What? I don't like the sound of that!" He turned to John. "What about you?" Daniel looked at John too, ready to hear the worst.

John said, "Well, I have a busy day today. I've got to dig some metal out of Michael..." Michael answered their looks with a nod and a shrug. John continued, "And I have to get to bed early. None of us slept last night... Fergus, I'll need your help and your generosity in packing. Daniel and I leave tomorrow and we have a long way." He turned a sad smile on the boy.

Fergus was sorry to hear it, but ready to assure John of anything he needed. "Oh, of course..."

Daniel said, "We do? When are we coming back? Fergus was going to show me how to make a cheese."

John said, "It won't be for a long time." Michael questioned him with a glance, but John didn't want to use a word like *never* right then.

Daniel said, "But, I thought we were going to stay here. Do you want me to stay until you get back?"

"No. I'll be gone for a long time. You have to come with me."

Daniel's head fell a little. "Huh, it's just that... I thought we were going to stay." The night before, his worst fear was that John would leave, and he'd accepted it. He hadn't considered leaving the Cauldron. Fergus and Margot had made it a home for him.

Fergus patted Daniel on the back. "You just keep him safe, John. We've got big plans for this boy." Margot hugged Daniel and kissed the top of his head.

12 In the Settling Smoke

On the steps outside of Betheford's inn, Biggs sat, wearing the fellowship's brown, wool trousers and white, linen shirt. He was watching an old laundress at work across the way. She sometimes peeked out from behind her fluttering sheets to frown at him. People walked by, greeting each other and gossiping at the shops.

Andalynn came up the street, waving, her blonde standing out from the native black. She wore local clothes as well, a white blouse and a long, brown skirt, but with goggles on her forehead and revolvers on her hips. She said, "Biggs! Biggs! I am a waitress!"

They shared a laugh, a hug and a kiss and sat down together. He motioned across the street. "Been watchin' this old girl for half an hour. Can't stop. Boy ran out a lil'while ago n' pulled down one a' them sheets. She hollered at him n' he took off like a jackrabbit. Didn't think I'd ever see regular people again, but here they are. Do'n the laundry."

It was more than that for him. The laundress reminded him of his wife, Marlene, who'd died five years before the Fall, before the bauran came. Their sixtieth anniversary was two months away. Biggs was eighty-three.

With Andalynn looking at her then, the old laundress' frown deepened. She wondered how many more of these *sailors* would come out to sit on Betheford's steps and stare at her. She thought they all looked quite suspicious.

Biggs said, "What'd you get?"

Andalynn said, "They are harmless. I believe Michael and John have described them faithfully."

"Yup, that's pretty much what we got too. Good ol' country folk."

Andalynn raised an eyebrow at him. "That being said, for a group with their history of persecution, I was appalled by some of the open speech I heard last night. They are racists."

Biggs chuckled. "Is that right?"

"And completely unashamed of it! They openly ridiculed a group known as the gunders, in the presence of one. I witnessed everything."

Biggs nodded facetiously. The fellowship's racism didn't make a *hill a' beans worth a' differ'nce* to him. "S'pose you can't have it all."

"You are very smug because you look like one of them."

Biggs shook his head just as facetiously. "Nope. Hair's brown."

Andalynn intended to have a good-old-fashioned argument with him. "I do not wish to criticize them too much, because they have taken us in, however, in response to you, I do not see any humor in prejudice."

"Why not? It's funny. It's natural. Shoot, ever'body's a racist."

"I disagree. I am not a racist."

Biggs cocked his jaw to one side. "Aint sayin' it's good. Sayin' it's natural. Sure it's dumb, but it's like somebody fallin' off his chair. S'alright to laugh at that. Don't have to hate him for it. Dumb ideas are a lot like fallin' on your butt, aint they?"

"That is up for debate. This humorous little quirk that you enjoy is a fundamental cause of murder, war and genocide."

Biggs shrugged. "Maybe. Maybe war's more about money. What do I know anyhow? Who cares if they're a bunch a' bigots? Bet most of 'em wouldn't hurt nobody. Be'n mean n' be'n ignorant's two differ'nt things." He turned back to the old woman. "Don't matter. Prob'ly aint enough folks left in the world to make it matter."

Andalynn had several lively counterpoints ready for Biggs' views on racism and the causes of war, but saw he was no longer in the mood. "Are you alright?"

"Nope. Found out sump'n else last night. Only five of 'em in that church, Lynn. This place can't handle what's comin. We got ahead of it some, that's all. Done come all that way just to watch it happen again."

They shared a moment of silence. Andalynn could not tell him then it was soon to be only Michael left in the church. She put her hand on his knee. "Have dinner with me tonight."

"Don't know, you're lookin' for a fight there a second ago..."

"No. I am only interested in enjoying what we have while we have it."

Biggs chuckled. "You're funnier'n a racist."

Andalynn leaned into him. "I was afraid for you in Meroe."

Biggs put his arm around her. "I know." They sat quietly for a while longer, watching the laundress work.

Biggs said, "Marlene n' me, we used to talk about what we'd do, if'n we could do it all over again. Used to say I'd a' done it all the same, the good n' the bad. Never thought it'd happen. Not like this, that's for sure. Truth be told, I was done. Lots a' times I wished Zeke never found me."

"The *Grace* would have been lost without you. It could be that you have a purpose you are not taking into account."

Biggs had been a deer hunter since childhood. He'd taught the other sailors how to handle their rifles. He chuckled again, in self-criticism that time. "Shoot..."

"A remarkable choice of words."

Ditch came out of the crowd, out of nowhere, brisk zippers and black leather, standing out like Andalynn's hair. Noticing his friends staring at the laundress, he sat down on the steps, waved across at her and yelled, "What's up!" She recoiled.

Andalynn said, "Good morning, Ditch."

Ditch said, "Whatever, man, it's like, noon. You guys slept forever. I been checkin' out these shops, you know, gettin' some stares..." He used his fingers to open his eyes extra wide.

Biggs grinned at him. "Buy yourself sump'n nice?"

"Pfft, with what? We gotta figure out how we're gonna fit in around here, you know? I gotta get a job."

"Lynn's got herself one already."

"You're kiddin..."

"I am a waitress. I have returned to my roots."

Ditch soured. "Man... I don't wanna mooch off Michael's dad." Then he perked up with an odd thought. "You know, workin's gonna be real weird around here. I bet you can't call in sick. What are you gonna say if you like, need a day off? They'll be all, *whatever, man, go to church.*"

Andalynn laughed. "I had not considered that. It reminds me, there is a town meeting tomorrow that all of us should attend. It will be a religious service, but there will also be an open discussion about the future of this community and our places in it."

Ditch said, "Yeah, they're havin' it up in here. Everybody's talkin' about it. They keep sayin' it's a big deal Michael's gonna be there, but I'm like, so what, you know? So what if *all five* of 'em are there... There's only *five* of 'em! I thought there was gonna be a whole mess a' these guys."

Andalynn decided that was as good a time as any to tell them what she knew. "The other four are leaving in the hope of saving additional villages, one each. Michael will be the only one to stay."

Ditch and Biggs' mouths fell open. After a while, the only thing Ditch could think of to say was, "Whatever, man, you know, like, pfft."

Biggs started chuckling. Sometimes the odds seemed so stacked against them he couldn't help but laugh. He pointed at Andalynn. "We're go'n on a date, to celebrate."

"Good for you, gramps. You guys want me to split? I don't wanna be a square wheel, or whatever."

Andalynn laughed. "I would enjoy your company this evening as well, Ditch. I have been instructed to bring my friends."

Ditch said to Biggs, "I'm totally comin' on your date, man. I'm a' mess it up. Where we go'n? Not here, right? Bleagh." He stuck out his tongue.

Andalynn said, "I will also invite Drake." The four of them had always gone ashore together.

Ditch scowled. "Man, I had enough a' him. He's sayin' all this stupid stuff last night, just to watch the hayseeds jump. Callin' his BOSS a boomstick, dumbass."

Biggs said, "Least he aint in your room! Goober'd better put a lid on it. Gon' get us all burned at the stake or sump'n..." He paused and frowned. "They don't do that around here, do they?"

Andalynn smiled. "They do not." She took a moment before continuing, to prevent herself from outright laughing at the expense of the fellowship's judicial system. "They enforce the peace with *shunning*."

They all laughed.

Ditch said, "What's that, like, they don't talk to you if you're bad?"

Andalynn relished it. "If you are bad, they do not speak to you and they turn their backs on your presence." They laughed again and sat back with some after-chuckles, thinking about it. She looked over the fine windows and double doors of Betheford's Inn, clean glass and white paint. "You do not enjoy the food here?"

"It sucks!"

"Really? I have had a different experience with Antiochian cuisine. *My* hosts were ridiculing this establishment." There was a little *nyah-nyah* in her voice.

"What'd they say?"

"Each in his or her own way, but essentially, *Betheford's eew.* Fergus, the proprietor of the Cauldron, was employed here as chef until he had a falling out with Michael's father. Fergus and his family have little regard for the man who replaced him."

Ditch said, "Me too!" and the three of them had another good laugh.

* * *

People packed the Cauldron's common room that evening. Andalynn and Biggs sat close to one another at the end of the table, sharing a private conversation. There wasn't a crumb left on their plates. Ditch and Drake laughed, drank and told stories in the center of the crowd.

Ditch said, "On top a' that, dingbat here," he pointed at Drake with his thumb, "puts a bullet in our best shooter."

Drake groaned. "It was a ricochet!"

Ditch said, "He butterfingers a round straight down into the bridge, *peeyow!* Shot pops up and tags Biggs *below the belt.*" The room gasped and cringed. Drake put his face in his hands.

Biggs said, "Shut up, Ditch! Quit tellin' that story!"

Ditch continued, "So that's real loud, right, and those turkeys are swarmin, so we gotta split. But whatever, Biggs took it like a champ and we just hustle up on the big boat for a turkey shoot. *Gobble-gobble, pop-pop,* you know?" Native heads nodded in approval of the strategy.

"That's how you do it."
"Shooting them like a turkey."
"Quite right. Very good."

Later that evening, when the crowd had thinned, Biggs had his arm around Andalynn. She was leaning into him. Marabbas was listening to another of Ditch's stories and Drake stood next to the fireplace, charming Sarah with tales of the marines' bravery. Fergus came out of the kitchen and his eyes narrowed on the tall, young sailor.

Drake stretched and flexed. "Yeah, we pretty much saved everybody."

Sarah was in love. "Wow…"

Fergus said, "Sarah! Your mother and *Daniel* need your help in the back." Sarah scowled and stomped into the kitchen. Drake leered at her rear end as she went and gave Ditch the thumbs up. Ditch shook his head no - *bad idea.*

Fergus moved in, shaking a finger at Drake. "Look here, young man, that's my daughter! And she's only sixteen years old!"

Drake laughed and gave Fergus the thumbs up. "Good job, dad!" Then he bit his lower lip, bared his big teeth and grunted three times.

Fergus drew back. Then he pointed at the door and said, "Get out!" The room started to pay attention.

Drake started to lose his drunken smile. "Wait, are you serious? I'm just playing around…"

Fergus was an angry statue. "Get!"

Drake looked around at the stares and scratched his head. "Well, alright, I'm sorry. Ok, ok, I'm going." He picked up his rifle from near the door. "I guess I'm going back over to Beefer… uh… Beeferthird's. See you guys." The bell rang behind him.

Fergus glared at the door. His face was red. Biggs leaned into Andalynn and whispered, "Goober's gone and done it now. Maybe Ditch and me'd better scoot." She nodded, concerned. Then a sound broke the silence, a sound Biggs often likened to that of a hyena in a henhouse.

It was Ditch's cackling laughter and his face was pure joy. "Man, *scraped!*" Fergus turned to him, surprised. Ditch said, "You're a beast, Fergus!"

Fergus started to laugh too. "Beeferthird's…"

Andalynn and Biggs relaxed and smiled at each other.

Ditch said, "Finally! Man, you don't know how many times I wanted to throw that kid off the boat." He celebrated Drake's expulsion and got cheers of laughter from the room by reenacting Fergus' iron *Get!* Then he mocked Drake. "*Uh… uh… Beefer! Beefer!*"

Marabbas didn't understand what anyone was laughing at, or why they continued laughing at it. He cocked his head at them and waited. Ditch had been telling an interesting story before the interruption. He poked Ditch to get his attention and then spoke, sounding like he had marbles in his mouth, "Talk about the boat."

Ditch was wiping tears away when he noticed. "What? Oh yeah, sorry, man. Hey, come on everybody, come on, I was tellin' him about this. This is messed up. Uh, what part was I at? Oh, yeah, yeah, man, they thought they could like, cure the rot later on, so they lock him up downstairs. You know, they wanna save him but they don't want him killin' everybody. Well, they don't want him to starve either, so this guy's bringin' him food."

Ditch rolled his eyes and took a drink. "Whatever, right? When food guy gets the rot, they're all like, *Oh no, how'd that happen?* So they lock him up too! They didn't know nothin, man. After a while, they figure it out. Anybody says *hey, I can't breathe down there*, or, *ow, my eyes*, gets the rot. But then it's too late, they're already messed up. They got 'em all locked up in the hold and can't get to their stores no more, you know, cause a' the smoke."

Ditch drank some more of his cider and then blinked with his entire face. "Last couple things he wrote's totally messed up. They're tyin' everythin' off cause they're runnin' out a' guys to work the rig. Then the whole crew's baurans and the captain and his buddy are locked in the deckhouse, just watchin' 'em through the portholes. That's when captain's buddy starts coughin. He knows that's it, you know, nowhere to go. So, last thing he wrote's *May good fortune bring us to shore.*"

Ditch emptied his mug. "The log book had blood all over it, man. The whole deckhouse did. From what he was writin, I bet the *Vesper*'s captain didn't even fight back. He still thought everybody'd get better. Anyway, that's what happened to Meroe. It wasn't no *good fortune*. A shipload a' bauran hit coast east a' the harbor."

Margot put her hands over her mouth. "Ooh, and the fishermen went out to help!"

Fergus said, "You were on that ship?"

Ditch said, "Yeah, man, with Michael. It sucked! Somethin' like that could a' happened to us too if it wasn't for Andalynn. See, she's with these soldiers for like, two weeks before us. They figured out all this stuff about 'em. She's the one who taught us to cover our faces and hold our breath, focus fire, go for the head. And when our guys got the rot..."

Andalynn suddenly realized what he was about to say. She sat up and her hand shot out. "Ditch, please, no!"

Ditch stopped. "What? Aw man... I'm sorry. I'm sorry, Andalynn."

She surprised herself, reacting that way, and was embarrassed. Biggs patted her gently on the back. The whole room wondered what had just happened.

Andalynn said, "I apologize, everyone, please excuse me." She touched Ditch on the shoulder before climbing the stairs to Sarah's room.

Ditch said, "Man, I suck."

Biggs said, "Come on, she'll be alright. I'm beat anyhow." He shook hands with Fergus and thanked the rest of them. Then Biggs and Ditch left the Cauldron, heading east.

Ditch said, "Biggs, that cider's twisted. I'm like, *hey, man, you got any water* but Margot queered at me like I was fruitier'n a nutbar, or whatever."

Biggs laughed. "Maybe the girls 'round here don't like you callin'em *man* all the time."

"Yeah... you know, they been sayin' that fwah to me."

* * *

Drake stumbled west, improvising a song, using too many syllables.

"She said he was his daughter!"
"Or, no, she was the daughter!"
"I don't know, he told me sooo!"

Clouds covered the moon over the dark and empty streets. He started to get cold and frustrated. Nothing looked familiar and the wind was bullying him.

A foul odor bent his face into a frown and Drake shouted, "Stink a' dink-dink! Wooo!" waving his hand in front of his nose. Then he clapped that hand over his mouth. He knew that smell. It made him sick and sober.

Holding his breath, he stole in the wind's direction, looking to turn out of it. He had both hands over his rifle's strap to stop its slapping and clicking. He stepped from toe to heel as quietly and as quickly as he could. The night hid everything farther than a few feet away. He couldn't tell if the sounds behind him were echoes or footsteps.

A turn came and he took it. The walls disappeared. Grass replaced cobblestone. He couldn't see or smell anything in the deepening black. Only the breeze and his pulse were in his ears. He shivered like he was freezing to death, but it was out of fear. After what felt like miles, he forced himself to stop and listen. A strong hand grabbed his shoulder and something stabbed into his back - *shuck.*

Drake cried out and struggled to get away but it dragged him down. The darkness was so complete, he couldn't see his attacker. The night itself seemed to be raking and tearing him. He knew what it was, though, and screamed imagining its black eyes. The thing above him imagined nothing. It saw only riin in a body of shadows.

* * *

Lot had been hiking and camping alone for fourteen days. He was fifteen years old. He didn't tell his family before he left home and didn't care if they worried. They would have tried to stop him. They would have said the church wasn't anything more than a fairy tale. That's what they said the year before and the year before that. Lot was determined to let nothing stop him again.

With Antioch only a few miles away at sunset, instead of camping that night, he decided to continue on through the forest. He thought it would make a strong impression if they found him outside of the church in the morning.

The city's streets were strange and dark but he knew just to head for the middle. As he entered the clearing, it occurred to him that a graveyard by moonlight could have been a very frightening place if not for the church. Then his long journey was over and Lot stood before the Circle's front door, smiling.

He sat down and opened his pack to have a snack of stale bread and salt pork in a sandwich. He chewed large mouthfuls, looking around, feeling proud of what he'd accomplished. Clouds passed over the moon now and then, dulling its light into nothing. When Lot heard Drake scream, he couldn't tell what it was for sure. He decided against knocking on the door, though, feeling that would have been a foolish time to lose his nerve, after everything he'd been through.

13 Andalynn's Scars

Andalynn sat on the edge of her bed, wearing a nightgown. Sarah crept in with a candle and closed the door. She set the flickering light on the dresser and then sat down cross-legged, opposite the sailor.

Sarah said, "Ditch is such a jerk, isn't he?"

"No. He meant no harm. He is a close friend."

"Why'd you get so upset?"

"I should not have left the room like that. It was childish."

"Oh no, I wouldn't call you childish. You're the bravest person I've ever met!"

"That is a strong compliment."

"You've done... I can't even imagine doing the things you've done, and you don't even talk about it. You didn't tell us any of this stuff yesterday. With all that, you brought Davies a drink and didn't even care." Andalynn smiled. It was a rare kind of praise Sarah gave. "And I love your hair, what a color!"

"You cannot possibly like it. I have been cutting it with a knife."

Sarah moved over to Andalynn's bed. "Wow! Mom would kill me if I did mine that way. I like it short!" Sarah's hair hung to her lower back in healthy, black waves. Andalynn's was roughly chopped above the shoulder; to Andalynn's surprise, the girl started handling it.

Sarah talked about hair for a little while and then said, "I hope Drake comes back. Do you think he will?" She bit her lip in a frown.

"I doubt your father would allow it."

Sarah groaned and flopped down on the bed. "Ugh! He wants me to marry *Daniel*."

"Preposterous. Daniel is too young." After saying it, Andalynn realized she did not know the marrying age in Antioch. Before, in what the sailors were starting to call *the old world*, there had been nations in which thirteen-year-old grooms and brides would have been perfectly legitimate. Andalynn had voted to raise the legal age to eighteen in her own district.

Sarah said, "Oh, not right now, when he gets older. Daniel owns land." She rolled her eyes.

"I understand."

"Daddy wants me to get Daniel to like me. I tried, but the only thing Daniel likes is frowning like a toad and moping around in the kitchen. He's so glum. I guess because his father and sister died." Sarah thought about it. "His mother's dead too... but Drake's been through worse than that and he's so mature about it! Ooh, what would you do?"

Andalynn paused at the discovery of someone who considered Drake to be mature. "It could be hazardous for me to advise you on this, Sarah. We have different customs where I am from. I do not want to cause any trouble for your family. Also, having never been married, my opinions on the subject are of dubious value."

"What about that man you were with tonight?"

Andalynn smiled. "Biggs. I like him very much."

Sarah sat up. "Is he your boyfriend? Do you kiss him?"

Andalynn raised an eyebrow. "I am far too old to gossip about kissing my boyfriend."

Sarah screwed up her face. "How old are you?"

Andalynn had to think about that. Telling Michael the truth about her age was one thing, but from what she had learned so far, the average person in Antioch would not believe it. Andalynn had trouble believing a mirror. Faced with the choice of answering the question, lying or avoiding it, she said, "Fifty-two."

Sarah's expression went flat. "Sure, ok."

Andalynn said, "It is the truth!" She then told openly about Zeke, his astounding ability and some of the other sailors' ages. Sarah was unsure but Andalynn spoke without a hint of humor.

When Andalynn finished, Sarah said, "That's really, *really* old. My grandmother's fifty-six." The way Sarah said *really, really old* made Andalynn feel ancient, despite Zeke's cosmetic hospital.

Sarah studied her. "Why didn't you ever get married? You kept your looks well enough."

Andalynn almost said she'd only had her "looks" for a year and that her "looks" were not much to speak of, but she did not want to fish any more compliments out of Sarah. Before having become *Armymom* and *Shooty McShoot-shoot*, Andalynn was known around the President's offices as *The Dumptruck* and resented ever being told she looked young or pretty. "I had an index of reasons but I normally cited my career."

Sarah had never heard words like index, cited or career.

Andalynn clarified. "Because of my work."

"Oh… sailors don't marry?"

Andalynn laughed. "No! I mean, yes they do, but I am not a sailor, not really. I loathe the water. No, before the outbreak I was an elected official. I sat on the President's Advisory Committee to the Grand Duchy of Englenov." She made an elegant gesture in the air with one hand.

"Wow, what's a doochy?"

Andalynn had always found the correct pronunciation of the word "duchy" to be rather comical, especially considering the grandeur it was often intended to convey. And, the Duke of Englenov had been such a ridiculous man that he could have been called a "grand doochy" without having to explain the meaning of the term's misuse or mispronunciation. Andalynn started to chuckle.

"What's so funny?"

"The word is pronounced *dutchie*. It is the territory governed by a duke or duchess."

"Oh…"

Andalynn smiled warmly and continued. "I cannot think of a better word for what I am now than *sailor*, but the truth is that my survival required I become one in spite of myself."

"Ditch said you were with soldiers before. Is that what you were? A soldier?" She was eager to hear Andalynn had been some kind of warrior.

"No, I was a politician… The soldiers found me hiding in the cafeteria of the capitol building. They saved my life."

Sarah screwed up her face again. "I don't understand. Why did you lead everyone ashore and teach them about the bauran? Why didn't the soldiers do all of that stuff?"

Andalynn's smile faded away. "Because they all died." Sarah crossed her legs again and waited for the story. Andalynn took a moment to decide if she wanted to tell it. Then she picked up her gun belts and put them on the bed. "These belonged to Sergeant Sebastian, referred to by his men as *Bas*. He gave me his pistols because he did not have enough rifles to, in his words, *waste one on a priss*. Despite my being a priss, he felt it was important for me to carry a weapon."

"Can I see one?"

"You may, but you must be careful. Do not point it at me."

Sarah held it in both hands like she was cupping water. "Wow, it's heavy!"

"Yes... pistols are interesting weapons. While rifles are useful for survival, these are only good for killing people."

Sarah became uneasy and handed it back.

Andalynn checked it with comfortable dexterity and then holstered it in her lap. "These are Three-Fifty-Seven Springstien Pythons. Bas liked to say that God did not make men equal, Springstien did. From what I understand, Captain knew him."

"Who, Bas?"

"No, Springstien. In the twelve days I traveled with Bas, I never fired these. We had a system for eliminating bauran from a distance that worked rather well. That part of the System did not involve the effective range of a pistol. And silence was always more valuable than target practice."

Andalynn looked away. "On that twelfth day, deep into the outbreak, we were searching an abandoned building for supplies, scavenging. A group of bauran happened upon us and followed us in. We tried to run through, to escape by the rear door, but... it was locked. We were trapped."

Sarah twisted her blanket into a knot. "What did you do?"

"Nothing. When the bauran attacked, I did nothing. I was too frightened. I cowered like a child and watched those brave men die, fighting. Then I died as well, without having fired a single shot."

"But..."

"I assume that is when Zeke found me."

"Oh!"

Andalynn checked the other pistol. "These will be empty before I die again."

Sarah said, "Wow," and sat for a while, thinking about the story and about how Andalynn had fled the common room before. "What happened when the people on your ship got sick?"

Andalynn nodded. "It will come out anyway. You must understand, they were not monsters at the time, only frightened people, but if I did nothing... they would have endangered everyone aboard."

"What did you do?"

"I used the pistols."

Sarah swallowed.

"We were incapable of treating the infection. We could not allow anyone to turn." Andalynn stared at the weapons in her lap, tensing the muscles in her jaw, thinking about Biggs in Meroe.

"Were you always the one... that... um..."

"No one wants to do something like that. From the first time, I could see it was my responsibility."

"Oh, that's awful. I'm sorry."

Andalynn gave a shrug of a nod. "I was afraid for it to come out like that earlier, so soon after our arrival, but what we did on the ship... what I did on the ship, was necessary. I had no choice. I apologize if I have disturbed you with this information."

Sarah shook her head. "I understand. I'm not a child."

* * *

Sarah lay awake for hours that night, flinching at small noises. When she finally slept, she dreamt of bauran in the common room. Had she ever seen one, it might have been a nightmare. Instead they all looked like her handsome fifty-six-year-old grandmother, someone Sarah deeply loved. Out of character however, the zombie-grannies slopped food on the floor, left poor tips for Sarah and called her a doochy.

Sarah hated the doorbell in that dream. It kept ringing. And every time it rang, another rude, frugal grandmother marched in to make a mess. Then one of them put a strong hand over Sarah's mouth. She couldn't get away. She woke up early in the morning, before sunrise, stifled by a real hand that smelled like sour milk.

Andalynn's lips touched Sara's ear. "Do not make a sound. Keep your head beneath the blanket. When I tell you to hold your breath, hold it for as long as you can and do exactly as I say. Do you understand?" Sarah nodded and Andalynn released her. A pistol clicked.

* * *

The doorbell rang. Margot sat up in bed next to Fergus. Chairs started groaning on the floorboards downstairs.

Fergus said, "I didn't lock the door. I forgot."

"Ooh, Fergus! What are we going to do? Sarah... and Daniel!" She put her hands over her mouth, thinking the worst.

"It's probably just... one of them, up for a snack. Or Marabbas. I'll go have a look." Fergus rubbed his face and got out of bed.

"Be careful..."

* * *

When the bell rang, Daniel woke up halfway, trapped between sleep and consciousness. He stared in the direction of his door, into the empty darkness. Then he heard footfalls on the stairs. The terror of the tree house returned. Daniel tried to move but his body wouldn't respond. He tried to call out but he couldn't make a sound. His door opened. A silhouette stood against the dull, red glow of the dying hearth.

From down the hall, Fergus said, "Who's there?" The figure turned.

At that moment Andalynn burst out of the door between them and opened fire, shouting, "Hold your breath! Hold your breath!" Fergus yelped and leapt back into his room.

The gunshots jolted Daniel into a fully conscious yell. The figure stumbled back as Andalynn blasted it, aiming with the pistol flash. It collapsed. She swapped out for her second revolver and emptied it into the corpse.

Then Andalynn ducked back into Sarah's room, shouting, "Everyone put a blanket over your head and get outside right now! Right now! Hold your breath! Hold your breath!" She repeated that at top volume while grabbing her own blanket. She couldn't find her mask.

Margot said, "Ooh, Fergus! Oh no!" and stepped over the corpse, feeling her way down the stairs behind her husband.

Fergus said, "It's ok, Pepper! Everything will be ok!"

Andalynn shouted at them, "Hold your breath!" and reloaded as she followed. "Keep your covers on! Outside! Outside!" When she felt the night air on her ankles, she ripped the blanket off. Three others stood in the street, blind, like they'd forgotten to cut the eyes out of their ghost costumes.

Andalynn clenched her teeth. "Someone is still inside!" She grabbed the shortest head. "Who are you?"

"Daniel, ma'am!"

Fergus and Margot gasped and pulled off their blankets. Their daughter was still in there. Andalynn ordered them to stay where they were. Back under cloak, she ran up the stairs, stumbling over the corpse at the top. Sarah was sobbing in bed. Andalynn grabbed two fistfuls of the girl's covers, nightgown and hair and yanked her to her feet.

Sarah blubbered, "Please don't shoot me with the pistols!"

At a loss for any other word, Andalynn said, "Unprecedented!" and dragged the squealing girl from the room.

They thudded down the stairs and out the door. That time Andalynn was relieved to find all four of them. Fergus and Margot snatched up their child frantically, bedclothes and all.

The clouds parted overhead, showing some of the street. Andalynn couldn't smell anything on the wind. She said, "Take the blanket off, Sarah." Sarah dropped it on the ground. Andalynn looked down at it. "Pick it up! You might need it!" Sarah dipped her knees to do as she was told, her face floating like a tragic-mask on a stick.

Andalynn said, "Fergus, we need to reach the church as quickly as possible. There is at least one more of those things out here."

Fergus said, "Follow me!" The five of them jogged away in their nightgowns, blankets tucked under their arms.

Daniel said, "How do you know there's another one?"

There was no emotion in her response. "Because that was Drake."

Sarah started to wail. Andalynn watched their backs as they went. She decided against telling the girl to be quiet. If there were any other bauran lurking the streets, Andalynn thought it best to lead them to Michael.

It wasn't long before she saw something in the night behind them, its movement before its shape, a steady, loping speed. It gained on them. As the bauran closed in, Andalynn noticed that much of its flesh had decayed. What remained swung like satchels from its frame, its leathery, skeletal form beneath. Its right hand was gone, baring the two jagged bones of its forearm like the fangs of a serpent.

Andalynn said, "How much farther, Fergus?" and fired a shot on the run. They jumped from the unexpected blast and shrieked when they saw what chased them.

Fergus said, "We're almost there!"

Andalynn missed again. Their bare feet left the painful cobblestones. They ran faster on the grass and the bauran slowly faded into the night behind them. Then they were dodging through the headstones.

Margot said, "There it is!"

The church took form in the moonlight ahead. Lot sat on the grass in front of it, gaping at the coming group. Behind him, the heavy door was shut. Andalynn narrowed her eyes on that door - it was locked, she knew it.

She snarled, "Get Michael! Get Michael!" turned and planted her feet. Daniel and the others flew by Lot and into the church; the front door was never locked. Lot watched them run in and then looked back across the yard at where Andalynn's pistol barked and flared in its smoke like a tiny thunderstorm.

Lot hopped up, shouted, "Fwah!" and bolted inside.

Bullets ripping through it, the bauran closed distance with every flash. It slammed into Andalynn and they both hit the dirt. Then it sat up on her stomach and started punching her with the barbs of its broken arm - *shuck, shuck, shuck.* Screaming, she shoved her pistol under the ghoul's jaw and pulled the trigger - *click.* It was empty.

John, Michael and Abraham leapt up from their mats in longhandles. Everyone had just burst in shouting urgent versions of what was happening outside:

"Andalynn's out there!"
"She's shooting at the devil!"
"I... I just arrived!"

John rushed to Daniel. Michael sprinted out the door.

The blasts and the screaming had stopped. Their bodies appeared to be still but Andalynn's second pistol was clicking into the ghoul's dead weight. She'd drawn it dearly. Michael flung the corpse away from her like a dusty rug. The clicking stopped.

The smoke touched his eyes and they glowed. "God's mercy…"

Andalynn's face had been raked from the bone. Her flesh hung in strips. Her breath rattled in her throat and hissed. Michael knelt beside her, gingerly replacing what he could. The light faded from his eyes until he couldn't tell blood from ink or earth in the dark.

Abraham arrived and watched them for a few tense seconds. He understood what Michael was trying to do. If he opened the way without replacing her flesh, the healed wounds would be grotesque. But, Abraham could also see - *from where he was standing* - the riin thinning to a shimmering thread within her. He said, "No time for that, Michael. She'll die. Do it now."

Michael put his blood-slick hand on her forehead. Golden light exploded through the churchyard.

14 Templar

Ditch woke up at five o'clock in the morning. Still dark outside, his room was a black hole. He rolled out of bed, hit the rug and started doing pushups. He'd woken up that way for twenty years. It didn't matter if he'd been sleepless in the creepy woods for three nights or if the sun was coming up at the wrong end of the day; he was awake and he needed to do pushups.

He settled into a rhythm, mouthing a song and hitting the beat with his breath. He tried to be quiet to avoid disturbing his roommate, another of the ten sailors at Betheford's. Across the darkness the roommate whispered, "Hey, Ditch, are you awake?"

Ditch frowned and kept working. "Yeah, man, sorry, didn't mean to wake you up." Then his frown bent into a scowl. *Didn't wanna wake you up at all, nerd. Now you're gonna talk talk talk.*

"That's alright. That's no trouble at all, actually!" He was excited to be sharing a room with Ditch, who he thought was just the coolest. "Hey, Ditch, why do you sing when you exercise?"

Ugh. "Cause I get bored countin' that high." Ditch would have preferred to bunk with one of the other marines but hadn't wanted to make a big deal out of it at the time.

"Oh, right!" The roommate slapped himself audibly on the forehead. "Because you can do so many! You're really strong, aren't you?"

Ditch cringed, unable to think of a way out of the conversation without being a jerk. "I'm real light." He weighed one hundred and thirty-nine pounds of lean muscle.

"Hey, Ditch, will you sing that one that goes, *hold you dooown, hold you dooown*? You know, the one you sang in the woods on the way here."

Ditch thought about it for a few presses. He was singing anyway, under his breath. If he sang out loud, the roommate would shut up... No one had ever asked him to sing before. He said, "Yeah, alright." He adjusted his breathing and his work to a more aggressive tempo and dropped his accent for the lyrics:

Black straps that bind them back snap,
And they strip the concrete up from the street,
Their raging pace rakes the road away,
And leaves hell to breathe a gravel wake.
-
The broken line behind them, smoking, hides,
The light of the sun, like night has begun,
In this eclipse, Apocalypse,
They break and run and make the earth quake.
-
Their skin is gnarled confusion,
Bruised and ripped in,
Revolution, used then,
To state the place that anger takes, they,
-
Faces blistered, fused and twisted,
Lose the reasons they resisted,
And regret,
And lament their hard and wicked visit...
-
They left a scar where they existed.
-
Even breathing your last breath,
The life is burning in your chest,
They try to hold you down,
And rip it out.

"Hey, yeah, that's the one!" The roommate said. He started to sing along.

"Even breathing your last breath,"
"The life is burning in your chest,"
"They try to hold you dooown,"
"And rip it ooout"

The roommate slapped the bedpost, keeping good time. They both sang louder and higher.

"Even breathing your last breath,"
"The life is burning in your chest,"
"They try to hold you dooown!"
"And rip it ooout!"

Ditch thought his roommate might be some kind of musician the way he handled the tune. He'd never known. *Hey, this guy's alright!* They shouted the fourth chorus.

"Even breathing your last breath,"
"The life is burning in your chest,"
"They try to HOLD YOU DOOOWN!"
"And RIP IT OOOUT!"

An angry banging came through the wall from next door. "Hey! You hold it down! We're trying to sleep over here!" Ditch and his roommate shut up, realizing they'd gotten carried away. Then they started to snicker like a couple of kids at a sleepover. Ditch kept doing his pushups.

The roommate's smile was in his voice. "Yeah, that's nothing like the music I'd heard."

"That's the Broken Toes. They were just startin' to build, you know. Could a' been alright, but..." Ditch blew a raspberry to represent the destruction of civilization, "Pppbbbttt."

"That song's from before? I thought it was about the bauran. What is it about?"

"I don't know, man, it's like, symbolism, or somethin." Ditch had often thought about the meaning of that song. He felt it had helped him to survive, in a way. But, he didn't want to get into any of that with his goofy roommate, musician or not.

"So, it doesn't mean anything at all?"

Ditch lost his rhythm and scowled again. "Yeah..."

"Hey, Ditch, I wish I could have seen them play."

"Yeah, but... I mean, they were ok, but their cello player's always go'n way over the top. Too much weedledee-wonk, you know?"

"Ugh! I *hate* cellists. They step all over everybody else, like they're the only one on stage."

Ditch couldn't help but agree. "I know! I just wanted to grab that thing and break it over his dumb head, like *SHUT UUUP!*"

The roommate laughed eagerly. Then he said, "Why don't you sing with your accent?"

"Nobody sings with a accent, man."

"Oh... So, were you a singer, before? Were you in a band?"

"Nah, just a fan."

"You've got a nice voice."

Ditch lost his rhythm again. "Uh... yeah, thanks."

* * *

Biggs woke up with the sun on his face. The other bed in his room was straight and empty. Worried, he dressed and went down the hall to knock on Ditch's door.

Ditch opened it wide and stood half-naked in the way. Tattoos snaked and dotted the length of his chiseled little body, weaving under his shorts. He had a straight razor in one hand and a puffy, white horseshoe of shaving foam on top of his head. "Hey, Biggs, what's up, man?"

The roommate poked his head into view from farther back, red haired, freckled and smiling. "Hey, Biggs, we were just jamming!" He waved his fist and sang, "Hold you dooown! Hold you dooown!" Ditch turned to chuckle at him and rocked out with his own fist.

Biggs said, "Seen Drake? Kid didn't come back to the room."

Ditch said, "Nah, man. Hope he fell in a hole."

Biggs gave a half-hearted wave and walked away. Ditch paused, struck then by the feeling that Drake might really be in trouble. He shut the door and started dressing.

Betheford's common room was much larger than the Cauldron's, with a high, white ceiling and pillars. Large, frequent windows filled it with daylight. Decorative red and white checkered cloth covered four long banquet tables and matched the curtains. People were gathering near the double doors at the entrance, Welles among them. He saw Biggs on the stairs and ran up to him.

"Biggs, bauran hit that little restaurant Andalynn's at! Let's go!" The two sailors pushed outside and ran down the street.

Hundreds crowded the courtyard across from the Cauldron. Biggs found Andalynn's blonde among the black. He pushed toward her. She had her back to him with her arms folded, watching the closed door along with everyone else. Strangely, she wore some kind of scarf on her head and her gun belts circled a baggy set of the church's longhandles.

Biggs shouted, "Lynn!" working his way through. "Lynn!"

When she turned he stopped. The makeshift headscarf slanted to cover much of the left side of her face. Jagged scars tore out from under it, outlining the strips Michael had replaced. She stood straight with her chin up, ready to tell Biggs about the evening's events and that she was fine.

Biggs' mouth fell open. "Oh, Lynn..." He went straight to her and embraced her. "What happened?" She stood rigid in his arms, eye darting.

She thought about pushing him away. She was trying to accept what had happened to her, feeling it was an appropriate punishment, some kind of cosmic justice for what she'd done on the boat. She did not want to be comforted or to pretend there would be anything between them now that she was so disfigured. But, she did not want to hurt him either, so she rested her forehead on his shoulder and let him hold her.

Biggs said, "It's alright, ever'thin'll be alright."

"Drake is dead."

"Aw no… What happened?" He held her like he'd held his loved ones in another life.

Andalynn described the flight from the Cauldron as a list of her faults: she was too slow, she was inaccurate, she made poor decisions. By the end of her story she had even apologized for her clothes, explaining that her nightgown had been ruined in the struggle and the long underwear was all the church had to cover her up.

Biggs offered his own point of view. "Took out two on your own. Them folks're lucky you was there."

She started to tear up and thought about how strange it was to cry out of only one eye. Ditch called their names across the crowd.

* * *

The Cauldron was dark inside except for the sunlight from the second floor. Fergus would've had it lit from the hearth by then. Puffs of the bauran's disease rose from Michael and Abraham's steps as they thumped up the stairs. At the top, Drake's body sat in a pool of ink, slumped against the wall with its chin on its chest. Smoke bled out of the bullet holes.

Abraham lifted Drake's head by the hair. It pulled like a bag. "She squashed him."

Michael was in full habit again, his sleeve repaired. He looked around and sniffed the air. "It's settled, somewhat..." He stroked his finger across the banister and tasted the leather. The smoke fizzled in his mouth against the riin. "But it's still deadly. A good place to try the milk."

Abraham harrumphed. "That sounds like a clan remedy to me. Still, these sailors have experience. You can't argue with experience. Advise Fergus and his family to stay out of here until you know it's safe. Also, keep in mind that you need to stay at the church, where you can be found easily. I don't know when you'll find time to clean a house."

Michael nodded. "Absinth and a cow are ready for you. That boy, Lot, is minding them until you're finished here."

"I'm taking him with me."

"Really?"

"I'll need the help. I'd just get lost, my eyes the way they are. And he's got nowhere to go. I can't send him home now, can I? It's convenient for both of us."

"Do you think he can be trusted?"

"Let's not get ahead of ourselves. I'll give him a chance to keep his mouth shut. He's earned that."

Michael paused and then spoke against his better judgment. "Sir, should anything happen to you, all of Salem will die. They won't stand a chance without someone who knows the way."

Abraham's manner went cold. "Yes, they certainly are in peril."

"Forgive me, sir, but, considering your age, perhaps you should... forgo the crucibles, only for Lot. Then he could..."

Abraham turned on him. "Salem will rot before I break my vows!" The templar wore his sword behind his back, at the waist, and had his hands linked above the hilt. His head seemed to float above his armor in the shadowy hall, like the skull of an ancient knight returned from death. A thundercloud of riin billowed out of him. "You've broken trust, haven't you, consecrate? Confess!"

Michael took a step back. "No..." He'd never felt such a wash of power. Then, he imagined all of Antioch lost to the plague because he'd spoken carelessly at the top of the stairs. Michael shouted, "No!" and opened the way.

He was a bonfire on the shore before Abraham's blazing *Vesper*. Michael's hand shot to his sword. There wasn't enough room in the hallway for a full swing, he'd have to stab for the head, knowing that thrust would not only doom the town of Salem but would thereby open a path for the bauran into all of the towns and cities of the north. *John warned me to be careful with him. I should have listened.*

However, before Michael's blade bared more than inches from the scabbard, Abraham's aura dispelled. He was a skinny old man in a loose suit of armor again. Abraham showed his palms and said contemptuously, "My hands are sheathed."

My hands are sheathed was an expression from the Reformation that meant loosely, "I'm not up to mischief," or literally, "I don't put people to sleep without their permission." It was a reference to why they kept their hands in their gauntlets and their gauntlets buckled to the sleeve. Most of them couldn't open the way in someone else without the touch of skin. In light of Abraham's ability, the expression was as meaningless as a quarter inch of leather, but Michael's sword clicked back into its housing.

Abraham glared at him. "Why don't you go find something to cover the boy? Let's get this over with."

Heart pounding, Michael slowly backed away from him and into Sarah's room. In all of his life, so much of it spent with Abraham and practicing the way, Michael had never felt riin come out of the air like that. It filled him with dread curiosity. *What technique had that been? What is he capable of?*

Abraham was still glaring when Michael returned. They wrapped Drake's corpse in Sarah's sheets. Michael lifted it, an end in each hand, like a grisly hammock. Then he carried it down through the restaurant, dripping ink on the floor and leaving strands of patient smoke in the air behind him.

He stopped in the kitchen. The door was open. Muddy footprints tracked the floor like a man had walked through on the balls of his bare feet. Michael turned to Abraham and said, "Marabbas has been in here..."

"Mmrnmhrn... stupid gunder. Come on. If he isn't dead already, he'll be out by the shed."

Abraham was right. Marabbas lurked near the smokehouse, beard and furs clumped with blood, crouched over an eviscerated deer. When Michael came out of the kitchen with Drake's body, Marabbas stood up and waved.

Away from the dinner table, the difference between Marabbas and a man was obvious. Standing on the fores of his very long feet, with stocky thighs and calves bent, his legs resembled a dog's. Leather braces on his arches left his thick toes and bony heels bare at either end.

Relieved, Michael tried to wave back, but it looked more like he was raising a toast with one end of the corpse.

Marabbas sniffed the air. "That's Drake. He's dead." He stalked closer, continuing to sniff.

Abraham strode forward.

Marabbas stopped, head cocked to one side, watching him. At five feet tall, average for a gunder, he was shorter than Abraham's shoulder. As Abraham approached, Marabbas felt threatened. His amber eyes flared and he tensed, ready to flee.

Abraham came to a halt ten feet away. Marabbas collapsed. Michael took note of Abraham's range, about twice that of a caligan. Abraham stood there, examining the unconscious gunder's reflection. Then he said, "Hmm, the smoke doesn't hurt him."

Michael set Drake's body down. "It didn't harm Ares either..."

* * *

Marabbas stirred. Then he stretched and yawned, emitting a faint, high-pitched whine. His mouth opened wide, twice as wide as a man's, and his long tongue curled between vicious rows of teeth. When his jaws closed his face seemed human again under all of that wild and bloody hair. He propped himself up on his elbows and looked around, doggish legs out in front of him. Michael and Abraham were discussing the smoke.

Marabbas listened for a while and then said, "That's the sailor smoke?"

Abraham turned, stroking his beard. "Yes…"

Marabbas stretched again, splaying his toes, and then got up. "A lot of that's inside. Is Fergus dead too? I have this deer." He pointed at the deer.

Abraham harrumphed and suggested to Michael, "You could use him."

Michael's expression lifted at the idea. "Marabbas, do you want to help Fergus?"

"Ok."

Michael spoke slowly and with his hands. "The smoke is in the house," he pointed at the house, "but Fergus can't clean it up," he mimed pushing a broom, "he'd get sick," he brought his hands up to his throat and stuck out his tongue. "Will you do it?"

"Ok."

"Good! I'll have a bucket of milk and a brush inside tonight. You go in and scrub the milk everywhere you smell the smoke, alright?"

Marabbas paused. "Scrub the milk." The idea tied his mind in a knot. *How do you scrub milk?* Michael gave him a long moment while Abraham's eyes rolled. The gunder scratched and said, "I have this deer." He pointed at the deer again. "Is Fergus inside?"

Michael slowed down even more and made even wider gestures. "*No*. He can't go - *inside* - until the - *whole* - house is - *clean*. He'd get - *sick*." Marabbas' face followed Michael's arcing hands like they were birds flying around in a room. Michael's expression went flat. "Come back tonight."

"Ok." Marabbas grabbed one of the deer's legs and bounded toward the forest. The two hundred pound carcass plowed through the fallen leaves and apples. Considering the unholy strength of the bauran, Michael was thankful he wouldn't be seeing any undead gunders.

Abraham said, "If you leave him alone with milk and a brush, he'll drink and scratch himself. Take that body out to the other one. I'll gather some wood."

In a private little clearing, they built a pyre out of apple twigs, branches and a large amount of the Cauldron's woodpile. On top they placed two bodies, both wrapped up to contain the smoke. Drake was bigger and heavier than the other, the monster that had killed him, the same one that had almost killed Andalynn. Michael stepped away from the intense heat as the fire started to roar.

Abraham had his own copy of the bauran book, his handwriting blocky and precise. He'd just turned from a page that gave basic instructions on how to properly burn a body with readily available materials and was on the passage that defined the incinerator. He'd copied detailed, technical drawings of the machine from the originals Captain made in Michael's book. He said, "Whatever is *pyrolysis*?"

Michael said, "This has taken too long. They're defenseless in my absence."

Abraham closed the book and tucked it flat against his lower back, under his sword. It was pleasantly supportive and tightened his belt. He motioned at the burning corpses. "You'll have your hands full once this gets out."

"I know."

"What are you going to do?"

"They're having service today. I'm going there to explain it to them."

"They won't hear it. They'll shun you again, this time for saving their miserable lives."

"What do you suggest?"

"Honor your vows. Even good intentions can tempt you away from them."

"How will that keep me from getting shunned?"

Abraham grimaced. "No, no, Michael! I don't care if you're *shunned*! I'm worried about what you'll do once these intolerable idiots are shunning you! You've no one left to advise you. You've no equal in this place. Our vows temper us and give us integrity. They make us fit to judge." Abraham pointed at him. "Honor your vows. I shouldn't have to tell you this."

"You don't. I'm not some kind of devil."

"Without strict, inhibiting law, that's *exactly* what you'll be! A devil. You almost pulled your sword on me today! Me! What foolishness are you going to justify tomorrow?"

Michael spoke freely, confident that Abraham no longer suspected him of heresy, in the strictest sense at least. "Perhaps you're right. But, perhaps men weren't meant to be so helpless. Please, be reasonable. With Lot you can..."

Abraham threw his hands up in frustration. "Fwah! Keep your advice!" He shook his finger at Michael. "You're a sorry successor!"

"I'm not. You're short-sighted. If you don't care about whether men live or die outside of the law, consider this, if everyone dies, there will be no one left to replace us. Who will protect the way then?"

Abraham put his fists on his hips. "If everyone is dead, it won't need protecting!" Michael dropped his hands to his sides and gave up. Abraham was just getting started. "This plague, these bauran, they're a crucible. I've never understood how someone like you could have come from this place, from *these* people. But *now* I see... Now I see you crumble and lose your resolve. You hide behind the letter of the law and mock its spirit. A true paladin takes the hard road. You're a disgrace!"

"Ah, I see, well, you could have consecrated your own acolyte, hmm?" He said it to be irritating.

It worked. Abraham had been at odds with Gabriel for a long time. "You know damn well why I didn't! Do you know what he said to me when he got back from Tabor, after having done *nothing*? I'll tell you what he said! He said *thou shalt not kill*. He actually said that to me! That's some of your father's gibberish, isn't it? What are you supposed to do with devils then? What good is a paladin that doesn't kill devils?"

"Quite a bit of good still, I'd think."

"Oh please. *Thou shalt not kill…* fwah."

Michael agreed but argued with him anyway. "I believe that only applies to men." He felt foolish right after having said it. Regardless of beliefs or having an accurate understanding of the fellowship's moral imperatives, it simply wasn't a good argument to have with Abraham.

"*Only applies to…* these people can only afford that sort of brainless morality because they built their houses on our doorstep! Do you think Breahg war parties stay away from here because they're afraid of being *shunned*? Do you think Tabor would be a better place if they had *God*? A devil's a devil, it doesn't matter what skin it's in! And I've never met - *anything* - so *evil* as a man!" He indicated Michael's scar. "Your devil's marked you, hasn't he?"

Again Michael agreed, but had by then developed a general disputatiousness that would not allow him to be silent. "The devil's mark is a silly superstition. This was an accident."

Abraham recoiled. "No, no, Michael! I know that! Don't be an idiot! I was making a point!"

A chorus of singing rose away south as Michael and Abraham argued. It was one of the fellowship's hymns. Service had begun. Abraham stopped and scowled when he heard it. "I can't stand these people. They've *God* instead of honor."

Michael wanted to be rid of him. "Before you go, may I have your key, sir? I'd rather not break the library door."

"So, that's how it's going to be, is it?" Abraham snapped the chain from his neck and dropped the key on the ground. "I'm not a saint yet. Honor your vows."

Michael linked his hands behind his back and waited - in the apple trees, the crackling heat of the pyre and the distant singing of the fellowship - for Abraham to leave.

15 Faith

That week's service filled Betheford's inn to the walls and almost three thousand more people stood outside, waiting for word of what would be discussed within. Seats had been saved for the sailors and Fergus' family. Betheford stood on the staircase, smiling and waiting for the whispers, chairs and shoes to silence.

Service started with a hymn. Betheford led their worship with a clear, powerful voice. The songs rose and fell in practiced harmony. An ocean of sound flowed from the fine, double doors and carried through the city on the voices in the streets.

Biggs leaned over to Andalynn and said, "They're makin' a racket." She nodded, frowning in her scars. All of the sailors shifted around, watching out of the inn's big windows, which seemed very fragile when they thought about it.

After the last song, the congregation settled and prepared for Betheford's sermon. Whispering near the entrance drew attention. Michael stood in the middle of the whispers, looking around the room. He hadn't attended one of his father's services in more than thirty years. Andalynn held up her hand. He held up her bundled goggles and surgeon's cover. She'd asked for them.

The man between Andalynn and Fergus stood up and offered Michael his seat. He shook Michael's hand with both of his own, smiling at him and welcoming him to the gathering. Betheford also smiled at Michael and waited once again for silence.

Betheford opened his arms wide and said, "Brothers and sisters, daughters and *sons*..." He went on, *and on*, to talk about friendship, family and accepting the sailors into the community. Though loquacious, it was a wholesome message.

Fergus was disgusted. He whispered to Michael, "Fwah! Look at him up there, that preachy, preachy…" Michael shushed him. Fergus frowned and turned to Margot.

Margot put a finger in his face and hissed, "Fergus! Don't embarrass us."

Betheford spoke about the importance of contributing to society and produced a list he'd taken the time to collect from the fellowship. It contained available work and more permanent living arrangements for the sailors. Betheford had just begun reading it when Fergus turned around and saw Ditch. Fergus twisted with his arm over the back of the chair and went, "Psst!" Ditch scowled.

Fergus whispered, "Do you see him up there? He's terrible! God *must* work in mysterious ways. Why he'd let *Betheford* speak for him I'll never know!"

Ditch said, "Look, man…" obviously not interested in anything Fergus had to say right then.

Fergus shushed him, motioning that he should keep his voice down. Then he went on to complain to his new friend in whispers about Betheford, quickly comparing him to both a toadstool and an old trout.

Ditch's face was a raisin. He wanted to hear what Betheford was saying and he didn't want to listen to any complaining. One of his friends had just gotten cut up. Another one was gone.

Fergus said, "Now I know how you sailors feel. I lost my home last night too. I don't know when we'll be able to move back in. So I have to sit here, drinking Betheford's sour milk."

Ditch snapped. With a little less volume than a shout, he said, "Hey! You lost a house, man! Everybody I know is dead! Now I'm tryin' to listen to this guy so, like, shut up!"

Betheford paused. The congregation turned to stare. Fergus rotated, sinking into his chair. Margot and Sarah covered their faces.

Ditch shouted, "Hey, man, sorry, can you go over the jobs again? I missed it."

Betheford said, "Of course!" and recited the available work. Then he moved on to the proposition of building a wall around Antioch and the donations it would require. The congregation grumbled. They didn't want to build a wall around their city. If something threatened their safety, the church would take care of it. A wall was impractical and costly, too much trouble. Also, such fortifications were against the king's law.

Michael shook his head at what he heard. Fergus turned around in his seat and scowled at Ditch. Ditch scowled right back, ready to bust Fergus in the mouth. Then everyone noticed a commotion outside. People were screaming.

Someone shouted through the doorway, "They're here! They're in the street!"

* * *

A gold and green meadow stretched east of Antioch, shimmering in the midday sun and breeze. Two rotten bauran limped through it. Their black eyes saw none of the meadow's rippling color. As their paths converged, the monsters appeared to one another as empty shadows against fields of gray. To one another, they were not important.

They didn't feel the sun's warmth or the coolness of the wind and they smelled neither wild flowers nor their own deathly reek. They heard the hymns of the fellowship, though - those were important - and hurried toward them.

Antioch's buildings and streets were a maze of sharp, black angles that had to be navigated to find the songs. The worship lulled into a steady, conversational thrum, but was still a sound stored in vital instinct, the sound of people. It came closer with every turn and at every turn the bauran's only desire became stronger. They were like men desperate for air, heading for the surface of the water.

Then the angles opened into a lane filled with riin, hundreds of tiny suns. Each light hovered within a shadow. The shadows started to scream.

Faith shrieked, "Oh my God, it's them! The devils of Meroe!" She was trapped. The crowd was a deep dead-end that held her in the alley for the two shuffling, jerking zombies. The people who saw them pushed against those who had not.

"Who's pushing? Stop that!"
"Get out of the way! Move! Run!"
"Help me! Please, help me!"

Faith pleaded and clawed at the crowd's backs. The bauran dragged her down. They bit and thrashed her as the fellowship pushed itself away. Terrible bony fingers ripped through her clothes and flesh, pushed into her chest and, with a horrible crack, pulled one of her ribs away from the rest like a lever. Her screams oscillated from the trauma.

Someone shouted through the doorway, "They're here! They're in the street!"

Two courageous men leapt from the crush to Faith's aid and wrestled the powerful ghouls. They grabbed one together and pulled it away, but then burned in its smoke and reeled.

Michael shoved through the retreating flow, knocking people down. He flattened three citizens to burst from the throng, pulled his caligan and took two, rapid strokes: the first sheared head and shoulders from the ghoul above the woman, the second split the other as the coughing men released it.

Michael dropped his sword and ripped his gauntlet from the mail before the second fiend fell. The blade clanged on the cobblestones in a shower of ink and ringlets. He shoved his bare hand into the gore under the bauran's vomiting trunk and reached Faith a moment before death. Light blazed from the horror.

Her new skin sealed around his fingers like a glove. He slid them out and pushed the corpse away. She'd been mutilated. Torn flesh swung in flaps from incomplete patches of hasty scar tissue. Her body had isolated pockets of ink in cysts. Broken bones were set at drastic angles, some exposed, like horns. She trembled in an abominable puddle.

The two rescuers retched in the poison behind him. Smoke rolled out of the baurans' cloven chests and burned into the retreating crowd. Eyes wide and glowing, Michael shouted, "No! Don't run!"

* * *

Biggs said, "It's a stampede!" looking out the window at the flooding citizenry. "What're they runnin' for? Michael's - right - there." He tapped on the glass, pointing at Michael, whose face flashed from one to the next: Faith, the convulsing men who had tried to help her, the smoking corpses and the fleeing crowd. He couldn't take care of them all by himself.

Ditch said, "They're buggin' out, man!"

Andalynn said, "Many of them have been infected. They cannot be allowed to hide."

Biggs pulled his bandana over his nose. "Michael's got his hands full. Let's round 'em up."

The sailors shouted quick directions to the congregation inside and then charged across the emptying street. The double doors shut behind them. They went into a courtyard out of the alley's breeze and shot their weapons into the air, beckoning with their free hands. The loud reports gained attention but only redoubled the frightened mob's desire to get away.

Ditch almost threw his rifle on the ground. "Aaah, come on, man!" He took off alongside the crowd like a cow-dog, jingling and chuffing from his pumping speed. Biggs ran after him, but wasn't half as fast. They both fired their rifles as they went and yelled for everyone to go back to the courtyard and to hold their breath. By the time Ditch reached the front runners, the people behind had started following orders.

Andalynn shouted, "Come out of the wind! Come out of the wind!" and waved them in. They filled the courtyard, some in the sun and some in the shop-awnings' shadows. Children sat on their parents' shoulders. A boy and a girl straddled the well's roof while other youngsters stood in a ring around the lip, looking out over the gathering. Across the way, frightened faces stared from the windows of Betheford's inn.

The two men who had tried to rescue Faith rounded the corner, reporting that Michael was dragging the corpses away. Several people shrieked and pointed at what followed those men. Someone shouted, "Look! Another devil!"

Faith cried, "I'm not a devil!" She was clutching Michael's tabard around her shoulders and chest, and trying to hide her face as she joined the group. Andalynn stared at her.

Ditch and Biggs came jogging back. Ditch spoke through a cough. "That's... all of em... I think... man."

Biggs said, "You're the fastest son of a gun I ever saw!" and clapped Ditch on the shoulder. Then he noticed the cough. "Caught it, huh?"

Ditch bent over and put his hands on his knees, gasping and retching into his respirator. "Yeah, man... It's like... hard... to hold your breath... you know." Coughs stuttered through the crowd as well.

Andalynn shouted orders to organize the afflicted. She asked for those who felt stronger to stand back and she failed to ease fears by saying, "Remain calm! You could have up to three hours before death!" People gaped, prayed and made holy signs.

Biggs shouted, "Come on y'all, the better we help Michael, the faster he'll go."

When Michael returned, he was the only one in the street. His naked mail's leather laces ran from neckline to waist. His left hand glistened red and black under the torn sleeve. He shouted, "I stowed them in the toilet! Stay away from the toilet near the inn!" He repeated himself and the crowd passed it along. *Don't use the toilet at Betheford's! Hey! Don't use the toilet at Betheford's!*

Michael scanned up and down the empty way, breathing. Then he said, "The lane is safe! We need to start curing the disease!"

They flooded out to him, begging for hospital. Michael worked as quickly as he could. As they lie down on the cobblestones, he touched them and moved on to the next. Each took no more than four seconds of his time, but long minutes passed in the presence of thousands.

He could not speak often at the pace he kept, but when he reached Ditch, Michael said, "Thank you." Ditch nodded through the wretched coughs and gave Michael a "don't mention it" slap on the arm.

Those who'd recovered or were waiting for their turn worried and questioned the sailors. Some asked about the bodies in the toilet. The answers were unsettling.

"Yup, gotta burn 'em."
"They, like, keep smokin, man."
"Their lungs do not die."

Word spread of blasphemy. Michael grimaced at the scandal while he worked. The sailors defended the necessity of the act and, though some citizens understood, many protested and spoke of damnation.

"It's terrible sin!"
"You'll deny their souls to rest!"
"They'll be doomed as ghosts!"

One pious man even refused hospital with a curt, "No thank you!" Michael grabbed that man's face and forced it on him. Then he moved on to the next. A runner knocked on the doors of the inn and passed word through to Betheford, who'd been watching out of a window. Listening to the tale, the deacon flashed a look of shock at his son.

It took more than three hours to cleanse the crowd. Michael could not be sure he'd gotten to everyone. Some people went twice. Others might have followed that pious man's example and removed themselves from the order on principle. No one was waiting for him, though, and he had not found an infection in a long while. The fellowship argued around him.

Michael raised his arms and shouted, "Everyone! Listen to me!" They gave him their attention. The torn chain gathered at his shoulder. "You're all going to die!" They gasped. A child started to cry. The arguments resumed.

Biggs said to Andalynn, "You n' Michael, sure know how to work a crowd."

She said, "What do you mean?"

Michael tried to get their attention again, to finish what he'd meant to say, that they were only going to die if they didn't make the necessary changes. But, it was too late. His voice drowned in the crowd's discussion and he ended up explaining himself to angry, frightened individuals for hours.

He didn't mind the work. The hours of talking to them and healing them did not frustrate him half as much as the conversation with Abraham that morning. The fellowship was made of friends and family, brothers, sisters and cousins among them, aunts, uncles, nieces and nephews. They were his history. Michael didn't share all of their beliefs, but he loved those people.

They were shaken to learn he was the only one left in the church. They were just beginning to realize the weight of the threat. The sailors' tales hadn't been enough. And after being attacked during service, most of them were ready to help however they could. They were ready to stand together and to protect each other.

Michael was resolved to teach them all, every one of them that wanted to learn. He'd already made plans to begin with Edward the following morning. He decided then he would teach Edward to teach. They would make the way as common as speech.

He took the time to answer questions and told everything he could, the open truth. It was a tremendous relief, like he'd been holding his breath for decades. In the corner of his eye, the lowering sun glinted gold from his tabard's circle. He turned to it and saw Andalynn speaking with Faith on the steps of Betheford's inn.

16 Gunders and Greer

Antioch's day of worship gave way to night and a full moon. The fellowship locked themselves in before sunset, just beginning their plan to survive. The entire city was on alert. Toward that, Marabbas stalked through the apple trees. At the glowing door of the Cauldron's kitchen, he smelled smoke, milk and Michael. He crept inside.

Michael's sleeve was at the forge again, but his caligan was next to him. He scrubbed the butcher table with a big bristle brush by the light of the fireplace. Another brush jutted up from a bucket of milk on the cold grill.

Marabbas crept closer, sniffing. "That's milk."

Michael nearly jumped out of his longhandles. "Aaah!" With one hand over his heart and the other over his weapon, he realized who it was. Then he picked up the brush he'd dropped and shook it at the gunder. "Marabbas! Stop… stop sneaking around!"

"Ok."

Michael hadn't been startled like that in a long time. He had to collect himself. Marabbas studied him and then looked back and forth from the bucket to the brush. Michael could tell he was thinking something through.

Marabbas said, "You're scrubbing the table, not the milk."

Michael smiled a little. "Yes, I've decided to see for myself if it works. The sailors said it gets the smoke out."

Marabbas snorted and sniffed his way through the kitchen. "I smell the smoke. It's different with milk on it."

Michael brightened. "It is? Can you tell if this is working? What do you smell?"

"Smoke with milk on it." Marabbas had a keen sense of smell but his speech was an unfortunate distillation of what it gathered.

"Ah..."

Michael stroked the butcher table and put his finger in his mouth. The infection didn't fizzle against the riin. Encouraged, he handed the other brush to Marabbas and the two of them scrubbed the kitchen together. As Marabbas sniffed around, Michael tested for the infection and they compared what they found. They soon discovered that the smoke was alive... and that milk killed it. Marabbas could point out the dead patches from the living by scent.

* * *

The front door stood open to the night, shining from the common room's fireplace. Michael sat scrubbing the stairs and Marabbas worked on the long table. Each had a mug of cider in reach and each was keeping to his thoughts.

Michael thought of Margot. How happy and grateful she'd been when he told her he would try to clean the smoke out of her house. She'd called him an angel. He'd always liked Margot.

Marabbas remembered eight years before, when he'd been only a beardless pup, making frequent visits to the inn's back door. Fergus was always there with something good to eat. Betheford would shout, *you'll have gunders at my door day and night! It's not right!* When Fergus opened the Cauldron, Marabbas got to sit inside.

Marabbas said, "I like Fergus."

Michael had been half-ignoring such childlike statements for hours. "I know you do." The ink on the stairs made his milk suds black.

Marabbas had an awkward, inefficient style of scrubbing, like an ape at the easel. He would also spend long moments in motionless contemplation. His progress was slow. He drank some of his cider, snorting in the tankard. "I like Margot."

Michael drank to that. It was delicious. "I do too. She's a fine woman."

Cider was the drink in Antioch and Margot's family made it the best. They'd been keeping secrets of body and flavor for generations. Michael thought of them as a sort of Cider Circle, with Margot as their mistress.

Marabbas absentmindedly scratched himself with the brush and then jumped at the touch of milk that trickled out of it. He sniffed it cautiously. "Margot says *ooh filthy beast go to the well.*"

The marble-mouthed impersonation of Margot made Michael laugh. "I don't blame her. I've seen how you track mud into the kitchen."

After a thoughtful pause, Marabbas said, "I was in the tree outside her window. Margot said filthy beast and threw her apple at me. I fell."

Michael put down his brush and covered a laugh. "God's mercy, Marabbas, what were you doing in the tree outside her window?"

"Looking at Margot."

"You shouldn't do that."

"Why?"

"Well, that's spying. It's wrong." Michael sighed and drifted into a memory of Margot's embrace, an innocent hug from her, but it felt *good*. He'd always liked Margot.

Then he imagined climbing the tree outside her window. There she was, the cider mistress. She opened up, but didn't throw an apple at him. Instead, she invited him in with a wicked grin, and he smelled her hair and held the soft weight of her flesh in his hands and tasted her skin. *Ooh, filthy beast.* It was an intoxicating fantasy. *And oh, what's this? Intriguing, someone's opening the door. We'll be discovered! Scandalous… Who could it be?* Fergus!?

Michael grimaced and shifted where he sat, coming back to reality.

Marabbas was off on his own as well. *Spying is wrong, don't do it.* But, he'd no sooner had the thought than it slipped away from him like a fish in the river. *If it's wrong, don't do it. Wrong means bad. But why is spying bad? I like it. Margot doesn't like it. Margot threw her apple at me and I fell. It's bad to get caught spying.*

Marabbas said, "I like looking in Sarah's window." That part of the tree had better cover.

"Marabbas!"

"What?"

"Don't do that! It's… inappropriate! God's mercy, she's a little girl! You should be ashamed of yourself! Don't do that ever again!"

"Ok." *Don't spy on little girls...*
Michael frowned, but understood it was only the gunder's natural curiosity. Marabbas didn't mean any harm. And, after more thought, Michael realized that Sarah wasn't a little girl anymore. *She must be sixteen years old now.* Marabbas was only ten. Though mature for a gunder, Michael thought it not unusual for a boy of that age to spy on a sixteen year old girl. Then he imagined himself in the tree outside of Sarah's room. She giggled and opened the window. Oh, how naughty it was to climb in and be alone with her. *But wait, who's this opening the door? Why, it's Margot...*

Michael lost several more guilty minutes to thoughts of Margot and her daughters before his conscience once again presented him with Fergus. *Fwah!* Samuel was right; it was foolish to remain celibate if he was going to break the most sacred vow anyway. Celibacy was a precaution, a way of ensuring his priorities, as were his vows of poverty and obedience. They were meant to keep worldly concerns from compromising his silence. Without silence, the other vows were meaningless.

It would be easy to find a wife... He was the most powerful and important man in Antioch. There was no use in pretending otherwise. Everyone needed him to survive. He imagined there would be a hundred women lined up at his door with fresh baked pies if he made it clear that he was *out and about.* He could have any of them. He could have all of them for that matter, if he wanted, and the fellowship couldn't say boo about it. It would be their suicide to shun him. In fact, he could have Margot...

No, no. Those are just fantasies.

It would be their suicide to shun me... He remembered the man who refused hospital earlier that day. *No thank you!* Michael frowned, seeing the man's pretense of sacrificing his life for his beliefs as a foolhardy and selfish gesture, inconsiderate of the consequences to others. *It must have come from ignorance.* No one could know about the bauran and hold to such a principle. Michael had wanted to break that man's neck at the time, not open the way.

Then he thought of a man willing to sacrifice any number of lives for the sake of his beliefs. *Salem will rot before I break my vows.* Michael envisioned driving his caligan through Abraham's head in the hallway, pinning him to the wall like a holiday decoration.

It made the most satisfying sound - *whock*. Hanging from the sword, Abraham's corpse spoke: *Without strict, inhibiting law, that's exactly what you'll be, a devil.*

Michael shook the image from his head. He couldn't keep violence out of his mind any better than he could keep Fergus out of his fantasies. It would always be there. Assuming every man had such a willful and disturbing imagination, and that actions were what truly mattered, he whispered, "No, no, Abraham… they're only my thoughts."

Marabbas looked up. "What?"

Michael said, "Ah, nothing. I was just thinking out loud."

The idea amazed Marabbas. He wondered if all men could do that. Then he started to wonder if they could "listen out loud" too and tried calling the man's name telepathically. *Michael? Can you hear me? Michael…*

Michael pulled his brush back out of the bucket. The milk was a dark, scummy gray. He stuck his finger in it for a taste. It was revolting, but it didn't fizzle. "Marabbas, when was the last time you dipped your brush in the milk?"

Marabbas looked from one end of the table to the other, thinking about time.

Michael waited. Then he said, "Is it still working?" but that caused the gunder another bout of contemplation. "God's mercy, Marabbas, smell the brush. Is the smoke dead on the brush?"

A quick snort and Marabbas said, "Yes."

Michael thought about it. Marabbas had scrubbed nearly an entire banquet table with one dip. The milk was strong.

* * *

On the lonely street outside, a frightened young man approached. He was coughing, rubbing his eyes and holding a torn note. Knowing what had happened in the Cauldron and that it was filled with deadly devil smoke, he stood far away from the open door to call through, "Michael? Are you in there?"

Michael answered from inside, "Ah, don't come in! Don't come in! I'm coming out!" He emerged, wiping his hands with one of Fergus' rags. The young man handed him the note. It read:
I am at the Cauldron - Michael

Michael's expression went flat. He offered hospital. When the young man woke up, Michael was kneeling next to him with the bucket of scummy milk. Marabbas crouched nearby. Michael dunked the young man's hands in the milk and told him about its strength.

Michael said, "Tell everyone about the milk. It's important. It's something anyone can use to protect themselves from the smoke."

"Yes, sir. I will. Thank you, sir." He started to go.

"Wait!" Michael slapped the note into the young man's wet hand and gave him a look of stern disapproval. "Put that back on the door of my church, please. It's not doing anyone any good over here."

"Oh! Yes, sir. Sorry, sir!" He scampered away into the night.

Michael hoped no one was waiting at the church, having missed that note. He didn't often call names and wasn't one to say *dumber than a gunder*, especially considering his company, but removing the note was such a remarkably poor decision. Michael thought of Drake and borrowed a word from Ditch. "That boy is a dookus."

Marabbas said, "What's that?"

"Hmm? Ah, It's a word the sailors use to mean foolish."

"Is it dumber than a gunder?"

"Marabbas... don't say that."

"Why?" Marabbas cocked his head to one side. Everyone said *dumber than a gunder.*

"I don't like it when you say that." Michael went to put a friendly hand on his shoulder but Marabbas flinched at the motion, ready to flee. Michael linked his hands behind his back. "It's a bad thing to say. It's wrong to call gunders dumb and to make light of them. It's... it's just not right." He went back inside. Marabbas followed, in a trance of thought.

When they'd finished milking the building, Michael locked the front door and moved back through the kitchen to leave. He imagined the Cauldron would smell like the biggest, nastiest sailor in the morning. At the back door, he remembered to reward Marabbas for the help.

"That was a fine hind you had this morning. Did you have your fill of it?" Marabbas looked confused so Michael tried to clarify. "You had that deer. Did you eat it?"

"No. I don't like it raw. I took it back to the greer."

"Ah, that's right. They do the hunting, don't they?"

"Yes. I like the greer."

"I'd imagine you do. You should be careful, stealing their kills away so often to Fergus. Surely they'll thrash you for it one of these days."

Marabbas thought about that. Then his face squinched up with glee and he laughed. The sound was as harsh and startling as the sudden braying of a mule. Michael took a step back.

Marabbas didn't laugh often among men. The way they spoke confused him, often meaning more or something other than what they said. He understood this time though, and it was ridiculous! His long, sharp teeth showed in his smile.

"No! The greer like me!" He was his pride's Apoc. He kept the other gunders away. The greer wouldn't attack him... not unless he startled them.

Michael had never spent so much time alone with a gunder. The evening had been enlightening. "I see. Are you hungry?"

All mirth vanished instantly from Marabbas' face, replaced by a focused, animal intensity. "Yes."

Michael took another step back. "Ah... Fergus told me, to thank you for helping, if you did, that you can have whatever you want from the smokehouse. So, have at it."

Marabbas' eyes popped and he shot out of the kitchen.

Michael shook his head and laughed. He leaned against the doorway, listening to the ravaging of the shed. The snorting, grunting and munching were pure. *That lusty gunder doesn't worry about anything. He just takes his meals as they come.* Michael felt a small pang of jealousy and then laughed at himself as well.

* * *

The sun hid under the trees, just on the rise, and Marabbas was stuffed. A wobble from the cider in his stride, he made his way home through the deep forest to the north, to the pride.

The pup, Barabbas, lounged in the bushes with his brother. Both of them were lean and shaggy-headed with long, toothy faces. Neither could grow a gunder's beard yet. They had bright, blue eyes as well that wouldn't turn amber until they matured.

Barabbas smelled his father on the wind and perked up. "Apoc is coming!"

His brother said, "Let's get him!"

They stalked the trail that led to the men. Their pupils were wide, black disks in the bordering leaves and their faces twitched toward any movement. They could see quite well at night, but they didn't see Marabbas. They held their breath to listen...

In a moment of dead silence, a sudden roaring and horrifying doom barreled through the leaves between them. The pups shot straight up into the air, twisting, hissing and screeching for their lives. It wasn't until their father's barks and snarls became his braying laughter that they stopped ripping through the brush to escape. Even then they stayed hidden, quivering from the icy fear he'd just poured into their veins.

Marabbas said, "Ha ha, pups! You can't get me... you're a dookus!" He moved on the tree, cackling like a drunken jackass.

Barabbas popped up and shared a look with his brother. Then they followed after their father, pushing each other into the bushes and mimicking his frightening roar.

The greer, six adult females, heard Marabbas coming from far away. He made sure of it. When he arrived, they were resting quietly around the roots of a tree as ancient and twisted as Daniel's oak. They were braiding each other's hair, sewing deer skin into clothing and relaxing, preparing to sleep through the morning and afternoon. They looked similar to women until their teeth.

Marabbas stopped in front of them, yawned and scratched. He had nothing to say. They looked up at him without anything to say either. So, since all was well, he vaulted up to his branch and made himself comfortable.

From a distance or in the dark she appeared to be a girl of Sarah's age, but Naila was only three years old. She'd been in season for the first time that summer and her belly was round with Marabbas' pups. She said, "Apoc smells like milk and mushrooms." It was an unnecessary thing to say, but she was young.

Barabbas' mother, Diana, stretched, flexed her thick fingers and toes and extended her smooth, hidden talons. Then she humored Naila with conversation. "That's man's food. The men feed Apoc."

"Why?"

"Because Apoc is strong and clever."

Marabbas settled into the crook of his bough and looked up at the leaves, hands behind his head. He thought about the word *wrong*. It was one of the more confusing words. Michael used it a lot. Michael said spying was wrong and *dumber than a gunder* was wrong. Betheford said it was wrong to feed gunders. Fergus said it was wrong to use shortening instead of butter. The word meant, *don't do it*, but it also meant why. It was the why in the word that made Marabbas curious, because that seemed to change from man to man.

Barabbas climbed up, crouched on the bough at his father's feet and said, "Apoc, what's a dookus?"

Marabbas lifted his head to look down at his son. Then he put a foot on the pup's face and pushed. "Get out of my tree."

Barabbas scrabbled to hold on, hissed and fell, crashing through the leaves to the forest floor. Marabbas reclined into thought as his son mewled below and the pride brayed like a herd of donkeys in the darkness.

17 Funerals

The sun reddened, low in the sky, as the fellowship hurried for home. Michael stayed in the street, answering questions in the thinning crowd. He would clean the Cauldron with Marabbas later that night. Andalynn, Biggs and Ditch stood together on the steps of Betheford's Inn.

Andalynn said, "I was surprised you confronted Fergus like that during the assembly."

Ditch said, "Yeah, I kind a' lost it, man. I was just sittin' there, thinkin' about how he tossed Drake out, starin' a hole in the back a' the guy's head, you know? And *that's* when he turns around and starts yappin' about whatever and sayin' he knows how we feel." Ditch couldn't believe Fergus' timing. "We just keep dyin. I didn't think this place was real, but it is, and it doesn't matter. We keep dyin' anyway. The stupid church splits up, makes it even worse. I'm gettin' the murks, man, bad."

Biggs said, "Did pretty good today, considerin. Just need to watch our step." He put his hand on Ditch's shoulder. "Not us, remember?"

Ditch nodded. "Yeah, not us." Andalynn said it as well. The three of them drew comfort from one another and went in. Bauran seemed impossible there, in Betheford's clean, red and white checkered dining room.

Despite the general rush to get home, to prepare for the inevitable siege of devils, the common room at the inn was full. Some had stayed behind out of shock, others were too scared to go outside but most just couldn't help talking about all that had happened that day. A group of sailors had gathered at one table.

As the three marines sat down with them, Biggs said to Andalynn, "Sure you don't wanna go on up? Figured you'd wanna be alone or sump'n."

"I am starving, actually, and I do not wish to be alone at all." The infection aside, she would not have survived such serious injuries in the old world. In the new, she could be mauled by monsters and go out to dinner the same day.

Ditch said, "The food here sucks, you know."

"I believe I can withstand the experience." She smiled briefly, drawing in as she felt the scars in her expression. Ditch and Biggs smiled back but then drooped with pity.

Locals rarely ate at the inn. The sailors ate better on the boat. Gray and salty clumps sat on their plates, some of it indiscernible as animal or vegetable. Andalynn said it could be loosely referred to as sustenance. Ditch said he'd told her it was going to suck. Biggs said it was free.

Instead of complaining about what was in front of them, a few sailors started exchanging stories about Drake. Some of the things he'd said and done seemed funnier then, looking back, than they'd been at the time. He'd been tolerated more than loved, but he was one of them and he was gone. Dinner that night became an informal funeral for their lost friend. In that way, they'd eaten many dinners like it.

The number of sailors in the dining room rose to twenty-four as they ventured away from their hosts in anticipation of such a gathering. Welles said, "Ditch, you knew him better than anyone else. Why don't you say something?" Many agreed and called for Ditch to say a few words.

Ditch stood up. "Yeah, alright. Uh, I don't know, man. I knew him from back home, you know. Just some dopey kid hung out at the gym. If I could a' picked somebody to bring with me, he'd a' been like, way in the middle a' the list. But it was him..." He trailed off. It was difficult.

The sailors looked around at each other. The tradition was to say something nice when someone died.

Ditch raised his glass of milk. "Kid had guts, you know, heart. Drake was a fighter." It was the strongest compliment he could give.

They all raised glasses of milk. "Hear, hear!" None of them drank.

Some later arrivals whispered at another table:

"How did it happen?"
"How do you think? Andalynn."
"Up to her old tricks."

They didn't know she was there. She let it go. Biggs did not. Angry, he stood up and faced them. "What's that s'posed to mean? Huh?" The whisperers were too surprised to answer. Everyone stared. Biggs said, "Yeah, thought so. When'd any a' you ever get off the boat? What'd any a' you ever do, 'cept take a ride? Y'all got some big mouths."

Ditch hadn't heard anything, but he put his milk down, his arms out and said, "Yeah, what's up!" It wasn't a question. If Biggs was in a scrap, he was in it too. Ditch felt like stomping somebody anyway.

Then one of the whisperers got up, rubbing his mouth. "Mmmhmm, we all know how it is with you guys. You think you're better than everybody else, don't you? Well guess what, we're not on the boat anymore. Let's go."

Andalynn recognized him by his voice. It took Ditch a little longer to see who it was. Bo wasn't wearing the mask he'd been known for on the *Grace* and he was groomed and dressed like a local. Only his volatility and his hatred were the same.

Ditch said, "Biggs, wait, that's Sue's guy." Sue had been the first of them to die.

Biggs groaned and withdrew. He didn't want to hit Sue's mourning lover. He didn't really want to hit anybody and felt stupid then for having stood up in the first place.

Bo didn't care. Someone was going to get it. Then he saw Andalynn. "Oh and look who it is! Isn't this just *GREAT!* I heard you got all carved up like a pumpkin, and you sure did! Hey, come on, Shooty, we're having another funeral. You can say something nice about Sue for us, ok? She never got one, remember? I know, tell us about how she got the rot. Remember that? But, maybe she didn't? Right? It's kind of hard to tell sometimes, isn't it? Especially when you've got to *pull that trigger.* Tell us about how you did it when she was begging you… to…" He choked up and trembled, which made him even angrier.

Andalynn said nothing. No one wanted to speak. Sue's execution had been terrible for everyone. It defined life on the boat.

Bo wouldn't let it go. "No? You don't want to say anything for Sue? You don't want to remember her, do you?"

Ditch felt bad for the guy, but enough was enough. "Come on, man. We all lost people."

Bo smiled obscenely. "Yeah... but not like that."

Biggs changed his mind. He did want to hit Bo.

Betheford, who'd been watching with worried curiosity, stepped in before it escalated any further. "Now, now, I think you've all had quite enough milk for one evening." It was an odd thing to say. He paused before carrying on. "We've got a curfew, from what I understand, so we all want to mind that, don't we? Anyone who isn't staying here should be on their way. Hurry along, now. Come along."

Bo raised his glass. "One last toast, then, to Drake." He stared right at Andalynn. "Kid wasn't a heartless son of a bitch." There were no *hear, hears* for that toast and Bo didn't wait for any. He left the inn with his glass as everyone shifted uncomfortably.

Betheford's mouth fell open. "Well, how do you like that? I'll have that glass back! Those are expensive. Who was that sailor?"

Andalynn said, "His name is Bo."

"And with whom is he staying?"

"I do not know."

Everyone was getting up and saying goodbye around them. A few more sailors snuck out with glasses of milk. Others took theirs up to their rooms. Betheford, waiting next to Andalynn, said, "You're the one that was with Fergus and his family, aren't you?"

"Yes."

"And... where are they now?"

"I do not know."

"My word, where are you going to stay then? I have to tell you we're quite full here."

Andalynn looked up at him, raising an eyebrow, but without the other her expression at that moment looked more like surprise than incredulity. Biggs answered for her. "She's with me."

"But... but..." Betheford leaned in and lowered his voice. "I can't have unmarried couples sharing rooms here. It's inappropriate."

Biggs almost laughed. "Oh! Right, yeah, don't worry about that. She's my wife. Been married for years. Confusion when we got here n' all." Andalynn smirked. Betheford paused and narrowed his eyes.

Ditch faked a yawn and stretched. "Man, I'm yawnin' like a yawny yawner over here." He got up from the table and said, "Night, Mrs. Biggs." Then, with a quick jut of his chin at Betheford, said, "Beefer," and trotted up the stairs with his glass of milk.

Betheford pulled his chin into his throat. "That's *Betheford...*" But Ditch was already gone. Several other sailors stopped by the table and called Andalynn *Mrs. Biggs* in front of the deacon. Some even touched her shoulder.

Welles said to her, "Bo was right about one thing, we're not on the boat anymore." He offered his hand to shake. She took it. After Welles left, Andalynn and Biggs excused themselves. Betheford's suspicious frown followed them all the way up the stairs.

* * *

Biggs shut the door. "Congratulations. I now pronounce us hitched."

Andalynn released one breath of a sad laugh. Noticing the scent of coffee, like a pot was on the brew, she looked around. The room was small and clean with two beds, two nightstands and a chest of drawers. It was lit by a single candle in a coffee cup. Dry, roasted beans filled up the cup around the wax, fragrant in the warmth of the flame. Every day before sunset, Michael's mother went to each of the inn's occupied rooms to leave one of those pleasant little candles for the night as an amenity.

Biggs motioned at the bed behind her. "That's his. If it's weird, take this one. I'll sleep over there."

"No. It does not bother me." She sat down on Drake's bed and placed her glass on the nightstand. Biggs did the same across from her. They started dipping their fingers in the milk and swabbing it on their eyelids and lips. Andalynn said, "I should have informed Margot and Fergus of where I was going. I am sure they will be concerned."

"Oughtta be with your friends tonight anyhow, not strangers."

Andalynn stuck a milky pinky in her ear. "That is true. It was delightful, reminiscing with Bo." Biggs stared. She said, "Tell me if I become too caustic. I am upset."

"Shoot, don't bother me none. Lemme have it. Been through the wringer, poor thing."

"It has been an exceptionally unpleasant day, all events considered. Ditch was right. Dinner certainly did suck." The headscarf was irritating. She wanted to take it off, but worried about what Biggs would think of her. She looked around the room for a mirror. "I have yet to see the damage other than in Betheford's window. I do not believe there is a mirror anywhere in this village."

"See if I can rustle one up." Biggs wandered around with the coffee-candle, trying to find a hand mirror for her. He didn't remember having seen one but thought she might appreciate the effort. Rummaging through the drawers, he said, "Does it hurt?"

"Not terribly. It feels strange, as though I am wearing a mask." She put the goggles on over the scarf. The black rubber made an airtight seal around her right eye and a drum of the cloth over the deep, empty socket on the left. "How fortuitous. My other mask still fits."

Biggs stopped and stared at her again, his false youth creased in the candle's shadows. He appeared much older for a moment.

She said, "I apologize."

"Don't have to say you're sorry. If'n it hurts or not, nobody's gon' be alright with sump'n like that happ'nin' to 'em. Want you to know, don't change nothin' for me." He resumed searching for the mirror that wasn't there.

She thought it was a gallant statement but did not accept it. "I have been foolish since we arrived. I thought I could start over here. I thought we could..."

"Aint foolish. It's good. Gotta move on, right?"

"Do you want to see my face?" It was a challenge. *How do I move on from this?*

He was on his knees, lifting up the blankets to look under his bed. "Seen it before." She took off the goggles and the scarf. He got to his feet and turned. "Don't think there's a lookin' glass anywhere in here, Lynn..."

She was staring at him. The candlelight made the scars even deeper. Half of her face was a dead skull, the other half a sad and vulnerable young woman. Neither was the truth.

He sat next to her. "Don't wanna say sump'n wrong."

"Bo called me a jack-o'lantern. Try to do worse than that."

Biggs took some time to build what he wanted to tell her. He didn't want the truth to sound like a lie. "Don't have a mark on me, 'cept where Drake put a bullet in my pants."

"Do you want to compare injuries?"

He smiled. "Had wrinkles n' liver spots before, n' big ol' tufts a' whiskers shootin' out a' my ears like pole cats. Had me some scars too. Not so good as yours, but some pretty good ones, n' the stories to go along with 'em. Was startin' to forget them stories, just from bein' old. Now, it's like… I'm erased. A clean slate."

Andalynn nodded. "And I have been doodled on."

"Huh?"

"I was referring to my slate. Please, continue. I believe you were in the middle of boasting about your physical condition."

Biggs cocked his jaw sideways and rolled his tongue through his cheek. "Look here, you, what I'm tryin' to say is, I lost a lot a' who I was. Them knocks n' dents are little reminders. Yours show courage."

"Courage is a euphemism for stupidity." She sighed, knowing Biggs was only trying to be kind. Then she gave him her best mechanical smile and let him talk.

"When Zeke found me, I asked him to take me home, to my family. He wouldn't do it, had bigger fish to fry. Course, couldn't get back there myself, would a' just died in the smoke like ever'body else…" He paused, remembering those he'd abandoned. "Thing is, Zeke didn't make me go with him. Followed him on my own. Took a long time to get over that, not knowin' what happened to 'em, but knowin' all the same. Thinkin' I's a coward and how I should a' tried to get back to 'em, but knowin, even if I did, I couldn't a' done nothin. Most ever'thin' we did on the boat, I was lookin' for a good way to die."

Andalynn could see it, looking back, and she understood.

Then he said, "Wish I had marks like yours."

18 Milk

The *Grace* was the only thing on the world other than water and sky. Drake was the only man on deck. He sat near the bow on a small, three-legged stool, trying to milk a goat into a bucket. The ocean breeze tousled his hair, a scarf covered his mouth and nose in tattered layers and an uncomfortable pair of goggles rested comfortably in his pocket.

The goat hated Drake. His cold, clumsy hands had her ready to run. She started but he caught her and grinned under his scarf. "Too slow, Eustace, too slow! Now hold still so I can yank on your boobs. Yank-a-booble-dandy." Her eyes and posture couldn't have been more severe if he was threatening her with death.

A man came out of the deckhouse along with the drone of a crowd until he closed the door. He approached on routine patrol, wearing the full gas mask Drake would own by the end of that day. The man shifted his rifle to one shoulder and tapped the mask's lenses with his fingers, attempting to indicate that Drake's eyes were not covered. "Wung, muggug, gugga gugga mung."

Drake said, "Sorry, what was that, Fritz? Am I getting too friendly with your girlfriend over here? Hah hah!"

Fritz chuckled in the mask, pulled it off - *foomp* - and repeated himself. "Hey, stupid, put your goggles on." Like all of them, he had the face of youth.

Drake looked around. "Why? We're in the middle of the ocean." He saluted. "I'm on a mission to milk the goat."

Fritz laughed. "The rules, kid. Armymom'll be all over you if she sees. Then she'll let me have it for not doing anything about it." He heard footsteps coming from behind and turned around, still smiling.

Then Fritz cried out, "Nyaaah!" He dropped his mask and fumbled for his rifle, choking a round into the air with a loud

CRACK! Eustace sprang away, sailing over the railing like it was a fence in a pasture. Milk erupted from the bucket. Drake fell backward off his stool, shocked by the chaos and by the goat going overboard. Fritz fell next to him, struggling and shouting, "Kid! Get it off a' me! Get it off!"

It looked like a woman had tackled Fritz to the deck. Her mouth was clamped into his arm. Drake froze, staring at her black eyes, recognizing her by the hair, Mullins. He'd spoken with her not long ago, after noticing her cough. Mullins had said *don't worry, it's not the rot. It's just a cold or something. I'll sleep it off and we won't need all the rigmarole, ok?* Drake didn't tell anyone.

Andalynn's boots came thumping toward them. "Hold your breath! Hold your breath!" At point blank, her pistol clapped. Ink exploded across the deck. She put a heel in the bauran's ribs and kick-shoved it away from Fritz. Her jaw clenched when she saw him unmasked. Her stare fell on his bloodied arm.

The shot was ringing in his ears when Fritz looked up at Andalynn's face - the goggles and surgeon's cover - the face of death. He covered his wound and started scrambling away from her. "Oh, no, come on. You gotta be kidding me!"

Feeling nothing under her expressionless plastic and glass, she shot him in the head without pause. Everything ended in an instant. The gathering crew moaned.

"Oh no, not again."
"That woman's done it again."
"Who was it this time?"

Drake was still frozen, sitting in a puddle of goat milk, unsure any of it had really happened. His eyes began to burn and he rubbed them with wet fingers. Then he noticed that Mullins' smoke was blowing out to sea across him and that Andalynn was looking at him.

Drake scooted away and put out his hand. "No, don't!" She followed him at a stride, aiming her pistol. He hid his head in his arms and pleaded, "Wait! I'll clean up! I'll clean up the… the… the thing!"

She hesitated.

"I can do it! I swear I'll do it, please…"

They had lost a good man during a disinfection before. The idea was repulsive to Andalynn, waiting to kill him while he swabbed the deck, and it would be a deviation from the System, but Drake's offer protected someone else from a deadly risk. He was not coughing. It was not in his lungs yet. They had some time. As she considered it, holding her weapon on him became increasingly difficult.

She did not know his name. She recalled someone having referred to him as *Goober* and then she remembered - he was young. He was not an old person in a new body like so many of the rest. He was an innocent, peeking out between his arms, waiting for her to make up her mind.

He was not like Fritz. Fritz had been her friend and she had killed him.

Andalynn's will broke. She holstered the revolver and said, "That is commendable." Then she turned away from him to organize the unhappy crew, calling for bleach and quarantine on Mullins' quarters. While they locked down the deck, according to protocol, Andalynn imagined that everyone would follow Drake's example from then on, to bargain for a few more minutes. What would she do about that? What could she do? They had to be as ruthless as the bauran to survive.

Drake got to his feet, shaking. He couldn't look at Andalynn. She had a bullet waiting for him. The thought of it haunted him as he got on the good side of the wind from Mullins' body. He held his breath out of habit and dragged the smoking corpse to a circular, iron hatch in the floor to the port side.

The hatch opened with a wheel that screeched in its rust, uncovering a steep chute that slid straight down through the hull and out to the ship's incinerator; the Coffin, Captain's design connected it to the *Grace* with chains and tubing but also held it at a flexible distance.

Drake let go of Mullins and watched her disappear into the chute, never to return. He saw his own mortality in that dark passage, and whispered, "That's where I'm going. I'm going down the hole..." He noticed Andalynn dragging Fritz over, grunting and straining from the weight of the body.

Drake wasn't about to help *her*. He left the hatch open, went to the guardrail and looked out over the wide ocean, contemplating jumping overboard. There was no land in sight.

Even if he somehow made it to shore somewhere, there would be nothing but monsters waiting for him. He wouldn't make it anyway. He'd be dead before long, regardless of Andalynn's pistols. If he jumped overboard he'd only bob along in the water behind them, blowing smoke into their wind. It was hopeless. He bowed his head and wept.

Fritz slid down the chute. Andalynn sealed the hatch and called for the Coffin's ignition. "Two down! Light it!" The incinerator's fuel lines gurgled and clanked like plumbing. The familiar roar of the blast nozzles sounded over the water, below the level of the deck. Andalynn was breathing heavily when she came to stand next to Drake.

She told a solemn lie. "Your bravery is inspiring."

He sniffled and wiped his nose in his scarf. "Yeah, I'm a real hero."

She felt badly for the boy and tried to comfort him with familiarity. "I am sorry about this, Goober."

He reeled, anguished to hear he would be remembered as *Goober*, and could hardly reply through his sobbing. "My name is Drake!"

She corrected herself, "I apologize, Drake." Then she let him shudder and sniff for a moment while she remembered what the smoke felt like, that invasive, rapacious burning. She understood at least some of what he was going through. "Your pain is severe?"

Why is she talking to me? He shook his head. "It's not that. It's that I'm... I'm dead. I can't believe it. How could this happen to me? I was sure I was going to make it."

Andalynn leaned on the railing, looking at the ocean with him. "There is little hope of that for any of us. This miserable ship is a prison. We are all sentenced to death."

He hadn't expected her to say that, or anything at all, really. Normally she just walked up, put her gun against someone's head and pulled the trigger. She was merciless. She'd been getting faster too. The first one had been a woman named Sue. Drake had nightmares about it - Andalynn, missing the mark with those brutal revolvers, butchering that screaming woman. Each execution after that had been quicker, up to Fritz, who'd barely had a chance to beg.

Drake slumped. "Why bother, then? Why not just let it happen?" Saying it made him think. Before Mullins, he hadn't seen one of those monsters in weeks. He'd been laughing and joking with Fritz only a few minutes ago. He didn't know if any of that mattered.

Andalynn said, "Because it is better to die fighting." Then she spoke her mind out of frustration. "This incident could have been prevented. Mullins deviated from the System. Had she come forward and informed someone of her infection, Fritz would be alive and we would not be having this conversation."

Drake decided against saying what he knew about Mullins. He didn't think things could get any worse for him, but it seemed like a dumb confession to make. "Maybe she caught it in her sleep and never got the chance."

Andalynn knew better than that. "Could you sleep through the pain you are currently experiencing?" Not actually being in any physical pain, he shrugged. Andalynn continued, "Our casualties will increase according to the distance we stray from the System. Bauran at least are predictable. We, unfortunately, are not. Now there is no knowing where Mullins' smoke has settled. More of us may be infected as a result of her error."

Drake couldn't stand the guilt so he tried to put it on her. "Are you just going to shoot me when I'm mopping, or wait until after?" His sniffling softened the question's aggression but the blame was still there.

She did not respond. Before becoming a plague-ship's executioner, Andalynn had been a lawyer and a politician. She had a modified notion of guilt. It suddenly occurred to her that she tended to assume rather reviled responsibilities in society. A tiny laugh died in her chest before it could get out.

Drake waited through her silence and then said, "Why don't you ever let anybody say goodbye?"

Grieving lovers and friends of the dead always attacked her with that question. She had once replied that unless someone else was willing to pull the trigger they should all be silent and stand aside. But, this time was different. She wanted to talk for a little while.

She said, "There is not a good way to do it, other than quickly. We do not know how long it takes for the infection to begin producing smoke. That must be avoided at all costs.

Immediate disposal must be our only consideration within the time we are allowed. Of course, I am saying this while deviating from the System myself." *At least he is not coughing.*

The rail dug into her arm. Andalynn shifted for comfort and Drake tensed. He thought she had talked herself out of allowing him to clean the deck and that she was reaching for her pistol. He didn't know she was procrastinating, that she needed a few more minutes as well.

He trembled, expecting her to draw and fire at any moment. "I... I don't think I have the rot. I got better."

"I saw you rubbing your eyes in the smoke. No one *gets better.* I do not blame you. Most of us would say anything for a little more time."

"My eyes aren't burning..." Drake's eyes were swollen and red and filled with tears, but he hadn't been rubbing them. Andalynn studied him. It should have been difficult for him to keep his hands away from his eyes. She had ground her palms into her sockets when it had happened to her. It was curious.

She pushed away from the rail. Drake cringed. His only hope then was that the bullet wouldn't hurt. She said, "I will return momentarily to assist you with the disinfection," and started walking away to the deckhouse. "Put your goggles on."

Drake almost asked why. They wouldn't help if he already had the rot. Then he shoved his hand into his pocket for those uncomfortable goggles like his life suddenly depended on them.

The deckhouse was a low rectangular room, fifty feet deep and thirty feet wide, contoured by small, porthole windows and built around the center mast like a tree house on the ground. Every one of the seventy five sailors inside was wearing a mask. They watched through the windows as Andalynn talked to Drake. They surrounded her when she entered.

Biggs was worried. "What's go'n on with the kid?" He'd sent Drake to do the milking.

Andalynn said, "He may be infected. It is strange, though..."

Bo pushed toward her in an intimidating respirator, a modified goalie's mask. "What do you mean *he may be infected?* I thought you *knew* if someone was infected or not! How can you wait for that jerk kid when you didn't wait for my Sue!?"

Andalynn backed away from him. She touched her pistol but then took her hand away, not wanting draw it in the crowded deckhouse. With her back against the wall, she braced herself. Bo was about to give her a beating. She was not going to ask for mercy, partially desiring the freedom that came from punishment.

Ditch darted in between them before that happened. He put a stiff palm in Bo's chest and said, "Hey! Cool off, man. I'm a' mess you up!"

Bo, a foot and a half taller and much thicker, said, "You bald little bastard! Get out of my way!" He grabbed Ditch by the jacket to throw him aside. It was as though he'd pushed the button on a machine. Ditch's hips twisted and he fired a hard knee from the torque into the larger man's groin. That would have been enough to put Bo on the floor. Ditch held him up and hit him with two more, just to make sure.

Bo dropped into groaning spasms. "Aaarrgh, you little... Aaah! I hate! Yeuuh!" He tried to fight his body's response to the strikes, tried to get to his feet. Then he threw up in his mask.

Ditch stood over him, ready to hit him again. "Man, every day with you! I'm sick a' this! We all lost people! This is what we got now! I don't wanna say, like, *get over it*, or whatever, you know, but, *come on!* Get over it!"

Everyone stood back and kept their opinions to themselves. Ditch made it clear early on that anyone who started a fight on the boat was starting a fight with him. He'd kicked more than one groin, had broken a man's fingers and once poked a guy in the eye during a nasty scuffle in a cabin. They'd all become wary of his dirty justice.

When it was clear Bo couldn't get up, his friends came over to help. They would take him back to one of their rooms, where they could uncover their faces and breathe, where they could curse Andalynn, Ditch and all of the other monsters and draw comfort from one another's company. Vomit leaked out of Bo's mask as they carried him away.

Andalynn composed herself and walked past Ditch to where Captain sat.

Ditch straightened his jacket. "*You're welcome!*"

She heard him but didn't turn around.

* * *

Outside, Drake was hard at work with a mop and a bucket of bleach. Andalynn had never given anyone a second chance before. Since he still wasn't feeling the smoke, he was starting to hope.

He found Fritz' mask and picked it up, wondering what to do with it. It was a valuable piece of equipment, probably the best respirator on the ship, but it could've been contaminated. He looked around to see if anyone was watching. The grumbling huddle of Bo and friends emerged from the deckhouse, stared at Drake for a moment and then went out of sight around the corner.

Drake, when uncertain if something had been exposed to the smoke, often relied on the two second rule. He understood the rule didn't work but, unless staring into the chute, he rarely considered the consequences of a risk. Also, if more than two seconds had gone by, he would sometimes use the rule's general invalidity as an argument against it. Since the two second rule didn't work, it didn't matter if he broke it. He brushed Fritz' mask off with his fingers and then exchanged it for his scarf and goggles.

Andalynn did not return to help. At first, she had been too busy, defending herself against the crew's criticism. Bo's outburst encouraged others to scrutinize her judgment. If she'd been ready to fire on Drake, but he'd convinced her to let him live, how many others might still be alive if only they'd been more persuasive? She told and retold the facts but had no explanation for why Drake wasn't showing signs of the rot. Then, after realizing how long she had been inside, she simply watched Drake through a porthole along with everyone else, like he was a firecracker with a lit fuse.

"Goober's got Fritz' mask..."
"I told you. He's a jackass!"
"Unprecedented."

The sun set five hours after the incident. Drake was fine, other than being cold, alone and nervous in the dark. He complained at the deckhouse door. "Hey, I don't have it. Can you guys hear me? I'm clean. Let me in!" The mask muffled his speech into honking gibberish. "Wung, mugunga mug. Gunna gung wumma? Wum gum. Wug munnung!"

They finally opened the door. Everyone backed away as he entered. Andalynn pointed at the mask and said, "Take it off." He did as he was told - *foomp*. She prodded and opened his face with her fingers like she was judging a dog in a contest. Confounded, she said, "I do not understand this. How are you not infected?"

Drake said, "I got milk in my eyes."

She clipped out a, "What?"

"I think, I was thinking about it, and I got milk in my eyes."

"Preposterous. Speak clearly."

"No, I mean I was thinking about it while I was out there cleaning. I was milking the goat when it happened. When the smoke got in my eyes, I rubbed milk into them by accident." Gasps and murmurs ran the depth of the deckhouse.

Andalynn drew back and turned to Captain. He was smoking his pipe again. It irritated her, but even when inebriated, which was often, Captain's education was impossibly deep. She said, "What do you think of that?"

Captain said, "It's interesting..." Everyone quieted to listen. He nodded thoughtfully and nursed his pipe. "It is. It reminds me, I'd an acquaintance once, long ago, an oenologist." He smiled inside of his wispy, egg-like cocoon, savoring the memory of a woman and her wine. Then he smacked his lips and continued. "She used milk as a fungicide. Mixed it with water and brushed it on the vines to treat them for powdery mildew." Captain tapped himself on the gauze over his nose. "The smoke might be a species of mold, or its spore, to be true."

Ditch said, "Holy crap! That's big, right? That's like, really important! Isn't it?" The possibility of having discovered a cure for the rot staggered everyone, even more so because the cure was so simple. Some sailors patted Drake on the back while others stood staring, vacantly declaring how much milk they were going to use.

"The whole rest of the way, I'm sittin' butt-naked in a bowl of it."

Biggs, however, rubbed the back of his neck, thinking. He was more familiar with what little livestock they had aboard. "Problem is, only got us the one milker. Right now she's good for six, seven pounds a day. No tellin' how long that'll last." His statement sobered the burgeoning enthusiasm. Still, one milker was better than nothing.

Drake said, "Biggs... um, Eustace jumped off the boat."

Biggs was slow to respond. "Aw, no, Eustace?" Then his frustration and resignation came out with a shake of his head and a gentle sigh. "Goober..." Drake put the gas mask back on to hide while everyone else deduced the identity of Eustace.

Captain said, "Have I gathered that our one milker had a man's name and that she's no longer with us?"

Biggs said, "Yup." The room deflated.

Ditch said, "Man, should a' got us some more goats. It's too bad we didn't know, you know. It's like, too bad everybody didn't know." It was a cold, emptying idea, that the cure had been there all along and that the world could have survived.

Andalynn gritted her teeth. "We need more goats." She turned to Captain. "Take us to land." Drake's discovery was forgotten in a surge of protests. Closer to shore meant closer to the smoke and that was unacceptable. Andalynn became frustrated with them, threw her arms out and shouted, "We shall find no goats at sea!"

Interested, Captain began ruminating aloud. "Mmm, we'd lose weeks to do it, and expose ourselves even more along the way. All without knowing whether it's worth it or not, whether it really works." The room stopped bickering to listen. Noticing their attention, Captain said, "At least, I can't think of an acceptable test, that is. Unless we've a volunteer to lick the chute..." He looked around. There was not a volunteer for that. "No? Well, I doubt we've any milk left anyway."

Andalynn announced her argument like she was in a courtroom. "We are presented with risk in either scenario. Since we are *dying*, we must consider the amount of time involved in each of our options. How long before we can expect to reach this Meroe?"

Captain said, "Months, most of a year, if Zeke's points are right, not knowing what other troubles we'll have. We're bound for uncharted waters. We've only just begun."

She then charged through the more peculiar particulars. "How long before we could reach a place that might have goats or sheep or some other sort of lactating beast?"

Captain snickered and drifted off on the effect of his pipe. His first mate was a cold-blooded killer but she was also an invaluable member of their improvised crew. There were a hundred of them left and there'd have been less or none without her. *Thanks for that at least, Ezekiel.*

When he remembered he was in conversation, Captain came back in good humor. He smiled, imagining the impatient frown waiting for him under the face of death. "We've been following the continent, roughly. My guess on that, as I've said already, would be weeks. Aye, indeed, not a bad gamble, maybe," and he winked at her, though she couldn't have seen it.

Andalynn used his faint approval to challenge the room. "Who here is willing to come ashore with me?"

There was mumbling and grumbling and some mentions of, "Nobody," under their breath. Not one of them considered going ashore with Andalynn to be any better than licking the chute.

Ditch said, "That's nuts."

Andalynn was about to say that if she had survived on open land for twelve days, they could do so long enough to raid an abandoned ranch for livestock. She needed to convince them it could be done. But, before she'd begun, Biggs came forward and said, "Yeah, me."

It surprised her. Biggs brooded lonesome days away with the ship's animals and was not one to speak out often. She did not expect much out of him but welcomed the support. If nothing else, he could hold the bag. She said, "Are you able to use a rifle?"

He shrugged. "Some."

19 Michael's Wall

Michael was asleep and dreaming of a memory. It was from twenty years into his past, a day in the forest with Gabriel and John. The two younger men, slim and unscarred, wore blank acolyte's tabards. Michael's covered the plain brown and white of the fellowship. Gabriel had a brilliant, cerulean blue shirt, the fashion of Meroe, under his.

John's hair was a bit thicker on the top and there was black in its iron gray but he would otherwise change little over time. He'd worn a paladin's habit for fifteen years by then and was well known in Antioch.

John said, "You're going to be strong, boys. That's dangerous without discipline. Look here." He patted a tall pine, ten inches thick through the trunk. "What do you think would happen if I struck this tree with my fist? As hard as I could."

Michael said, "You would knock it down." He thought John could do anything.

Gabriel scoffed under his breath, "I'd like to see him try."

John laughed. "No! I'd break every bone in my hand, that's what would happen. Not to mention the hand would glue itself back together in a mess. Oh, no, this tree is much tougher than I am." John drew his caligan. "I could hurt myself in striking such a formidable thing, even with this. A bad swing could shatter my wrists. The strength you'll have is a danger to you. It's difficult to control. It takes discipline, practice and technique to use it on your enemies instead of yourself."

John winked, turned and swung through the pine. Michael would never forget the sound of it - *whock* - a deep, rich expression of destruction, compressed into an instant. The heavy tree slipped from its diagonal stump, punched the earth with a tremor and then leaned into its neighbors' branches, raining needles.

Gabriel shrugged. "Not bad."

Michael said, "Not bad? That was more impressive than Abraham's sleeping beetle."

"Shame about the tree."

"Pines are a nuisance."

John said, "Watch your heads, boys!" and tossed some burlap sacks at them. "Look at all the pine cones! The discipline it takes to fell a tree like that in one stroke starts with smaller tasks, like, oh, say, collecting and shelling pine nuts for our dinner! Hop to it." John lectured them while they gathered and the two students carried on a private conversation in whispers.

Gabriel said, "The beetle was only a demonstration. You don't need to be a sword master if your enemy is unconscious."

Michael's chin pulled into his throat. "God's mercy, how dishonorable."

"Really? Do devils deserve such regard?"

"Well, perhaps not, but honor isn't for others. It's for the self."

Gabriel said, "And you question Abraham's?"

Michael drew back. "No! No, of course not. That's not what I meant. You're always putting words into my mouth and trying to get at me. Stop it."

Gabriel smirked. "Well, at the risk of being *honorable*, I have to tell you something else you might not have considered. There's little hope of becoming templar as John's acolyte. You might want to reconsider your opinion of Abraham while you still can. Ordination isn't so far away for us now. I'd hate to take unfair advantage of a humble coffee beaner like yourself."

Michael frowned. "I don't care about that. And don't call me a beaner."

Gabriel smiled broadly. "You don't care about that *right now*." Then he vanished.

John's lecture was coming from farther away. "...because you don't want to make the same mistake I did. Remember my finger! Assume you'll only have the time for one strike. Make it your best..." Michael looked around but couldn't find John. "...and put it through the middle." Then John's voice was gone as well. The chill forest was empty. It didn't seem right. Michael wasn't supposed to be alone...

...and he wasn't. He was lying on his mat on the cold, stone floor of the church. There had been a small noise or a brush of air or a smell, nothing identifiable, only enough to tell his body that something was in the room with him and to wake him with a pinch of fear.

Then, anger. Michael opened the way and sat up, ready to destroy whatever had dared to molest him in his sleep. He didn't need his sword - he didn't want it! He could snap a bauran's spine with his bare hands.

Sunlight and cold air were rushing in from outside. The door was open. Edward sat on the next mat, beaming.

Michael ceased channeling and frowned at him. "Edward! Be careful! You startled me. I might have harmed you."

"But, you told me to meet you here this morning."

"I didn't tell you to hang over me in my sleep like a devil, though! Did I?"

Edward flinched. The sight of him made Michael even angrier. Michael rose to one knee and put his hand over his face, trying to understand why his urge to beat something to death wasn't going away. He needed to clear his mind.

Edward's smile crept back as he watched Michael meditate. That was going to be *him*. He was going to be a knight of the church too! Just like Michael. Unable to contain his enthusiasm, he said, "When do we start?"

Michael's temper broke along with his concentration. He stood up, frowning in his long handles, towering over the boy. "I was wrong to approach you the other day. I didn't give it enough thought."

Edward's smile disappeared. "What do you mean?"

"I need someone responsible and mature by my side, to help me with serious matters. These are serious times. I do not need a careless boy."

"I'm not careless!"

Michael pointed around in a huff. "I wake up in the cold, my door's open, look at the hearth's dead, and you, you spooking at me like an owl on a mouse! You should've brought a log in! Think of someone other than yourself, child."

"That's not fair! How am I supposed to know..."

Michael cut him off. "That's enough! It's done! Go!"

Edward got to his feet in disbelief. Michael had done it to him again. He made fists and said, "You know what, Michael? To you, Fwah!" Then he stomped out of the church.

Michael didn't like what Edward had meant by that, but the anger was already abating. Perhaps it had been unnecessary to call Edward a child, and an owl... Michael thought about it and scratched his chin. His whiskers were three weeks old.

Edward was a poor choice, the gathering consequences of which had bothered Michael more than he realized. He put it out of his mind. He'd make it up to the boy some other time.

Michael put on his boots, tabard and belt. Then he opened the library with his key. Using it, the key seemed so foolish. *Who would steal books they couldn't read?* He left it on a shelf, muttering, "The lock should've gone on the front door." He took down a bottle of ink, a goose quill and a piece of parchment and sat at the round table to write: *I am at Betheford's Inn - Michael.*

A cold new day waited outside. He walked through dewy grass on the way to the forge. It was too early for Jacob to be there. Michael's sleeve hung on the wall in mid-repair. He dug through the smith's tool box, found a hammer and a spike and then returned to the front.

Michael shut the door, palmed his note against it and notched the spike between his fingers. With the hammer raised, ready to nail his words to the church, he noticed another spike already there. It was the one he'd used the night before when he'd been at the Cauldron. He just pushed his note onto that instead.

* * *

Michael didn't need to knock. The inn's doors weren't locked. Securing them behind him, he crossed the empty common room to the fireplace. It was lit but had never really been enough to heat the size of that space, especially with how his father conserved wood. Michael took a seat next to it for warmth and waited, listening to the just-before-breakfast bustle of his family in the kitchen.

Betheford came out with a cup of coffee, surprised to find his son there. "Why, Michael! How delightful... wait. Has something other dreadful happened?"

Michael said, "Not that I know of. I'm here to see someone."
He gestured at the front. "You didn't lock your doors."

"My word!" Betheford started toward them.

"No need, I took care of it for you."

"Oh, thank you, son. We're not quite used to that yet, obviously. What a terrible mistake. I understand that's how it happened at Fergus' place." Betheford sipped from his cup. "Who are you here to see?"

Michael darkened - *coffee*. "A sailor named Biggs. Can you tell me what room he's in?"

Betheford nodded quickly and with a charming smile. "Mmm, I can. It's not the kind of thing I'd tell to just anyone, of course, but you're you, aren't you, and I don't even lock the doors so who am I?" It was an attempt to win a smile out of his doughty son. It failed. Betheford sat down. "I'm afraid, though, as soon as I do, you won't have a reason to speak with me anymore and you'll leave."

Michael used his manners to be rude. "What would you care to discuss, sir?"

"Well, you're very formal. Perhaps we should talk about defiling the dead? Thou shalt not do it, you know."

Michael exhaled to calm his anger. "I've already had that discussion with Abraham. I'd rather not have it with you. I'm pressed for time. I shouldn't stray from the church for long."

"And I don't blame you for that at all, not at all. Abraham is a fanatic. I wouldn't care to hear his opinions on the matter either. Michael, I don't want to force my company on you... oh, would you care for some coffee?"

Coffee! COFFEE!? Not if I breathe! Of all the thoughtless... "No, sir, thank you. Just the room..." *irreverent, irresponsible suggestions! The blood of our forefathers is in your damned cup!*

Coffee, though traded from town to town, grew in the north. For Michael, it was an everlasting symbol of the fellowship's persecution there. For Betheford, those events happened more than a hundred years ago; coffee was delicious and good for business. It was one of many old differences in values that the son couldn't trust his temper to discuss and that the father had forgotten about.

Betheford said, "Son, when you asked for my help the other day, well, it was for the sailors of course, but you haven't asked me for anything in thirty years. I was so happy to be able to do it. I want to help you. I can do more than I have, in fact. I can make everything you need to do so much easier. Don't you know that? I happen to be a very influential person around here." He reached out with his charm again.

Michael's eyes narrowed. "Yes, sir. I know it well."

"It was such a pleasure to see you at service yesterday. That's all I want. Come to service."

"Are you bargaining for my attendance with the lives of your flock?"

Betheford nearly spilled his coffee. "What? What is wrong with you?" He put the cup down and shook his finger at his son. "You got that surliness from your mother. My word. That's not what I'm doing at all! Of course I'm not going to hinder you, in any way."

Betheford raised a solemn finger and quoted doctrine. "*Thou shalt not defile the dead*, son, but, *thou shalt - also - not knowingly endanger thy brothers.*" It was an odd way to say it. He paused and then carried on. "Burn every corpse you've a mind to! It won't be the first time doctrine's given way to practicality. Listen, Michael, you must know that I'm proud of what you're doing... *but*, you should reconsider holding your back to God. You need Him now more than ever. We all need Him to be in your heart."

Michael hadn't heard a word of it. He only smelled the wretched coffee. He stood up and linked his hands behind his back, putting his golden circle at the height of his father's eyes. "I really shouldn't stray from the church for long, sir."

Betheford sighed. "Michael, please. We've had our differences, but don't let your opinion of me, whatever that may be, stand in the way of a relationship with God." Michael softened some.

Then his mother came out of the kitchen, gushing. "Oh, Michael! It's so good to see you!" She was seventy years old but could still carry a thirty pound tray of plates on one shoulder. She set it down with a clatter and gave him a big hug. "Ooh, that feels so nice without your crunchy shirt! Have you come for breakfast? Why, you haven't eaten here in ages, not that anyone else has either since our good Fergus left, that poor, dear man." Betheford's eyes rolled as she spoke. "Do you know that I can't blame them?" She lowered her voice hardly at all and put a hand to one side of her mouth. "Your brother's an idiot in the kitchen!"

Michael's older brother, Junior, had come out behind her, had been smiling and had almost said hello before she'd called him an idiot. Junior scowled, threw his arms up in the air and left the room without her knowing he'd been there at all. Michael's visit wasn't a special occasion for Junior anyway. He saw his brother whenever he wanted.

Michael was embarrassed for him. "I'm sure he isn't that bad..."

Their mother said, "Oh no, he is! Awful. *Dreadful!* Are you out to catch yourself one of those bugaboo devils today?" She sounded like she was speaking to child on his way with a basket to pick berries.

Michael almost failed to respond. "Ah, no, ma'am, not... yet?" A pained croak came out of his throat and he turned back to his father. "Thank you for your advice, sir. May I have that room now, please?"

Betheford harrumphed. "Sailors. Do you know the little one called me biffer, or what was it, hmm, boffer?"

"Beefer, dear."

"Oh, quite right, beefer. Now they're all calling me that. I'd say it's rather disrespectful considering how much I've aided them. Room and board for ten, you know, that's expensive."

Michael wanted to run away again.

Betheford said, "Fine, one last question then, before I direct you to your libidinous sailor." He stood up. Other than his long, beard and his age, he was Michael's mirror. "One final, burning inquiry haunts me." He looked into his son's eyes, reading them for lies. "Honestly, Bing's outhouse is right across the street. Did you absolutely have to put those beastly things in *my* toilet?"

"Yes, sir. I did."

* * *

Biggs woke up to knocking. He got out of bed, opened the door wide enough for his face and peeked out under a mousy-brown mess of hair. "Hey there, Michael. What's go'n on?" He picked some sleep out of his eye.

"Good morning, Biggs. My apologies for disturbing you. I'm looking for Andalynn. Can you tell me where she is?"

"Alright, yeah. Hold on a sec." Biggs shut the door, leaving Michael in the hallway.

After a while, Michael leaned in close and said, "No need to bother dressing, if you could just tell me where she is..." Fergus and Margot hadn't known. Michael assumed if anyone did, it would be Biggs. He wasn't prepared for what he saw when the door opened again.

Andalynn stood there in a fresh headscarf, wearing a man's shirt for a nightgown. Her legs were bare. "Good morning, Michael. How can I assist you?"

Michael's face opened. "I... I didn't know... I..." He stared at her legs. Andalynn put her fists on her hips, raised her eyebrow and waited. He thought, *God's mercy, she's a harlot,* but couldn't see how that made any difference. So, he gathered himself, looked her in the eye and said, "Andalynn, I want to teach you."

She stood speechless as she started to understand.

From behind the door, Biggs said, "What's go'n on, Lynn? Y'alright?"

"Michael wants *me*..."

"Tell him you're married."

Andalynn looked over at Biggs and said, "He wants to teach me..." She shook her hands like she was drying them. "To be like them!"

Biggs came to the door again, equally surprised. "Wanna come in or sump'n, Michael?"

Michael said, "Oh, no, I couldn't, that would be... inappropriate. I should have... Ah. I'll wait for you downstairs. I need to speak with you both." He gave a hurried bow and left. Andalynn and Biggs shared wide looks as they closed the door.

* * *

Michael only took one bite of his breakfast - too much salt. Eavesdroppers milled around them, mostly sailors but also a few locals who'd noticed something was going on. Michael said, "I don't know where to start."

Andalynn said, "Why me?"

"Because of the Cauldron. Truthfully, I've quite a few reasons, but it would be disrespectful of me to pour compliments onto a man's wife." Michael turned to Biggs. "Forgive me. All of this is very unconventional. I didn't know and I certainly didn't mean to offend."

Biggs laughed. "You're alright, Michael, don't worry about me! We're not..." He turned to Andalynn as he spoke. Looking at her, he didn't want to make it clear they weren't married. It meant something to make that distinction. "We do things a little differ'nt overseas." Andalynn smiled at him.

Michael said, "I see. Thank you. I must say I have a deep respect for what you sailors have done, what you've survived with such courage. Your story is similar to our own fellowship's history, in a way, except that yours was an enemy impossible to face. My ancestors fled because they refused to fight."

He exhaled and poked at his food. "I promised a boy I would instruct him. We were supposed to begin this morning but things didn't go well. It was his youth. He was inconsiderate. He didn't even bring me anything to eat. Honestly, I was so angry with him I changed my mind right there on the spot."

Andalynn found Michael's impetus amusing.

He said, "It wasn't just that, though. I needed to make a better choice. I have to make the best choice." He stared at her. "I had a discussion with Fergus and Margot about you yesterday. You disappeared after the assembly. They're worried for you."

"They are excellent people. I regret not having informed them of my whereabouts."

Michael smiled. "I would have approached you right away if you weren't a woman."

Her eyebrow went up again. "An understandable hesitation."

Michael laughed. "Well, it was a difficult option for me to see. There's never been a woman in the Circle. We had a law against it. But, the Circle is gone, and so are those laws. Now my first priority is Antioch. I need someone else who can say that, someone who can put others first and make this city their priority. Can you do that, Andalynn?"

"I can. I have, since the day I boarded the *Grace*."

Michael nodded. "That reminds me. I thought you'd want to know what this really says." He took out Ezekiel's note and flattened it on the table, pointing out the symbols as he read them aloud:

"Armageddon is arrived."
"Break your silence."
"Open the library."

He sat back, expecting a reaction. The sailors only looked confused. He said, "And this last mark here is his real name, Ezekiel." The terms and their significance didn't carry the weight he'd thought they would.

"So," Michael clarified, "we're going to start a new order and make new laws. This will be our first stroke. We'll put it through the middle. I want to change everything. With dedicated practice, you'll be ready to teach someone else within a year. In ten years, we'll have a thousand paladins in Antioch."

No one was eavesdropping anymore. They'd all gathered around to pay close attention, excited by what they were witnessing. It was the planning of a new age for humanity, right there, over a red and white checkered table cloth.

Andalynn was inspired to be a part of it. "Unprecedented. An astonishing proposal. Tell me, what is that word, paladin? Is that what you are?"

Michael said, "It means protector." Until then, a paladin's highest priority was to protect the way. They were going to change that too. "Do you accept?"

She felt a rush of pride to say, "I do."

Ditch said, "Holy crap!"

Michael flinched, disgusted by the expression. People started congratulating Andalynn but Michael wasn't finished yet and he called for their attention. "That's not all! Listen to me! This is the most dangerous time for us. I must stay in the church, where I can be found without trouble. I can't be gallivanting around the town. Now, the fellowship can build a wall, we've good stone masons here, but they're not fighters. They'll need an organized guard. You sailors must do this. Patrol, answer calls for help and protect this community. We'll stand together against these devils." The room cheered, unified behind him.

Ditch put his fist in his palm with a smack. "Right on, man! That's what's up!"

The Circle had avoided political power since the Reformation, seeing it as a source of corruption. Michael saw no choice but to abandon that point of view, along with his other former priorities, and take command. In a bold move that depended on people accepting his authority, he held out his hand to Biggs and said, "Sheriff the guard for us."

Biggs was taken by surprise and slow to accept. He did though, and congratulations came for him. "Yeah, alright." He laughed. "Yeah, do the best I can, Michael."

Andalynn put her arm around Biggs and gave him a fierce smile. Then she turned and found the same expression on Ditch. There was a future in what Michael had proposed, something other than death and something more than just survival.

Michael stood and told Andalynn, "Get plenty of sleep. Come when you can. I will always be in the church." Then he left his father's house and all but that one bite of his breakfast.

20 Acolyte

Davies pulled back the curtains enough to see who was knocking. It was still dark outside and his milk shop wouldn't be open for hours but he'd been up anyway, getting a cow ready for John, whom he expected later that morning. It happened to be John at the door, and Daniel, who was scowling and holding the reins to Michael's white stallion, Ares.

Davies said, "Uh oh, the beggar's here with his hand out."

Beth took a peek out the window with him. "Ooh, Davies, you're so rotten." She swatted his backside and squeezed a handful of it. "Give him some milk!" He grabbed at her but she slipped giggling from his clutches and then bounced up the stairs. "Bring him in! It's been at least a week since we had the boys done. I'll get them up!"

Davies opened the door, leering from thoughts of his wife. "Morning, John. In the market for a milker?"

John didn't care for that look on his face. "Hmm... Yes, well. I've brought Ares here in trade, if you don't mind."

Davies smiled broadly. "You know, all this time I thought his name was Daniel." He slapped the doorway and laughed. "Sorry, John, I wouldn't trade a good cow for anything from Breahg!" Daniel's scowl turned a clenched shade of purple.

John said, "None of that, Davies, please. We're in a hurry. I know I'm early, but can you get one ready for me?"

Davies waved humor aside and came out to pat the horse. "I have done already. I didn't expect this great brute from your end, though. He's Michael's, isn't he? Won't Michael be needing him?"

"Michael isn't planning on traveling any time soon."

Davies became serious for a rare moment. "What's going on?"

John looked up and down what he could see of the street. "I'm sure you'll find out everything at service today. I really don't have the time to get into it right now and we shouldn't be lingering outside."

Beth called out from the parlor, "John, come in and do the boys for us, won't you?"

Davies smiled. "Do you have the time for that?" John sighed and nodded. He wouldn't refuse a request for hospital. Davies motioned for them to enter. "Alright, go on. I'll switch beasts with you while you're at it." John started in.

Daniel wouldn't budge. "I'm not going in *his* house!"

John paused. "Daniel..."

Davies smirked. "It's fine, John. He can come around with me!" He ruffled Daniel's hair playfully.

Daniel ducked away, batting at Davies' hand. "No I won't!"

John said, "Daniel, please..."

Davies laughed. "How about you go around to make the trade then, Breahg? We'll put you to work while your uncle puts *the whammy* on us."

Daniel's eyes and mouth popped open in his scowl. *Fergus told him about that!? How come Fergus had to go and tell him about that? Fwah!* Then the scowl fell away and Breahg's fables leapt out of Daniel's imagination to challenge reality. He didn't know how he hadn't seen it before - *Uncle John's a wizard! He's been puttin' the whammy on everyone the whole time...*

Davies took out a ring of keys and twirled them on his finger. "What do you think, old man? Can we trust him?"

John frowned then - at everything that had happened, that was happening and that would happen. "Oh, just do as he says, son. I'll only be a minute in here." He went inside, expecting them to still be arguing when he returned.

Davies said, "You do know what a cow looks like don't you?"

Daniel's teeth grated.

Davies tossed over the keys. "She's the noisy one in the barn around the way. Just leave your old nag in there and bring her out."

Daniel snatched the keys out of the air and stomped off with Ares. "Stupid milkman. *Can we trust him? Do you know what a cow looks like?* Calls *you* an old nag. We ought to fix him!" He wrenched keys in the lock until one of them worked. Then he threw open the gate and ran his eyes over the buckets, bottles and breakables inside, searching for a suitable way to wreak his vengeance. The complacent cow therein watched and chewed.

Daniel yanked Ares in after him. "I bet if I strung up one of his clangitty, clang... clang milk buckets on your bridle you'd wreck his whole place! Wouldn't you? How'd you think he'd like that?!"

The stallion's nostrils flared and he snorted. The boy's ranting was agitating him. The cow stopped chewing and backed up. Fortunately, Daniel knew better than to spook a horse in close quarters and saw he was doing just that. He calmed himself, shushed and cooed, and Ares calmed with him. Daniel gave him an apple and stroked his powerful neck. "You'd just hurt yourself worse than Davies' dumb old barn anyhow."

When he returned with the cow, he shoved the keys back into Davies' hand.

"Ouch! Careful, boy, my palm's not a padlock. Say, you don't look very happy! Is something the matter?" Davies had a baiting grin.

"Fwah! Michael's horse is worth twice your old milker!"

"Fwah yourself, fisheyes. Michael's horse will be pulling my dung cart tomorrow. Ha ha! *Yes!*"

John came to the door with one hand unsheathed. "Alright Davies, your turn..." He paused at the sight of his grandson's quivering rage. "I think you'd better let the boy alone."

Davies said, "It's alright. We were just discussing poor Ares and his short, miserable future of hauling my manure. I suppose when his back finally breaks, he'll be good for nothing but Fergus' table." He clucked his tongue at the shame of it all. Then he let a little bit of a laugh slip out of the back of his nose.

Daniel exploded. He wound up all of his strength and weight and threw his fist like a rock at the milkman's head. Davies didn't see it coming. The blow caught him hard in the nose with a crushing pop. It tied his face into a leaking knot.

Davies brought his hands up to the pain and moaned. His nose was broken, bent sideways by Daniel's fury. "Aaah! Gaaah! You little savage! Why'd you do that?"

Shocked, John made a hasty decision. He came up from behind, covered Davies' mouth, flashed him with riin and lowered him to the ground. If he'd been fast enough, Davies might not remember any of it.

John stood up straight and stiff, looking around like a criminal for witnesses. It was dark enough that he didn't have to worry about the neighbors, and Beth was still asleep on the parlor's couch, but... her five fine sons had seen everything. They'd gathered in the milk shop's doorway, gaping like a silent choir.

Daniel spat on their father.

John shooed him away. "That's enough, Daniel!" It was an embarrassing end to John's life in Antioch but nothing could be done about it. He dragged Davies in out of the street and made the rest of his stops in more of a hurry.

* * *

Miles away, the sunrise behind them, Daniel sat frowning and with folded arms between a brace of fat pannier bags on the cow's back. John led them from his pinto, also packed for travel.

Daniel said, "I don't see what's so special about her," talking about John's horse.

John's shoulders rocked with his filly's motion. "Well, she's my horse. That's as special as she needs to be."

"You didn't even give her a name."

"I haven't thought of one yet. Maybe you could name her?"

Daniel's frown and arms tucked in tighter. "We should've brought Ares instead, if Michael doesn't want him anymore."

"Oh, it's not that Michael doesn't want him. He loves that horse. It's just that we need the cow and Ares was all we had left to trade. At least Michael will get to see him this way."

"Davies wants to ruin him!"

"I told you, he isn't going to harm that animal. He was only trying to upset you..." *And he sure got what he was asking for!* John looked away, controlling an urge to laugh, not wanting to encourage that sort of behavior in his grandson. "Davies knows livestock and keeps them well."

Daniel thought about that and saddened. "All of ours must've starved to death in their pens."

"No, I don't think so. The pigs had dug out on their own by the time I went back. And I opened a few gates."

"You went back?"

"I did, on my way to Meroe."

"Why?"

John paused. "I went back to bury them."

"Oh..."

"I buried all of them on that hill by the pond."

"That's where Ma is, and Grandpa Isaac."

"Much of our family's on that hill."

Daniel noticed then that John had said he'd buried *all of them* not *both of them*. "Did somebody else die out there on the farm, Uncle John?"

"Hmm? Oh, yes. I don't know who it was, but I think your father cut his head off with a shovel." Daniel made a frog face. John went on without realizing what an unsettling thing that was to say. "Must have been the one that brought the plague there."

"You buried some *bauran* up on the hill? With Becca and Pa? Why'd you do that!? He's the one that killed them!"

John turned in his saddle to look back at Daniel. "He didn't mean to do it, son. He might have been a good man before all of this happened. It seemed like the right thing to do."

Daniel struggled with that in silence for a hundred yards of the cow's pace while her stamping and complaining about her swollen udder became more noticeable. She needed to be milked. John looked at her and then turned around to look back. Satisfied no one was following them, he said, "Let's go ahead and see to this one. I have a lot to tell you and I don't want to do it while she's bawling at us."

They stopped and tied their animals to one of the sturdy thorn bushes that were beginning to dot the countryside. Then they set down a pail and milked the cow together, to her relief. Daniel kept peering at John from the other side of the udder, waiting for him to talk. Steam drifted up from the pail in the morning's chill.

John rubbed the back of his head, scratched his beard and kicked at the ground. Then he came out with it. "Horace was my son."

Daniel's mouth fell open.

John told the hard version, trying to be honest. "When I met your grandmother, I'd already been sixteen years in the church, earning my trust. I'd have been thrown out if our relationship came to light, so we kept it a secret. When she told me she was carrying my child, I was distraught. I confided in my brother,

Isaac. He offered to marry her and to claim the baby as his own, for my sake." The regret was plain on his face.

"What'd you say to that?"

John thought it was quite obvious what he'd said to that and had to look twice at Daniel before answering. "I brought her to the farm to meet Isaac and... she accepted. It's hard for an unwed mother, especially in Breahg. I took my vows and they raised my son."

"Fwah... and Pa never knew?"

"Oh no, he did. That's what we fought about eighteen years ago. That's when he found out."

"How come he never told me?"

"I don't believe he ever told anyone. I think he might have been protecting me."

"Huh?"

"Had Abraham found out... Well, the penalty for what I've done is serious. I think your father kept my secret with that in mind."

"How come you're telling me?"

"I don't want to keep the same secret from you. Things might have been different had I been honest."

Daniel thought about the story. Then he said, "Do you wish you hadn't done it, Uncle John?"

John sighed. He didn't expect Daniel to start calling him "Grandpa" right there on the spot, but *Uncle John* was a significant name to bear. It was the only one his son had ever called him. "I've often wondered what life would have been like if I'd stayed home and raised a family instead, if I'd have been happy on the farm or a good father. Isaac was happy. I visited them often. I think your grandmother fell in love with him."

"No, I mean, do you wish you hadn't done it with Grandma?"

John grimaced. "Fwah, Daniel, that's coarse..." But, it wasn't a good time for a lecture on social graces. "No, I'm glad to be here with you now. And really, I've never regretted your father. I had no reason to. He kept me from nothing that I wanted. My only regrets now are the things I wanted. Those change over the years, you see. Eventually, I became jealous of my good brother and sorry I'd chosen the church."

Daniel thought some more and nodded. "I guess we'd be dead if you didn't." He drank raw milk out of the bucket. John was surprised by Daniel's response, having expected outrage or disappointment. Daniel said, "What are we gonna do with all the extra milk, Uncle John? We'll get three or four buckets a day."

"Oh, spill it out when we move on, I suppose."

"Did we bring some vinegar? Fergus showed me how to make a cheese."

John laughed. "*Cheese?* I don't think we're packed for making cheese!" He drank some of the raw milk himself and wiped his mouth. *That's that then.* His secret was out. John stood up and looked around. "We need to get moving. Listen, Daniel, I can't go the whole way without sleep this time. I'll be staying up at night. You'll have to stand watch during the day to let me rest."

Daniel's expression took on some frog.

John said, "There's nothing to worry about. There's no safer place in the world than with me. If you see anything, just wake me up." He motioned at the milk. "Have you had enough?"

"Yes, sir."

John poured out the bucket. "It's time to go then. There are no roads from here to Golgotha. I'm hoping we can cover twenty miles a day."

They plodded mostly west and slightly south over browner and browner hills stubbled with those dense, thorny bushes. John had stories about the Circle, devils and heroics. Daniel had stories about growing up on the farm with Rebecca and Horace. Each was fond of the other's.

That evening they tethered their animals on a windless hillside. There wasn't room enough between the brambles to lie down and Daniel wondered how they were going to sleep. Before the boy could ask, the old man stooped, shoved his armored hands into a stout shrub and ripped it up with its roots out of the earth and rocks. He tossed it aside like a weed and pulled another.

Daniel gaped. "You're strong as a donkey, Uncle John!"

John laughed and continued chucking shrubs away from a broadening patch of ground. Daniel flattened it out. Then he gathered dry branches and leaves into a pile in the clearing's center and went to work with his tinderbox. John stopped him.

"Watch this, son." He struck one of Captain's matches on his gauntlet. The boy stood transfixed on the hissing, spitting, little stick's ignition. John enjoyed Daniel's reaction. "It's a sailor trick! They call it a lucifer." It lit the tinder easily.

"I didn't know sailors could do stuff like that!"

"Oh, they're full of surprises. Do you want to do some? I've got a whole box."

"Yes, sir!" Daniel sat and struck match after match, each brimstone flash more fascinating than the last. When the flames neared his fingers, he'd toss it into the campfire and draw another. "Where does the fire come from? How do they work?"

John unloaded the animals, hoisting a hundred pounds at a time. "I don't know. Captain called it chemistry."

"Wizardry..." The matches snapped, sparked and smoked.

The surrounding bushes started to glow on the fire's side against the dusk and made twisted, black talons in the darkening shadows. John's gauntlets hung from his belt as he rummaged through their grounded baggage. He took out a skin of cider, a jar of pickled apples, a package of venison jerky and an acolyte's tabard.

John said, "Daniel, I want to talk about why we had to leave."

Daniel turned and saw John inspecting the blank garment, holding it up from where it would fold over the shoulders. It was a brilliant, white strip in the firelight against the night-blue sky. Daniel's match singed his fingers and broke his stare.

John folded the cloth over his arm and brought it over with the food. "We're going to start a new church. I'm going to teach you everything I know."

Daniel pointed at the tabard. "That's for me?"

"Oh, yes, I thought you might like it." John tossed it into the boy's lap.

Daniel held it up, his face wide open. "I'm going to be in the church?" Then he narrowed. "What about that old rascal Abraham? What's he gonna try?"

"Don't worry about Abraham. We're never going to see him again." John opened the jar and the package on the ground between them, drank from the cider skin and passed it to Daniel. "Every time we stop for the night, we'll practice a little, after dinner." John smiled and popped a pickled apple into his mouth. His smile cinched up like a drawstring pouch. *Tart!*

Daniel was mesmerized by the tabard. The taste of spicy, chewy meat and sour apple slices stayed under his racing imagination. He put food into his mouth automatically.

John said, "I want you to know that I'm not going to lie to you."

Daniel descended from a fantasy. "What?"

"I want you to know you can trust me."

"I trust you, Uncle John!"

Uncle… John shook his head. He questioned the decision he'd made to tell Daniel the truth. *Is he too young for such things? Was it the right thing to do? Does it matter?* Regardless of the answers to those questions, John would never have to worry about Daniel finding out on his own. "Ok, put that thing on. Let's get started."

Daniel stood and pulled his head through the collar. The garment swung loose from his front and back like long lily petals.

John smiled at him. "Good! But we can't have it waving around like that."

Daniel was wearing brown-and-whites with suspenders. He looked around, trying to figure out how to tie the tabard to his waist. John went to the packs again. He came back, unrolling a thick leather belt that had a sturdy, steel buckle in one heavy, riveted end.

John handed it over. "This should work. It's made to hold a sword."

Daniel held it, appreciating the weight and craftsmanship. Jacob had punched neat and even pairs of prong-holes near forty inches, fit for John. When Daniel wrapped it on and tightened it to twenty five inches, he found some rougher holes John had stabbed through the leather with a nail. A pair of them fit well and he tucked the extra length downward through the inside.

John nodded. "Mmm, now you look like an acolyte. Here, lie down." Daniel lay back on his blanket, curious about what sort of exercises he'd have to do to get strong enough to rip thorn bushes out of the ground. Even his massive father couldn't have done that. John knelt next to him and said, "All you have to do is try to stay awake, son. If you feel you've fallen asleep, try your best to wake up, ok?"

That sounded easy enough. "Yes, sir."

"We'll have to wait a few more minutes, though, now that I think about it."

"Why?"

"Otherwise you won't remember what I just told you to do!" John laughed but Daniel had to think about it.

When John placed his hand on Daniel's forehead, the boy suddenly felt he'd fallen asleep. He opened his eyes. The sun was rising and John was kneeling next to the campfire, having made breakfast.

Daniel sat up. "What happened?"

"Oh! You're awake." John's joints cracked in a stretch. "Did you dream?"

Daniel pointed at himself, at the blanket and at John. "I was just... I just... you JUST... Did I fail?"

John tried to reassure him while yawning. "Oh, no, no, no. No one gets it right away. You have to get used to it. Don't worry, we'll try again tonight. You'll get closer each time." He brought over a warm, cast-iron skillet filled with crusty bacon and potatoes. Then he went to his own blanket and fell down. "I'm so tired! Milk the cow for something to do. Keep an eye out. Wake me up at noon..."

John was asleep before the confused and discouraged boy could say, "Yes, sir." Daniel had gone from one instant to the next without so much as a dream. John's bestial snoring began and the cow called for attention. She *was* noisy. Daniel frowned, ate and then went to get a pail.

He became uneasy, squatting down behind the animal's mass. She blocked too much of his field of vision. He went to the other side, hoping to be more comfortable there, but the top of the hill was much too close. There could be an army of bauran just over the rise. He'd have to watch that. John's snore put them in constant danger of attracting attention as well. It took Daniel almost two hours to fill the bucket because he kept poking his head up to look around after every few squeezes of the teats.

No monsters appeared. The animals grazed in the shrubs. It was still a long time before noon. Daniel drank some milk and started to get bored. Then he went to rummage through the packs.

"Uncle John, where are those pickles?" He said it absent-mindedly, not intending to wake him.

John rolled over, the torture in a dream transformed by his grandson's voice. "No... nooo... it is... a pickled pork chop..."

Daniel had no idea what that meant and gave it only a moment's consideration before continuing his search for the apples. Halfway through the first pack, he found one of John's tabards; not the plain, blank designation of an acolyte, but the high-collared, golden-embroidered standard of a paladin. He felt suddenly like a thief to touch it. He opened it up and traced his fingers through the Circle's insignias, one on the front and one on the back, each half an inch deep and six inches wide on the inside. *This might make a good strainer...*

Inspired, he put it aside and unloaded the rest of the bag to the bottom, discovering it was watertight. *I'll have to put a hole in that.* He needed something sharp, like a knife. Daniel's eyebrows went up and he turned to look at John's caligan. It lay on the ground next to John.

Daniel crept over and picked it up. Jacob had replaced the scabbard that John had burned. The weapon felt much more forbidden and valuable than the tabard. It was heavy, like lifting an axe, a spade, a pick and a pitchfork all at the same time. Daniel slid the bright steel out of its sheath and handled it with careful awe. It was beautiful.

He posed with it and scanned the horizon, thinking he might just *kill* a bauran if he saw one, rather than wake John. Surely he could destroy anything with such a sword. His eyes narrowed on one of the thorn bushes. Daniel brought the blade back and swung with all of his strength, expecting to cut the bush in half, for branches to fly from a flat cleft. The springy shrub disappointed him, absorbing his attack and twisting the grip in his hands.

The caligan felt then more like a heavy club than a sword, and Daniel's arms were getting tired. He dragged it over to the empty pannier bag and used the point to work a hole through the leather. Then he put John's weapon back and eventually found the pickled apples in another bag.

Daniel spread out the tabard on the ground next to a bucket of milk, surveyed his work and nodded with satisfaction. Everything was ready. "Me's in place." He poured the pickles and their vinegar into the milk, which curdled right away. He poured that into one of the tabard's golden circles, where it made a lumpy pile of curds and apple wedges. Folding it all up into shape with the tabard's second circle, he put it into the bottom of the punctured pannier bag and repacked on top of it, to press the whey out of his cheese.

He woke John at noon and they set out again. An ease developed between the two of them. John was happy Daniel was accepting him. Daniel looked forward to surprising John with what he'd done.

When they stopped that evening to camp, Daniel brought out his pressed curds. John was taken aback. The old man examined the damage to the bag as the boy bragged about his improvised *mise en place* and about overcoming all odds to make cheese in the wilderness. The bag and everything in it smelled like apple cider vinegar.

John didn't understand how Daniel could have treated their equipment like that. "But, but, you made *cheese* in our saddle bags!"

Daniel's face fell. "I... I'm sorry, I didn't mean to..." He started to fear he'd be punished. He sure didn't want a wallop from someone stronger than his father.

"And you've used a *tabard of the Circle*... as a *cheese cloth!*" John started laughing. "It does make a nice round, doesn't it?" Daniel didn't laugh. He was still too nervous. John put a hand on his grandson's shoulder. "Son, this is the first official cheesecloth of the church of Golgotha. That calls for a celebration. I'll get the cider."

John came back with a cider skin and the cast-iron skillet. "You've got to brown a sacred wheel like that. It's the only way to do it right."

"Fergus browns it too!"

"Well, he's the one who showed me to eat it that way." The cheese was two inches thick and the width of the circle across, with pickled apples snug in its shape. "I've never seen him put apples in a cheese, though. Was that your idea?"

"Yes, sir. I thought it might taste good to leave them in."

"Mmm, I think it will."

John held the pan over the campfire, using his gauntlet as an oven mitt, and gave the cheese a rich, brown crust on each side. Then he turned it out onto his other hand, sat down and broke it into halves. They tasted it at the same time, both to mild disappointment.

Daniel said, "I forgot the salt!"

John looked sly. "How could you? It's the most important thing in the kitchen."

Daniel laughed.

John went on, "Would you say this needs butter or salt?" Daniel rolled his eyes and took another bite of the bland, crusty, sour, apple cheese. It had a pleasant density and meatiness. There were some good things about it. John's half was gone before Daniel's.

John said, "You should make it again tomorrow. I've some salt packed. We've another three jars of pickles. There's certainly enough milk to get it right."

"When you saw I poked a hole in the bag, I thought I was in for a wallop."

John gave him a kind smile. "Never be afraid of that. Are you ready to practice some more?"

"Yes, sir!"

Daniel lay down stiff with his fists at his sides, concentrating. *I won't fall asleep this time. I won't fall asleep this time. I won't...* John put his hand on Daniel's forehead.

Daniel woke up with the sunrise. "Fwah! What am I doing wrong?"

John laughed and yawned. "Nothing, you have to get used to it. Did you dream?"

"No. How long before I can do it?"

John fell onto his blanket. "Milk the cow. Make cheese." He left a pouch of salt and a jar of pickled apples on top of the official cheese cloth, which was in a tidy fold. John had assumed the tabard and the bag would start to stink of sour milk, but they didn't. Everything still smelled of apple cider vinegar.

That night John fried the cheese and it was perfect. He was impressed. He finished his half first again and then tried to steal some of Daniel's. The boy laughed, holding it out of the old man's reach.

21 The Road to Golgotha

Andalynn awoke. She sat up from her mat on the church floor. The door was shut. The hearth's fire was the only light. Michael knelt on the next mat, deep in thought.

Noticing her, he said, "Did you dream?"

She spoke blankly, preoccupied. "I did."

"This is it then. What do you feel?"

Andalynn felt a radiating calm and acceptance, its character like the taste of water. The closest she could come to it in a word was, "Nothing."

"No... that's not right. You should be having an overwhelming emotion, one strong enough that it grips in your body. I assure you, it is quite profound."

"This is a profound and overwhelming nothing."

"But, *nothing* isn't an emotion. You can't open the way with *nothing*. What sort of things were in your dream?"

"I was in a tunnel of light, surrounded by images and voices in the walls. They concerned the death of a woman named Sue." Though it had been a difficult memory before, Andalynn found herself examining the details of it with clarity and without the urge to look away. "She was the first of our crew to be infected after we separated from Ezekiel. I killed her."

"I see."

Michael could not argue. Awakening, as they referred to it in the Circle, was always the same, a golden tunnel of memories accompanied by a powerful emotion. She'd woken from the dream. From Michael's explanations of it, she'd expected to dream of that night in the graveyard, when the bauran had raked half of her face away. She now wore a black scarf over the damage. It looked less like a bandage.

He said, "There is no certainty in the path we'll choose. Important events from our pasts will shape that choice but it is often unexpected. What do you think it is?"

"Perhaps I cannot do this. This… nothingness… could mean I am unable." She seemed wholly unaffected by the prospect.

"No, I don't think so. It's a way that you feel. That's all that matters. Emotions can be difficult to put into words. Of the six beginnings, which would you say is closest to what you're feeling now?"

"Repeat them please."

"Hate, love, sadness, anger, fear or joy."

Considering each, Andalynn said, "This is not derivative."

Michael shrugged. "They're just words, only helpful in study. The name of what you feel isn't as important as feeling it."

Andalynn sat still, being, without an opinion or a question. Her body functioned and her five original senses provided her with information, none of which interested her attention. A new sense captivated her. She could feel riin.

Michael studied her for a minute. It certainly was a strong physical expression of nothing. She wasn't doing anything at all. And, she only spoke when he asked her to. *She might sit like this all day if I let her.*

He said, "I wouldn't worry about not being able to continue. In all the history of the church there's never been a man who couldn't do this. The newly ordained are usually concerned about it… Are you concerned about that?"

"I am remarkably unconcerned."

"Ah, of course. If your path is truly *nothing*, then I suppose you won't be feeling much of anything for the rest of the day…" He gave her opportunities to converse. "In case you were wondering… how long, of course… you're going to feel like this."

"I was not."

Michael chuckled. "This feeling is your path, what you'll use to open the way. It will always be near to you because of that, but not so strong again as it is now. It's normal to be overcome by it the day of the dream and then to simply sleep it off. That's how it happened with me. Mine is a path of anger, but it's no more vexing to me now than, oh, say, buckling my belt. Well, perhaps that's a bit of an understatement. However, I can say that I've -

never - been angrier than the day of my awakening. John found it rather humorous."

Andalynn said, "I have never felt more at peace."

* * *

Golden images of Daniel's mother flashed and swirled around him. His favorite bedtime story echoed through him in her voice: *But the wizard didn't drink his blood, because the little boy's mommy woke him up, just-in-time.* She touched him on the nose. Then a shimmering Becca played in the field, a tiny version of their mother, squealing and trying to get Daniel to chase her: *Be the horse, Danny, be the horse!* Then his father, huge and strong, taught him the importance of responsibility: *Never sleep past sunup, Dan. It's a sin to waste the day.* Daniel remembered then that he was supposed to wake up if he'd fallen asleep. He knew he was asleep and he chose to stay that way.

John was cooking bacon for breakfast when he noticed Daniel stir. "Well, that was the sleep of the dead! I haven't seen you miss a sunrise before. Did you dream?"

Daniel said, "Yes, sir," but something was wrong. Something horrible was swelling inside of him.

John was delighted. "Oh, that's good! How did the dream make you feel?" He put his sizzling skillet on the dirt and rubbed his hands together with anticipation.

Daniel hid his building turmoil by rubbing his eyes but answered John's question with the truth, "Sad..." Though the contents of his dream had been happy, on awakening, the stark reality of his family's deaths confronted him, like he'd never felt or understood them before that moment.

John didn't notice the boy's distress and continued brightly. "Really? I use a branch of sadness myself. After the way you put it on Davies, I'd have sworn you'd be one to use anger, like Michael. Oh, you should have seen *him* wake up. He was hopping mad!" John laughed. "This is exciting! But, we'll need to narrow it down a little before we can really get going. Would you say it's more of a grief or a remorse that you're feeling? I don't know if you're aware of the difference between the two."

Daniel couldn't hide his feelings anymore. They came sobbing out of him with tears and shouts. "What are you talking about!? What's happening to me!?"

John suddenly understood and hurried over. "Oh! Oh, no… forgive me, son. How careless of me. I forgot to tell you how strong it is the first time. I should have warned you. It's going to be alright. Don't worry!"

"I feel… I feel like they died! They died again and… *they're never coming back!* I know they're nooot!" Daniel wailed and hugged his knees. "They're gone! No! Nooo!"

John knelt next to him and held him. "Shh, shh. It's alright. It's alright. I'm here, son. I'm here. Don't worry." Daniel was inconsolable. John didn't sleep that day.

The next, Daniel woke up with the sun. There was a large breakfast ready for him with milk. He needed it. He couldn't eat or drink at all the day before and had cried so much the muscles in his face were sore. John waited for him to speak.

Daniel finished eating first. "I don't want to feel like that ever again. I don't want to learn the way anymore."

John said, "I'm very tired. Give me an extra hour or two today. Ok?"

Daniel had expected an argument. "Yes, sir."

That afternoon they traveled deep into a pine woodland and had little conversation along the way. That evening, before settling down to camp on the dry needles, they noticed the air was hazy and smelled of wood-smoke. It had accumulated gradually but was on the verge of causing them to cough. John feared a forest fire was coming.

"What is this, Uncle John? What's going on?"

"I don't know. Go ahead and set us out something to eat. The air's cleaner near the ground."

Daniel did as he was told. John left the animals packed. Throughout dinner, as it had been all day, the boy was ready to refuse practicing but the old man never brought it up. John stayed watching the direction of the wind. Their campfire's light reflected from the haze and turned the trees into tall, glowing sentinels. John felt he could have seen farther in the dark.

Daniel said, "I'm going to bed now," assuming that would bring out the argument.

But, John didn't even look at him. "Goodnight, son. Get some rest."

Daniel lay down, feeling like a complete disappointment, feeling about to cry again. Despite John's assurance it had been normal, it embarrassed Daniel to have wept a whole day away. He frowned and sat up, fighting back the tears. He didn't really want to stop learning. "Uncle John, what's riin?"

John turned from his vigil to respond. "Oh, well, that's important. We should talk about that." He scratched his beard and gave it some thought. "You know, honestly, I don't know what it is."

"Huh?"

"I know what it does, but I don't really know what it is. No one does, though they'll certainly say they do. For instance, Gabriel believes riin is our connection to God. That it is our spirit flowing out of God. Do you believe in God, Daniel?"

"Pa said Ma wouldn't have passed on if there was a God. So, I don't guess there is." John couldn't respond to that. Then Daniel said, "What about Michael? He's pretty smart. What's he got to say about it?"

John smiled. "Michael once told me he thought it was time."

Daniel's face opened and he put his hands on his head. "Because time heals all wounds!" Then his hands came down and he looked as though he held a giant, invisible ball, helpless before its wonder.

John stared at him for a second. "That's not... yes, that was why. It's difficult to discover the truth about a thing when only a handful of men can discuss it. I know this much, when I give you hospital, I'm letting riin into your body, a great deal more than is normally there. You always have riin inside of you, you see, but for some reason, your body's natural response to a lot of it, is to fall asleep. When you can overcome that response, you can begin learning how to control and channel it by yourself."

"Will I always be sad when I do it?"

"Never like that again, I promise you. But, you will feel sadness more than you did before. Sometimes it's something you try to avoid feeling that comes forward on awakening."

"What do you feel when you do it?"

"Regret."

"About what, Uncle John?"

John sighed, scratching his chin. "Abandoning your father and your grandmother... honestly, son, did you even have to ask? And please, stop calling me *Uncle John*. That's gone on long enough."

Daniel frowned but conceded to have been a bit thick. "Sorry." John nodded pensively, keeping his hand at his mouth; it was his left and it was uncovered. Daniel had been meaning to ask him how he'd lost his ring finger.

John said, "We're each of us given a path, only one, never to know what it is until awakening. It becomes a defining influence in our lives. Some even allow for strange abilities, like Abraham's. His path is contempt. That has its beginning in hatred. It doesn't make him a bad man, of course... Hatred is something all of us feel. What was I saying? Oh, he discovered that it lets him open the way in others without needing to touch their skin. Oh, that's important too. When we do that to someone else, that's actually their riin coming into them. We call that *pulling*. It's a more advanced technique."

"How'd you lose that finger?"

John shook his head, realizing Daniel hadn't been listening. Then he held up his hand. "My little devil's mark? I got this from a nasty pest that was fouling a farmer's well - by living in it! Poor fellow's wife refused to come home until it was gone. This thing was like a frog and a man all jumbled up into one. And slimy? You wouldn't believe."

"Yeeuuh..." Of all the devils John had told him about, Daniel thought a slimy frog-man who would live in your well was the most disgusting by far. He didn't want to think about what it did in the water.

"Mmm, I've never seen another one like it. Dying breed I suppose. Well, I was green at the time and had this notion it would be a lot easier to put him to sleep first. So, I gave the bucket-line a tug and here he comes, scrabbling up out of the dark, all claws and teeth. About the size of a dog, I'd say. I thought, *simple enough*, reached in there and grabbed him."

Daniel's eyes bulged.

John felt a pinch at the knuckle, remembering it. "Only, he didn't want to hold still for hospital. And those teeth, those were sharp. That was an important lesson for me. If you want to kill something, keep your hands sheathed and use a sword."

"Did you get him?"

"No, he got the best of me. But, I think I scared him near to death, yanking him out of the well like that. He certainly cleared off to find a safer place to live! The farmer got his water back anyway and his wife. And, if I remember, gave me a sack of apricots for my trouble." John looked at his hand again. "Poor trade."

* * *

"Uncle John... Uncle John, wake up. It's time to get up. The smoke's gone."

The haze had blown away. John was relieved. He had trouble getting to sleep that morning, worried Daniel wouldn't be able to keep a good watch in those thick trees, but the threat of a forest fire seemed to be over. They headed west before one-thirty that afternoon and by three o'clock found the ruins of a small village, where the haze had come from.

The cottages were reduced to blackened frames and ash. A few broken heaps still smoldered, but the violence was over. Villagers lie dead in the lanes dividing the wreckage.

John wanted to shield Daniel from the sight, to take him away from there, but he knew there might be people in need. He couldn't leave the boy alone. Daniel would have to come with him and be branded by the tragic scene.

Daniel gaped at the indiscriminate casualties, men, women and children. "Was this Golgotha?"

"No. We won't reach Golgotha for another few days. That's an old city, made of stone, larger than this and on a hilltop. I don't know what this place was, a newer settlement, maybe. This is terrible..."

Daniel started thinking out loud. "We were too slow. The bauran got here ahead of us because I couldn't handle waking up and we lost that day." He started to cry.

"No, son, don't say that. Let's think. This doesn't look like bauran to me. They don't leave bodies behind. I don't know what's happened here yet, but maybe there's someone we can help." Daniel nodded, sniffling.

They called out as they walked their animals through the ruins, searching, but no one answered. The buildings had been burned with torches and oil. The people had been slashed and run through. It was the work of men.

John had seen enough. "There's nothing we can do. This was over yesterday." The sun came through the trees to the west. "We're losing light. I don't want to be anywhere near here after dark." Daniel agreed.

A broad track led away from the village in the direction they were headed, the first thing close to a road since Antioch. It made an easy way for them and they followed it to make better time. But as they went, they couldn't help watching its ends and feeling it was more dangerous on it than off.

Less than an hour from the slaughtered village, four men on horses guarded the way ahead. They wore sleek, black uniforms with silver crosses threaded into their chests, striking against the forestial greens. They didn't notice John and Daniel.

Daniel whispered, frightened, "Uncle John…"

John was frightened too. On his own he feared very little, but with Daniel, danger had a different meaning entirely. He didn't know if they should back up and try to take cover, thereby looking suspicious if spotted, or make themselves known by calling out. His uncertainty was short-lived. The horsemen started shouting in a language other than Meroan, drew out thin, silvery rapiers and charged.

John felt his filly close to bolting. He did the only thing he could think of to protect Daniel. He leapt to the ground. "Get off the cow! They'll ride you down!" Daniel jumped. With the horsemen only seconds away at a furious gallop, John shouted, "Hold on to the tree!"

Daniel didn't understand - *which tree?* John seized him from behind by the collar and the belt and swung him into the air. The world lurched. Daniel hit the sticky bark of a pine, fifteen feet off the ground, and latched on out of instinct.

Below, the rush of hooves arrived. John's caligan struck flesh and rang four times in the length of a heartbeat. Then there was squealing, hollering and a rolling crash like a landslide.

Daniel inched and twisted to see, not knowing what he'd heard. The riders were staggering up from the ground. An unimaginable volume of blood leapt in arterial rhythm from their dying mounts. John had struck down the horses.

One rider landed on his feet, sharp and poised to fight, as though his mount had been cut out from under him a thousand times before. He took a bow from his shoulder, nocked an arrow and shot in one flawless motion. The shaft stopped with a thud in John's chest.

John looked down at it, said, "Oh?" and took a threatening step forward with his bloody sword. The sharp fighter took a step back. The other men shouted some more and then all four ran away into the woods.

Daniel shouted from the tree. "You killed the horses!? Why'd you kill the horses!?"

John tore out the arrow with a blast of light. He looked up and shouted back. "I don't know who those men are! Better to kill a horse if you've got a choice!"

Daniel slipped and clutched, feeling like he was going to cry again. "Those… those are the ones who did the village that way!"

"We don't know that! Did you understand anything they said?"

"No!"

"Well, neither did I!"

"You killed the horses!"

"Fwah! Get down from there! We need to get out of here!" The pinto hadn't gone far. John ran out to catch her.

* * *

They didn't make a fire that night and settled down far away from the road. John knelt and watched. Daniel wept in his blankets. They knew they were being followed.

Daniel whispered, "Why did you kill *the horses*? You could've gotten them right then."

John said, "Son, what if those men were from the village?" Daniel hadn't considered that. He doubted it, but it made him think. John had second thoughts as well. "I did the best I could."

The four unhorsed men kept their distance, whispering their different language in the bushes. The one named Fagan said, "Did you see how he threw that kid into the tree? That man isn't normal. He could have killed all of us if he'd wanted to, even you, Judas. You hit him dead-center!"

Judas didn't agree. "We'll see. I'll hit him in the face next time. I just couldn't resist that yellow circle. It was too much of a target."

"Next time? Doesn't it mean anything to you that he spared your life?"

"It means he has questionable judgment. I would have killed me."

Fagan couldn't argue with that. "I want to find out more about them. If he wouldn't kill us, I doubt he's going to cause any trouble in town. We'll follow them in and tell Bishop what we saw."

Judas shrugged. "It's your decision. Bishop is going to be angry with you. You've found another reason to disobey orders."

"It's not my fault! We're done here without the horses. Besides, Pierce's arm is broken." Fagan motioned at Pierce, who sat with his arm in his lap and his face dripping with sweat. He'd fallen badly from his horse. Fagan said, "We need to get out of these damned woods."

Judas calculated everything. "True."

Over the following two days, those men regretted having forced John and Daniel off the road into the wilderness. They didn't have any milk or bacon or pickled apples stowed in those handsome black and silver uniforms. They were exhausted, thirsty and brush-beaten when they finally came home to their tall, stone city.

And the sky burned red at sunset. From another way around, John and Daniel stopped at the foot of Golgotha's hill. Tall crosses made of pine picketed the rocky incline. Hanging in the centers of those looming, black shapes were the shadows of the crucified.

John bowed his head. "This is an evil place." He feared it was wrong to have brought Daniel along and thought of the life the boy could have had in Antioch.

Daniel couldn't look away. "These people are devils. We ought to let the bauran have them."

22 Angelus Bells

A gray sky spanned cold over the cobblestones and made them slick with drizzle. There were no more windows in Antioch; all had been boarded over. Ditch and Captain walked together, the only two people on the street. Each had a rifle on his shoulder. It was noon on a Tuesday.

Ditch shrugged. "They called me *The Assassin*."

Captain wore his long, auburn waves tied back in a loose tail and had a handsome cut of brown and white under his coat. "Oh, aye? Who did that?"

"Nobody... that's what I'm sayin, man. We picked our own nicknames. It was stupid. I picked assassin, just like everybody else, cause it's like, sinister, or whatever. But when there's a dozen assassins runnin' around, it kind a' loses its punch, you know? When I got in the cage, the announcer'd be all, *in this corner, Ditch, The Assassin!* And, that's cool, but not if he's like, *and in the other corner,* whoever, the assassin."

"Aye, indeed."

"Some of 'em saw we're all callin' ourselves that, so they'd stick somethin' in the front to change it up. There was a Murder-Face Assassin and a Peewee Assassin and the Honkin-Dogone-Tonk Assassin. That guy was dooked."

Captain repeated the last one, tasting the words. "Honkin-Dogone-Tonk."

"I don't know, maybe that one's legit. Still, that's a lot a' assassins. Guys shouldn't be pickin' their own nicknames."

Captain smiled. "Did you ever find yourself staring across the cage into the eyes of another cold-blooded assassin?"

"Yeah, one time."

"Did you win?"

"Nah, man, I got DQ'd for low blows. That guy was a crybaby. He's all, *waaah, ref! Waaah, ref!* Pfft. Suck it up, you know? Be a man. Don't cry to the referee, crybaby."

Captain laughed. "The Crybaby Assassin. Did Drake have a nickname?"

"No..." It was a lie. In the old world, if a professional fighter could take a lot of punishment while still coming forward, they were called a zombie, as a compliment to their toughness. The term had come from a time when the idea of such a creature was a fantasy and even a joke. Drake earned that nickname in his first amateur fight, because of the beating he took without giving up. *Dang man, you're a zombie!* Ditch respected it but hated the thought of it in conversation. "He was just trainin, you know, gettin' started."

Captain nodded. "Too bad, too bad and too bad for everyone, across the board."

"It's weird. I didn't know I'd miss him."

"There's a brotherhood that comes from being at sea, all packed in together like that. You get to know the breadth of good and bad in a man instead of what he wants you to know. Sailors are like a family that way."

Ditch nodded. "That's the truth. I was locked in that bathroom with him for all that time too."

Oh aye, here it comes. Captain knew Ditch liked to brag about how long he'd been in the bathroom. *Twenty-three days was it, Ditch?* "I'd forgotten about that. You were in there for what, three days?"

"Twenty-three days, man!"

Captain drew back. "Twenty-three days! That's a hell!"

"Yeah, kept markin' the stall with a pocket knife, you know, keepin' score. We knew we were dead, just wanted to see how long we could go. One last fight. Every day we'd check on each other to see if we're still kickin."

Captain tapped himself on the nose. "Mmm, terrible. Still, people have been known to go a lot longer than twenty-three days without food."

Ditch frowned at him. "Man, what would you know about it? I bet you never been one day without somethin' to eat."

Captain tried to remember if he had. "You might be right about that. Still, people have been known to fast for forty and fifty days at a time, if they've access to water. Twenty-three isn't so much compared to that. And, you *were* in a bathroom."

"Man, whatever, man! You know… You're a real know-it-all, you know?"

Captain laughed at him. "I'd say I'm more of a know-a-lot." Then he patted his stomach and smacked his lips. "You're making me hungry. Where is this place?"

"You're sick. It's right over here."

Captain bowed with a flourish. "My thanks for the escort."

"Yeah, whatever, man. Where you been?"

"Establishing my financial future. I'm now partners with the chandler. We're making a killing on matchsticks."

"That's gross. Go pull some shifts on the wall. Biggs is on it double-time."

"How much does it pay?"

"It pays respect. That's what it pays."

Captain jingled his hand in his pocket. "I've already made a purse-full of this town's respect. Are you sure I can't buy you lunch?"

Ditch was refusing (he still didn't want anything to do with Fergus) when the Cauldron's doorbell rang. Marabbas came out under the sign, about twenty yards down. Captain's mouth fell open at the sight of him, the gunder's legs and step. Ditch waved. Marabbas waved back and then bounded away, toward the center of town.

Captain said, "That's… That's…"

Ditch helped him out. "Marabbas. He's one a' them hairy dummies, gunders, you know?"

"Fascinating…"

"You gotta get out more. Look, the wall's over that way for now." Ditch pointed northwest. "Think about it, man. See you around." Ditch tapped him with a back-hand to the chest and then jogged toward the construction site, leaving Captain alone in the dreary lane.

From the center of town, the new church bell tolled - *Ka-Kang, Kang. Ka-Kang, Kang.* It was Michael, bringing in the dead. The bell sounded in the morning, at midday and in the evening but not to mark the hour. It was intended to attract any bauran wandering in or around the city.

Captain shook out a chill and crossed to the restaurant's door. It was already locked. *Ka-Kang, Kang.* He knocked and watched up and down the way, tapping himself on the nose. *Ka-Kang, Kang.*

The latch's - *click* - gave him a rush of relief. Margot opened up, smiling. "Ooh, the black man! You must be Captain. Come in, come in!"

Captain said, "Aye, indeed. My thanks, madam." The door locked behind him. He turned and smiled at her. "And you're Margot."

"I am! It's a pleasure to have you. We've heard so much about you from Andalynn and Biggs since they moved in. I've been looking forward to a visit. They've made you out to be a right pirate!"

"Arrr..."

Margot waited three seconds and then asked, "Are what?"

Captain left his little foreign joke at that. "Any pleasure in our meeting, dear lady, is entirely mine." He bowed and then looked around the low, dark common room. The smell of sour milk lurked in its nooks and crannies. "Reminds me of home."

"What a nice thing to say!"

His eyes adjusted to the firelight and he found the bowls of apples on the table. "Ah, Malus. May I?"

"Help yourself!"

"Here's a nice, round fruit." He sank his teeth into it and broke a chunk away with a snap. Tart, sweet juice and saliva flooded his mouth. "Mmm, wonderful genus." He sighed and grounded himself with its flavor and texture. "I've just beheld my first gunder. It's comforting to know that wherever you go, some things stay mercifully the same, no matter a cataclysm around them."

"Ooh, such a pretty way to talk. You've some extra luck then too. We've got *fried chickens!*"

Captain looked over the apple at her and chewed, contemplating what she'd said. There had been a stereotype in the old world that black men were abnormally fond of fried chicken. It was a strange leftover from the race-wars before the unification of the Great Nations, long before the Fall. Though a fairly harmless notion, considering some of the others, still... *No, there are no black men left in the world, other than the few of us sailors. She must've meant something else.*

Margot said, "Biggs has gone on and on about how much you black men love fried chickens! It's his recipe Fergus is playing with. It might just be fate that's brought you by, seeing as we have them." She nodded and winked.

Captain cleared his throat. "Madam, *everyone* loves fried chicken."

"Ooh, I know. It's grand! Shall I get you a plate?"

Amused by her innocence, he took a seat. "Please, that would be lovely. I'm just glad it's not ham. I hate ham."

"I'm fond of a pork chop, myself."

Fergus called out from the kitchen, "Pepper, have we got a guest?"

Margot put her fists on her hips and shouted down the hall. "Fergus! It's Biggs' friend, Captain!"

Fergus shouted back, "The black man? Tell him we've got fried chickens!"

She said, "I have!" and Fergus *hoo-hoo*'d as he got busy on the meal.

Captain tapped himself on the nose until she faced him again. "Margot, it's neither fate nor fried chicken that's brought me here today."

"No? What was it?"

"My old friend, Biggs. He's told me this is the only place in town worthy of celebrating an occasion with a cider."

"He's right! What are you celebrating?"

"My birthday."

"A happy birthday to you, Captain!"

"Thank you."

"You'll get one on the house for every twenty years. Now, I know you sailors can hide it. How many do you have?"

"Six hundred and two."

"Ooh!" Margot laughed and clapped. "That's rich! You like a drink, do you? Business is dead so I think we'll have one with you. Be right back."

She and Fergus returned with a banquet for three. Captain said the cider was the finest he'd had in years and that *that* was coming from a connoisseur. The bread's crust made a pleasant crackle as Fergus cut, but he didn't squash the loaf, and soon had soft pats of butter sinking into its steaming slices. They shared bowls of the Cauldron's signature stew, like hot comfort from the cold, deep with nutrition and the flavor of the second day. And then, *the chicken* - a new world interpretation of an old world favorite - served cool, picnic style, and tender with a spicy, crunchy fry.

Fergus and Margot enjoyed Captain's renewed enthusiasm after he tried each of those things set out before him. They talked for hours. When the conversation turned away from food, Margot said, "All by yourself on your birthday, that's sad. Why didn't you bring some friends?"

"I'm not so by myself, am I? I'm with a fine couple." He raised his drink. "To new friends."

The three clanked flagons, said, "Cheers!" and drank to one another's company.

Then Captain declared, "I'm stuffed to the gills!" He leaned back, pulled out his pipe, a bag of leaves and a box of lucifers.

Margot said, "What's this?" He struck a match as an answer. She cried, "Mercy!" at the burst of flame.

Fergus smacked the table. "That's that *fire-in-a-stick* I was telling you about!"

It was Captain's turn to enjoy reactions. He lit the pipe, waved out the match and puffed. Then he pushed the rest of the box over to them. "Please accept these as a gift, from one business to another. Just be careful not to burn your business down."

Fergus was pleased. "We'll make it a trade for the meal!"

Captain smiled. "Fair deal." He liked Antioch. He could get anything he wanted for a box of matches. Handing them out and bartering with them were also good ways to introduce them around town and boost sales at the candle shop.

Margot was delighted, until she smelled the pipe. "Ooh, they're brilliant! How kind of you... Oh... *Ooh*... that's got a bit of a funk to it, doesn't it?" She'd grown accustomed to the sour milk. Now this - the sailors were a stinky crew.

Captain closed his eyes and breathed. "Mmm, that part of a thing that makes it unseemly against a more common notion of beauty, its funk, as you say, is often in what we'll find perfection, to be true."

Margot said, "It's that grand, is it?"

"Oh, aye."

Fergus said, "It smells like a devil."

Captain said, "This'll make more money than lucifers, I'll wager." Then he offered the pipe with a devilish smile. "Would either of you care for a try?"

Fergus was cautious but Margot was game. She said, "Alright, I'll give it a go!"

Fergus said, "Careful, now!" But, once she had a hold of it, Margot put the bit in her mouth without qualm and sucked. Captain hadn't been fast enough to give her any instructions.

Her eyes clenched and a violent cough blasted out of her. "WAAAGGGHH! WHHUUFFFF, hoof, hoof! AAAaahhh!" She grimaced with her tongue out and held the evil thing away at arm's length, waving her other hand in front of her face. "Och! Tekitawee! Tekitawee!"

Fergus grabbed it and said, "Pepper! Are you ok?"

Captain snickered. "I'd no chance to explain! A chance to explain!"

Fergus gave him the chance to explain, along with an iron glare.

Captain said, "The first puff's... a little rough," then snickered at his own explanation. Margot fanned herself, eyes watering, sure it was one of those coughs that would last forever.

* * *

Captain's chemistry was a boon for Bing's candle shop at a time when only the strongest desire could get people to leave their homes. Those profits were nothing next to the rise in value of milk. Davies was squeezing gold out of the teats those days.

And he rode the white horse, Ares. Each was a powerful picture of his kind, though the milkman's nose bent a little to the side. Hooves pounded moist turf as they rounded Antioch's western reach, heading north past the thorny expanse John and Daniel had traveled - *puh-puh-fwump, puh-puh-fwump, puh-puh-fwump, puh-puh fwump.*

Coming around to the northwest, they approached the hundred yards of wall so far completed, a stone and mortar section eight feet thick and eighteen feet high. Biggs sat atop a scaffold with his Springstien BOSS, keeping watch for the hard working masons below. Andalynn sat with him, having brought lunch. They all waved when the horse and rider passed, just like they did every day.

Davies and Ares took a turn into the city at the north, rather than dodging through the apple orchard, and the hooves hit cobblestone - *Ca-ca-clack, Ca-ca-clack, Ca-ca-clack, Ca-ca-clack.* The clatter was so piercing that the milkman was nearly deaf for those few seconds he reined Ares in to keep from trampling Ditch in an alley. He couldn't hear the bell ringing - *Ka-Kang, Kang.*

Ditch flattened himself against the wall and shouted, "Hey, watch out! Every day with you! Where's your guard?! You're s'posed to have somebody with you, bucknard!" *Ka-Kang, Kang.*

Davies couldn't hear any of that that either. He held up one hand and said, "Out of the way, Mitch! Official church business!" Then he charged through the space Ditch had given him - *Ca-ca-clack, Ca-ca-clack, Ca-ca-clack, Ca-ca-clack.* The little sailor shook his fist as they left him behind.

They shot out of town and tore into the turf again to the northeast. Davies roared a challenge to the world, "Heya! Ares!" and the horse built to a thrilling speed. On a good day, in season, they would have been galloping through a vast, gold and green meadow that spread from there almost all the way to the road south. That day, the field was a sullen adversary, made of mire and dampening air, but still couldn't thwart their spirit.

It wasn't until Davies saw a figure off in the foggy distance that he brought Ares to a halt. "Whoa, boy. Whoa, there." Ares didn't want to stop. He wanted to run! He stamped and pitched to make that known. Davies clucked at him and patted his neck while staring at the misty shape. It was too big to be a man. They trotted toward it.

Closing in, the figure revealed itself to be a horse. Davies recognized him. It was that red roan, Rascal. Davies laughed. "Thrown another thief, have you?" He rode up alongside and took the reins without trouble. "Let's get you home." Right away he noticed some hesitancy and a limp in Rascal's step. Davies stopped for a closer look and found a long, festering gash on one flank that continued partly through the saddle. He inhaled with a hiss. "That's a nasty cut. Come on then. Michael will fix you up." He dismounted and walked the horses in. The mud plated his boots.

They were slow to cross the wet field and through the lonely, narrow streets before coming to the graveyard. Michael was inside by then and it was silent but Davies was far too saucy to be afraid of bauran. When he finally arrived at the church, he dropped both sets of reins and tiptoed toward Michael's bell, grinning.

The bell hung six feet off the ground on sturdy posts with a rope to swing the clapper. Massive, gray and the depth of a man's chest, it was unadorned but well-made and had the voice of God if you were standing next to it. Michael planned on hanging it higher to save his ears.

It was the largest of five bells. The smaller ones were stationed around the city for signaling Michael in case of trouble. They had been made by and represented the effort of the entire community. Sailors and citizens alike donated inspiration, time and material to found them. The bells were the heart of a new Antioch.

Davies crept up with an eye on Michael's door and gave the clapper one good pull - *KWABONG!* The horses flinched.

Moments later, Michael stomped out with an angry frown. "How many times do I have to tell you people that's not what the bell's for! Ah, Davies, of course." Then he saw Rascal. "What's this? Is Samuel here? Joseph?"

Davies said, "No, just the horse. He's hurt. Come have a look."

Michael removed his gauntlet and went around. The heat of an infection glowed from the wound. It was as long as Michael's arm and two inches deep. Running his fingers through the cleft in the hard leather saddle, Michael didn't need Jacob to tell him it could've been done by a caligan. Abraham had planned to go through Tabor on his way to Salem.

Michael moved in front of Rascal and said, "Hup! Hup!" He swatted the loose chain on his forearm as part of a command and threw his gauntlet on the ground. "Lay down! Lay down!" Rascal went to his knees and rolled onto his side. Michael was a little surprised. "I've never seen him so obedient." He knelt, put his hand on the horse's head and opened the way.

Davies said, "I wish John had been that careful with me." His boys had told him who'd broken his nose but he preferred to say that John had dropped him. "It's trouble this one's back, isn't it?"

Michael stayed on his knee, thinking. "It's not a good sign, of course, but they're trained to come home on their own. Rascal wasn't trained to go home to Tabor, so, I can't be sure what's happened. I'll admit it has me worried. That was a serious injury."

Davies didn't have anything useful to say, so he said, "I'm worried too. Sam's my favorite out of the lot of you."

Michael smiled and stood up. "Thank you for bringing Rascal to me. Do you want to take him? Finish that trade for the cow?" Davies, believing the church needed at least one horse in its stable, had given Ares back to Michael the day John and Daniel left.

"No. That deal's done." He collected an empty milk can from the church doorstep and then went over to pat the white stallion. He was quite fond of Ares.

"Thank you then, for everything. With two horses in the stable now I'll need more help for sure. Find a boy for me, won't you? I'm sure this has been hard on you."

Davies took on a skeptical air. "I don't know... he'd have to be a brave one to come out here so often. Not to mention, a mighty rider to work this great brute. Someone like that could take a long while to find. Mmm, I doubt there's such a hearty soul in the whole city." Michael chuckled at Davies' bragging, which ended with, "Ha, ha, *yes*."

"Fergus was right. Nothing can cork your sauce. If you won't get me a stable boy, at least stop ringing my bell."

The milkman grinned, ran over and struck the bell with his can - *KWANG!* It woke Rascal and startled Ares. "See you tomorrow, brother!" He waved goodbye as he walked home.

Michael laughed, shook his head and waved back. Then he watched Rascal get up. The wound's crust and pus sloughed away, disconnected from a canyonous scar. Michael's worry returned to the surface. He hoped Samuel and Joseph were safe.

23 Death and Taxes

Captain and Jacob met during the incinerator's construction. They became good friends during the founding of the bells. Demand for their expertise had them meeting frequently to *do science*, as Jacob had become fond of saying. One afternoon, after having done science all morning, they sat against the wall of the church, pooling their thoughts.

Captain held the smoke in his lungs. "I like… burning things and… explosions. And plants. I like plants."

Jacob nodded. "I like food. And women."

Captain exhaled. "Uncommonly common claims to make, Jake. Everybody likes them."

Jacob giggled, said, "I know," and inhaled from the pipe.

"Oh, ok then. I liiike… cider."

"Fwah, that's a good one. I like Rachel."

"Who's that?"

"A woman."

"You've already said women!" They laughed at each other, hunching over and shaking their heads. Captain slapped his knee and pressed on, "I'll take money, then. Money's like the score in a contest, except you buy things with it." He paused, seemingly on the precipice of a great discovery. "And the contest… is life."

Jacob offered him the pipe. "I like smoking." They hissed and snorted like little boys.

Michael, having heard them through the wall, came around the corner, frowning. Wearing his long handles under the tabard again, looking like he was about to tell them that Armageddon had no place for sitting or laughing or pipe-smoking, he said, "Forgive me for intruding. I'm curious about how my sleeve is coming along." He managed to mean the other as well.

Jacob blew smoke and nodded. "Today." Then he pointed at Captain. "He's distracting me."

Captain said, "Back in your jammies, Michael?"

Michael's eyes narrowed. "Jammies?"

A snort of laughter slipped out of Captain. "Jam jams."

"I see. Well, when you can, Jacob, thank you."

The blacksmith got up with a laugh, said, "Of course, sir," and went back to work.

Michael looked down at Captain. "What about that thing you've been working on? Jacob's told me about it, your exploder."

Captain snickered at the term. "The design's in its infancy but growing like a weed."

"Ah, very good. I've been thinking we could use something like that at the wall." Michael linked his hands behind his back. "As soon as possible." He stood there, expecting Captain to hop to it, like Jacob had. Captain reclined, making it clear that wasn't going to happen. Michael frowned at him again, said, "Carry on, then," and walked away.

Captain waited for him to be gone. Then he strolled over to the forge, where Jacob was using a special pair of pliers to twist and pinch around a rip in Michael's mail. Captain tapped himself on the nose and watched. "Jake, who pays you to do what you do?"

Jacob smiled. "I don't get paid for this. It's an honor." The smith's nimble wrists and fingers were the only sober parts of him. They moved in tight patterns over the damage and made slow, consistent progress. Captain imagined that if time sped up the torn chain would pull together like a zipper.

Jacob rambled while he worked. "My family's always been smiths for the church. Right now, I'm the one. It's me. I can walk into any of these… shops, hey, and they'll say, *there's Jacob, the armorer.*" He nodded with pride. "You must feel something of the same. Sailors are the cow's teats around town… *and you're a big cheese!*" His face clenched up as though he'd pinched himself with the pliers and an infectious giggle squealed out of him.

Captain couldn't help joining in and had to lean against a post to recover. "*Weee! A Big Cheese!* Aye, indeed, we're all well-loved. Does that get *you* anything for free?"

"Fwah, no! Well, sometimes." They shared another laugh and Jacob went on, "My brothers and my father have the town smithy for making money. They'll take care of me while I'm the one. When one of them is ready to serve the church, I'll take care of him. I don't mind selling... hammers and... nails."

"So, nothing's changed for you. The Circle's gone, you know. It's only Michael in there now."

Jacob prickled some. "Oh, ho, only *Michael* in there is it? Let me tell you something, hey. If it came to it, your life or your love's, you'd offer *Michael* everything you own. And do you know he wouldn't take it? He wouldn't even ask for thanks. While there's a man like that in it, I'll serve the church."

Captain looked as though he'd smelled a fart. "Oh, aye? That's... ok, fine, but I'm a bit bothered by what they've done, myself." He pointed at himself. "I'm mad. You should be too. So should everyone be! They've duped us! They've held part of us hostage in their little clubhouse, hiding it from us, like, like..."

The stream of frustration that poured out of him then wasn't something Captain often shared. "They think they can just pop back in every few decades and make you good as new and that *that* makes everything alright. But nobody understands *that*, do they? Nobody knows what's happened to you when it happens and they want the truth, or they think you're a warlock. So, you have to run away and start all over again in some new place with new people who don't know your face and don't have a torch or a pitchfork. Better just to stay away from them all, because it's easier than the other... easier than living... You'd think you could say no, wouldn't you? But you can't. You can't say no to a god. And he never lifts you up more than a head taller than the crowd... and that's only so you can do for *him* better."

Jacob didn't know what he'd just heard. "Is it like that?" It certainly hadn't been about Michael or the church. But, seeing his friend so put out, Jacob offered the best advice he could. "Maybe I could be mad about... something. What good would it do? Michael's doing all he can. That's what I'll do too." He nodded some encouragement at Captain and went back to mending the sleeve.

Jacob started talking about something else but Captain's thoughts went adrift behind a pout. *Who does Michael think he is anyway? The Circle, hmph. A circle of children playing ring around the secret. Secret notes in secret languages for secret civilizations across the ocean...* "Kafferway's Llama!"

"Hey?"

"Oh... sorry, Jake. Go on, about... that," Captain submerged into contemplation again. He'd been marooned. And it confounded him why Ezekiel had bothered to do it. *Zeke, hmph.*

He supposed the reasons didn't matter. He'd doubted from the day they'd set sail that Ezekiel would find enough people after the *Grace* even to man another ship. *He's marooned himself as well, for an eternity in the wasteland.* The thought settled on him. Michael didn't have a candle of Ezekiel's power. Eternity, for Captain, meant death.

If Antioch somehow survived the army of bauran fermenting in the south, he guessed he might have another sixty or seventy years of natural life, at most. He was finally among the people with whom he would age and die. Captain smiled. He'd grown fond of them and their simple ways already. Dying had started to seem like something that was supposed to happen.

Jacob had been rambling on. "...because he's never had a penny, despite being the deacon's son. It'd be nice if he could go a day without ripping his damn sleeve, but I've nothing really to complain about. Other than the end of the world, hey?" Jacob smiled too.

Captain clapped him on the shoulder. "Jakers, you're priceless. Even I couldn't afford you."

"Shop's doing well, is it?"

"Aye, indeed, but I'm coming out of the past. Here, let me show you something about wealth." He pulled a golden ring from his pinky finger and handed it over. "Oversea, that was worth more than the *Grace.*"

Jacob examined it skeptically. "This little thing. Against your ship? The one that carried you all across the water? Go on." He wondered what other tall tales glittered and dangled in Captain's outfit, a fashionable and bejeweled variation of traditional brown-and-whites.

Captain said, "It's true! The value's in its history. Before I got it, that ring had been passed down through generations of royalty, dynasties. Men have killed each other for that. I've even seen some afraid to pick it up, believing it to be cursed."

Jacob handed it right back. "Ooh, well, ah, how'd you come by it?"

Captain waved the particulars aside. "Bought it as part of a collection. No one here could possibly comprehend the kind of wealth I've commanded. Riches, indeed. I've abandoned troves of such baubles as this. None of it'll ever have value again, not in the span of a man's life anyway. Without its history, here, this cursed thing is just a harmless circle of gold. I might could trade better with a box of lucifers, to be true."

Jacob nodded. "Fire-in-a-stick. I'd go for them first in a deal myself."

"Aye... that's because a matchstick's value's in what it does. It *does* something." Captain held the ring up to his face and stared through its hollow, having another moment of pipe-induced clarity. "This doesn't - do - *anything*..."

Jacob said, "You know, you're right. Look at it. It isn't doing anything at all!" They both burst into giggles again and Captain slipped the ring back onto his pinky.

* * *

The wall inched its way around to the north. Captain had never seen it, having been preoccupied until then with more centralized affairs. But, a seed of worry grew in him that he could no longer ignore; it had him following second hand directions through empty streets on his own, his rifle and a rolled up schematic in hand.

When he reached the construction site outside of town, the massive, stone barrier came as a surprise. It was too big, well more than enough to hold back any number of bauran. It was a true fortification, a military wall.

The masons saw him coming and called out.

"Look here. It's Captain!"<br/>"He's come to give us a break."
"Bring your pipe, old boy?"

Captain met them, smiling, relieved by the company. "No, not out here, lads. I'll want my wits if I'm to sit in your crow's nest."

One said, "Fwah!"

Another swayed back with his hands out and made an appeal to common decency, "Yeah, come on, man, fwaaah." It was an unmistakable impersonation of Ditch.

Captain laughed. "Oh, aye? Fwah to you then!" The masons laughed too. They all exchanged a few more local curses and called each other dumber than gunders.

Biggs looked down over the edge of the scaffold. "Hey, Cap! What's go'n on?"

Captain waved. "Biggs, I'm coming up."

"Alright."

The scaffold wasn't as firm as Captain would have liked. It creaked and bent with his weight and in the breeze. Biggs held out a hand to help at the top and that turned into a friendly embrace once Captain was aboard.

Biggs said, "Glad to have you, partner."

Captain was about to say something of the same but the view stole his attention away. Twenty feet off the ground, he saw fields and trees for miles, the church in the city's center over an alley of lower rooftops and a length of the dirt road to the north that spoke of their community's isolation. It was a panoramic touch of being on the open ocean.

Captain became nostalgic. "The Cauldron took me back to the deckhouse, but this takes me back to the deck, to be true." The *Grace* had been dear to him.

"Sure does." Biggs smirked. "Heard you liked that chicken."

Captain's eyes rolled. "That's only funny to you."

Biggs chuckled and pointed at the schematic. "What'cha got there?"

Captain unrolled it and held it up so they could both see. "Jacob's named it *the exploder*." Intricate mechanical drawings of a broad-barreled gun and bomb shells accompanied notes about propellant densities, regional materials and explosive velocities.

Biggs said, "Dadgum, Cap… what's that? Some kind a' mortar?"

"Something like that. Now that I've access to a forge and a competent smith, I can make us a useful weapon against groups of bauran. However, I'm starting to wonder whether I should."

"What d'you mean?"

"Michael mentioned something the other day that's got me thinking. You've not had many bauran this way, have you?"

"Not a one. Right now they're only comin' out the south. Michael's catchin' him some on the big bell now n' then. Don't know how long it's gon' stay that way."

"Mmm, nothing from the north."

"Circle's plan's got a hole in it for sure, hopin' the smoke won't make it up there on its own. Shoot, just that n' the wind would a' wiped this place out a long time ago. First one to come out the north's gon' be a heartbreaker, Cap. Lot a' folks up there. Way more'n here. King n' a castle n' whatnot. Hope's all we got for 'em."

"So it seems." Captain lowered his voice. "This wall's a bit sturdier than what we'd need for bauran, don't you think? Looks strong enough for a siege."

"Yup, n' there's a reason. King's got this law 'gainst forti-fi-cation. Anythin' good enough to stop the bauran's gon' be against the law. So, Michael wants a wall good enough to stop the law too."

Captain lowered the schematic. "Unbelievable. We're to be involved in a revolt as well?"

"S'pose so, if'n the king finds out. North don't come down this a' way much. Wanna get the wall done 'fore any a' that. When it's up, Michael figures one a' us with a BOSS gon' be a lot nastier'n a whole bunch a' the king's boys."

"Despicable."

Biggs shrugged. "Kind a' ticked me off too when he told me that, but, what choice've we got? Don't matter what comes out the north now. Soldiers, bauran, gon' be a mess either way."

"There's more to it than that, Biggs. No one's to leave town, according to Michael's orders. We're locked down."

"Well, yeah. Who'd wanna leave town anyhow?"

Captain rolled up the schematic. "Aye, indeed, we wouldn't want to send out a word or a warning now would we?"

Biggs leaned on the railing and looked away.

Captain said, "It wouldn't matter if anyone outside of town knew about the milk, of course. The smoke took its toll on us in spite of that the whole way here. The truth is, if they knew about any of this, well enough to protect themselves, they'd just start coming, wouldn't they? In droves."

"S'pose so."

"There're only a few small spheres now in which nature allows human life to exist, like ships on the ocean. Michael's at the helm of ours. He means to keep it from sinking under the weight of its crew."

"Well, what d'you want him to do? Had to pick somewhere. Picked his own kin. I'd a' done that too."

Captain gestured with the schematic. "But could you fire one of these at men? After what we've been through?"

"Depends. Aint some killer, Cap, but the right side a' this, for us, is with the beaners. They're the ones took us in."

The situation made Captain's stomach turn. He didn't know how far he could go in designing weapons for the city's defense if those designs might be used on people. He'd sworn never to take part in a war again. At the same time, Antioch was remote and the land around it was undeveloped. They wouldn't have enough room or food to provide for a very steep increase in population. If too many people surrounded Michael, everyone would starve.

Captain sighed. He preferred botany to ballistics. "Survival's a murderous business."

"Yup."

They shared some silence. Then Captain said, "Ditch told me this is how you've been spending all of your days."

"Pretty much."

"When you make yourself useful, you get nothing but used, to be true."

Biggs raised an eyebrow at him. "That right?"

Captain smiled it away as a joke. "It's a thoughtful place to sit, though, isn't it? Perhaps a turn or two of this would do me some good. Would you care to have me fill in for you from time to time?"

"Sure, alright."

"It wouldn't make me *sheriff*, of course. More of a *captain* of the guard." He hadn't wanted the responsibility, and would have refused it, but it bothered him a little that Michael hadn't asked.

Biggs chuckled. "Wouldn't call myself much of a sheriff. Just set up here a lot. Ditch n' Welles n' them other boys come by now n' again, let me know what's go'n on. They're the ones do'n all the work."

"What would you call yourself then? Michael's made you the highest authority in town, next to himself."

"Aint give it much thought, tell the truth. Sure don't feel like a aw-thorty, way old Beefer's on me."

Captain spent a few seconds trying to decipher that. "What do you mean?"

Biggs' eyes widened and he exhaled a little frustration. "Guess that aint gotten round to you yet. Lyin' bout bein' married to Lynn's got old Beefer in a tizzy. Says we're *livin in sin*." He wiggled his fingers and rolled his eyes. "There's some talk 'round town bout us gettin' shunned."

"Pshaw. Who'd go along with that?"

"Don't know. Turns out, marriage's right significant round here!" They shared a chuckle and Biggs went on to the part of it that bothered him. "Gettin' out of his inn sure wasn't good enough for him. Now it's hurtin' Fergus n' Margot just to have us there. Not that they'd complain. Fine people."

"Biggs, Betheford wouldn't dare. The both of you are too important. The fellowship would no sooner turn their backs on you than they would on Michael."

Biggs cocked his jaw to one side. "Guess you don't know about that neither."

"They've shunned Michael? No, I was just there. Jacob didn't say anything."

"Naw, it's old mess, thirty years. But, kind a' tells you sump'n, don't it? He's just a kid at the time. Beefer shunned his own son n' the whole town went along with it."

"Why?"

"Lynn said it's on account a' some *fundamental differ'nce in beliefs*. Beefer brought it down on him hard, thinkin' he'd bend. Never did. Split the two of 'em like a cedar in a storm."

"That's a fool's shame to bear."

"S'pose. But, what now, with us? Shoot, aint enough else goin on? Old Beefer's on edge n' makin' trouble just to make it if you ask me. Ever'body's scared. He aint the weight round here no more. Inn aint gon' run without Meroe..." Biggs paused.

Captain become nervous, thinking Biggs had spotted a bauran. "What? What is it?"

"Just thought a' sump'n. Can't believe I didn't put it together before. Ditch said Beefer's been talkin' about the town's taxes. Caint nobody take 'em north, on account a' the lockdown."

The meaning of that passed between them.

Captain swatted his rolled up schematic in hand. "And so it follows, certain as death, that we're to be expecting a visit from a tax collector."

"Gotta know one's comin' for sure. Gets one look at the wall, gon' blow the lid off early's what he's gon' do." Biggs scratched his head. "Can a' worms."

Captain stuffed his design into his coat and brought out his pipe. "I'd meant to keep a clear head today, but a puff or two should give me some ease."

Biggs leaned back, amused by Captain's method of dealing with crises. He'd seen the pipe come out like that many times before, in addition to the regularity with which it normally came out. Biggs didn't care for it himself, but didn't mind others the indulgence. The masons smelled it and started whispering.

"They're having a smoke."
"Keeping it all to themselves."
"Fwah, selfish sailors."

Captain puffed and nodded. He'd have paced as well, given a larger platform. Eventually he said, "When the inevitable taxman comes, we'll welcome him in with a fine meal at the Cauldron, and enough cider to make a difference." He offered the pipe. Biggs smiled, motioning a refusal, and Captain went on, "There we'll explain the dire circumstances facing the world today, in compelling fashion, and invite him to start a new life here. What do you say to that, sheriff?"

"S'all we gotta do, huh?"

Captain shrugged and took in the view. "Why not?"

Biggs engaged the proposition. "Say taxman raises a fuss. Gotta figure he's a stinker, right? Mean, come on, boy's a taxman." Captain acknowledged the possibility with an expression of interest, as though it was an overlooked variable within a mathematical theorem. Biggs continued, "So this one's a nasty piece a' work n' all he wants to do is run on home n' tell the boss on us. What then?"

"Incarcerate him?"

"Aint even got us a jailhouse, Cap. Shoot, what if there's more'n one? Some's gon' keep comin' for that money anyhow."

"I believe there's a decent way around anything if you care to look for it. Decent - not blasting people to bits with bombs."

Biggs kicked at the platform. "Alright, I hear what you're sayin. Could try slippin' him a little extra, keep his mouth shut about the wall, just not mention the other. But, maybe your way's a little nicer."

"We'll never know until we know. Our hypothetical taxman might have family he'd never dream of leaving behind."

Biggs shifted and withdrew. "Sump'n to think on. Reckon a little good come out a visit anyhow. It'd mean all them folks up there's alright."

"Aye, indeed."

They shared the view but not their thoughts. Then Biggs changed the subject. "Thinkin' 'bout makin' it official with Lynn. Get some that other mess out the way."

Captain grinned in a wreath of smoke. "A wedding?"

"Well, yeah, you know, just for looks. Smooth things over with Beefer n' the beaners."

The grin got bigger. "She's agreed to it?"

"Aint asked her yet. Figure she'll up n' say no, on account a' her face." Biggs wagged his hand at his own face as if that didn't make a difference.

They considered what had happened to her. Then Captain said, "And you don't care about that?"

"Shoot, no. Lynn's got a good butt."

Captain sneezed out a burst of smoke and laughter.

"Aint told nobody yet, 'cept you n' Ditch. What d'you think?"

Captain nodded like an old hand at love and exhaled a curling plume. "Mmm, mmhmm, romance. How've you planned on going about it?"

"Say again?"

"How are you going to ask her? You've got to bait your hook, lad, if you want to catch a fish."

Biggs hadn't considered how to do it, only if he should. "Don't know. Maybe cuss at her n' spit. Think that'll work?" They chuckled.

"Have you got a ring?"

"Well, no... Whole thing's just for looks anyhow."

"Aye, and at the same time you're afraid she'll refuse. Even if it is *just for looks*, in fact, especially so for that, make it look good."

Captain removed the ring from his pinky and offered it. "Here, give her this."

Biggs took it and looked it over, ignorant of its value. "Sure is a pretty lil'thing. You know, that's real nice, Cap. Thanks." He flicked the ancient seal spinning into the air, snatched it sideways and then stuffed it into his pocket.

Captain's eyes went wide at that handling of it. Then, with a smile that went much deeper than it showed, he clapped Biggs on the shoulder. "May it make her yours forever. I'm curious, what was Deputy Ditch's advice to you on the matter?"

"Said I's bein' a wuss n' to just do it."

Captain laughed. "Oh, aye? Indeed, Biggs, now that it's on my mind, you really are a great wuss. She's always had an eye for you." Biggs grinned - and then frowned, wondering if that had been an eye joke.

Captain smoked some more and then said, "Mmm, show me what to do up here. Not that I'll be doing it today of course. I've been impaired and shouldn't be responsible for the welfare of others." He winked with the pipe in his teeth and tapped himself on the nose.

"Alright. Aint much to it, really. Keep a look out. If'n you see sump'n, get these boys scootin' on over to the church first, to be safe. Then give ol' Tinkerbell here a shake." Biggs directed Captain's attention to the scaffold's signal bell. It was identical to the one at the church, though a third of the size. "That way Michael's sure to get tell. When he does, he'll let out a clunk-a-clunk on the big'un to let you know he's a' comin' with the truck."

Captain hadn't seen any of the smaller bells in more than a month, not since their founding. "Tinkerbell. That's precious. She's loud enough?"

"Shoot, lil'ol'bell's louder'n Lynn! Gotta keep her up here now, though, and don't let nobody mess with her. See, these beaners just love foolin' with the bells, but Michael, well... he hates that."

24 All the King's Men

"**W**hat do you mean, *none of them?*" said the king's senior advisor, sure he'd misheard. He lifted his attention from his desk's papers to focus on the royal counting house clerk.

The clerk repeated himself, "None of the southern counties have remitted their taxes, sir. Not a single one below a line you could draw from Salem to Golgotha. All of those funds are late by more than two months now. One late here or there wouldn't have been much cause for concern, of course, we'd have handled that with our own investigators. But, all of them at once... Well, I thought you'd want to know about something like this." He handed over a list of the delinquent counties.

The advisor looked at it and then rubbed his temples, not wanting to think about what it meant. The entire southern third of the kingdom had in unison stopped paying its dues. "Yes, you're right in bringing this to my notice. I'll inform the king straight away. We'll be managing the collection for every place on this list until we notify you otherwise."

The clerk bowed, said, "Thank you, sir," and left the advisor's chamber, glad to have been relieved of the responsibility. He suspected the absent funds might be a sign of anarchy or rebellion in the south and he didn't want to send any of his men into such potentially hazardous situations.

The advisor suspected the same. So, putting on his flowing, scarlet robes, he sought audience with the king. In that meeting he counseled the prudence of a quick display of strength.

That was why a small army was on its way south. Slow formations of fifty each rode under four commanders, bearing the king's scarlet standard, a wolf's head. They were invulnerable soldiers in ornate, plated suits of armor, sitting high on barded horses. They were the King's Men, trained to be incomparable warriors, equipped by the depth of the royal treasury and sworn to ruthless loyalty.

Cornwall, a respected veteran of the order, was one of the regiment's heads. When they came to a halt, he lifted his visor and called out, "Gladstock! Channing! Cumberland! Here's the part! Let's show these southern counties sovereign law does not abide rebellion!" The three men he'd named and their units saluted and split off in separate, direct routes across the countryside. It would take weeks to reach their destinations.

Cornwall then shouted at the rest, "And we're for Antioch! Time to teach those beaners not to pay their taxes, eh brothers! What, what!" His company answered with shouts of *hoo-rah* and *damn beaners* as they resumed their horse-march south.

Harold lifted his own visor and cantered up to Cornwall's side. "Don't you mean teach them *to* pay their taxes, sir?"

Cornwall raised an eyebrow at him. "You're a King's Man, Harold. Don't pick at someone's grammar if you've understood them."

Harold laughed. "Do you really believe there's rebellion in Antioch? My gran-gran always said they wouldn't throw a stone. Her great grandfather drove the squatters from the coffee fields, you know."

"Is that so? A lot can change in a hundred years."

"Do you think highwaymen could be robbing the couriers?"

"Across every route from the coast to the lee? And at the same time? That's a stretch. No, I think they're either part of a rebellion or more likely they're being molested by one. We've some sorting out to do."

"I think it's going to scare the living daylights out of them when we arrive, sir, whether or not they've done anything wrong!" That got a chuckle out of Cornwall. Harold smiled and chatted away. "What about these white wizards eh? I've heard they can suck an evil ghost out of your face if you're haunted. That's exciting, isn't it? I'm looking forward to meeting one of them!"

Cornwall laughed. "You've a good nature, Harold. That'll make it a short trip. What other stories does your gran-gran have about the south?"

"Oh, well, let's see... There's a little man named Gunther who steals your shoes if you leave them out at night. The tale is that he's very small, but his feet are so big that he can't get any to fit, so he tries on every pair that he can find."

Cornwall chuckled again. "I've a mind to see how this Gunther fellow likes the feel of a sound, king's-issue boot then... on his backside, what!" He slapped his thigh - *clank* - and bellowed.

Harold laughed with him. "Hoo-rah, sir."

* * *

Michael's only usual company, Andalynn, was off getting married. So, assuming she wouldn't be coming in to train at all that day, he'd spent most of it sitting on a mat, rereading his library between the lights of the open door and the fire.

He closed his book, feeling restless, like he'd forgotten something critical. Then he noticed a faint sound coming from outside - *clang, clang, clang, clang...* one of the signal bells.

Afraid of how long that had been going on, he ran out into the yard, listening for the sound's character and direction. It came from the north, from the wall. Michael rang out with the church bell to let them know he was on his way. Then he sprinted toward the stable to hitch Ares and Rascal to the incinerator.

* * *

Biggs and Andalynn's marriage was a small ceremony with everyone in humble brown and white. She wore pants and an acolyte's tabard. Betheford conducted the affair from his common room's steps, a look of narrowed disapproval on his face. Fergus and Margot were among the witnesses, as was Sarah, who'd cut her hair shorter to look more like Andalynn's.

It could have been romantic that bells started ringing after they took their vows, had the bride and groom not grabbed their guns and run out of the inn.

Biggs said as they went, "That's Tinkerbell for sure!"

* * *

Captain leaned and yawned up on the scaffold. He would have preferred to attend the wedding but everyone who wasn't on the wall that day had agreed that the wall couldn't afford a day off. The masons were restless below.

"Fwah, pass down the pipe!"
"At least! There's a good sailor."
"We'll celebrate here!"

Captain laughed at them from above. "Fwah, yourselves! We'd get so boogered, the bauran'd get us and we wouldn't even care!" They traded some good natured cursing and Captain shook his head, smiling. Then he gave the countryside a responsible scan. He paused. Was that movement on the road? He picked up his rifle with a sudden chill.

Captain aimed at the clump of trees where he'd seen it. He didn't want to sound the alarm without being absolutely sure he was right, and he desperately hoped he was wrong. There'd still been nothing from the north.

Then Harold stumbled into view, that time magnified in the rifle's scope and crosshairs. Teetering like a drunk in his armor, he fell to his knees and crawled.

Captain worked into a shout, "Go... Go home! I mean, go to the church, lads! Get to the church!" He started yanking the bell's chord - *Clang, Clang, Clang, Clang...* The masons looked up at him, at each other and then gathered at the edge of the wall to see what they could see.

After a bit, one of them called up, "Shouldn't you be shooting him like a turkey?" Captain cast a look of shock down over the edge and kept ringing. He didn't stop until he heard Michael's response - *Ka-kang, kang! Ka-kang, kang!*

Ditch got there before anyone else and shouted at the masons. "Come on, guys! What're you waitin' for? Let's go! Let's go!" Any bell meant *get off the street.* They conceded to follow him away from there. Before they left, Ditch called up, "You alright, Cap?"

Captain didn't show his face when he shouted back. "I... I am! I've got it!" He kept his aim on Harold but didn't touch the trigger. He stayed that way until Andalynn and Biggs arrived, shaking the scaffold with their ascent.

Biggs said, "What's go'n on, Cap?" took a knee on the platform and brought his own rifle to bear.

Captain said, "Don't shoot him! I don't think he's turned."

Andalynn climbed up behind them and found the distant target with her naked eye. "What evidence do you have of that?"

Captain turned for their opinions. "He didn't come to the bell. He stayed following the road." They nodded and kept watch with him, helpless to do anything else. Minutes later, an ear-shattering racket of hooves and banded wheels swelled up from the cobblestones.

To make it mobile, they'd built the incinerator out of a wagon, bolting black metal into the wood. Pipes and tubing coiled over its welded mass and a glowing heat raged behind its grate. That and hauling it had a sweat rolling down the white and red stallions' hides. Michael was deaf in the driver's seat, holding the reins and a whip.

Biggs, Andalynn and Captain pointed and shouted from the scaffold.

"Over that a' way!"
"He is from the north, Michael!"
"Go! He's still alive!"

Michael couldn't hear anything they said but nodded and drove the incinerator in the direction of their pointing, rumbling to a stop where a *King's Man* was on his hands and knees. Michael leapt down, glaring at the scarlet heraldry. It was they who'd driven the fellowship from the coffee fields so long ago, slaying Michael's ancestors out of blind loyalty to a greedy master.

Biggs clapped Captain on the back. "Reckon you just saved taxman's life."

Captain smiled. "I've kept in mind how you lot spared Michael because of the way he moved. So, I'll wait until I see the ink in their eyes." He tapped himself on the nose. "I'd hate to catch a bullet just for being three sheets to the wind, myself."

Andalynn said, "How are the two of you so certain that is a tax collector?"

Biggs shared Captain's smile and said, "Just guessin."

Andalynn held out a hand for her husband's rifle. "May I see?" Biggs passed it up. Shouldering the stock, she found

Michael standing over Harold in the scope. "He is not removing his gauntlets."

Harold was almost paralyzed, coughing and muttering at Michael's feet. "There's... sickness... in... in the woods... my brothers... my brothers... are sick..."

Unmoved, Michael thought, *you and your brothers are damned.* He knelt and lifted the visor on Harold's helm. There was only a man under the armor, pale and black-haired like everyone else. *Your loyalty makes you no better than a butcher's tool, doesn't it, King's Man? How dare you come here, begging me for hospital? Would you have listened to cries for mercy? This is retribution.*

Harold said, "Don't... don't go... into... the woods. It's... dangerous..."

Michael frowned. The man wasn't begging for hospital. He was using his dying breaths as a warning. It was an ignorant, disastrous gesture, of course, having accomplished little more than carrying the plague, but in response to it, Michael was disarmed. He couldn't help but unbuckle his gauntlet and question his own convictions.

Captain was convinced the north-man was alive and that Michael was about to throw him into the incinerator. Michael was going to pull the lever on a living person and there was going to be screaming mixed with the sound of the blast nozzles. Unable to watch, he gave his rifle to Biggs and sat turned away with his hands on his head.

Biggs spoke from the aim. "See, there he goes, Cap. Told you Michael's alright. Taxman's gon' be fine." Captain's expression lifted and he smiled.

The three sailors watched, passing two rifles around, as Michael waited for Harold to wake. The distant pair had a short conversation and then both climbed into the incinerator's seat. When they reached the scaffold on that deafening machine, Harold's face was bloodless and full of dread.

Michael motioned at his own ears and shouted up, "Don't bother! I can't hear a word! Find Marabbas! Send him to me!" The sailors nodded that they understood. Michael cracked the whip, called, "Heya!" and rumbled away.

* * *

It was Naila's first night back among the greer in months. She'd been away on her own to give birth and to nurse and had returned with two healthy pups old enough for the pride. When she discovered what it was they were hunting that night, she spoke out of curiosity. "Apoc says it's wrong to hunt men. It makes the church hunt us."

There wasn't any need to talk about it, but Diana humored Naila in whispers as they padded through the brush. "No. It's good now. Apoc wants us to. The church wants us to."

The greer slunk through the forest in the moonlight, following a mingled scent of death and fungus toward a scattered group of King's Men - bauran by then - that struggled in their new bodies and suits of armor, falling over themselves and the terrain. The greer quietly took positions around them.

Naila said, "I've never eaten man before. What does it taste?"

Diana said, "The taste is bad. Then you like it." Her breathing deepened on the scent and her lips curled up over the canines. Though it wouldn't be the first time she'd eat human flesh, it was the first time she'd do it with permission. She coiled up with the same focused intensity Marabbas had for the smokehouse. She said, "I like this new way." The others agreed.

"We hunt the dead men."
"They don't run from us or cry."
"No one misses them."

They crouched and waited for the signal to attack, that being the first of them to rush in. One of them did and then all sailed through the leaves. They tackled their prey, gripping with talons, biting down with gaping rows of fangs and raking with powerful legs. They were shadows falling on shadows in the dark.

An angry hissing and screeching rose from the fray as their natural weapons failed against the plate armor. The bauran flailed and swatted at the greer's dancing light; riin was arcing everywhere.

Naila leapt away from hers, discouraged. "It hurts! The clothes are hard!"

Another bit down as savagely as she could, trying to get through. A painful - *crack* - and blood flooded her mouth from broken teeth. She howled, "Aaowrr! My teeth are dookussed! Run away!"

But, Diana already knew how to get around a suit of metal. She roared, "No! Twist their hats! Like this!" In a flash she was on Cornwall's back with her talons in his visor's eye-holes. She wrenched and jerked ferociously until his helm faced backward. Cornwall collapsed as his ink lost pressure. Diana called out to the others, "Break them in the middle! Like rock-fish!"

The greer crept back to twist and snap the spines inside the armor. They left nothing to move. In the peace after the kill, they discovered leather fastenings and straps they could cut with their claws to get through. The armor held no mystery for them after that.

And, with the baurans' flesh exposed, they fed. It was their place to feed before bringing kills to the pride's tree. They broke open rib cages with the raw power in their hands. Michael had asked through Marabbas that they start with the lungs. None of them had a problem with that.

Their return to the pride drew the elderly and the young in out of the forest. They gathered around, reluctantly pawing and sniffing at the offering of corpses. Barabbas took to it right away. His mother had raised him on such. His brother, however, was hesitant and had to be convinced to try it.

Marabbas avoided raw meat anyway so he stayed up on his branch, lay back and listened, waiting for a song. While the others ate, the hunters sat in a circle and started a sort of rhythmic humming and howling chant. They kept a slow pace, reminiscent of the stalking calm before the chase, and waited for one of them to stand. She who stood would sing alone.

Younger greer preferred the song's beginning because it was always the same and put less pressure on the soloist. The first to stand was a frightened, three-year-old killer:

"The hunt is breath and blood."

After her, the rest came together in chorus:

"The hunt is good."
"The kill is good."

They gave the song time to develop, waiting for another to stand and sing over the drone of the chant. It was Naila then. She sang the name of what they'd hunted, but in an unusual way:

"Apoc says to hunt the men."

Despite having mentioned Apoc in a line reserved for the hunted, she'd been on time. It made the others smile at her wit. The pride patted her pups and pointed out their mother's skill. The greer came in together:

"We hunt the men."
"The kill is good."

The next part of their song was performed as statement and response, describing what had happened. It was considered to be the most challenging and exciting part and had an element of competition to it. Diana stood up right away, to ensure her place, and on the timing growled:

"The clothes are made of stone!"

There were nods. Pieces of the armor were being passed around. A sad, broken-toothed hunter stood up to volunteer a response:

"They break our teeth…"

And then Diana roared triumphantly:

"We break the clothes!"

Lips curled back in fanged smiles. Donkey-calls blurted out around the tree. Barabbas and his brother stopped eating and flared their eyes at each other. Diana had impressed! No one was likely to stand after that, unless she wanted to get hissed.
The chorus came in:

"The hunt is good!"
"The kill is good!"

They let the chant drone until it was clear no one else would stand. Then, one after the next, they gave credit for their success. *Diana made the hunt* was said again and again, woven into the chant until it became the last chorus:

"Diana made the hunt."
"The hunt is good."
"The kill is good."

They were so happy with their song that the last of it broke up into braying laughter before they finished.

25 Burying Saints

Andalynn and Margot were gossiping in the kitchen and packing picnic baskets with leftover fried chicken and jars of pickled apples. It was convenient for Michael that his acolyte lived at the Cauldron. She always brought plenty of good food when she came to practice.

Andalynn said, "Faith comes to see him almost every day, and brings a pie." She had that small, self-satisfied smile that comes from understanding someone else's motives.

Margot clucked and shimmied. "Sounds to me like she's courting him!"

"Is that how it is done, with pie?"

"Well, you've got to let the great bollgres know somehow, don't you? But, I knew better than to bake a pie for Fergus."

"Does he dislike it?"

"No! He bakes a wicked apple, ooh! No, no good to make him something he'd make better for himself. I gave him a stout cask of the family recipe instead. That got his attention."

"An intelligent maneuver."

"It was love at first pint!" They shared a laugh. Then Margot gestured at Andalynn's left hand. "Biggs has put a pretty little fellow on your finger, hasn't he? Is that how it's done oversea?"

Andalynn admired the ring for a moment. "Yes, though it is unusual to receive the royal seal of an Antithian dynasty as an engagement ring."

"That's posh."

"I do not believe he knew the value of what he was offering me." Biggs snuck into the kitchen while she was speaking and stood behind her. He wore a heavy fur coat and a big furry hat.

Margot smiled at him. "Ooh, I don't know. He seems pretty sure of himself."

He said, "That's right. It's a ol' family heirloom, cause I'm sump'n a highfalutin' tithaneen." He gave Andalynn a peck on the cheek. "Mornin. One a' these for me?" He motioned at the baskets.

Andalynn could not have imagined many of the things that had come to pass over the last year and a half, not even in the darkest of her nightmares. Out of them all, her packing a picnic basket to send a red-necked husband off to work seemed among the most absurd. Embracing the ridiculousness of it, she said, "Yes, this one. Have a good day, dear."

Biggs paused. Then he smiled and looked around the medieval kitchen like he was seeing it for the first time, despite having slept upstairs for months. He scratched his head and said, "D'you just say that?"

She blurted out, "I did!" and surrendered to laughter. Biggs understood right away and laughed with her. Margot smiled at the pair of them and continued packing. They made a fine match in her opinion.

Biggs kissed Andalynn again, on the mouth that time, with his hand on the back of her head to make it count. She was grinning when he pulled away. Her life was absurd but it was not altogether unpleasant. Her gallant cowboy slung his rifle over his shoulder, headed for the door and said, "You have yourself a good day too now, darlin."

He opened it to the outside. A gust of cold and swirling snow - and then he jumped back against the stove. "Eeuuh!" Andalynn and Margot started when he called out. Biggs stomped his foot. "Dadgum it, Murrbus! Quit creepin' around!"

From outside, "Ok." The three humans shook their heads with relief and waved goodbyes. Biggs left for his perch at the wall. Marabbas poked in through the doorway, hairy face caked with blood and ice. He stared at the other picnic basket. "That's fried chicken."

Margot waved a finger at him and moved to prevent him from entering. "Marabbas! Don't you even think about it, ooh, filthy beast! Get off to the well!" She couldn't stand him tramping all about and making a bloody mess inside, even if he had brought a carcass to Fergus.

Marabbas spent a moment wondering if he could stop thinking about something at will. Then the scent wafting from the basket refocused him. "I want it."

Margot put her fists on her hips. "Well, that's too bad then, isn't it? Because you can't have it! That's for Michael and Harold. Now, get!" Marabbas' face fell as though he'd been delivered the most horrible news.

Andalynn took pity on him. "It is alright, Margot. He may have a piece. Here, Bas." She tossed him a thigh. She had taken to calling him Bas in part because it reminded her of Sergeant Sebastian. Unfortunately, the nickname tended give Marabbas pause and the chicken hit him in the face. Then it fell on the ground. Andalynn's hand went to her mouth.

Margot said, "Ooh!" and started laughing. Marabbas saw what had struck him, snatched it up off the floor and devoured it. Margot covered her laughter with one hand and shooed the gunder with the other. "Go wash up at the well - ooh - before you come in! *Ooh!*"

Marabbas bounded away. Margot turned to laugh with Andalynn, whose head was bowed from doing so. It was a good start to the day.

* * *

The morning sun sparkled on the distant rooftops. Snow crested the tombstones and crunched under Andalynn's boots. Walking through the graveyard always gave her gooseflesh. She took the same path every time, the one they had that awful night, because it was the most direct. The hollow under her black scarf ached from the cold and from the memory. When she arrived at the church, a woman had just closed the door to leave, bundled against the weather in humble brown and white.

Andalynn rounded the bell and said, "Good morning, Faith."

Faith shrieked in terror, "AAAiiieee!" and backed into the wall, clutching her chest. Andalynn stood there with a picnic basket, sorry to have caused such a fright, and decided to make her presence known from farther away next time.

Michael burst out, fully armored except for one hand which held a messy piece of gooseberry pie. After looking them over and realizing everyone was safe, he said, "God's mercy! I thought the bauran had come back." It had been more than a month since one had answered his bell, two weeks since the last infection.

Faith breathed into her hands, embarrassed. "Oh, I'm sorry. Oh, Andalynn, I'm sorry. How silly of me. You must think me such a cowardly ninny." Fear released her like a clawed grip, leaving pins and needles behind.

Andalynn said, "I do not," and stepped forward. "This is a frightening place. You are courageous to come here as often as you do." Faith managed a sheepish smile.

Her face hadn't suffered jagged cuts like Andalynn's. Faith could hide most of her wounds under her clothes. However, Michael had realigned a few of her broken bones - having broken them again by hand to do so - and ridges from some of those second fusions showed beneath the skin of her cheek. Andalynn saw a rugged beauty in the damage, evidence of what had been survived. It was easier to appreciate in someone else.

Michael nodded, respecting what Andalynn had said. "Ah, quite right. And you visit me without any sort of want or need. That's not only brave, but selfless. Good show, Faith."

Faith became even more embarrassed than she'd been before. She curtsied to excuse herself and scuttled away, picking an awkward path home through the frozen graves. Michael stared after her for a moment. Then he held the door open and said, "It's the candle again today." Andalynn nodded and went in.

The contents of the library cluttered the church. Michael had emptied that back room out to make a prison cell for Harold. The round table took up the space of three sleeping mats. Books piled from floor to waist in seemingly random columns around the hall. Scrolls and loose papers crowded the corners along with ironbound chests and a few hardwood practice swords, carved to the measure of caligans.

Harold's shield, emblazoned with a scarlet wolf's head, leaned against the wall, his broadsword behind it. His plate mail suit sat on the stones like an empty, metal man and Harold himself sat on a stack of displaced mats near the hearth. Gaunt in his donated clothing, he didn't look up when they came in.

Andalynn said, "I want you to eat today, Harold. I have something excellent in this basket."

Harold was a soldier who'd lost everything but his honor. "No, thank you." He'd taken nothing but water since he'd survived and he rarely spoke unless it was to politely refuse the kindness of his jailer. Michael hadn't kept him locked up for very long. Harold didn't seem like he would try to escape. He'd even given his word that he wouldn't when Michael asked him for it. There was nowhere for him to go anyway and it had grown too cold to keep him in the back room.

Andalynn and Michael shared a look of concern but Harold was in no immediate danger from his self-imposed fast. So, Michael lit a candle from the fireplace and sat down at the round table with the rest of Faith's pie. Andalynn prepared a quick plate of chicken and pickled apples and set it on the floor next to Harold, who slumped when he saw it.

Michael said to her, "Let's see how much you can do by yourself first." She rolled up her sleeve and took a seat in front of the candle. She'd earned a hairless patch on her forearm from this exercise. Harold turned to watch.

Andalynn sat in calm concentration, her first goal being to achieve that feeling of nothingness. She did so by remembering the faces of unfortunate sailors like Sue, Fritz and Drake. Andalynn had discovered by then what her path truly was; it was the void she needed to feel in order to pull the trigger. The nothingness was a suppression of emotion. But in that way, it was also part of the realm of ideas and of feelings and of the will, and so was subject to the Circle's techniques.

She was improving. It took her less than a minute to follow the nothingness to its source, where it was a perversion of riin - that strange, limitless influence that inexplicably enters reality to cause life. She had learned to perceive these things outside of her other senses and was able to pull at the source with her will, widening it just barely more than its natural gauge. Thus, she opened the way, slightly. Additional riin flickered into her body, like tongues of ghostly fire.

Success. She held her arm up to the heat, close enough to burn, and riin coursed toward the damage on its own. It was an exhilarating sensation, like a champion had taken the field for her, certain of victory. She couldn't release the sheer amount of power that Michael could, though, and held her arm too close. It started to hurt. She lost focus, hissed and withdrew.

Michael said, "You're doing it again. Don't try to defeat the candle. You'll only damage yourself that way. This exercise is about growing accustomed to riin's ebb and flow. Hold your arm only close enough to feel that." She nodded and readied herself for another try, but definitely harbored intent to defeat the candle.

Andalynn channeled steadily against the flame for a minute at a time, a rivaling glow under her skin. Michael sometimes put his hand on her forehead and observed her reflection while she did. Now and then, he would use his more advanced technique to pull a comparably tremendous amount of riin into her body, thereby helping to reveal to her the invisible locks and tumblers that allowed for such access. With his assistance she could hold her arm directly over the flame and riin flared into the world from her with blinding radiance. They practiced like that for two hours while Harold sat in silent amazement.

Then they took a break, ate and discussed what they'd done and how she could improve. And, they noticed Harold eating as well. The three shared solemn smiles. Harold's curiosity had finally overcome his willful depression. He was filled with questions. In becoming open to ask them, he also became open to a meal.

Harold said, "You were right. This is excellent. Thank you."

Andalynn was glad to see him coming around. "You are welcome."

Michael held up a drumstick. "Fried chicken is my favorite. I think it's even better when it's cold. Would you care to try some of this gooseberry pie? It's also quite good." He offered the dish.

Harold accepted it. "Yes, I would. Thank you." Though his first bite in weeks let hunger rage into him like an animal, Harold kept a ceremonious and reserved manner when eating. King's Men were not barbarians to scarf their food. He consistently invalidated Michael's preconceptions.

Harold said, "May I ask some questions about what it is that you're doing?"

Michael said, "Certainly."

"Thank you. Can anyone do that?"

"Yes."

"There's no part of ancestry to it?"

Michael prickled some. "As there is with royal entitlement? No, certainly not."

Harold proceeded cautiously. "Why are there so few of you who possess this ability? How can I have never heard of this skill before?"

"That is a long story about my order's ignorance, secrets and misguided loyalty. Suffice it to say, the plague forced us to correct that, and hopefully not too late."

Harold nodded. "With just a few more of you, the entire kingdom could have survived. I don't say that to cast blame. I can tell you're acting in the right. It's just such an overwhelming tragedy..."

They waited for him to speak again while he picked up a book and turned through it. Harold had been educated at the royal academy and was fond of reading but the Circle's library confounded him. Not one of the books was written in Meroan. Some contained drawings of wicked-looking beasts and demons. "What are these about? I've never seen such symbols."

Michael said, "Much of this is bestiary. It's a collection of devils and how to deal with them."

With a mixture of sadness and interest, Harold said, "Do you have one for the bauran?"

"I do. I wrote it." It was the second book Michael had written for the church. The first hadn't been very useful. He stood up, went straight across the room and retrieved the original book of bauran from one of the piles. He handed it over, curious to hear more of what had been on Harold's mind for the past two weeks.

Harold weighed it in hand, guessing it was the most valuable book in the world. It was an inch thick, bound in leather and encoded with a solid volume of vital information. "You knew right where this one was."

"I know where all of them are. I've read and reread this entire collection since the plague began, searching for some record of the man named Ezekiel, the one who guided the sailors here." Andalynn did not know Michael had been researching Zeke. It roused her interest.

Harold said, "And you've found nothing?"

"Not much more than the loose notes in that book."

Andalynn said, "May I see those?" Harold handed them up. It almost gave her a twinge of seasickness to unfold the one from the *Grace*. She could not read it, learning the script was not a prudent use of their time, but she knew what it said.

Armageddon is arrived.
Break your silence.
Open the library.

She said, "Is it possible that he contributed to any of these volumes without leaving his name? Would you recognize his handwriting?"

Michael said, "He does have a peculiar hand. There's a sweeping, artistic quality to his style. The only place I've found its like is where he signed the ledger of ordination."

Andalynn said, "May I see that?"

Michael went three piles over, lifted four books from the top and placed them on the floor next to the others to preserve whatever bizarre order he had them in. Then he brought the ledger to Andalynn and flipped right to Ezekiel's signature. "For most of us, this is the first time we ever use the script, in signing our names to this book. Look at how clumsy the others are, but not his. It's an obvious match."

"Yes, even I can tell. Look at how much of the page he uses compared to everyone else. That is an arrogant signature by any standard. What does it say here around it?"

"Those are the dates of his ordination and of his supposed death, where he was from and where he's buried in the churchyard."

Andalynn was surprised. "Ezekiel has a marker outside?"

"Yes. I've visited it. I'm sure I've told you."

She raised an eyebrow. "You have not. That is interesting. I wonder who is buried there…"

Michael shrugged. "I suppose we'll never know."

Harold said, "Where was he from?"

"Meroe."

Harold darkened. Despite his previous withdrawal, they'd explained much to him already. The loss of Meroe, believed by some scholars to be the birthplace of civilization, was what had convinced him there was no hope for the kingdom. He knew the smoke had bridged the gap and had gone on to destroy everything.

Andalynn said, "That grave makes Zeke a liar."

Michael said, "Maybe."

"How else can you explain the marker?"

"I don't know."

"A man calling himself by the name on a tombstone is concealing something. Possibly a murder or... it might even be evidence of a conspiracy. Now I am beyond interested."

Michael sighed. "Honestly, a murder? Ezekiel saved your lives."

Andalynn smirked. "Very well. If he is who he says he is, then no one else is buried there, so, what is?"

"What? Was that a question?"

"Exhume what is there. Find out."

Michael's chin pulled into his throat. "God's mercy! What an awful suggestion! Why would I do something dreadful like that?"

She chuckled at him. "Out of curiosity. For the sake of inquisition. As a way to spend your time? You have read and reread your library looking for him. That is no light endeavor. There is a stone outside with his name on it. Look for him there."

Michael remembered having had a similar conversation with her before. "Desecrating the grave of a saint... It's a mortal sin." And not only that - *thou shalt not defile the dead.*

In Meroe, Andalynn had been wary of Michael having strong religious beliefs, knowing how dangerous such things often are. Since then, she had come to see such ideals as a loose kind of innocence in him rather than a threatening dictator of behavior and she was comfortable speaking freely with him on the subject.

"Who is left to punish you for your sins, Michael?"

He frowned at her. "That is not the point."

* * *

Regardless, Ezekiel's grave became an earthen hole in the snow. In it up to his hips, Michael heaved out dirt with a shovel. Andalynn and Harold stood watching nearby with their breath curling in the air. They'd been going in and out of the church for warmth since Michael had started.

Harold rubbed his arms. "I can't believe he isn't exhausted yet. He's been at it forever."

Andalynn said, "Michael is able to draw considerable stamina from the way."

"If only I could. Is there a place in town we can get a cup of coffee?"

Andalynn smiled. "Yes. I would like that. However, I should warn you, since you are staying with him, the mention of coffee tends to sour Michael's mood."

Harold understood. "Noted."

Andalynn called out that she and Harold were leaving. Michael waved for them to go ahead, not concerned at all. Once he'd decided to unearth Ezekiel's mysterious remains, he could think of nothing else. The other two had been gone for half an hour when his shovel struck masonry.

Michael scraped at it and then stood back for moment. Saints weren't buried in stone. Unless the ways had changed, it should have been a coffin made of pine and it should have rotted away long ago. Even the caligan and sleeve would have been nothing more than rust after two hundred years in the ground. He returned to digging and scraping, searching for the edges of what he'd found.

* * *

Andalynn and Harold returned two hours later, after one of those long talks over coffee that so often turns compatible personalities into thick companions. They were still in lively discourse as they approached Ezekiel's marker.

Harold chuckled at her. "You're a disturbing person."

Andalynn smirked. "Do you think so? I consider myself a free spirit."

It seemed from a distance that Michael was no longer there. He could not be so deep in the hole that none of him showed. Andalynn wondered if they had lost track of time and if he was already back in the church. As they got closer, the gooseflesh started to rise. At fifty yards she shouted, "Michael!" There was no answer. She stopped and looked around, feeling exposed.

Harold said, "Is something wrong?"

"I should not have called out."

"He's most likely back inside, wouldn't you say?"

Andalynn's jaw clenched and she nodded.

Harold rubbed his arms from the cold. "Perhaps we should go inside as well."

So, they did and Michael wasn't there. Andalynn drew her pistol and pointed it at the door. They were in danger, she knew it. Overreaction was impossible. If Michael was not at the church, everyone was in danger, and if a bauran walked through that door, it could kill both of them.

She said, "Stay here. Lock yourself in the library."

Harold said, "Not likely," and grabbed up his broadsword and shield.

Andalynn ran outside with Harold on her heels. They were far away from the church before she stopped, far away from anything concealing. She would not let one surprise her around a corner.

She said, "They do not make any sound. They just come. You have to watch every second, everywhere around you." Harold followed her lead, keeping his eyes open.

Andalynn could think of no other explanation; Michael must have answered a signal bell. They would have heard the wall's bell from Betheford's, she had before. The eastern bell was even closer. But, she might not have heard the western or the southern - and the southern bell was the most ominous of them all. That would be the one that rang when the remnants of Meroe and Breahg and every other settlement sacrificed south of the Circle's arc finally marched on Antioch.

And, when that army of the dead came, it would be old. Andalynn remembered Ditch saying, *I hate the fast ones, man. They're like, spiders, or somethin, you know? Hard to hit.* It was accurate. She hated to think of them.

But no, she had not heard the church bell. Michael would have rung out with that before answering any of the others. Out of frustration she shouted, "Michael!" No answer. "Michael!" No answer. It was infuriating. Every time she called for him, she told the bauran where she was.

Harold said, "Let's check the marker again, just to be sure."

They ran to it. As they got closer, what seemed to be a second headstone was jutting up out of the excavation. It was actually a massive, four hundred pound slab, tilted up out of that hole like a lid. Its cold, gray seat, streaked with earth, framed a rectangular pit in the foot of the grave. They couldn't see the bottom.

Andalynn yelled into it, "Michael!" and jerked to look around, still expecting silent stalkers at any moment, so haunted for her was the churchyard's white desolation. Her heart beat like a bird's wings in her chest.

Harold peered into the darkness. "My goodness. He must be down there."

"Michael!"

Before she could call a third time, Michael's face appeared in the light of a candle twenty-five feet down. "I'm here! Is everything alright?" His voice was faint and far away.

Aftershocks of anger and fear rippled through Andalynn's body. She could only walk through the graveyard in the mornings because she knew Michael was in the church. When she didn't know where he was, there was no more terrifying place in the world. She put a trembling hand over her face and said through gritted teeth, "Yes. Everything is fine."

Michael called up again, "What? There's a ladder! Come see what I've discovered!"

Andalynn shoved her revolver into its holster. She would not yell up and down the depth of that hole with him. She would go down there and tell him exactly how irresponsible it was for him to be out of earshot for so long. Her boots clanked on the wrought iron ladder as she descended. Harold followed, his shield on his back.

She harangued Michael as she went. "You cannot hear anything down here, Michael. We have been calling for you. What if there had been an emergency?"

He waited for them with his candle, disappointed in himself. "Ah, quite right, of course. I must have lost track of time. Has something happened?"

She reached the floor and dusted her hands, snapping her words at him. "No. Fortunately. What is this, a burial chamber?" The air did not move at all down there and tasted stale and dry. What they said stayed alive in a sepulchral echo.

Michael said, "I found this," and handed her a very old book.

She opened it, thinking, *wonderful, more sacred script.* "I cannot read this. What is it?"

"Ezekiel's hand."

She held it up and reexamined the telling strokes. Then, as her vision adjusted, she saw shapes over Michael's shoulder. He moved toward them, revealing rows upon rows of ancient bookcases. Flat columns, filled with literature from the stone floor to the stone ceiling, planed into the darkness of a room that neither the depth nor the width of which could she determine by the candle's light.

Michael said, "Every one of them so far. See?" He took down another tome at random and brought it to her. Therein was Ezekiel's hand.

Harold whistled.

Andalynn's mouth fell open. "Unprecedented. What kind of information do they contain?"

Michael gestured helplessly at the shelves. "Where should I start? There must be thousands of them. That first one I gave you is page after page of the emotional impact an apple had on him, as far as I can tell."

Andalynn squinted at him. "An apple?"

Michael nodded like Ezekiel must have been insane. "It is explicit, to say the least."

Harold said, "It must have been some apple."

Michael looked sideways at him and then turned back to the books. "I might have to read a few of these just to put them in some sort of context. Ah, I've no idea how they're organized..."

They stood in speechless appraisal of the discovery. Michael carefully replaced the books and then took down another. Opening it and skimming a page, he feared he could devote every day of his life to reading, from sunrise to sunset, and never finish what Ezekiel's tomb contained.

Michael said, "I think this is the library. When he told us to *open the library*, I think this is what he meant. And I'm the only one who can read it."

Andalynn had seen enough. "Collect a few of them for investigation. We are deaf in this hole." Michael agreed and picked the first five off the top shelf farthest to his left, hoping that was where they started.

As they climbed out, Harold offered, "If you want some help with it, I wouldn't mind learning this script of yours." Michael frowned at him.

26 The Second Pendulum

This one's full of more off-hand references to the second pendulum again.
Whatever does that mean?
I don't know, something about riin's tendency to ebb and flow, I suppose.
Oversea, the sailors used pendulums in machines to tell the time. Ah
well, I think I'm done for the evening.
You go ahead. I'll take notes if I find anything on my own.
Thanks, I'm sure she's got dinner on the table already.
I'm sure mine does too. See you tomorrow. Oh, hang on... This is
interesting. Here, before you go, listen to this:
"Emotional paths have such complex and dynamic arcs because they are
further removed from the source and do not possess the pure force of
instinctual paths, which are, of course, forbidden."
..Well, well, what do you make of that?"
Let me see that one!

* * *

An old man, dark-skinned and topped with tight, white curls, walked the busiest avenue of a city about to die, mindless of the thousands of passersby. Dapper, horse-drawn buggies cruised the lane off the walk and the populace surrounded him with pocket watches, parasols and petticoats, fine suits, top hats and bustles. He wore plainer clothes and carried a brown paper bag.

He stop-started through the revolving doors of Main Street's most expensive hotel, *La Fleur du Sud*, where he and his wife had been staying for a week, a lavish extravagance in celebration of their thirtieth anniversary. Every surface inside seemed to be cream colored within a gilded lilt. The front clerk greeted him with her pretty smile and waved. The bellhop drew back the elevator door like an accordion. Its brass matched the buttons on his red velvet uniform.

The bellhop's nametag read Beauchamp. He'd come in early for a double into the night shift. "Welcome back, sir! Did you find what you were looking for downtown?"

The old man thought, *he looks more like a Richie or a Timmy, but, in fairness, no one really looks like a Beauchamp, do they?* "Why yes, I did, right here in this bag. Thank you for inquiring after me, young man."

"Very good, sir. It's too bad about our paper here."

Don't patronize me, Beauchamp... "Yes, it is unfortunate. But, we all do the best we can..." *I could turn you inside out like a baked yam, boy.*

"Happy anniversary, sir!"

And then up to room nine-ten. Its interior, crowded with finery and everything sculpted or draped, looked more like a still-life than a living space. Elizabeth, his wife, adored it. She was out with her - *cringe* - relatives, preparing for the - *cringe* - party and would be back later on. Right then he was alone. He sat down at a writing desk, so decoratively carved that it should rather be called an escritoire, and from his paper bag removed a bottle of ink and a sheaf of paper.

They were special examples of those items. The paper had to last as a book and had to flip from his thumb, just so. His work required longevity. *This isn't just something to be scribbled on hotel stationary and then forgotten, thank you very much, Beauchamp.* The ink was rare. Modern inks faded after only a few decades and would therefore never do.

He tapped his pen in the well and at the top of the first leaf wrote, "Dear Diary." Then he hunched over, laughing. He'd wanted to do that for years. He chuckled and smiled to himself for a while before putting the pen to paper again.

> Eleven hundred and fifty-nine, September thirty-first: Seven o'clock in the evening
> I'm remembering seeing Elizabeth's "doctor," Jones. I called him Mr. Jones on purpose, expecting him to correct me. He didn't. Good for him. I think it was in the paper later that he'd beaten his wife with a poker. Or, it might have been that I'd heard someone had beaten him at poker. I really can't remember. I answered his questions as truthfully as I could at

the time. He diagnosed me with depression and suggested that I keep, of all things, a diary! Every time I think of that man, it makes me laugh. It makes me laugh to think anyone could imagine themselves qualified to recommend that I keep a diary. Still, since it does make me laugh so, perhaps he had an ancillary effect on my temper's improvement. The man might be a genius.

I still can't stand the sight of anyone other than her, though. And, her family is particularly base. I don't know how someone like Elizabeth could have come from people like them. They won't stay away from us, either! Would that they were dismembered. She's been making an effort so I don't have to see them too often but the more time I spend away from them the more I want and the worse it is when I am forced into their company again.

Oh, they're not evil people, of course. They're just people. Their every word makes me cringe. They suggest meaning with a language their mouths don't deserve to form. Every movement and every breath. I wouldn't destroy them like paper nests, like bug houses to disintegrate, their flesh falling away from their skeletons while they gape at themselves in horror. No, if they were collectively helpless and I could ignore the opportunity to aid them, I suppose I would not even do that, because they mean so much to her. But, if I could live with Elizabeth in a world with no one else, oh, that would be paradise, such everlasting beauty is in her spirit. That, for her, however, would be hell. And, without her happiness, what would be the point of anything? Perhaps I've never been fit to live in this world, for which Elizabeth's family seems so perfectly designed, hagfish in the slime.

Fwah! All things considered, these last thirty years seem to have had a profound effect on me. It's so odd that I'd need to experience them in order to come to this night, but it's true. It really is true. I'm actually afraid of the evening at hand. That's quite encouraging!

Elizabeth remarked that I seemed more tolerant today. I honestly love her. Success! How can I hate everyone as much as I do if I can have this boundless love for her? That's dishonest, I don't hate everyone, of course. I'd feel terrible if those rare friends of mine thought that, or the children. Perhaps I hate myself.

What part of me is it that chooses what I want? Why do I want things that make others unhappy? Why do I want others to be happy? Why can't I simply be comfortable with their disappointment or their violent deaths and seek my own happiness? Elizabeth's sister is like that. She's vile, bouncing along without any concern for the displeasure she creates in others. In that way, she's stronger than I am. Her carelessness brings her happiness. My honor brings me misery.

Oh pish posh, enough of this, poor me and my poor honor, Elizabeth's sister flayed and screaming, all things coming into their own and so! Currently I am excited, afraid and expectant. That pretty little clerk waved at me a moment ago on my way in. What a disgusting display! She most likely despises her occupation and would prefer that no one came in at all. How dare she lie to me with her smile? And that damned bellboy is an idiot. I am angry and murderous...

The door *ka-chunked* and rattled and then opened. Elizabeth came bustling in, out of breath, arms full of packages and bags, and a smile in her voice. "Help!"

She was sixty-five years old, and looked so. She was natural. Her hair was pulled back into a bun of black and gray springs and her deep, brown eyes were lined from experience. She wasn't a youthful sixty-five but she'd been strong and healthy for the last thirty.

He laughed and went to her, leaving his work on the table. "Lizzy! Here, give me some of those. You'll hurt yourself." He lifted them from her until she could move like a person again.

There was someone else in the hall with even more items on a cart - *Beauchamp...* He wheeled them in and unloaded them. The old man gave him a large, meaningless tip - *Currency...*

"Thank you, sir! That's very generous of you!"

"You're worth every penny, young man."

Elizabeth beamed at her husband. "The big day's tomorrow! I can hardly wait! Everything's going to be perfect. Oh, never tell me where you got the money!"

He smiled and closed the door. "Alright."

"Don't be ridiculous. Tell me right this instant where you got the money."

He laughed. "I've told you, it's a surprise." He sat down on the bed and started looking through the bags. "Let's have a good night, tonight. I'll need it to face the hagfish tomorrow."

"G'oh! I hate it when you call them that. That's my family. Can't you just call them *the in-laws* like a normal person?"

There's sure to be a box of sweets in one of these... "I'll call them whatever word you like, but whatever word you like will taste of hagfish."

"You're awful." She saw his paper on the table and picked it up. At first glance she thought he'd been writing something. On closer inspection she was perplexed. "What are these symbols, Zeke? Did you write this?"

"What's that? Oh, yes, it's art. I've decided to throw it all away and become an artist. This hotel's inspired me."

She frowned at him. "You're such a liar. This isn't Continental. It's strange looking... cultish. Tell me what it is."

"Do you know, I think it might just be the sacred script of an ancient cult?"

She raised an eyebrow at him. "I'm not joking, now you tell me what this is." She knew her Zeke didn't study obscure, foreign languages. He was a common, hard-working man, not a scholar.

He cleared a space for her on the bed and patted it. "Come sit next to me, my dear." She did and he kissed her - *oh, soaring joy of love! Success!* "I'll tell you about everything tomorrow. Not only the secret of our newfound wealth, but another secret or two that will surprise you."

Elizabeth paused, staring at him. "Zeke, I'm... I don't like this. We don't keep secrets from each other. The money's one thing, but this writing, and you not telling me, this isn't right. It's frightening."

It was in his old, familiar face: *how could you possibly be frightened of me?* "Trust me, Lizzy."

She relaxed. Of course she trusted him. They'd been through everything together. "You didn't need to do any of this, you know. You could have just gotten me flowers. I like flowers."

So beautiful... "What I'm going to share with you tomorrow will be better than flowers. I promise."

She loved him too. She always had. They sat on the bed together, talking and laughing about their plans and the celebration and how he didn't really want to go to the party, but how he'd do it just for her. He liked to keep secrets with the truth. A few times that evening, she tried to trick him into revealing something about their sudden, outrageous fortune. It made him smile. She couldn't have known how good Ezekiel was at keeping secrets. He even taught her the script for the word "love" and had her write it in the book, without really revealing anything at all.

Later, as they lay together in the dark, he waited patiently for her to fall asleep on her own. It didn't wake her when he rose. It rarely did anymore. Over the years, she'd grown accustomed to sleeping alone. She didn't know it, but she'd never actually seen him asleep. She'd seen him with his eyes closed, certainly, but the truth was that Ezekiel hadn't slept in millennia. After age, sleep was the first thing he'd striven to overcome, mostly to keep from wasting the time.

He'd overcome many of what he considered to be the frailties of life. Poised to do so with another, he lit a kerosene lamp with a match and sat down to write.

Eleven hundred and fifty-nine, September thirty-second: One o'clock in the morning

We've lived the perfect life. Not too much, not too little, just enough to appreciate what we've meant to each other. It has created love, true love, I'm sure of it. If I feel it, she must. Combined with her excitement over coming into a little money and the intrigue of new possibilities, she must be dreaming out of love right now. If only I could know those precious fantasies. If only I could know her mind like I know her body.

I'm afraid of losing her. Everything is exactly as I thought it would be. I'm not ready yet, though. I'll wait another hour, to prepare myself. That's not very long, each stroke of my pen being part of a second, each book then a part of a year. What a strange thing time is.

When the hour passed he looked at her without his eyes. A shimmering reflection slept on the bed. Seeing her like that, there was nothing else in the room. He hesitated. *Perhaps, one more hour?*

No. Resolve. No more accidents, no more uncertainty, no more loss of control. Nothing out of hand. She can live forever, if I'm strong enough to learn. I must be resolved.

He exhaled and then, from where he sat across the room, closed the way in her. Elizabeth's reflection went out like he'd turned the knob on a lamp. Only the tiniest lives were left smoldering in her body. *What if I fail?*

"Liz..."

Ezekiel's heart broke.

That was the feeling he'd spent the last thirty years to achieve, the loss of a lifetime's devotion. He went to its source in a single stride, a giant in a land of dreams, and tore his grief and love loose until the riin was a hurricane around him. He stood up from his chair in a seizure, eyes rolling back into his head. *Now, return to me.*

He created a rushing, ethereal wheel out of the release, every strand of it masterfully woven to tear the way open again. But, it skidded through dead flesh without effect. *It isn't working.* He gave it time, slipping into apprehension. Then he grabbed at facts from his memory and rammed them together, searching for a desperate combination that would accomplish what his careful planning had not. He couldn't let her go. When every emotional influence failed, he resorted to raw power.

Ezekiel's despair led him to channel from paths that yielded chaos and misery in the past, forbidden paths of instinct and fundamental intent. He shocked Elizabeth's corpse with bursts of that terrible current.

She wrenched and flexed on the bed, but went still when he stopped. He tried over and over, pushing and pulling, rowing those energies through her, until he realized she would not be revived. The way would not open. She would never live again. Her face was blank. She would never look at him again.

He fell into his chair, trembling, questioning why, questioning everything. Then, though it pained him greatly, Ezekiel forced himself back to the desk. He could not allow his grief to change or to fade. His tears dotted and warped the page as he recorded what he felt.

* * *

The sun peeked into the hotel's lobby. The gold and brass were dull brown borders around the cream. The elevator bell rang, the gate shrank to one side and Ezekiel hurried out with his manuscript, wanting to leave that place behind forever.

Beauchamp approached dutifully to extend the hotel's courtesy. Without breaking step, Ezekiel ripped a cord through him that unbound the young man's body. Beauchamp melted under the velvet into skin and bones, blood and grease - with the speed of gravity.

Ezekiel chastised himself as he waited through the rotating doors. *I shouldn't have done that to him. That was wrong.* Then he joined the street's sporadic, early morning flow. In an hour it would be teeming. He had to reach his children before they heard news of their mother's death. He had to keep trying until every path of his thirty years' work was exhausted. The key to resurrection could be within any of those relationships.

He didn't know what he'd left in room nine-ten.

Ezekiel usually ignored the reflections of the smaller lives, those tiny things passing through moments of existence allowing bigger things to function, those voracious little beasts that eat their host from the inside when it dies, mold from the ceiling of the apartment he'd shared with his wife for the last eleven years - those sorts of lives.

He didn't know he'd created a new kind of life, on a cellular level, by smashing the ones left in Elizabeth together. It wasn't the first such offshoot he was responsible for, not by far, nor was it the first to happen by accident. But, this one was different from all of the others. It was awake. Ezekiel had awakened it by channeling through instinct.

While the relatively reserved and graceful influences of emotion would have been imperceptible to it, instinct was fundamentally understood. Through instinct it could draw power directly from the source and each of its pieces would inherently know the way. It was a being without curiosity, its abilities and purpose defined by coincidental design. It could consume and reproduce but only in a bed of human flesh. It could spore and take root and it could use its dead hosts like machines to carry it to the living.

The morning desk clerk sent for every emergency service in the city when he discovered Beauchamp's horrifying remains. Management wished he hadn't. They didn't want *La fleur du Sud* to become one of those cheap tourist attractions, one of those haunted hotels. Yes, there had been a tragedy, but you don't just throw everything away because of it. Even as the coroner's office, the police, emergency physicians, guests, journalists and the simply curious gathered downstairs, housekeeping was expected upstairs to carry out their duties.

And, Gélise had a family to care for. She knocked on the door to room nine-ten and said, "Housekeeping. Do you need service?" Her voice told that her heart wasn't in it that day - *poor Beauchamp.*

Thump, thump, thump, thump, thump, thump, WHAM!

It sounded like someone had charged across the room headlong into the door. Gélise stepped back, already on edge because of what was going on downstairs, and then made the connection; whoever - *or whatever* - was inside room nine-ten could be the one who'd done Beauchamp that way in the lobby. Her hand went to her mouth.

The door handle rattled like an animal was learning how to turn it - *chiclick, clack, chick, clickack.*

Gélise left her cart right where it was and went apron flapping in a half-walk-half-run scuffle for the elevator. *Zut! Zut et zut, that's the killer in there I just know it! What am I doing up here? Who stays at work on the day of a murder? Stupid, stupid, stupid...*

The door opened in the hall behind her, followed by footsteps - *thump, thump, thump, thump...* and the dull resonance from the carpet of an empty, upper story hallway.

Gélise turned around, bolt-upright, fearing it was a man with a long knife. Elizabeth's black-eyed, smoking corpse was much worse. Gélise' face peeled back in a scream and she staggered into the elevator alcove, swatting at the gate. "Open up! Oh, God, help me! Please! Help meee!"

The shadow was screaming. Elizabeth reached out for its shining heart. The wall behind it slid away and they fell together to the floor. She caught it! It was right in front of her, so close, but the shadow was in the way. The shadow kept her from touching the light. She smashed it, bit into it and tore at it, trying to get through. The screaming stopped. The light went out.

The elevator bell rang in the lobby.

> Hundreds of lights, so bright,
> They swept away like the tide.
> She ran to them.

While everyone else retreated, brave policemen stepped forward to capture Elizabeth, who was quite obviously a homicidal maniac. They overpowered her, handcuffed her and dragged her struggling out of the hotel. The coroner stayed, wiping his burning face, baffled by the two deaths that were left; what seemed to have caused one didn't seem likely to have caused the other.

The hotel would have to be evacuated. Those passing through the lobby carried the smoke away in their bodies and on their clothes. Gélise rose later in the morgue. So began the Fall.

27 One Thirty Fivers

Antioch's stone masons completed the wall at the end of summer, less than a year after they started. Before the wall's ends met, the city hadn't seen a bauran in months. Everyone felt it was the calm before the storm, that an army of smoking devils was out there roaming the countryside, gathering in number, and that it was only a matter of time before the siege. Michael had rung the church bell for months without an answer. It wasn't until the wall was finished that he was finally able to relax.

He stood opposite Harold in the graveyard, each wearing the brown wool pants and white linen shirts of the fellowship. They saluted one another with their weapons, Michael with a two-handed, hardwood practice-sword, Harold with a skinny apple-branch, holding his wolf's head shield in his other hand. A dead leaf twirled by on the gentle, autumn breeze.

Jacob sat watching them from the stump by the forge. His apprentice, Ditch, sat next to him. Since the sailors' other responsibilities, the patrol and defense of the city, had basically come to an end with the wall, Ditch was taking the initiative to learn a trade.

Jacob flashed him a quick grin. "Michael's got him this time."

Ditch said, "No way. Harold's too good."

Harold stalked, almost in a crouch, swaying in and out of the wooden sword's range. Michael stood upright, poised to strike with power. Harold kept trying to bait out an attack; he'd fake to go in and then he leapt back. Michael wasn't falling for it. Then, suddenly, Harold swept by and tapped Michael on the inside of the thigh with the branch.

Happily out of range again, he said, "Touch-point!"

So taken by surprise, Michael had barely moved to respond. He groaned and lowered his sword. "What was that?"

Harold tapped his own leg on the same spot. "There's a blood line through here. Draw an edge across it and the fight's over."

"Ah, of course, I know the one." Michael took position and saluted. "Again."

Ditch nudged Jacob. "Harold knows what's up."

"Fwah. Michael's just taking it easy on him. He doesn't want to hurt him, that's all."

Ditch laughed. "Whatever, man. Harold's gonna school him all day. Watch." Jacob frowned at Ditch and then focused in on the action, shifting and ducking with his fists up, as if he was one of the combatants.

Harold swayed back and forth out of range again and then head-faked Michael into a cautious swing - *whoosh.* The King's Man spun aside under his shield and came to a graceful stop with the tip of his apple-branch poked into Michael's ribs near the armpit.

"Touch-point!"

Michael acknowledged the hit. "Ah, and from there to the heart. You're a difficult target with this *fencing* of yours, Harold."

Harold bowed. "That's gracious to say! Such is the fencer's endeavor. Every attack should be coupled with defense. In fact, that's where the name of the art comes from, the word *defence.*"

"Is that right?"

"Quite!" Harold whipped and brandished his apple-branch athletically. "A true fencer is the deceiver in a quarrel. He seeks first to avoid the point!"

"Ah..."

Over on the stump, Ditch nudged Jacob again, jutted out his chin and said, "What's up?"

Jacob laughed. "You're smug!"

Ditch laughed too. "It's all that feintin' Harold does, man. Michael's used to fightin' stuff that comes right at him. He doesn't know what Harold's gonna do."

Jacob nodded, recollecting past repairs to the sleeve. "That's true."

"Michael's all about that one big shot too. In the gym we used to call that head-huntin. Like when a guy's got a good right hand but that's all he throws, always go'n for the K.O. You're a lot easier to read if you only got one move." Ditch sighed. "Man, I miss gettin' in a good fight."

Jacob paused at the mention of *head-hunting.* "You *miss* fighting?"

"Yeah! It's fun, you know? When you're good at it n' the other guy's good at it. Watchin' a good fight's fun. Trainin's fun. I miss all a' that."

"But you were a slave!"

"Huh?"

"Captain told me you were a pit-slave oversea..." (Captain had been trying to generate a little sympathy for Ditch, in order to help him get the apprenticeship. He'd also inferred that Ditch's tattoos were a type of branding, like the DB Davies put on cattle.) "What was it he said? ...He said you'd been *forced into a blood-sport for the amusement of your unscrupulous masters.*"

"Man, *Pit Slave's* the gym's name. We got paid to fight."

"Whatever for?"

"Cause people like watchin' *these.*" Ditch made fists, bit his lip and sneered at the awesomeness.

"Who'd pay to see those, hey? Fist-fighting's for... savages and... naughty children."

"Pfft! Whatever, man! This is you." Ditch opened his eyes wide and mocked Jacob's earlier shifting and ducking with his fists up, as if he was one of the combatants, only goofier.

Jacob laughed. "I don't do that!"

"Yeah you do! Everybody likes a good fight. Look at you out here watchin' these two."

Michael and Harold guarded, turned and parried, dodged, spun and thrust.

Jacob said, "Sure, but they're not trying to hurt each other."

"We didn't fight to hurt the other guy, man. It wasn't just for the money either. It's about competition, gettin' better, showin' everybody what you can do. For a fighter, that's totally worth a bloody nose or whatever. You know, even if we hated each other, a lot a' times after a fight we'd get this mad respect for the other guy, cause he stepped up. Some a' my best friends were guys that smashed my face."

Jacob thought about it, fighting for the joy of it, not to make war or to kill. It didn't exactly fit the fellowship's definition of violence, to which they were religiously opposed, and Jacob thought it brought up some interesting questions. Then he started thinking about how much had changed over that last year. *Michael's in brown-and-whites for God's sake.* That alone was a shocker.

Despite the horrors of the plague, the sailors were causing a cultural revolution. The fellowship devoured art, literature and philosophy from oversea. Stout farmers braved a life outside of the wall to bring in crops to trade for technology. And as far as any of them knew for sure, they were the only people in the world. Not only had the bauran and the infections disappeared months before, there hadn't been a stranger from any direction in just as long.

Ditch said, "It's cool to see how styles match up. What's Michael's called?"

"What?"

"You know, Harold's got that *fencin*, right? What's the name of Michael's fightin' style?"

"Oh, I think it's called *cutting things in half.*"

"For real?"

Jacob laughed. "No. I don't know that it's got a name. John taught him how to use the way with a sword. He's terribly strong. Michael can't *really* take a swing at Harold, not even with that wood waster. He'd break him through the shield."

Ditch believed it. "Power's no joke. Sometimes head-huntin's fine if you got enough swat. Seen it plenty a' times. Guy's losin' a fight, then - *blough* - out a' nowhere, you know, like a bolt out a' the balloon, it's all over." He waved his arms in the traditional fashion of an old-world referee stopping a bout.

Jacob didn't understand any of that. "Hey?"

Ditch went back to watching the sword-play, wistfully missing his old career. Before the Fall, he'd been thirty-six and mostly in retirement, coaching. His injuries had accumulated and prize-fighting was a young man's sport. But at thirty-eight, with his body carved into its twenties again and his competitive spirit at its peak, it was instead the entire fight-game that had been retired. *Whatever, man.*

Ditch pointed at Michael and Harold. "*That's* what it's all about, right there. You get in there, get a good sparrin' partner and just make each other better. That's the best part."

Jacob scoffed. "Not if your *sparn-partner* flits about like a nesting tit with a wee twig, chirping it up. *Touch-point! Touch-point!* I don't see how that's making Michael any better at anything. He's a devil-slayer, not a dancer."

Ditch laughed. "What d'you want him to do?"

Jacob held up his meaty, blacksmith's fist. "Stand strong. Go blow for blow! Then we'd see who's the better man, hey?"

Ditch rolled his eyes. One minute Jacob was saying *fist-fighting's for savages and naughty children* and the next he wanted Harold to stand in the pocket with Michael and get his clock cleaned. There was too much wrong in there to argue with all of it.

"Look, Michael's your boy, so you don't like seein' him lose, but only bums go in to trade punches. Harold fights smart. Take that stuff he's sayin' about the blood line or whatever, that's straight up *physiology*, man. He's talkin' about the femoral artery. You kick a guy there, put some hard shin on it, you can shut down his footwork and get a real advantage. Inside leg-kicks win fights."

Ditch said the last as a detached aphorism with a shrug. It was something he'd often said when coaching in order to discourage fighters from head-hunting. He smiled, remembering calling it out from the corner. *Inside leg-kicks win fights! Inside leg-kicks win fights!* He could almost feel the canvas and almost hear the cheering crowd.

Jacob said, "If you're going to kick a man there, why not just kick him in the peaches?"

Ditch paused. Then he leaned forward and started cackling with his rapid-fire, raucous laughter, like a hyena in a henhouse. It distracted Michael and gave Harold an opening.

"Touch-point!"

"God's mercy!"

Ditch giggled through an explanation about the fight business for Jacob. "Cause that's against the rules, man! In the street, yeah, kick 'em there all day, but nobody's gonna pay to see a couple guys bustin' each other in the balls!" Jacob laughed along with him.

* * *

A sun-bleached skeleton was tangled in the thorn bushes to the west. Its tattered clothing had outlasted its flesh. Once, it had been the smoke's instrument of death, a dreaded bauran, but those only consumed themselves. Over time, its nature and exposure had worn it too spare even to pull itself free.

John's pinto passed the skeleton coming in toward Antioch. The rider slowed to have a look. Under a hooded cloak, he wore a sleek, black uniform with a silver cross threaded into the chest. A rapier hung from his hip. He spurred the horse on.

The closer he came to the wall, the larger it looked. He trotted up next to its eighteen-foot height and realized he wouldn't be able to jump it even if he stood on Sarah's back - he'd caused much dismay by naming the horse that. He'd have to find another way in.

It took him an hour to ride around the entire town. There wasn't a single tree close enough to help him over, and the four gates - North, South, East and West - were each as unscalable as the rest. Each also had a cord leading up above to a bell. He guessed those were for ringing to get in but he didn't want to announce his presence like that, not until he knew for sure if that old rascal Abraham was in there.

He rode to the orchard in the north and got down to share some apples with his horse and to think. It was in the same season of the year before that he'd first come to Antioch after losing his father and sister to the plague. He was that year older, taller and thicker. And, hidden in the shadows of his hood, Daniel's eyes had lost some of their froggishness.

The north gate would be the closest to the Cauldron, where he wanted to go first. He trusted Fergus. All he had to do was figure out a way to get in. So, he sat there until dusk, eating apples, feeding apples to Sarah and staring at the wall without a clue. He'd almost given up and was about to ring the bell when a marble-mouthed voice startled him from behind.

"Are you going in?"

Daniel spun to his feet in a whirl of cloak and silver, his rapier drawn before he'd seen or asked who it was. Barabbas backed up, eyes wide in a shade between blue and amber. A sparse scraggle of a beard was coming in around his neck and didn't hide his teeth yet. From far away and in the fading light, they could have been boys of the same age, one groomed in a uniform and the other wild in furs.

Daniel lowered his sword and frowned. "What do you want, gunder?"

Barabbas sat down, scratched and thought for a moment. "I want my own pride. I want to sit in the tree."

Daniel turned away disdainfully, sheathing his elegant weapon. "Go sit in a tree then. I don't have time for a gunder like you. I'm on an important mission." While Barabbas contemplated what would happen if he tried to sit in Apoc's tree, Daniel stared at the wall and recalled those first words: *Are you going in?*

"Gunder, do you know how to get into the city?"

"Yes."

Daniel waited. Then he sighed. Then he lost patience and said, "How?!"

Barabbas queered at him. Having already dissociated that question from the last, he wondered what the little man meant by it. It was such a broad thing to ask, how. *How... how... how what?*

"Fwah! How do I get inside?!"

Barabbas was shocked. *He's listening out loud!* "Jump over the wall."

Daniel groaned. "I can't jump over that wall. It's too high for me."

"Ring the bell."

"I can't do that either!"

He can't ring a bell? "Are you dookussed?"

"What? No! I don't even know what that means!" *Stupid gunders and their stupid words that don't mean anything! I'll just have to figure it out on my own.* Daniel settled his gaze on the wall again as though it was a masterful opponent in a game of strategy.

Barabbas was bamboozled. The little man wasn't dookussed but couldn't ring a bell or jump over the wall. It was a difficult set of problems. *How is he going to get in? Hmm... how... how... Oh! The little man might know.* "How are you going to get inside?"

Daniel threw his hands up and shouted all of his words into one. "*Aaahstupidgundergetawayfromme!*"

Barabbas hissed and cut out of there in a scramble. He stopped three trees down, peering back. *The little man is dangerous.*

Daniel gave up. He'd just have to ring the bell and take his chances. *If Abraham comes, there's gonna be a fight, and I'm ready for it.* He took up Sarah's reins and led her to the gate. Then, right when he was about to pull the cord, he got an idea.

"Psst! Gunder!"

From back where he'd stayed watching, Barabbas said, "What?"

"Come jump over the wall and open the door for me."

There was a pause. Then, "Ok."

Barabbas shot out of the trees, kicking up leaves, vaulted into one step off the wall and then easily over the top. He landed with a soft thump on the other side. The guardhouse and the watch platform were empty. He had the gate unbarred and opened in a minute.

Daniel walked his horse through and said, "Thanks," in passing. Barabbas scratched and waved. Neither of them considered closing the gate.

* * *

Daniel left Sarah by the smokehouse and crept like an assassin toward the kitchen. The doorway glowed in the darkening night. He pulled his hood back and listened. Fergus was talking inside.

"Hoo-hoo! Then our little pixies go to work and scream us up a batch of good dough for the baking!"

"Grandpa! I'm not a dummy. There's no wizards or pixies."

Daniel frowned, guessing that was one of Davies' boys.

Fergus said, "Oh, ho, there's not, is there? Well, what do you think makes the bread rise then, *not-a-dummy?*"

"God?"

"He's the one that makes the pixies, isn't he? Put some good lungs on them too. Just listen... *Help me! Heeelp meee!* Oh, no! Did you hear that? Poor devils."

The little boy laughed. "That was you, Grandpa!"

Fergus chuckled.

As they spooned yeast into the dough-bowls to bloom, the little boy asked, "Grandpa, is there really magic?" He didn't think of hospital as magic of course. He'd been around that all his life, just like everyone else in the fellowship.

Fergus said, "Sure there is! Here, let me show you some. Give us a hug."

Daniel guessed from the following silence that they were hugging and thought he heard Fergus whisper something. Then the little boy said, "I love you too, Grandpa."

Daniel felt less then like he was being cautious and more like he was spying. He stepped into the kitchen and knocked on the door. When they looked up, he raised a black-gloved finger to his lips and went, "Shh…"

Fergus beamed at him and exclaimed, "Daniel!" as loud as anything.

Daniel's eyes bulged and he started waving frantically. "SSSHHH!"

Fergus laughed, went over and embraced him. "What are you doing, boy? You're hissing like Barabbas!"

"Is Abraham around?"

"What? No! No one's seen hide-nor-hair of him since the lot of you left! I'm so glad to see you!"

Daniel exhaled and got another hug. The little boy stared up at him from behind the butcher table, not placing the black-clad stranger as the one who'd punched and spat on his father a year before, but getting a bad feeling from him all the same.

Fergus said, "Where's John?"

"He's back in Golgotha."

Fergus realized then that Golgotha had survived and that other towns might have survived as well. He thought about what a dangerous trip it must have been for Daniel. "What are you doing here?"

"I'm on a secret mission. I'm here to get a book from the church."

Fergus frowned. "Does John know where you are?"

Daniel paused long enough to reveal the truth. Then he lied. "He's the one that sent me."

Fergus let it go. Daniel was safe right then, which was the most important thing. Instead of confronting him for the lie, Fergus said, "You must be starving. Let me make you something to eat."

Daniel ate there in the kitchen and then out in the common room too (which was quiet compared to the time he'd spent there but much busier than when Michael's bell used to ring.) He answered questions from all sides wherever he went. Margot squealed, "*Ooh!*" hugged him and asked about John. Everyone asked about bauran. Harold was there, desperate to know if any King's Men had made it to Golgotha and Captain sat smoking and listening.

Daniel told that John was fine and sent everyone reeling with the news that they'd seen neither a bauran nor a king's soldier the whole year. There were hands on heads across the room and a general discussion about what it all meant. Daniel removed himself from it. He'd found something more important, Sarah, the girl. She was more beautiful than he remembered.

Daniel offered her a chair. She was happy to sit with him and to talk, ready to catch up like old friends. She didn't ask many questions, though, and kept on and on about some boy named Edward, who Daniel didn't want to hear about.

Daniel strove to impress her. "I won't be here for long. I've got a big job to do back in Golgotha. I'll be leaving soon."

"Wow, that's neat! Edward's got a big job too. He works the church's stable for Michael. He was doing it even before the wall was finished. Andalynn said it was very brave of him to go out there every day through the graveyard, and she's the bravest person I know, so that's really saying something."

Edward... "I've been riding and camping by myself for two weeks. I didn't have a wall."

Sarah gasped and covered her mouth. "You must be tired! Where are you going to sleep? I'm in your old room now, Andalynn and Biggs have mine. Ooh, I know, maybe you could stay with Edward! I'm sure he'd let you. He's ever so generous."

Edward again? Daniel pointed at himself. "*I'm* on a secret mission."

"Really? What is it?" Sarah loved a good secret.

Daniel divulged it readily. "I'm here to get a book that will help us kill a devil in Golgotha. It's an evil rascal called a *gaffot.* Everyone is depending on me." He puffed out his chest and made himself look important.

"Wow! That is a big job! But, at least you don't have any bauran there, like you said. Nothing could be worse than them. You can be thankful for that no matter what devils you've got." Sarah nodded wisely and then started thinking about Edward.

Daniel was annoyed. The conversation was not going as planned. It was hard for him but he didn't care for any more chit-chat so he got right to the point. "I'm not just here for a book,

Sarah. I came all this way for you, to take you back with me. We're supposed to get married, remember?"

Her mouth fell open.
The room began to listen.
Daniel said, "What's wrong?"

Sarah squirmed. "Ooh... uh, I... Daniel, wow, that wasn't... eeuh." Aware of the silence around them, she lowered her voice. "I'm seventeen... You're thirteen..."
"Fourteen." He didn't know why she was being so stupid. He was a year older too.
Sarah froze. Then she rose slowly out her chair. "I just remembered. I have to go upstairs." She turned her back on him and scooted away, a straight line of uncomfortable girl.
Daniel didn't understand at all. Recalling some advice Judas had given him, he stood up and shouted, "I named my horse after you!" as if that was delightful and would bring her right back.
Sarah accelerated, up and out of sight onto the second floor's landing. Daniel dropped his hands to his sides, confused, and stayed that way for a long time, watching that spot on the stairs.
Everyone else drew together, cringing and whispering, their greater concerns briefly muted in that moment of humiliating rejection. Then Daniel overheard their conversations. The whispers revealed that Sarah had been courting Edward for some time, that Fergus had been baking his wicked apple pies for them left and right, and that she hadn't ever shown much interest in John's nephew.
Captain strolled over to Fergus, blew smoke and said low, "Boy's named a horse after your daughter."
Fergus nodded sadly and reached out for the pipe. "I guess he has."
"Is that something you do around here?"
"No."
"Mmm, seems a dubious compliment to pay a young lady..." Captain tapped himself on the nose. "Still, better than a boat I suppose."
Daniel slumped into his chair and stared at his empty plate, just beginning to feel like a fool. Then he covered his face - he

knew it was coming and he couldn't stop it - he wept in front of everyone.

* * *

The church door opened and Michael looked up from the round table where he wrote by the hearth's light and a candle. He'd been translating script into Meroan every evening after Andalynn left. Pillars of books surrounded him on the floor, twice the number that originally came out of the back room. They'd been bringing up more from Ezekiel's tomb.

Harold walked in out of the night with Daniel, whom Michael didn't recognize right away in that black and silver uniform. Harold said, "This boy has just arrived from Golgotha. He says he knows you." Daniel frowned at the introduction.

Then Michael knew who he was. "Daniel!" He hurried over to take his hand, asking right away about John. Daniel liked that much better and told everything as he had at the Cauldron. Michael darkened almost immediately, listening to the rest with cold scrutiny.

When Daniel finished, Michael said, "Harold, would you mind giving us a moment alone?"

Harold did mind. He wanted to know what Michael was going to do. He wanted to explore beyond the wall and to find out if anyone in the north had survived. But, he also had a soldier's respect for authority and Michael was the Lord of Antioch.

Harold said, "Certainly. I'll just take a few ledgers with me to practice the script." Michael nodded, keeping a hard look on Daniel, who was starting to get nervous. Harold collected his things and closed the door as he left.

As soon as they were alone, Michael said, "You're lying."

"No I'm not, I…"

"Don't lie to me! John would never have sent you all that way by yourself. Tell me the truth."

Daniel paused, about to lie again, but Michael's glowering disapproval frightened him. "Ok, you're right. He didn't send me."

"Does he know where you are!?"

"No. I didn't tell him, but…"

"He must be beside himself! Do you have any idea what you've done? No! No, of course you don't! How could you, you careless child." Michael radiated anger and disappointment. He could only hope John hadn't left his post to look for Daniel. *No, John wouldn't do that.*

Daniel felt about to cry again. *Not in front of Michael, please, no...* The whole trip was turning out to be horrible. "I'm going back! He just really needs that book. I was afraid he'd come after me. That's why I didn't tell him where I..."

"Why would you be afraid of John? What's happened between the two of you?"

"No! That's not what I meant! I was afraid to tell him because I know he can't leave Golgotha and he wouldn't've let me go if I asked. I heard him talking to Fagan about the book, but they couldn't come to get it, because of the smoke. So I came to get it for them."

It didn't sound like the whole story, but Michael saw some sense in it. If there was something vital in that book, if they did need it in Golgotha, Daniel would have been the only one capable of coming after it, provided he'd learned anything from his master. "You can open the way?"

Daniel said, "Yes," though he often wished he couldn't.

"Well, that's something at least. You weren't completely defenseless. Can you pull?" That skill was more complicated. He doubted Daniel could do it. Andalynn, though a rapid study, was still in the practicing stages of it.

Daniel looked away, wiping tears out of his eyes.

Michael saw the truth. "It's more difficult to do for someone else than it is to do for yourself, isn't it?"

The boy choked up.

Michael was disgusted. "Are you crying? Stop that!"

"I can't! It's my stupid path. I cry all the time now. I hate it!" Daniel hid his face and did everything he could to stop. Then he cried even more because it didn't matter; he'd already looked like a fool in front of everyone.

Michael paused, understanding. A path could be strong and difficult to control for a long time after awakening, especially so without diligent practice. He'd forgotten about that because Andalynn's was so unusually calm. "What is it, some kind of sadness?"

Daniel sniffled into his elbow. "Sorrow."

Michael pitied him with a sigh. It wasn't hard to guess why Daniel would have a path like that. And, being so young, he would grow into a man under a cloud of its influence.

"Don't look at me like that! It's not my fault!"

"I know. Sit down." Michael motioned to a chair at the table and went to one of his pillars of books. He lifted five off the top, set them aside to preserve the order and then picked up two more, one in each hand. "So, you've got a gaffot in Golgotha, do you?"

"Yes, sir."

Michael nodded. "It's always something. I've this one copied into Meroan as well. You'll be able to read it on your way back, unless John's taught you the script, of course. Then I'd prefer to hold on to the translation."

"No, he hasn't taught me, but I can't read Meroan either, so it doesn't matter."

Again Michael pitied him. He put the book of script in front of Daniel and returned the other to its place. "Ask him to. He taught me, you know." Michael went to a different stack, pulled out a different kind of book and sat next to Daniel. "I want you to take this one as well. It was the first thing I thought to translate when I started doing all of this. Have John read it to you."

"What is it?"

"It's called *The Six Beginnings*, written by the saint, Matthew. It's more than a hundred years old now but I've found it to be a useful study on the nature of paths. It helped me to understand some of the things I went through with my own. Shall I read some to you?"

"Ok."

Michael flipped through to a specific passage. "Ah, here it is. Matthew says: *Sadness is the noblest of these emotions, because it is through our own sadness that we understand each other's pain. Only one without sadness could ever truly be alone. The known paths of sadness are…*"

Michael read on and Daniel sat listening, not so sure this *Matthew* knew what he was talking about. Daniel felt both sad *and* alone, terribly and all the time. But, he was also glad Michael didn't seem to be angry with him anymore.

Daniel spent that night in the church. Michael suggested he stay and rest for a few days, but Daniel said there was no time, that he needed to act. Michael remembered saying something similar to John once.

* * *

The next morning, Michael left a note on the door so they could share a mediocre breakfast at the inn. Daniel didn't want to eat at the Cauldron. Michael didn't argue with him about it.

Their conversation was spare. Michael prodded the bad food, remembering the last time they'd eaten together. That had been a bitter-sweet affair for them all. He said, "Ah, I know. What's the best thing in the kitchen, Daniel?"

Daniel said, "Not this," without a trace of humor and ate it anyway.

Michael chuckled. "Do you know, I think I'd like to send a letter to John. Could you stay long enough for me to write one?"

"Ok. Maybe Grandpa won't be so mad that way. I'll get my horse up while you're at it."

"There won't be any need for that. I've the stable-boy outfitting her as we speak." Michael smiled, happy to lessen Daniel's burden.

Daniel paused, bug-eyed, having just taken a mouthful of salty eggs on toast. *Edward* was the stable-boy. Daniel didn't want *Edward* saddling Sarah - *at all*. Food blasted from his mouth as he shouted, "Fwah! No thanks! I'll do that myself!" He jumped out of his chair.

Betheford, who was coming over, cried, "My word! What's that language for the breakfast table?"

Michael did something of the same. "God's mercy! Go right ahead then!"

Daniel had already run out of the inn's double doors. While Betheford's common room recovered from the inappropriate outburst, Michael thought he remembered that Daniel *might* have just referred to John as *Grandpa* a moment before. He'd have to ask him about that later.

By the time Daniel reached the stable, it was too late. The pinto was shoed, saddled and brushed. He found the precious books in her pack and some good food from the Cauldron too, which meant Edward had been through his things. Daniel burned with hatred.

Edward walked out of the back. He was seventeen, tall and thin. Daniel was three years younger but on his way to being a giant like Horace. They both weighed one hundred and thirty five pounds. Edward smiled at him. "She's all yours!" Then, just as he left the stable, just within earshot, he snickered.

"What's so funny?"

Edward paused and then turned around; there was a little too much challenge in the way Daniel had spoken. "It's just that, you named the horse *Sarah*. That's so stupid!" He laughed, not necessarily trying to be mean, but genuinely amused. It was obvious he'd heard everything.

Daniel was mortified. His large eyes started to water.

"I'm sorry. You're not going to cry, are you?" That was Edward being mean.

Daniel did cry. He followed his path to the source, ripped it up like a thorn bush and let the rain fly. Then he grabbed Edward by the shirt and slammed him into the wall. It could have been Ares kicking the stall the way the whole stable shook. Bridles and tack trembled to fall and a jar of shoe-nails crashed to the floor.

Edward blacked out for a split second and then gasped from having the wind knocked out of him. He swatted and scratched to get away but Daniel was too strong - impossibly strong. It seemed like an ax would've bounced off of him. Twisted with sadness and rage, tears spurting out of his ducts, Daniel had the expression of someone who was very, very sorry for being about to rip another person apart. Edward was terrified.

A burlap sack of horseshoes dropped to the ground behind them - *clank*. "What're you do'n, kid?"

Daniel turned around with that terrible face.

It was Ditch, in a sweat from the forge. The pictures on his skin snaked out from under his tank top and dipped into the clefts of his muscles. Though small for a grown man, he was a beast next to these teenagers.

Daniel shouted, "Go away, you stupid sailor!" and turned back to Edward, who was so firmly pinned he might as well have been impaled.

Ditch nodded, *alright*, promptly walked up and kicked Daniel between the legs from behind. It was beyond Daniel's ability to concentrate through the pain. He let go and doubled over in the dirt.

Ditch said, "Get out a' there, Ed," which Edward did, gladly. Ditch had heard Daniel was back in town. Guessing the kid was *all pumped-up on the way, or whatever,* like Michael, it didn't seem fair to let him stomp the stable-boy. Ditch put himself between the two and said, "You wanna fight? Fight me."

Daniel wanted to do exactly that. He found his path again and tore it loose. It was the quickest recovery from a groin-shot Ditch had ever seen. Daniel charged, the intentions plain on his face: *Let's see how* YOU *like it!* He brought his foot all the way back to Golgotha, ready to punt Ditch through the roof.

Ditch almost laughed as he circled out of the way. Daniel flew past like he was jumping a hurdle. *Yeah, they always wanna pay you back with the same,* Ditch thought, strutting out into the open. He looked back over his shoulder, pretending to be thoroughly unimpressed.

Daniel charged him again. Ditch circled out and - *smack* - slapped him in the face.

It wasn't the hardest slap but to Daniel it was worse than a low-blow, it was more personal. Only his father had ever hit him in the face like that. He was too shocked to concentrate. The sudden loss of riin's strength caused a weird shift in his momentum and he dropped onto his hands and knees in the dirt again, crying.

Ditch walked away. "Keep it up, kid. You're gonna learn how to get hit, that's all."

Ditch didn't want to hurt him. He wanted to break his spirit. He figured Daniel was already in tears, so it wouldn't be long before he gave up. Then he'd show him a little respect and they'd all go get something to eat together and be friends. *Pfft, I might even make up with Fergus while I'm at it.* It seemed like a good day to kill a feud.

Edward cheered, "Yeah! Give it to him, Ditch!"

Daniel headed for Edward then, who shouted and ran for his life.

Ditch out-paced them both like it was child's play, hook-tripped Daniel and sent him sprawling into the dirt on his face again. Walking away, he said, "Don't worry about Ed. I'm your problem."

Daniel went berserk. His strength was useless. It didn't matter what he did, he couldn't lay a hand on either of them.

Ditch was too fast, circling out of the way, slapping him, tripping him and pushing him down, over and over, all while Edward laughed and cheered. The dirt and tears turned into mud on Daniel's cheeks. Then he remembered his rapier. He drew it without a second thought, ready to kill that stupid sailor.

Ditch's eyes narrowed. Playtime was over. He saw the weapon as a three foot reach advantage with a hard, sharp edge. He thought about backing off, that it might be smart, but instead decided to teach that clumsy kid a lesson about fighting dirty.

Unfortunately, Daniel wasn't clumsy with his sword. He feinted once, spun and shoved it up to the hilt through the sailor's lung. Then he ripped it out and walked away, paying Ditch back with a look.

Ditch was stunned. He couldn't believe it. The breath hitched in his chest and he put his hand over a sputtering hole. His lung collapsed, filling with blood. Something Jacob had said popped into his mind: *John taught him how to use the way with a sword. I think it's called cutting things in half.*

Edward didn't know what to do. That silvery steel had been sticking out of Ditch's back and when it pulled through, Edward realized something awful. "Ooh, you're a *murderer*... Michael's gonna cut your neck off!" He sprinted for the church to tell.

Ditch fell to his knees. It was excruciating to breathe. He thought Daniel was about to kill him, or worse, heal him. *If that kid tries to put the hospital on me, I'm a' get him. I'm a' get him in the eye.*

Daniel sheathed his sword, tears streaming. He didn't know how any of it had happened but he knew he couldn't face Michael. *I'm a murderer.* He wished he could take it all back, or that he could heal Ditch, but he couldn't. He could only run away. Daniel wailed, "I'm sooorry!" and ran into the stable.

Ditch coughed and wheezed, bewildered. "Man... that's messed up..."

Daniel tore out of there on Sarah, his cloak fluttering behind them. He rode hard and didn't look back, hoping the sailor wouldn't die, that Michael would reach him in time.

Heading west out of the clearing, he decided not to use that gate. It was the shortest path to Golgotha. If he had any trouble leaving town, if they somehow managed to catch him, it would happen there. *They'll look for me there... because I'm a murderer.* The north gate gave him the same doubts and he couldn't bear to pass the Cauldron so he turned south on the city's streets.

Sarah's hooves clashed over the cobblestones like the world was coming to an end. She wasn't the skittish thing she'd been before. Under Daniel's hand she was a bold charger. People dodged out of the way. Daniel tried not to worry about them. They didn't know what had happened and wouldn't know to tell anyone they'd seen him, not until he'd escaped from Antioch.

The southern guardhouse and watch platform were empty, to his relief, but that gate was much different on the inside than it was on the out. Flowers, old and new, in wreathes and arrangements, leaned against its base like gifts. When he leapt down to lift the bolt, he saw words chiseled into the wood all around.

Daniel couldn't read but, as he opened the gate and the arrangements fell over, he began to understand. They left a bouquet on his mother's grave every year on Becca's birthday. Those words were names. They were the names of loved ones lost to the plague. The southern gate had become a memorial. It was Meroe's tombstone.

All of those people, they were never coming back. Overcome by his path again, Daniel went to his saddle bag. He took out a rough carving of a pig and left it among the flowers.

28 The Third Meridian

zekiel looked at himself in the mirror of a window-lit
public restroom. He had failed. He could hold life in his
hands, bend it into shapes and even stop its flow, but
he couldn't bring it back once it was gone. Not yet. He felt he'd
come closer every time, with each of his daughters and his son
and then his grandson, but resurrection remained just out of
reach. There was an element he was missing.

Perhaps the solution lies in those forbidden paths. But no, he
wasn't insane with grief anymore. He knew the dangers of those.
In those paths he risked himself. Venturing into them for
Elizabeth had been a short-sighted mistake. *She was going to die
anyway*, he told himself, *eventually. She never would have loved me if
I'd just kept her alive. I've learned that much from the others. Truly,
loving me was the only purpose she served.*

No, he'd simply have to try again within his boundaries.
What was thirty years anyway? He couldn't remember how old
he really was, certainly much older than this man in the mirror.
He imagined that if he were to look his age, he'd be no more than
a fragile column of dust, ready to fall apart at the slightest breath
of motion.

He needed to change. The waitress out in the restaurant was
pale and black haired. He'd make himself look like that. He hadn't
looked like that in a while.

The color drained from his face, leaving a shade of waitress in
its wake, down into his shirt collar. Under his clothes it did the
same, pulling out of every surface and collecting into his left arm.
That hand became darker and darker with lightness creeping
down above it. The tip of the index finger began to distend,
swelling with melanin like a blackberry. When he was almost an

albino, he plucked his previous hue and left it on the sink, encased in his fingerprint.

He squeezed the basic structures out of his recent meal, began dissolving and growing bone and sprouted straight and black hair under his old, tight and white curls. The skin elasticized on his strengthening frame as the materials of his appearance exchanged. The energy behind the shift was limitless. When he was finished, he took out a pair of scissors. He looked ridiculous.

Ezekiel paid his tab as a different man with a sloppy haircut and stepped outside into a warm breeze. The waitress queered out at him through the window. The restaurant was a quaint little building with the bark still on its pillars, built cozily into a grove of trees. Seeking out the last of his blood relatives had taken Ezekiel deep into the country.

An annoying stinging in his left eye made him squint. He brought his fingers up to rub it at first. When the irritation persisted, he examined his reflection. Something small and vicious was growing by division in his eye, rapidly.

* * *

All of the Great Nations' militaries were either ignorant or at critical security, there was no in-between. The plague was faster than the post. Major cities across the continent evacuated on their own accord. The safest response, however, was to stay out of open air.

General Alexander, his crisp uniform armored with decorations, led a group of soldiers and scientists from the headquarters of an underground system of bunkers. Those surrounding him were alive because of his quick and tough decisions. They were absolutely loyal to him and busy at their tasks, ready for his orders.

Then, suddenly, every one of them collapsed, hundreds across the room. In one moment, rifles clattered under combat fatigues, coffee arced from dropping cups, and papers spilled to the floor to float in low, slipping courses. Alexander stood alone in the middle of the event. He understood what had happened. It had been twenty years, but he'd seen it before. Ezekiel was coming.

He considered drawing his pistol and holding it on the door. But, he didn't and then the door opened and Ezekiel came through in his latest disguise. The altered appearance didn't come as a surprise. Alexander had seen him in countless faces. He could only hope this version would be useful.

"Oh, Alex, thank everything you're alright. You're the first one I thought of when I found out what was happening."

Alexander was unreceptive. "Are they dead?"

"Well, I don't know. Like I said, you're the first one I came to see."

Alexander frowned and indicated his fallen company.

Ezekiel said, "Oh, that. No, they're asleep."

"What do you want?"

"That's fairly obvious isn't it? I'm here to help you."

"Good. I'm working on the *best* response to the plague, the *best* way to move around above ground and the *best* way to aid the suffering holdouts on the surface. I assume you're immune to this disease." He strode to the wall map with his pointer. "You can find and bring in survivors from sector seven-G."

Ezekiel paused at having been given orders. "But, we can't bother with *these*," he said, gesturing at the sleeping men and women. "We have to find the others. They're in danger."

Alexander put his hands behind his back. "I don't care if they are. I'm not interested in abandoning my responsibilities. You can stay and help me with what I'm doing or you can carry me out of here."

Ezekiel was taken aback. *He really means that... How sad.* Alexander had always been his favorite, the oldest and wisest of his glorious immortals, his rare friends. *He looks rather like a bellboy in that uniform, a fantastic genius of a bellboy. If he hadn't met me, he'd have ruled the world for a time.*

Ezekiel conceded. He had to hurry. The others needed and might even want his help. But before leaving, he'd do everything he could for this one. He found a pen and some paper in the mess and started writing. "I won't do either, Alex. I know of a place where they can cure this, whatever this is. You should be safe at sea." He stopped and looked up. "It's very far from here. Your only other option is to come with me."

"I'll take directions to the place if that's the choice."

Ezekiel sighed and went back to writing. "Be careful with the men there. They're dangerous. They'll destroy you if they even suspect that I've instructed you."

"So, it's finally a good thing you never did." Alexander turned away to check on his soldiers.

"Like I said, even if they *suspect*. You must appear absolutely ignorant. Promise me you will do so."

"They're like you?"

Ezekiel's eyes darted. "Somewhat. They're called the Circle. You must deliver them this secret note. No... have one of your, one of *those* give it to them." He flicked his fingers at the sleepers again and went back to writing.

"When did you last meet with them?"

"The last time I collected my books from you I suppose. When was that?" He didn't look up from writing to ask.

Alexander put his palm over his face. That was over two hundred years ago. Ezekiel seemed to have no concept of how long that was or how much could have changed. The Great Nations were little more than warring, ethnic tribes two hundred years ago. The place in reference might be a wilderness or even a crater by now. Then again, outside of appearances, Ezekiel hadn't changed at all in much longer than that.

Ezekiel took out a leather-bound journal from behind his back, the record of his latest work on resurrection, and put it on top of the two notes he'd written. "This place, it's where I take the books. You do it this time, but remember - *you don't know anything.*" Alexander nodded. Then Ezekiel said, "Good luck, Alex," and left.

Everyone started waking up when he was gone. They found Alexander sitting in study of what Ezekiel had left behind. The first note had directions in Continental that led to a land outside of discovery, past the endless ocean's mythical third meridian, and ended in a place labeled, "Antioch."

So, this is where he takes the books. How many times has he crossed this impossible distance? How does he do it? He flipped through the journal. It appeared to be yet another tedious volume of Ezekiel's psychotic babble.

Alexander had secrets too. He'd deciphered the script on his own, long ago. He put the journal aside and read the second note to himself. *"Armageddon is arrived,* that's the truth, no matter what you believe. *Break your silence...* hmm. *Open the library."* He rubbed his face in contemplation.

Corporal Lyons wobbled over to him, still recovering. "Sir! What happened, sir?"

Alexander made up his mind right then. "Send out my command to ready the fleet, corporal. It's time to evacuate all non-essential personnel." He handed her the journal. "Add this to my private collection and have all of it loaded onto the *Vesper*. She'll serve as a flagship." He handed her the directions. "Give this to her captain and have him report to me immediately for briefing. I know it's slower but use the tunnels from now on."

He'd meant what he said. He wouldn't abandon his responsibilities. But, if there was a safe place in the world, he knew of a few thousand refugees who deserved a shot at it.

Lyons gave him a bleary salute and then looked at the directions. Her face opened with surprise. "This leads across the third meridian! No one knows what's out that far!"

Alexander frowned at her. "Do you need me to repeat your orders, corporal?"

Lyons recovered herself at attention. "Sir! No, sir!"

"Carry them out."

"Sir! Yes, sir!"

* * *

The *Grace* was anchored off the coast. Captain, the only one aboard, lay back in a folding lounge chair on the front deck with his long, auburn waves in a greasy draggle. He'd a beautiful green macaw perched on the headrest behind him and a brown bottle of rum in hand. He would spend weeks at a time out there in solitude, except for the company of his bird, drifting in and out of a drunken stupor.

He offered her a soda cracker over his shoulder. "What do you say there, Beatrice, if you drink and smoke yourself to death, that doesn't count as a suicide, now does it?" He'd been asking her that all day.

Beatrice held the treat in one foot, nibbled it and whistled. Then she blasted out, "Rrrawk! Smoke yourself to *DEATH!*"

The shocking volume of it made Captain duck. Then he laughed, delighted with her. "Oh Aye? That's a new one for you!

There's a good girl." Beatrice didn't have a very large vocabulary. Captain thought that made what she said all the more important, so he took her advice and lit his pipe.

He smoked for a good long while and fed crackers to his bird. She liked the salt in them. Near dusk, Ezekiel climbed over the railing, soaking wet, like a devil out of the depths, and spluttered, "Noah! Thank everything you're alive!"

Screech - "Smoke yourself to *DEATH*" - *whistle.*

Ezekiel gasped at the bird.

Captain didn't bother to look up. He'd gone by a lot of different names but there was only one person left in the world who knew him as Noah. "Kafferway's Llama! What? Do you need money again already?"

Ezekiel said, "No..." thought, *not this one too,* and missed Elizabeth. "Have you even moved from that spot? Don't you know what's happening?"

Captain glanced at him and then recoiled. "Gaaah! You're an ill sight every time, to be true! What do you want?"

Ezekiel went to him and told of the devastation on land. It had taken him a week to reach the *Grace* from Alexander's bunker. The plague was wiping out towns and cities as fast as he could travel.

Captain had to believe it, considering the source. He took it all in with a depressed horror and then resignation and a drink. "The end of the world. Maybe it's time for that."

"No! We have to find the others! All of you can gather around me to survive this!"

"Oh, aye? No, I don't think I'll be going in for that. I'll just stay here and let what happens happen." Noticing Ezekiel's frustration, he said, "Do what you're going to, of course. I can't stop you. But, you'll have to carry me every step of the way."

Ezekiel conceded once again. "Do you have paper and a marker?"

Captain made a lazy motion at the deckhouse door and returned to his chair. Ezekiel came out later with two notes similar to the ones he'd written for Alexander and gave the same instructions. Then he said, "Good luck to you, Noah," and headed for the side.

Having given everything a little more thought, Captain said, "Oh, ah, before you go… I might have some trouble getting to this place of yours. You see, I've no crew aboard."

"How many do you need?"

The *Grace* sailed well with twenty. She could comfortably house sixty-five. Captain said, "I'll need a hundred and thirty or so, without a doubt." He figured they could double up in the bunks.

"A hundred and thirty! I don't have time for that! I have to find the others!"

"Aye, indeed you do. You, you go on ahead with that. I'll just go ashore and try to find a crew by myself."

Ezekiel hated his choices. "Fine! I'll need your lifeboat." It sat twenty.

Captain almost grinned. "Here, let me help you with it." When they had it in the water and Ezekiel had the oars in place, Captain shouted down, "Don't bring me only men, now! That makes for a dull voyage!"

Ezekiel didn't respond to that foolishness. There wouldn't be much to choose from anyway. He rowed the dark water into glistening ripples on his way toward a blacked out city under the moon. There, in its deserted alleys, his eyes flashed as they rejected random trails of infection. His perception stretched out through the walls like a search light. He saw any life within a hundred yards.

When bauran came upon him, they didn't cast the shining reflections of living people. They had dull, smoldering glows, like dead bodies. They were alive enough to unravel, though, and weren't much of a threat. Curiously, when he pulled their riin through for the death stroke, it felt as though it came through a sieve. He didn't know what to make of it and still couldn't spare the time to investigate. His immortals' lives were too important.

Ezekiel filled the lifeboat with survivors and rowed them out in slow trips. The delay tortured him. Many of the people he found were so old and feeble that he simply kept them unconscious and carried them, because it saved time. Their bodies were soft bags around delicate frames, just a flinch from being crushed in his grip.

Captain stood waiting for them on the *Grace* with lanterns in place to light the way. When Ezekiel headed back out to the city, the survivors woke up and wandered around, wondering where they were and how they'd gotten there. One old man came up and said, "Scuse me there, scout. Where'd that Zeke get to?" Captain held up his hands as if he didn't know anything and went around trying to convince them all to lie down. The front of the ship started to look like a field hospital.

Every time Ezekiel returned, everyone but Captain fell unconscious, some with the brutal thud of their flesh hitting the deck. It kept them out of the way. Captain wondered if it was possible for them to be injured like that, despite being within Ezekiel's power when it happened. It was unpleasant, no matter, and played havoc with their memories.

Ezekiel's arduous trips continued until a few hours after dawn, when he returned with the last ten, making one hundred and thirty exactly. He could have fit ten more in that boat. Captain didn't want to think about that.

Ezekiel glared. "That's all of them you asked for."

"Without a doubt, every one, but... I still can't make it all that way without provisions, now can I?" Captain had a cargo list prepared that would stock the ship for an impossible journey, for a hundred and thirty. "Here, I've written down the things I'll need."

Ezekiel's mouth fell open when looked at the list. He was still gaping when he looked back at Captain.

"Oh, now, you can improvise on some of the items I've marked, of course. Like this one here, see? Aye, indeed, it's quite a lot. We could go ashore and get it ourselves, but, well..."

Ezekiel questioned whether it would have been easier to carry the man around after all, or just let him die. No, too much trouble for one and too valuable for the other. He'd already contemplated whether any of his rare friends would be appropriate for attempts at resurrection, since their loss would be so dear, and had come to the conclusion that thirty years of common love was one thing to sacrifice, centuries of reliable genius was another. No, he'd no way of knowing if any of the others were still alive. He had to do as much as he could to provide for each one he managed to find.

He held up the cargo list with an empty threat. "There'd better not be anything else after this!" Then he went back down in the lifeboat. It took him two days of constant work to return with everything.

Captain didn't drink or smoke in the time between trips. He pretended to be one of the survivors, using their stories to add essential items to the cargo list, things like goggles, respirators and bleach. A fifty-one year old Andalynn was a valuable source of information. When she asked about guns and ammunition, Captain assured her the *Grace* was already a floating arsenal. "She's spent some time as a... munitions vessel, you see."

All the while, Beatrice shouted at them to smoke themselves to death. *Smoke yourself to death, smoke yourself to death, screech, whistle.* It was disconcerting to everyone but her master.

Ezekiel came in from his last run, bringing two hundred pound barrels aboard with ease. Though physically tireless, he was emotionally exhausted. "This is everything you wanted."

"Well, almost."

Ezekiel reared back with a fearful scowl. *"More essential items?!"*

Captain said, "No, no, I've everything I need, not to worry. But, this crew, they're old as the hills and there isn't a seaman among them. I'll need them young and strong if I'm to make it out past the third meridian." He tapped himself on the nose.

"Fine!" Ezekiel pitched into a violent trance, eyes rolling back. The sleeping bodies around him began to pop, squelch and transform, wriggling from the inside like larvae. Captain cringed. It was the sound of a classroom cracking its knuckles and squashing grapes by the bucket. It went on for grisly minutes.

When Ezekiel was almost done, Beatrice blasted out from her perch on the chair. "Rrrawk! Smoke yourself to *DEATH!*" The volume of it shocked him out of his trance and the simmering pops and squelches stopped.

Captain turned to smile at her, just in time to witness a burst of Ezekiel's temper. The bird's eyes sucked back into her skull as every living cell in her body split open and separated. She fell in a wet mass of once beautiful feathers.

Captain winced and looked away. He'd had Beatrice for years. He couldn't say anything that would make a difference. It occurred to him that every moment near Ezekiel was a moment away from death, for almost anyone but him. For him, Ezekiel made life a prison.

Out of vague self-criticism, Ezekiel said, "You could never love me, could you, Noah?"

Captain didn't waste any time trying to understand what that meant. He just said, "No, indeed," and lit his pipe. After a moment he offered some flat praise. "But, you can still be proud of all the good you've done."

Ezekiel was on the edge of a personal crisis. "All the good I've done?"

Captain motioned at his new crew. "Look at all the lives you've saved from the plague."

"The lives I've... *these?* You don't understand *anything* about life!"

Captain blew smoke. "I could say the same to you."

Ezekiel screamed. He couldn't take anymore. He dove overboard without another word and without completing the crew's rejuvenation.

29 Mission

Thomas wore a traditional sleeve, the gauntlets and boots buckled in. His white tabard had the same high, clerical collar, but instead of a golden circle, two broad, cerulean blue chevrons pointed up like cresting waves across his back and chest. It was the habit of Gabriel's new order of paladins in Calvary, *The Walls of God*. A bag of ashes hung from his belt and, secretly, Thomas endured a chafing, horse-hair shirt under his longhandles.

He arrived in Antioch with the coldest wind of autumn that year, three weeks after Daniel. Like Daniel, he'd come looking for a book from the bestiary, but he found more than that. Michael offered him stacks of sacred script to take back. Michael valued his translations more than the originals, believing it better to start a library anyone could read than to bother teaching a dead language. So, any volume with a sister in Meroan was Thomas' for the asking.

Thomas knew the script by then, he had a gift for linguistics, so it made no difference to him. He sat at the round table with an ancient text of Ezekiel's, wearing a delicate pair of spectacles to read. He was astonished.

Harold sat across from him, fairly astonished as well, not because Calvary had survived or because of the ease with which Thomas had mastered the script, but because of the way Thomas spoke. After barely more than introductions, Harold was convinced he'd never heard a more impressive barrage of gargling diction and ejaculatory I-saying than what issued from that man.

Thomas closed the book. "I say, I'm quite a bit jealous of you, Michael. I am. This has become a place of profound learning, discovery and advancement in our absence, hasn't it?"

Michael nodded. "It has."

"Quite so. Underground reliquaries, fire-in-a-stick and what-have-you. However, I *must* say that in Calvary we've a great deal of heathen people to our credit. Such an opportunity as that is a righteous wealth in and of itself. To have so many souls in desperate need of saving, I am observably content with my station there, you can be assured, and am proud to think of myself as *Gabriel's Wall*, in honor of his institution."

Harold's mouth fell open.

Thomas leaned in mischievously. "I've a confession to make, though. Do you know that I've decided to stay another three days, in order to attend one of your father's services?"

Michael smiled. "I'm glad, Thomas." He was.

Harold thought three more days of Thomas might be something of a challenge. It was a small church.

Thomas went on with humble pride. "Our mission, in Calvary, is fashioned after the spirit of the fellowship you understand. Only, my sermons aren't quite so rousing as your father's, of course, and I should like very much to hear one of his again before I leave, and take from that good example something to improve my own."

Michael said, "I've been escorting Faith to service on Sundays lately. We'll save a seat for you inside."

Thomas thought that was rather scandalous. "*Escorting a woman?* I say, it's good that you've taken an interest in the service, but that's a bit of a bold statement to make, isn't it? One might get the impression that you're, dare I say, *out and about?* I should think the implication quite inappropriate for men of our station and most desirously to be avoided! Such an impression might lead to disquiet or... irreverent rumors within the community, only serving to lessen the impressiveness of our advice, and thereby its influence. Wouldn't you say?"

Harold's hands were on his head.

Michael guessed *The Walls of God* had held on to a few of the Circle's vows. Instead of explaining that he no longer intended to remain chaste, or that he was more interested in Faith than religion, Michael politely repeated his offer. "Would you like to sit with us?"

"Oh, quite right, I should like that very much. Very much, indeed."

Harold couldn't restrain himself any longer. "I say, I should think, and quite rightly so, that I too find it most inordinately trying to tolerate Michael's indiscretions!"

Michael coughed out a laugh.

Thomas looked sideways at Harold. "Indeed? That sounds like cheek to me, sir."

Harold recoiled. "Surely you don't say!"

Thomas turned to Michael. "That's your man's cheek, is it?"

Michael put a hand on Thomas' shoulder. "Let's go have something to eat. You've been on a long road."

Harold gasped with pleasure. "Oh, I say! I rather should think a cider at the Cauldron would be most agreeable at the moment, and quite, actually, considering such wealthy conversation!"

Thomas frowned at Harold. "You, sir, shall soon find me to be thoroughly unobliging in *that* regard."

Michael laughed, but mostly because he was so happy to see Thomas. He ushered them out the door and they crossed the churchyard. He didn't leave a note behind. It didn't seem necessary anymore. Antioch hadn't seen an infection since the previous winter.

Thomas said, "I say..." and then paused self-consciously. Harold grinned. "I've been meaning to mention... Blast! About that bell! Do you know Gabriel used a horn to do the same thing in Calvary?"

Michael said, "Is that right?" and linked his hands behind his back. Thomas did as well and they walked side by side, a Wall-of-God and a brown-and-white. Harold followed, listening with interest to both Thomas' tale and the way it was told.

"Quite so. Gabriel trumpeted a stalwart vigil on it day and night for months, constant as the sunrise. The villagers started referring to him as *the rooster* near the end of it there - and not to flatter him either. But, the bauran's attacks finally did cease. That was a nasty business altogether with them. I should think we're quite content to exchange those troubles for the ones we have at present. And, that we've much cause for rejoicing to know that this good place still stands, along with Golgotha, as you've said. Yes, there's cause for much rejoicing indeed. *And...* won't Gabriel be surprised when, upon my return, I inform him that you've chosen for *your Wall* - a woman? I say!"

* * *

Andalynn was washing dishes in a tub behind the Cauldron, scrubbing them in the suds with a big bristle-brush. Thirty-five years before, when she was eighteen, she worked as a waitress for a woman named Mont'lemayor, also called Money-May. Money-May kept busy around the restaurant's kitchen, helping with the dishes and floors despite being the one in charge, and often said, *if you've got time to lean, you've got time to clean.* Andalynn respected that message: if work needs to be done, don't wait for someone else to do it - do it.

At that time on any other day, she would have been training with Michael. But, since he started attending services, she had Sunday mornings to herself. So, there she was, proudly washing dishes like Mont'lemayor. Shortly after service let out, she heard some children playing around the corner. They sang a song that sounded like something to skip rope to:

Churning in the morning
Up before the sun
clap- clap
Sister Sophie's courting
So she's never done
clap-clap
She'll be picking berries
A basket of the black
clap-clap
Butter churned and ready
Flour in the sack
clap-clap
The plunger made her blister
The pie turned out to burn
clap-clap
Sophie said to sister
I hate that butter churn!
clap-clap

Then one of them started to wail as though mortally wounded and the others fell silent. Andalynn assumed it was over nothing but went around anyway, just to be sure. A tearful little girl sat on the Cauldron's doorstep surrounded by her friends. She'd stubbed her big toe on the cobblestones while running around barefoot. The tip of it hung open in a bloody flap.

Andalynn said, "You have injured yourself. Do you need assistance?"

They hushed and stared.

Though the sailors had been in Antioch for a year, they were still mysterious strangers to the town's children, who'd spent much of that time carefully hidden away indoors by their parents. The sailors weren't just foreign to the children, they were alien. Andalynn's blonde hair and copper skin made her unlike anyone else in the world. The scars and the black scarf made her look dangerous. And, she wore pants. A few whispers passed through the group that she was the one who'd joined the church.

The girl with the toe was only six years old and too shy to answer. Andalynn sat next to her and said, "May I offer you hospital?" That was the way Michael would have said it.

The girl nodded.

Andalynn craned over the injury, checking it for grit, careful not to touch it yet. Then she put an arm around the girl's shoulder. "Lean into me. I do not want you to fall." The girl did. Andalynn patted her knee. "Put your foot up here where I can reach it."

The girl was frightened. "Don't touch it! It'll hurt if you touch it!"

"Yes, it will. But, not much and not for long. You do not want to lose that chunk of toe, do you?"

The girl reluctantly did as she was told and when asked if ready, nodded again, grimacing. Andalynn held her close with one hand and pressed the toe back together with the other. The girl took in a hiss and then suddenly fell asleep in Andalynn's arms. A shimmering line of gold sewed the toe back together under the shadow of Andalynn's hand. The other children gave appreciative *oohs* and *aahs*.

It would be about a minute before the girl could wake up. Andalynn held her rather than leave her on the ground. A boy sat down next to them and said, "My mom always says to wear shoes on the cobblestones."

Andalynn smiled at him. "Your mother gives excellent advice."

Others spoke their minds as well:

"My ma says to eat peas."
"Mine says to stay away from sailors!"
"That's dumb!"

Andalynn laughed and talked small with them, which for her was something of a challenge. When the girl woke up, her friends told her what had happened and she said, "Thank you, miss."

"You are welcome." As Andalynn said it, she felt a sudden urge to cry. She controlled it expertly with her path, like closing a curtain over the stage, but the thoughts behind that feeling remained; she was a healer. She brought comfort to those around her. She would never represent the System again.

The System was gone forever.

Andalynn expected the boys and girls to run off and continue their game but they did not. They stayed, asking questions and sharing random, embarrassing facts about their parents. Andalynn was entertained to be their entertainment. It wasn't long before it had been the most time she'd spent with children since having been one herself. She would have spent longer.

When Michael came looking for her, they all smiled up at him, said hellos and waved, Andalynn in a copy of their innocence, like a class and a teacher welcoming a visitor to school. Michael acknowledged all of that through a dark concern over another matter and cut the greetings short. "I've been waiting for you at the church. We need to speak."

Andalynn stood. "Is something wrong?"

Michael said, "Yes," and started walking.

She followed him, leaving the children behind. "What is it?"

"Over the last three days this has been weighing on me more and more. That's two of them now, Thomas and Daniel. I've been thinking about Samuel and Joseph in Tabor."

"Do you believe one of them will come looking for a book?"

"That would be a great relief, but we can't afford to wait for it."

"What do you mean? You want to go there?"

"No. I want *you* to go there."

Andalynn paused. He kept a brisk pace toward the graveyard. She caught up with him again and said, "Why?"

"To find out what has happened there, of course…" There was something else too.

"Is that really necessary? I am almost ready to take on a student. Our plan was to focus on teaching."

"I know. This is more important right now. Come, I've gathered a council. I hadn't expected you to put off training all day to play with children. We've been waiting for you. Better to discuss the rest of this with them, in private."

When they entered the church, Andalynn saw that the "council" was only Biggs, Harold, Captain and Ditch. They sat at the round table with a map spread out in the center. There was no humor among them. She took a seat there as well.

Michael closed the door. "We are not to repeat what we discuss in this meeting. Agreed?" The sailors nodded apprehensively. Harold already knew. Michael sat with them and said, "When the Circle split apart, we hadn't thought the plague would end like this. We anticipated lifetimes of its misery. Now that we're receiving visits from the others, we need to find out for sure if Abraham is in Tabor."

Captain said, "Why would he be?"

Michael explained. "The shortest path to Salem runs through there. Ever since that horse came back, I've been afraid something happened between Samuel and Abraham. Abraham undoubtedly still guards the secrets the rest of us decided to share. He won't hesitate to kill over that. If those two fought and Abraham won, he might have chosen to stay in Tabor. As strange as it sounds, he may have felt obligated to carry on Samuel's task in his stead."

"Why not just leave him alone then?"

"Tabor is only four days away. If the plague has truly ended, he might find some reason to come here, like the others have. We can't wait for that to happen and be taken by surprise."

Captain said, "Surely we'd be able to reason with him if he did. It's a different world than it was…" But as he said it, he thought of Ezekiel's warnings about the Circle, the ones that had originally made him so leery of Michael.

Michael was incredulous. "If Abraham is in Tabor, he killed Samuel and left all of Salem to die! You don't know him like I do. I nearly fought with him myself the day he left. Sometimes, now, I regret not having killed him then, when I had the chance. No. We have to strike first."

The sailors rubbed their faces and shifted.

Andalynn said, "You want to assassinate Abraham?"

"As ugly a word as it is, yes."

The table fell silent. The sailors looked around at each other as if to make sure they'd all heard the same thing.

Captain said, "If you do it, you might as well be doing the same for that entire town. The bauran may seem to be gone, but who's to say some spore of theirs isn't hiding under a leaf somewhere, ready to start it all over again?"

Michael said, "Better there than here."

Andalynn was disgusted. "We are not assassins! How could you think we would agree to this?" There was hesitation behind her words. *How could anyone think I would not?*

Michael said, "I appreciate your reluctance, but we would be foolish to think of Abraham as anything other than a devil now. If he comes here, he'll try to kill me. He'll try to kill Andalynn. He'll destroy everything we hope to accomplish and any security *our people* now have against the smoke, solely to uphold his vows. Truthfully, he would be much, much worse than a bauran loose in the city."

Biggs didn't like the idea of someone coming to kill his wife. He felt he could put a bullet in a man for that and walk away from it.

Ditch had almost died three weeks before; on his knees there in front of the stable, he'd unexpectedly welcomed it. Facing death had altered his perspective on life. He said, "If the guy's such bad news, let's just take him out."

Andalynn covered her face and groaned, wanting nothing to do with it. She wanted to be back on the doorstep with those little boys and girls or doing the dishes or doing anything other than talking about an execution. "No!"

Captain had seen more death and destruction than any of them. He believed himself, through his inventions, to have caused more suffering than any single person in the history of the world. He hated war. But, for every one he'd taken part or profit in, he'd been a recluse on the outside of society. Antioch had become dear to him as a home and Michael was convincing him it was threatened.

Harold said, "Abraham isn't the only reason to go. Commander Cumberland was on his way to Tabor with fifty King's Men at the same time my troop was coming here. I mean to find out what's become of them. Cumberland, the Circle and the bauran were all in the same place at the same time. Also, Michael's told me a band of outlaws was already there causing trouble. Anything could have happened."

Michael nodded. "The Carter-Miller Gang. I can't imagine a few outlaws being of much consequence to those others, though. There's no need to worry about them."

Ditch had an unsettling thought and leaned over to find Tabor on the map. "This place is four days out?"

"Yes."

"Might be nothin' but a mess a' bauran there now, man. Back on the boat, if things got nuts, we'd just put the water 'tween them and us, you know? But if we get too many a' them little skinny ones out in the open like that, we're gonna be dead, no escape. We can't run four days straight. They can."

Michael hadn't considered that.

Captain slapped the table. He was coming in. "You won't need to run. You'll have more than milk and rifles on your side this time. Aye, the more I think about it, the more I'm inclined to support an expedition. We'll learn a lot from it. And, we've got a lot worth fighting for here."

The others nodded. Then all of them looked at Andalynn.

Michael said, "Hopefully Samuel and Joseph are fine and only missing a horse. Hopefully, the plague has run its course. But I'll not rely on hopes or prayers where Abraham is concerned. If you refuse, I'll go myself."

Andalynn closed off what she felt about that. "I do not refuse."

Biggs said, "Oughtta try gettin' the line back together for sump'n like this."

Ditch said, "Right on, man."

Harold said, "I'm coming with you. Count on that."

Captain said, "Well, I'm not one to get in a dinghy, but I've other ways to lend a hand. I'll just need a few days to make them happen."

Michael said, "It's decided then. But all other concerns aside, we must be agreed on this - if you see him, use your Springstien

BOSS. Kill him on sight." He looked around for arguments. Though it was hard for the others to hear it like that, they agreed.

Michael was satisfied. "It shouldn't take much. He's just an old man when he's not channeling. That being said, it would be unwise to go within ten feet of him. Now, you can take a wagon along this route here…"

He pointed out the way. They gathered around and spent the rest of that day plotting the death of Abraham.

* * *

Captain had a lab behind the candle shop. It contained a jungle of local plant life that he'd collected for study. Shoots, creepers and cuttings flowed from pots and troughs all around the work benches and hung from the ceiling. He brought a few precision machine tools off the *Grace*, lathes and the like, capable of threading, boring and rifling metal. They hid among the leaves and the vines like miniature silver cities in a wilderness.

Tendrils of smoke curled up from his pipe through the greenery. It was the middle of the night and he was cleaning a homemade grenade launcher by candlelight, the exploder. Its revolving, six-shot chamber whirred and clicked easily. It was a product of his terrible genius, more advanced than anything he'd contributed to warfare in the old world. Each round of its ammunition was a cylinder the size of two hen's eggs end to end. It could deliver its payload from a thousand yards.

Captain looked through the barrel's hollow, examining the way for imperfections, and said to himself with a morose sort of resignation, "It's not a war. It's only a murder."

* * *

In the dark before sunrise, Andalynn stood looking out of her bedroom window. She'd seen movement in the tree outside. Biggs woke up and watched her from their bed. Her naked shoulders looked strong in the moonlit blue.

"You alright?"

"No. I am not." She was holding a sword.

Before Daniel or Thomas came, Michael asked Jacob to make that sword, as he would have done for any other acolyte. It was only a token of the Circle's history, however, in honor of both their new imperatives and of Andalynn's accomplishments. She did not know anything about swordplay and was not inclined to learn.

It was slimmer and a few inches shorter than Michael's, but still as heavy as a sledgehammer. Jacob considered it to be a feminine caligan. Traditionally, those weapons had four symbols etched into the blade's fuller, the script for a paladin's vows: Silence, Obedience, Poverty and Chastity. Andalynn had often poked fun at those promises. When Michael and Jacob presented her the sword, they pointed out three different symbols etched into it, the script for Knowledge, Healing and Peace.

She thought it was a beautiful sentiment and that Jacob's craftsmanship was that of an artist. Michael said he'd chosen the symbol for Peace to represent her path, because that is what he believed it to be. It had been touching at the time.

Biggs sat up in bed. "Could just let him go. Was his idea in the first place."

"No. He was right in bringing this to me. Michael's family is here. Mine is on its way to Tabor today. I have no choice in the matter."

Biggs got out of the covers, went over and put a warm arm around her. Her skin was cold. He didn't know how long she'd been standing there. He said, "This is sump'n's gotta get done. We'll just get it done n' then come on home, alright?"

She nodded, lost in thought.

"I love you, you know."

"I love you too."

* * *

Ditch did his pushups on the rug as the sun came up. It was the same room he'd been in for a year but now he had it all to himself. The roommate had moved out.

His workouts didn't last half as long as they used to, even less if he tried to sing. He kept it to himself but it felt like he had a hole in his tank. There were two short, thin scars, one on each side of his body, where Daniel had skewered him.

Ditch shaved, put on his leather jacket and went downstairs to have a bad breakfast, trying not to think about all the things he should have done differently. *You can't win a fight if you don't throw a punch, you know? Yeah, but what if you shouldn't a' been in the fight in the first place, dummy?*

Then he was out the double doors, ready to go. The old laundress across the way had just started to work. She smiled at him and waved. "Good morning, Ditch! What is up?"

* * *

At ten after nine, Welles kissed his wife goodbye. He'd married a local girl and was in her family's employ. They had a baby on the way.

Welles had outright refused to take part in the mission at first. But after giving it more thought, he decided that by going they were protecting their new homes and their new families. He didn't know that he could live with himself if he stayed. He headed toward the east gate with a duffel bag, his mask and his rifle.

30 The Massacre at Sawmill Proper

Harold said, "I'll just have to see one in action before I'll be convinced, that's all. I can't imagine one of those tubes being more effective than a stout king's-issue crossbow. Mine was on my horse or I'd show you."

He was speaking to a wagonload of sailors armed with rifles and a grenade launcher. Biggs and Ditch shared a look. Welles clicked his tongue at their cows from the driver's seat. Andalynn and the other two kept to themselves.

Since no one else felt like talking, Harold closed his visor and sulked in his armor, the full suit of plate. "I'm only trying to make conversation... This is going to be a long trip." His speech was muffled some in his helm.

Ditch felt sorry for him, Harold being an outsider among them, so he said, "Who does this guy remind you of?" The sailors chuckled. The muffling helmet and the general, unwanted chattiness were a little similar to Drake. Ditch decided to cut him a break and talk shop. "Look, man, some old-timey bow shot aint nothin' next to a BOSS."

Harold lifted his visor. "*Old-timey?* I assure you, the king's-issue is state of the art."

The sailors chuckled again. Ditch had a wide grin. "Oh yeah? It's good a one huh?"

Harold's manner took on some strut. "Well, that depends on who's shooting of course, but *I've* been known to keep my shaft in a hay bale at *sixty paces.*"

The sailors laughed. Harold had offered himself up as the butt of the joke, in more ways than he knew. The mood lightened some.

Welles reined the cows in to a stop. "Whoa there, whoa! Time to milk these two. Whose turn is it?" They all got out of the wagon, some with buckets and some to stretch their legs.

Ditch leapt out and said, "Thing's kind a' like a dinghy, you know, but you gotta milk it a couple times a day."

Harold said, "Whatever is a ding-gee? That sounds perverse."

Ditch laughed, took out his rifle and motioned for Harold to follow. "It's a little boat. Come on, man. I'm a' show you somethin' cool."

Andalynn had just taken a seat at the milking stool. She popped up and said, "No shooting!" Ditch gave her the thumbs up, as did Harold - a stiff, metal man with a smile - and the two walked off the track into the woods together.

Ditch said, "We gotta find a spot where we can see real far." They could tell the trees broke a little way to the south so they headed in that direction. When they stepped out of the forest, they looked down on a vast, grassy slope that descended into the valley, dotted with white rocks under a clear sky. The great expanse of blue meeting green was a reminder to them that the whole world still existed.

Ditch whistled, impressed. "Man, that's somethin." Harold had to agree. It was a spectacular view. They were unaccustomed to such space, having been confined in the city for so long.

Ditch pointed out and said, "Alright, see that big rock over there all by itself? That's like, what, about four hundred yards?"

Harold said, "Impossible. Nothing can shoot that far."

"Pfft, we could shoot way past that if we wanted to. I'm just givin' you somethin' to look at." Ditch put the rock in his scope and looked for a distinguishable mark on it so he could brag about how a BOSS could hit that mark at that distance accurately, over and over. He planned to explain that he'd never even fired one before Biggs had taught him how on the *Grace*, showing how easy a BOSS is to use, and therefore making it a whole lot better than some old-timey-crossbow-shooter. But, at the base of the stone, Ditch saw a human skeleton in the moss and the grass and all of his plans changed. "Oop, found a bauran."

Harold drew his sword.

"Nah man, it's dead. It's all the way out at that rock. Here, take a look." Ditch offered him the rifle.

Harold had never looked through a telescope before and found it awkward to shoulder the rifle in his armor. It took him a few moments of confusion and wonder before he found the remains. "Ooh, I see it!" He looked without the scope for comparison and then through it again. "This is amazing!"

"Yeah, let's go get Andalynn. She's been waitin' for one a' these."

Not long after, Andalynn and Biggs went down the slope toward the corpse. He was carrying a pail of milk. When they were almost there, she said, "You might not want to see this."

"Woman, I's guttin' n' skinnin' deer 'fore you were born. Some ol' bones aint gon' bother me none."

Andalynn knelt next to the remains, took off her glove and stroked her finger through the inside of the fallow rib cage. It came out coated with a grimy residue. She put that finger into her mouth.

Biggs put his hand over his stomach and turned away, blowing out a breath on the edge of sick. He hadn't known she was going to do that.

She felt the infection take root in her tongue and fizzle against the riin. It was a bitter victory. "Captain was right. The spores are still active, even with the rest of it in this advanced stage of decomposition. We cannot be sure of the bauran's dormant lifespan."

Biggs shivered. "Eeeuh... You done?" He hadn't turned back around yet.

"I am."

He offered the pail. "Here, wanna take a swig a' this?"

She did and then dumped the rest of the milk out into the skeleton's chest. "I apologize if I have disturbed you."

He shook his head. "Nope, nope. You were right. Should a' listened." As they started back up the slope, he tried to shake away the image of what she'd done. Then he said, "I did not want to see that."

* * *

Though the nights were frightening, they were confident in one another. They took turns standing watch and were able to get some sleep. Harold became an honorary sailor along the way.

They were ten miles from Sawmill Proper on the morning of the fourth day, rolling up the track not knowing what to expect when they got there.

Harold said, "We'd thought this was a more important town, actually. Antioch doesn't produce anything, you see, and the Circle, well, certainly sounds like a fairy tale, doesn't it? We really could have ignored the fellowship not paying its taxes. Tabor, however, supplies lumber to a few communities of note in the north. Or, at least they did. The place was built around its sawmill. That's why it's called *Sawmill Proper* in the books. *Tabor* is the name of the mountain."

"Been here before?"

"No, but I've been told you can hear the whine of the sawmill blades from miles away. They're somehow powered by the mountain's stream."

They never heard the sawmill blades and when they arrived on the outskirts of Sawmill Proper, they didn't see a wall, which would have been a primary goal for Samuel or Abraham there. They decided to back up quietly, leave their wagon out of sight and get a better view of everything from a ridgeway trail. It was after noon. Looking down through their scopes and spyglass, the tiny town appeared to be deserted. It was one dirt lane with wood plank buildings in rows on either side.

They spoke in close whispers.

Biggs said, "Wanna let out a clear-call n' see what happens?"

Andalynn said, "No. We should wait a little longer before we... there, one o' clock."

Harold noticed them all aim in unison at her mention of the time. He followed their line of sight. Something in a suit of armor had stumbled out of the town's south side, partially hidden behind a sign that read, "Logan's Tavern."

"Is it bauran?"

"Don't know. Look, he's do'n somethin. What's he do'n?"

"Is he drinking? I think it is a King's Man."

"Let me see! Let me see!"

"Shh!"

"Give him the spyglass."

Harold looked down with hope that turned into disgust. The man below tilted so far into his drink that he fell backwards. Then there was a pathetic struggle to get up. Harold saw the beard of a slob and armor that was filthy, dented and piecemeal. One of the man's hairy legs was bare.

Harold said, "That's no King's Man. That's a drunk."

"What's he do'n down there?"

"I believe we can rule out bauran at this point."

"Maybe the King's Men stayed here with Abraham or Samuel."

"That is *not* a King's Man."

"But if Abraham or Samuel's down there, why isn't there a wall around the place?"

"Maybe they didn't..."

Harold raised his voice just enough to gain their attention while remaining within the whisper range. "Hold! I am telling you, *that* is - not - a King's Man."

Biggs said, "How do you know? Y'all all look the same to me."

Harold opened his arms. "Do you not see the dignity of my bearing?"

The sailors' expressions ranged from amusement to impatience, but any of them would have admitted Harold was immaculate. He'd traveled for four days through the woods in a wagon, wearing his armor the entire time, and that armor sparkled. So did his teeth. He was clean-shaven and completely confident he was saying the truth.

Harold said, "I represent the king. I do not conduct myself like *that*." He pointed into town.

Biggs laughed.

Harold's face went flat. "Yes, well. I think he's one of those outlaws." The sailors passed glances around, considering it. "And, since I am an officer of the law, I should go down there and have a word with him. So," He saluted and started down.

Biggs stopped him. "Hold on now, that aint such a bad idea. Bein' a local boy n' all, maybe you can find out a lil' sump'n too. Maybe even get ol' Abraham to come on out into the street?"

Harold said, "Certainly," impatient to head down.

Andalynn said, "Be careful, Harold. If that man is an outlaw, I doubt there are any King's Men in town. They would not stand for such an imposter, would they?"

"Certainly not."

Ditch started loading the grenade launcher. "Don't worry, man. If a bunch a' goons jumps you, we got your back."

Harold gave him two metallic thumbs up and then clanked down the trail. When he arrived in the street, the suspect was still on his back but no longer trying to get up. Harold leaned over him, blocking out the sun, opened his visor and smiled.

"Hellooo! You're quite drunk aren't you? From whom did you steal that armor, my good man?" Harold kicked the bare leg - *clank*.

"Aaah!" The drunk winced and groaned, tried to get up and failed.

Harold kicked him again - *clank!*

"Aaah! Stop!"

Clank!

"Stop! Stop it!"

Biggs had them in his crosshairs. "Looks like Harold's gon' beat it out of him."

Andalynn said, "Four more have exited the tavern. There appear to be five... six now. More..."

Ditch watched through the grenade launcher's scope. "Uh oh, Harold's in trouble, man."

Biggs flinched when he caught sight of the launcher beside him. It looked like one of Andalynn's Three-Fifty-Seven Pythons had swollen up into a bazooka. "Dadgum, Ditch! Careful with that! You even know what you're do'n?"

"Yeah, Cap showed me. You just put the thing in the thing and pull the trigger, man. It's not rocket surgery."

"Well, don't point it around him! You... you know what? All y'all just back up. I'll cover Harold. One a' you crazies gon' put a hole in the boy. Or blow him up."

The drunk groaned at Harold's feet. Fifteen men, all of them filthy and some in dented pieces of king's-issue plate, had come out to have a word with Harold. Both Harold and Andalynn had been right; none of them were King's Men.

Harold put his fists on his hips, proudly displaying his wolf's head shield, and stared those men down. "The Carter-Miller gang, I presume?"

The biggest, dirtiest one in the middle couldn't help but laugh at how this lawman would kick a helpless drunk in the street in front of everyone and without any fear of reprisal. There was a double-headed woodsman's axe over his shoulder. "It's my gang, now, eh. Carter's dead."

"I'm glad to hear it! Where did you steal all of this armor from, you great oaf?"

Miller and his men looked at each other in disbelief. Then Miller said, "I gotta respect your grain, fella, but we don't like the king's men around here. We kill the king's men around here." He brought his axe down into both hands.

Harold drew his sword. "Blackguard! Where is Cumberland?"

Miller had said enough. He charged.

Harold swept away with a grace that defied the encumbrance of his armor and flicked out his sword at the same time. The stroke was barely more than a gesture but it left a cut three inches deep in Miller's throat. Miller had just enough time to notice a spilling sensation over his chest before he collapsed. The gang was shocked.

"He... he killed Miller..."
"What are we going to do?"
"I don't know, get him?"

Harold closed his visor and lowered his posture, almost into a crouch. He intended to slaughter every single one of those outlaws. It baffled him how such a group of disorganized miscreants could have defeated even one King's Man, let alone Cumberland and a force of fifty. Then he noticed the other two hundred former lumberjacks that had come out up and down the street, many of them wearing pieces of the king's-issue. A crowd of townsfolk gathered to watch as well.

The outlaws murmured, "What are we waiting for? Kill him!" in a hundred different ways. The ones closest to Harold advanced, axes in hand.

A bullet slipped through the air. An outlaw's shoulder exploded a few yards from Harold and a roaring call like distant thunder came down from the mountain. The man screamed in the blood, his arm hanging from his body by the meat. Then, in an explosion of bone and brain, the man next to him was headless. High thunder rumbled from the mountain again.

Andalynn looked away from her spyglass to Biggs. He was completely committed. He'd never taken a person's life before having just done it twice in the space of five seconds.

Biggs locked in a third round and waited to see what the others would do. He'd come to kill Abraham, not a bunch of lumberjacks. If he had to, though, he'd imagine them as mindless zombies to make it easier.

Harold straightened up, having to guess that he'd just witnessed one of the sailors' rifles in action. Everyone backed away from him, thinking he'd made those men explode. The screamer bled into shock. Some people said, "Witchcraft..." Others shouted, "Get away from him! Shoot him!"

All along the street and on the porches, the outlaws brought out king's-issue crossbows and were aiming to loose. Harold ducked under his shield and braced himself. The bolts, six inch iron spikes, came in a rain. Most skipped and glanced off of him, many missing entirely, but a few hit the right angles to get through. One nailed his shield to his forearm - *ptank!* Another pierced his armor at the ankle - *ptank* - and lodged in that cluster of bones like a horrible hinge. Harold cried out and fell to one knee.

The outlaws started winding up their plundered crossbows with cranequins, cranked gear-boxes with a rack and pinion. It was the only way to draw the tremendous weight of those weapons' cords.

Before they could release a second volley, Ditch took aim on a group of them with the grenade launcher. "I'm a' put one in them crossbowers."

The launcher kicked hard, like a BOSS. The grenade punched through an outlaw's body so rapidly he didn't even shudder and it was deep in the ground behind him before it detonated. That man never really experienced the egg-sized hole it left in his stomach. There wasn't enough time.

The blast was a dome of light. It demolished the nearest building, a two story brothel with six rooms - blew it away like dandelion seeds. It left a crater that spanned the street and obliterated twenty-seven people instantly. The shockwave sent Harold crashing through a porch railing on the other side of town. Men and women were shredded and dying everywhere in the debris. Others had their hands over broken ear drums, screaming and running for their lives.

The sailors stared down, awestruck. Ditch set the launcher on the ground and backed away from it. Captain had warned them not to use it on anything closer than a hundred yards, but none of them had expected it to be so devastating. Andalynn took off down the trail toward the destruction, ignoring Biggs' shouts for her to come back.

Biggs decided not to chase her. He'd cover her instead. "Alright, alright, alright... ever'body just stay calm. We're lookin' for Abraham now. That oughtta bring him out."

Ditch trembled and swallowed. "What'd I just do, man?"

The crew watching from the ridge, Andalynn sprinted to Harold first and lifted his visor to touch his skin. They'd have to pry the bolts out of him later. There was no time. People were dying everywhere. The closest one from there was the drunk lying in the street. When she opened the way in him she saw that, somehow, in the midst of all that crossfire - bullets, bolts and blast - he'd been completely unharmed. She'd done little more than put him to sleep.

Andalynn almost kicked him. She ran to the next body and then to the next, sometimes sealing bloody stumps in golden light, sometimes arriving too late. She didn't know it, and wouldn't have congratulated herself for it, but she saved more lives that day than she'd taken on the *Grace*.

Abraham didn't come. Most of town had run for the woods as fast as they could and didn't look back. When the drunk woke up, he stared at the crater and the empty space where the brothel had been. Others woke up to discover they were missing limbs, friends or family. The blast-site swelled with cries of anguish.

When she'd done what she could for the wounded, Andalynn decided to interrogate that drunk. At first sight of her he said, "Fwah! Who're you?" He'd been sobered up by the hospital and completely bewildered by the scene.

She tried patient lies at first. "A traveler. I require..."

"What happened to your face?"

"I was injured in the blast. Tell me..."

"What blast? What's go'n on around here? Where's the cathouse?"

The wailing sadness around them became too much for her. Andalynn snatched a fistful of his hair, gripping hard enough to scalp him if she wanted to, and growled at him through clenched teeth. "Answer my questions!"

He grabbed her arm but she was blazing with riin. He couldn't have budged one of her fingers. She twisted her grip and he felt a pop on top of his head like the flesh was pulling away from his skull. "Ow! Yeah! Ok! Ok!"

"I am looking for a man in a white sash with a gold circle. Have you seen anyone dressed like that?"

"Yeah! Yeah! Bout a year ago! Let go! Let go! OoowOOOW! Seen a couple of 'em like that! Aaah! One caused a bunch a trouble, real old fella, looked a bear'd pawed him! Othern's a big fella, preacher! Aaah!"

Andalynn released him. "What about a man named Samuel? He would have come into town last fall with another man named Joseph."

The very sober drunk rubbed a patch on his head like he was trying to start a fire there. "Sss! Didn't meet no Samuel or no Joseph. Old fella had a kid with him. Preacher's by his self. OooOooh... Lady, you're a jerk!"

Andalynn asked him a few more questions. Harold limped over. Later, up on the ridge, she told what she'd learned. The drunk, whose name was Sawyer, had never even heard of anything like a bauran. Abraham had only passed through. Sawmill Proper had survived the plague for an entire year without a wall or a healer.

31 Armageddon

Only one man was fishing off the piers that morning. The other fishermen were either at the festival or sleeping it off. When he saw the warship *Vesper* on the horizon, he stared at it for a full minute before realizing he'd dropped his good pole into the water. When he noticed his hands were empty, he didn't care.

"No one's going to believe this..." Pirate ships sailed in children's tales by the fire. They didn't *exist*.

He took off up the boards into town, shouting, his brilliant, cerulean blue shirt fluttering from his suspenders. "There's a ship on the sea! There's a ship on the sea!"

A few merry-makers were curious enough, or drunk enough, to go have a look. Word spread and Meroe started to gather - *for the first time ever* - to watch a ship come in. And, it was coming in fast. They followed the cliff's ridge as a gawking mob, watching as the minutes passed, as that heavy moment built until the ship would crash. Their hands went to their heads with gasps and exclamations.

The *Vesper*'s unbelievable bulk hit a full, raking stop, breaking its hull on the coast in an explosion of white geysers. Its sails rippled and bent as the crew spilled forward on the momentum over the rails and into the raging collision.

The natives rushed down to help, taking familiar paths, and the undead crew saw their coming as stars shooting out of the darkness. The pitching waves couldn't bend the light of riin. Ink washed in. Then thin, black-eyed pirates crawled out of the spray, bones jutting from their wagging skin and hoops of clothing, smoking from their silently open mouths. Their breath made the wind burn.

Meroe ran.

They ran back to town, shouting, warning that evil ghosts had risen from the sea. The ignorant watched out of their windows in disbelief, but also in cold dread that they were about to witness what could not be. At those first wiry fiends that scuttled into view on skeleton's hands and feet, many couldn't help but scream.

It was already too late for some, those who'd unwittingly brought doom into their homes, in their bodies and on their clothes. Others chose to stand and fight. They fell. No matter courage, skill or implements, it was a rout in which the corpses overwhelmed the heroes.

Meroans climbed to the highest parts of their houses and shouted to each other from the rooftops and balconies like they would during a flood, trying to decide what to do. Bauran gathered below the voices. The town divided into two desperate efforts with those shouts:

"Wait for Gabriel!"
"No, we must make for Breahg!"
"Gabriel will come!"

Most made one of those choices.

They, who stayed, hid and listened to the others run away, a shouting and stamping descent into gravid silence. They'd locked themselves in to wait. Some looked out over the hours with hope torn into horror at their neighbors coming back to life in the streets. The sun set. All throughout the night windows shattered and people screamed as the dead broke in and broke out. Some changed their minds and ventured into the poison, always to return. Some gave themselves away by weeping. The sun crossed the sky again before a more lasting quiet fell over Meroe, a stretch of silence in which the staunchest holdouts in the safest corners met their inevitable ends from dehydration.

The flight to Breahg Bog faced two sleepless days by foot over the heath, chased by tireless ghouls. But, they had a favorable wind and there was a cruel certainty in their numbers and the distance if they kept moving; at over two thousand men, women and children, there simply weren't enough of the fast ones to catch them all.

A mass of younger bauran set the flight's pace to a hard walk, any slower than that were caught. The older bauran skittered in the gap, like spiders on the web, straight to the weakest and the loyal. They'd spend precious time with their captured lights, turning them over and picking at the shadows while the other lights swept away.

Those who died on the walk did so holding onto a strong desire: *We must make it to Breahg.* They made other final wishes, prayers and pleas, but *that* desire was particular to what they would become. It told where to go. When their eyes filled with ink and the smoke rolled in their lungs, that desire remained as an instinctual memory: *Something important is in the bog.*

* * *

To the north east, where the green heath dipped into misty peat before it elevated into the gray mountains, Clan Breahg had built a village of simple, circular huts out of mud bricks, bone and hide. In the past, they'd followed herds of giant elk across the countryside as a way of life, terrorizing the towns and settlements in their path and earning reputations as savage warrior-nomads and thieves. Over the course of generations, they domesticated the elk, started a settlement of their own and left the past behind.

The elk were seven monstrous feet tall at the shoulder and had palmate antlers that could serve as banquet platters, sometimes twelve feet across from furthest point to point. They were the center of Breahg culture. Called "great war-moose," (though really a deer) they were meat, milk and mounts, shelter, weapons and living symbols of strength.

Lonny sat high over his, Wroughtvahk, on a tremendous bone and leather saddle that was almost a throne, hinged into the antlers with levers and thongs for driving. Lonny was a typical clansman, hardy, beard and hair long and untamed, clad from throat to toe in coarse elk-fur, brown and black. He looked like he'd burst out of his animal's back. The pair rode in surging leaps over the spongy turf, up a low rise into the village and right to the hut of the chiefs.

Lonny climbed down a ladder of stirrups and then punched the door a few times. It was a hard-leather shield and, from the way it took his knocks, looked like it could stop a kick from Wroughtvahk. The chief of the men, Histain, opened it and came out naked. Bulging and hairy, fat and strong and gray, his posture challenged anyone to find a better man than him.

Lonny grinned and bit his tongue before he said what he'd come to say. "You're not going to believe this, but I think *Meroe* is coming at us."

Histain put his fists on his hips and laughed. "What? You've been in the huckleberry jug, haven't you?" Huckleberry whiskey was the drink in Breahg. They drank a lot of it.

The other chief - the clan's sexes governed themselves - was an ample vision of creamy skin on the dark furs inside, named Haukrith. Reclining with her own nude confidence, silver streaks in her tousled hair, she said, "Get out of here, Lonny."

The insides of their huts were like the outsides of their elk, musty fur and antlers everywhere. Under an opening in the roof that kept and let the rain and the smoke out, a peat brick fire smoldered in a ring of stones. Next to it was a water-well. Their homes were symbolic of their values, the elk and the earth sheltering the halves of life together, fire and water next to one another like man and woman. The peat held meaning for them too. It was a piece of earth that burned even in the damp.

Lonny stopped himself from ogling the one chief to keep the other from punching him. "Uh... sorry to be a thorn, but you should come have a look. And, we should bring some friends."

Histain turned back to Haukrith and shrugged. She rolled her eyes, waved him away and started dressing. They'd have time later. Their children were grown and in huts of their own. They'd nothing but time on the bog.

Lonny led the chief and eight other elk-borne warriors bounding out over the miles to where what appeared to be an army was trudging through the mist. It was difficult to tell at that distance, but there seemed to be two or three hundred of them, blue dye popping out like patches of sky in a muddy river. The riders passed glances at each other, considering the odds.

Lonny was disgruntled. "Told you we'd need more than ten..."

Histain soured at their concerns. *Cowards...* Then he decided to show them. "Breahg! The fire still burns! Look at me! Look at my heart!" He pulled a lever to flick spurs into his nineteen-hundred pound beast-machine, Hrothvel, and leapt toward the beleaguered Meroans. He'd cut a road through them. He'd show the others, those *youngsters*, that warriors still fought with their hair blazing in the wind. "Heya! Hrothvel!"

They were impressed. Histain heard them following. But, the first Meroan he was close enough to make out was only a woman holding a baby. He pulled back on the levers and slowed to a stop, looking down from Hrothvel's antlers like a man in a tree.

The woman gave him a rabidly determined stare and kept walking, clutching her bundle in both arms to her chest, her veins standing out and her teeth bared and clenched. Histain was speechless at the sight of her. She was fleeing something at a fierce walk, having crossed her body's thresholds to save her child. Neither said a word in the passing.

The other riders pulled in to watch the strange invasion firsthand. Almost all of them were women with children. There were no men, only a few boys and those had their little hands hitched in their mothers' veiny grips. The Breahg called down to ask what was happening.

The Meroan women's throats were so parched they couldn't speak above whispers, and none of them would stop the march. If they'd been able, they might have wailed that their beloved men had sacrificed themselves to give their families more time. Thinking about it made them want to die. Only the urge to protect their young had kept them alive.

Some rasped, pointing backwards, but most had driven themselves beyond the ability to communicate. They could only go. The Breahg scratched their heads and then rode around to see what hounded the women. Fifty yards back, a ruddy skeleton scuttled out of the mist on all fours, its muscles cords that creaked like twisting leather. That time Histain was among the hesitant glances and it was Lonny who took action.

Lonny said, "It's me! It's me! Heya! Wroughtvahk!" and bounded toward the bauran. To the others' surprise, it made no attempt to get out of the way - it changed its course to attack. A hush came over them. *It charges the great war-moose...* Wroughtvahk's antlers lowered, pierced the skinny little devil like a bug on a fork and lifted it wriggling into the air.

Histain cupped his hands to his mouth and shouted, "Brain him, Lonny!"

Lonny was on it, having already drawn out his bone-hammer, a club with a blade of stone lashed into one end. He reared up in the stirrups and brought it down in both hands on the bauran's head - *spack!* A black gout spat out of its skull and its body went slack.

Wroughtvahk flicked it away like trash.

Smiling and spattered with ink, Lonny raised his weapon and shouted, "Breahg!" They all cheered his victory. And, when more of those devils appeared, the Breahg took up the fight. They weren't idle, whiskey-drinking hut-men then. They were a war party. They leapt onto the skittering fiends, stamping them to pieces under the hooves, tossing them from the antlers and smashing them with bone-hammers, all while riding high above the meager smoke. It was easy, until the rotting army of the young approached, fifty to one.

The warriors nodded eagerly. Odds like those, how welcome they'd become, how *good.* The great war-moose would cut swaths through *them,* like grooves into the fallow to make bricks - like rolling thunder in the shadows - riders striking from the saddles. *Battle!*

The war party charged, slamming into the crowd of corpses, knocking them into the air, cutting them apart and trampling them. One elk plowed into the middle, spearing too many to lift. His rider drove him hard into a rut of flesh until they stopped, bauran spilling into their wake. The smoke curled up thick and churning from the young. One warrior and then another fell, gasping for breath into the grasping death.

The elk-borne didn't mourn their fallen. They were fighting - *killing* - not protecting anything or anyone. They were killing because they loved it and they were purified by the violence. If they bled they'd let it flow and nod their heads and swing again. If they burned they'd *let* it burn them - *burn them black* - and swing again!

The mass of young divided, some limping after separate elk, some broken to a crawl and some destroyed. The bog was a smoking massacre. The war party bounded over it with lusty battle-cries. *Heya! Grithsdel!* The giant elk launched and landed with destruction. *Heya! Nathanseffer!*

Hrothvel and Wroughtvahk crossed the field back and forth into exhaustion. They took in too much dirty spore. Their mouths foamed, their great lungs rattled and mucus hung from their nostrils in ropes. They'd given everything and were dying.

Lonny and Histain knew it. They'd been fighting side by side. But, there were still bauran in the mist, a few in cerulean blue now. They decided to ride their elk clear, to avoid crashing at the enemy's feet. As they plodded, out of breath in the saddle, their hair clumped with sweat and their faces burning from an infection they didn't understand, Histain quoted an old something his father used to say:

"There we stood, ten against a thousand."
"They rushed us..."
"And, we slew all ten."

He finished it with a wicked grin. Lonny grinned back and they laughed and coughed. While their beasts drifted on, the riders climbed down and jumped off, bone-hammers in hand. Hrothvel and Wroughtvahk fell less than a hundred feet apart, with the tremor of giants returned to earth.

An hour's walk away to the north, there were comfy huts, good, frisky women and whiskey. To the south there was only battle. Lonny offered a more common Breahg adage in response to what the chief had said. "If you're gonna get dirty, get filthy."

Histain bared his teeth. They charged back into the smoke together, shouting, "Breahg!" Three answering cries came from the elk-borne alive and one of those still rode high, raining blows.

* * *

Haukrith's black and silver was pulled back into a bun with bone hairsticks, the ends beautifully carved into elk skulls. Her cold gaze narrowed in the firelight on a Meroan she had by the collar. She gave her a little shake. "Where are our men?"

The woman's eyes rolled under their swollen lids like bloody eggs. Her mouth stayed open when she spoke. It was a breathy, feverish whisper. "They're dead..."

Haukrith leaned in closer. "Who killed them?"

"Ghosts..."

Every Breahg in the hut groaned. No one believed *that* but *that* was all any of these Meroans had to say. Haukrith dropped her the six inches to the fur and stomped outside. The entire village had gathered around, learning of the emergency.

Haukrith shouted, "This one's got the same story as the rest. Put all the google-eyes together and stay away from them. They're sick or something. Start locking yourselves in. Whatever's done for them's on its way for us." The women nodded and went about their business. She'd been barking orders at them since the Meroans arrived. The men, however, just stood there looking confused. Histain or Lonny usually told them what to do.

Haukrith shouted into a fury at them. "Your chief is *out on the BOG! GO GET HIM!*" They passed glances around at each other to see if any of them would follow a woman's orders. There was a lot of open-handed shrugging and head scratching until they did. Then all forty-seven remaining warriors readied their saddles.

Haukrith pulled her son out of them and said, "If your father's dead, kill the ones who did it, and after that - *take it back to their blood.*" She'd want an evil vengeance for Histain's death. And, though only seventeen, her son quickly swore that he'd grant it.

* * *

John knelt in the church, meditating on the past. He reached a point of clarity, stood and went right to knocking on the library door. When Abraham opened it, John said, "I need two weeks to go home for a visit." He hadn't asked for leave in more than eighteen years.

Abraham didn't give it a moment's thought. "Go right ahead. Take three."

John nodded and strode out, an embodiment of determination. From back in the library, without a mark on his face, Michael said, "May I have some personal time as well?"

Abraham frowned at him. "Wherever would *you* go?" Michael never really asked for leave either, but the church was practically surrounded by his family.

Michael knew what he was about to say would irritate Abraham. It gave him pleasure he tried not to show. "This month is that festival for Gabriel in Meroe."

Abraham grumbled. "Mmrnmhrn…" Then he held up two rude fingers. "*You* get *two* weeks." Michael pulled his chin into his throat at the sight of the offensive gesture.

He walked into the stable while John was saddling the pinto. The older man offered an explanation without being asked. "It's been so quiet lately. I keep thinking of my nephew. It feels time to heal the breach."

Michael nodded on his way to saddle Ares. "Ah, very good. I'll ride out with you until we part ways then." There was unspoken warmth in their friendship. John had been almost a father to Michael over the years and Michael had been close to a son.

They shared some agreeable riding, campfires and conversation. Then they stood next to their horses at the crossroads where the dirt lane led off through the field to John's farm. The southern sky darkened on the horizon from the coming of an oceanic storm. They'd be soaked before long.

John swung into the saddle with a sad smile. "Wouldn't it be something if Horace just walked out and waved?" He didn't expect it to happen.

Michael got up too. "I hope he does."

John gave him a curious smirk. "What could possibly interest you at that festival? All you'll do is brood."

Michael smiled. "It was the company on the ride out I was interested in!" They laughed. "And, I don't mind their music. They play those lutes. Hopefully it isn't ruined by a bunch of drunken partygoers. I really do hate parties."

John said, "Oh, I hate them too," pleasantly mocking the other's attitude.

Michael glanced south and saw someone staggering toward them on the road. "God's mercy, here's one of them now… barely on his feet. Just look at that blue shirt… garish. Meroans really have no humility whatsoever." He shook his head and clucked his tongue. Then a lash of smoke crossed his face. He brought his hands up and started coughing.

The spores brushed into the pinto at the same time and she gave a start. John's eyes widened - his skittish filly was about to bolt. He took a firm hold on the reins, immediately and completely concerned. "Easy girl… Fwah."

She took off to the north with John shouting, "Whoa! Stop! *Stop!* Gah! You stupid horse!"

Michael had endured the pain long enough. He opened the way, seeing in that moment what it was. "Plague…" He snapped a look at the staggering Meroan, jumped down from Ares and ran over, unfastening a gauntlet as he went.

They met before his hand was free. The bauran's aggression and appearance came as a shock. Michael had to shove it away to get the glove off. It came right back at him and they wrestled, him trying to heal it, it trying to bite and thrash him. Michael was stronger. He threw it down and pinned its rotten head against the road with his bare hand, searching, confounded. It was empty.

He tried and tried to find the way as its poison bled into the wind and as he neared the decision to destroy it. Whoever it had been before, it was a devil now. He picked it up by that blue shirt and flung it twenty feet out into the field. It flailed through the air, smoke tracing an arc behind it, and then - *flump*. It got right back up and kept coming while Michael went to Ares for the sword.

When John returned, the pinto was unconvinced and ready to bolt again. Michael stood in a pint of ink between the bauran's smoking halves, wiping his blade.

John didn't know what he was seeing. "Michael... you killed him?"

Michael turned around, showing his naked hand. "No! It's plague! The way wouldn't open! It wasn't there..."

John snapped a look at the road home.

Michael's mind was racing. The corpse boiled contagion into the air. He knelt to examine it and said, "John, go to your family. See that they're safe from this."

"I can't... I..." If it was plague, he couldn't justify going home to a remote place like the farm. It was days away from the larger populations at risk. *I can't go home, can I? Is my son already dead? Is the last of my blood gone?*

Michael stood up with a golden glow in his eyes, mail sparkling on either side of the white. "John, as the templar's consecrate I command you to investigate the farm down this road. Go."

John's emotions fought against his sense of duty. Though he wasn't a model paladin, he'd given up much for the Circle and believed they stood for the right. The crossed roads were too many. He let Michael's order point the way, turned his pinto toward the farm and rode.

The storm came and went.

* * *

On a woodland path east of Antioch, birds on the chirp, Samuel and Joseph rode toward Mount Tabor Sawmill. They'd left the church the day before. Samuel sat astride his red roan, Rascal, worrying that Abraham would be the one to go to Salem, knowing the way to there led through Tabor. *What will Abraham do when he discovers I've betrayed him?*

Joseph bounced along in tow on the DB cow. "You know, after I failed loyalty, I almost gave up and went home to Summerset. I was devastated."

Samuel smiled, missing those front teeth, and put his other thoughts aside. "You hadn't failed loyalty, Joseph."

"Oh yes I did. Abraham let me have it in the worst way! I don't know where you were…"

Samuel chuckled at him. "No, you didn't. It's that crucible that's a betrayal. You're told you failed for one unfair reason or another, to test your resolve with the injustice of it. Why was it again, that Abraham *let you have it?*"

Joseph's face was open disbelief. "For eating at the Cauldron on a Tuesday!"

Samuel laughed.

"It's not funny!"

"You didn't think that was strange? A little too picky?"

"I thought it was something I'd missed in my studies! I've been killing myself over that!"

"Well, it's a good thing you didn't go another year with that attitude. Abraham would have held you back again if you didn't at least complain."

Joseph shook the bulk of the lie from his head. "Loyalty takes more than a year?"

"Oh yes, it's the long one. You never really fail it, unless you give up."

That made Joseph angry. "I don't see how that tests a man's loyalty at all."

"It doesn't, of course."

"What?"

"Well, none of them do. You can't test for a man's virtues. The crucibles are meant to have one or another in mind but the only thing any of them really find is resolve. We're not especially honest or loyal or *tolerant...*" Samuel chuckled, remembering Gabriel's dynamic failing of that one. "We might have some of those qualities, sure, well... not *all the time,* of course..."

"What are you saying?"

"The crucibles only test your determination. That isn't the spirit of them, now, they're intended to find virtuous men. But, the reality, what I've come to find, is that determination was all we ever needed."

"Do the others see it that way?"

"Only Abraham believes in the Circle's righteousness anymore. Even Michael's had his eyes opened."

Joseph was shocked. He'd counted himself among the virtuous elite, among the white knights, since he was thirteen years old. "All these years... I've... I'm... Well, there it is."

Samuel nodded. "Even then, it's the templar's decision in the end. If he doesn't think you're worth ordination, he won't waste any time with you at all. Where's the virtue in one man's opinion of another?"

"I can't believe Thomas didn't tell me."

"Thomas is a prat."

Joseph shook his head, the shock becoming amusement. "You didn't tell me either."

Samuel gave him a beefy, cheesy grin.

Joseph said, "At the very least, I can take comfort from Abraham having wasted so much time on me. He must have really liked me after all." They chuckled and then they laughed.

They rode east and up into the mountains toward the deep forest on the northern face of Mount Tabor. Samuel divulged other interesting secrets as they wound through the rocks and the trees. Then, to Joseph's further confusion, Samuel turned them off the way onto a smaller, wilder path that descended southward into the valley.

Joseph looked back, scratched his head, looked at Samuel and then back again. He said, "Sir, I think we're going to lose time if we go around the mountain first."

Samuel smiled but it was a sad distraction. The secrets he had yet to tell were harder for him. "Have you ever had huckleberry whiskey, Joseph?"

Joseph paused. "I can't say that I have..."

ANTIOCH 323

Samuel nodded, remembering the taste. "Best drink in the world. It's because of the peat smoke. When you dry the grain over a peat fire it makes the liquor earthy later on. Gives it a... peatiness."

"Peatiness. I see. Shouldn't we be getting to Tabor? We're headed the wrong way. What's going on?"

Rascal stayed the course. "I never planned to go there. We're going to Breahg."

Joseph's eyes expanded. Then his arms flapped out and he said, *"Why!?* Why in the world would you want to go *there - now?"*

"Because I think they're still alive."

"But you'll be days out of the way! Tabor will fall, the smoke will get through and everyone in the north will die!"

"The smoke travels on the wind. Saving Tabor won't make a difference."

Joseph had a creeping fear that his master had gone insane. "Does saving *Breahg* make a difference?"

"It does."

"Why!? This doesn't make any sense! Those savages aren't worth breaking the line for!"

"I disagree."

"Oh, well, that's all that matters then, isn't it?" Joseph clenched and turned away. The original plan had given him hope for his own people in the north. Samuel was abandoning them. Joseph felt that he couldn't argue and that he had no choice but to follow. He was powerless.

Samuel tried to explain. "The smoke is on the wind. We can't stop it. Nothing can. Wherever I plant myself, that's where people get to live. I'm not going to waste that on filthy, lawless Tabor. When everything ends, I want this to be the decision I made, right or wrong."

"But why *the clan*? I agree with you about Tabor, to hell with that place, but why not go to Summerset, where I'm from? They're good people. Why go to Breahg?"

"Because I'm Breahg."

Joseph was stunned.

Samuel handled it gently. "Shave and a haircut, we look like everybody else."

Joseph didn't know what to say, so he said something stupid. "But... But, Breahg isn't allowed in the Circle."

"Well, I lied to get in, didn't I?"

It took Joseph a long time to respond. Out of the five, he'd always been closest to Samuel. He knew now there'd been lies between them, but he'd known Samuel's kindness and patience as well. Those hadn't been lies. Joseph hadn't known he'd ever met anyone from Breahg. "I feel like I've never known anything."

"I'm sorry, Joseph." It was only an apology.

The silence between them didn't last long. They were still friends. Some things just had to be accepted. Samuel answered Joseph's questions and they spent two days on the ride putting the pieces into place. At night, by the campfire, Samuel read his book of bauran out loud. By the time they reached the hillock over which they'd be able to see the village, Joseph's hopes were on Samuel's side. They left their animals at the bottom and dropped to a crawl at the top to spy.

The earthen huts out and below were surrounded by hundreds of Breahg and Meroan bauran. Peat smoke came out of some of the openings in the roofs. The people within had been burning chunks of their walls to keep warm.

Joseph said, "Look at all of them gathered around the huts. You were right. They're still alive!"

"And those devils are waiting for them, just like Horace under the tree."

"I can't believe they haven't starved."

"You can last a long time without food if you've got water. Those huts are built strong with their wells inside."

Joseph was encouraged. "Surely this is an even better cut-off than Tabor."

Samuel nodded. "It's much further south. And, the plague will stick in this bog's valley like flour in a wet spoon."

"Alright, what are we going to do?"

"We aren't going to do anything. You need to stay as far away from this as possible. I won't be able to stop fighting to give you hospital, or protect you while you're asleep." Samuel rubbed his mouth, thinking. "There are hundreds of them down there. I can't handle them all at once. Michael says they pile on top of you until you can't move. I have to split them up somehow."

Joseph got an idea. He looked back at Rascal for a moment, the horse known to throw paladins, and gauged his own horsemanship against his chances. "I can ride Rascal through and draw them out. You can take them once they're scattered."

Samuel said, "That's too dangerous..." but he couldn't think of a way to do it alone.

"What are you going to do then?"

"I don't know…"

"Let me help you."

Samuel paused. "Are you sure?"

Joseph remembered what Samuel said two days before: *When everything ends, I want this to be the decision I made, right or wrong.* "It would be an honor."

Samuel's chest swelled with love and respect and he embraced Joseph. Then he said, "Rascal's no great war-moose, but you've the fire of a rider!" Joseph didn't fully understand what that meant but it sounded like a powerful compliment. They smiled at each other and went about forming a plan.

The cow could graze. Samuel left his scabbard on the hill. Joseph sat in Rascal's saddle. Samuel reminded him, "Hold your breath when you come through and don't bring them back around until I'm out of sight. We don't want to give them too much to think about."

Joseph nodded.

Samuel went on, worrying over his young friend, "And don't spur him too much or jerk him, that's what makes him pitch. Rascal likes to have a say in where he goes."

Joseph nodded again, ready.

"Good luck, Joseph."

"You too." Then Joseph screeched out, "Heee-YAAAW! Raaascaaal!" and galloped toward the village, whooping, hollering and raising a ruckus. Samuel stayed low and watched.

Sure enough, the bauran peeled away from the huts and went after the horse, some of them with surprising speed. Samuel noted to himself, "Those must be the old ones." They flooded out of the village like ants out of a mound. Then Samuel ran down without a sound and destroyed the few that had stayed.

His technique wasn't as clean as Michael's. Samuel swung a caligan like a club. He swatted them around, breaking more bones than he cut, but he got the job done. Then he hid behind a hut and waited. Rascal and Joseph shot by a few minutes later, kicking up mud and leading a line behind them. "Heee-YAAAW! Samuel! It's working! It's workiiing!"

Samuel smiled at Joseph's bravado. Then he rushed out at the line's end and chopped twenty of them to bits without as much as a grunt. The rest pulled away and he ran back in to wait for the next pass.

A nearby door opened a crack and gaunt faces peeked out. Samuel turned on them, eyes glowing, and slammed that door shut. From behind the hard leather, they asked him who he was. Samuel replied, "Shh… I'm a wizard. So, you'd better stay inside." They gasped and repeated it to each other.

Horse and rider flew by again and again in a wide figure-eight that crossed at Samuel's hiding place. Samuel popped out to destroy the end of the line each time. The corpses piled there. They were little more than skeletons under blue shirts and elk furs and they hardly smoked at all.

But, they did smoke. A cloud built at the intersection and Joseph rode through it like a breeze, carrying it with him. The infection would have been impossible for him to avoid, no matter how long he could hold his breath. His boisterousness lessened as the painful spore crept into his body through his eyes, nose and mouth. The paralysis began.

Joseph leaned forward in the saddle farther and farther until he was lying down, clinging to Rascal's mane and cooing deliriously, "You're a good boy… aren't you? You're not a… bad horse. There you go… there's a good boy… only one… or two… more…" While Joseph faded away, Rascal kept playing the game, trailing them in a figure-eight, unguided. Then Joseph's grip failed and he fell, but Rascal stayed the course.

The bauran didn't have long with Summerset's light.

The horse passed by without a rider. Samuel's face turned the color of ash. He rushed out, saw the last of the monsters gathered in one spot and started screaming at them, "Here! It's me! To me! Here!" They came. Samuel finished them like Michael's story, moving in a backward circle.

Joseph lay motionless at that path's end, his yellow plaid and acolyte's tabard torn and muddy. Samuel rushed over to him and knelt, fumbling with a gauntlet, but he could already tell it was too late. He tried to open the way but his brave, young friend was dead. Rascal trotted up and snorted.

Samuel snapped. "You threw him, didn't you!? You threw him! You miserable animal!" He stumbled up with his caligan and took a vicious swing on the run. If Rascal hadn't flinched, the stroke would have opened him from ribs to tail. Instead it bit two inches into his flank through the saddle. The horse squealed and took off, spraying blood. Samuel dropped his weapon, fell to his knees and moaned into his hands.

He was a dark man when he returned to the village that night. He walked from hut to hut with a torch, punching the doors to knock. If they answered from inside, he'd give them hospital and made sure they stayed safe. If they did not answer, if they pounded and scratched and tried to get out, Samuel put his torch to the hut and turned it into an oven. Since the walls were made of peat, they smoldered even in the damp.

32 A Crucible of Resolve

Abraham rode a gold and cream palomino named Absinth. When the fellowship's hymns stopped, he looked over his shoulder. He'd never imagined leaving Antioch by any way other than death. He felt relieved to have those people behind him. His only regret was what had happened with Michael. He'd always been fond of Michael.

With better vision, Abraham might have spotted the two bauran shuffling in from the field toward town. Even if he had, though, he'd have just dismissed them as beaners late to service.

"Good riddance! You know boy, if there really was a God, there wouldn't be any damned religions."

Lot scratched his head, not sure what to take from that. He sat between their DB cow's bags, the leash tied to Absinth's saddle. "Sir, I have something to ask of you."

"I know. You want to go on crucible."

"How did you know that?"

Abraham rolled his eyes. "That's the only reason boys your age seek out the church. Did *you* know you only get to try once a year?"

Lot paused. "Yes, sir..."

"What was that business last night then?" Abraham mocked Lot's first words from when he'd burst into the church with Fergus. "*I... I just arrived...*" He turned around to look at him. "I knew you'd been sitting out there."

Lot slumped. "How?"

Abraham gave him a spooky stare. "I can see through walls..."

Lot hung his head in shame and defeat. Then he immediately made up his mind to follow Abraham around until next year, to try again. *Everyone's always trying to make me quit. I'm never going to*

329

quit. It all showed in his pulse and in his temperature, in his reflection.

Abraham was impressed. He chuckled and said, "Everything a child does is dumb and obvious. I remember when Michael was five years old. I swatted him on the butt to play. He said, *stop it,* and stalked away from me, looking all standoffish. He wasn't playing at all. He was serious! I'd offended his sensibilities."

Lot didn't care for being called a child, dumb and obvious, but kept it to himself.

Abraham said, "You're not the first boy to try making an impression like that. *Ooh, look at me, who knows how long I've been out here, ooh.* You can't go on crucible unless you've an advocate in the church. One of us has to sponsor you."

"You mean I haven't failed?"

"Not yet."

Lot's faced opened with delight. "Will you sponsor me, sir?"

"Mmm, I suppose I could. But then I wouldn't have anyone to talk to. It's a long way to Salem. I'll have to think about it."

All that day and into the night, Lot did everything. He milked the cow, saw to Absinth, made the campfire and made them a meal, salt-pork sandwiches. Lot did the very best he could to make sure Abraham didn't have to do anything, except relax. Abraham ended up with plenty of time to do that, but the boy's incessant conversation made it impossible. *Oh, sir, did you know... Oh, sir, I really want... Oh, sir...* It had the old man grumbling and rubbing his temples.

While cleaning up after dinner, Lot said, "The others left with their students too, sir!"

"Mmrnmhrn, is that what you think?"

"Oh, yes, sir. That's obvious. I've always really wanted to join the church, myself. Oh, sir, did you know..."

Abraham had had enough. He interrupted Lot with, "*The Crucible of Resolve...*"

Lot shut up.

"...is symbolic of everything you'll do. *Silence* is more important than - anything - boy. You're hoping to one day take the same vow of silence that I have. How old are you?"

"Fifteen, sir."

"Mmm, fifteen... you'd be thirty if you never failed. You can't even imagine the pressures of being a man, much less those of being in the church. Do you know how old I am?"

Lot found it difficult to tell when Abraham was talking to him and when he was talking to himself. He replied, "No, sir."

"Eighty-seven. I don't think I'll be alive in another fifteen years. Do you still want to do this?"

"Yes, sir!"

Abraham nodded and became very serious. "Then you must obey me. Do you understand?"

Lot couldn't believe it. It was happening! "Oh, yes, sir!"

"More important than that, today is September thirty-first. From *right now*..." He let that sink in. "...until sunset of this day next year, you may not speak. Do you understand?"

Lot nodded vigorously.

Abraham was impressed again. Over the years, he'd witnessed many initiates answer that second question. They'd say, "yes, sir!" or, "anything you say!" or, "*my liege.*" He had nothing but contempt for when they said *my liege* and was glad to see them fail that way, for any spoken answer broke their silence. The Circle was not interested in a boy who couldn't follow that one, simple rule: keep your mouth shut.

Abraham lay down on his blanket. Already the night was more serene. He went to sleep without any trouble, listening to the fire's crackle and the hooting of an owl. Lot had been expecting more ceremony than that. He sat on his feet, overwhelmed by his good fortune and didn't sleep at all that night because of his joy.

By the time Abraham woke up, rubbing his eyes and stretching, Lot had breakfast made, salt-pork sandwiches. The animals were packed and ready to go.

"Mmm, we're still alive. Good of you to keep a look out, boy."

Lot yawned in a smile.

Abraham said, "Careful..." and then chuckled to himself as Lot's pulse quickened.

That day, Abraham enjoyed the quiet for the first few hours. Then he became lonely for conversation and started trying to trick Lot into speaking. It was his duty to test initiates anyway.

Abraham searched in his pack as they rode along. "Do you want an apple, boy?"

Lot nodded but Abraham stayed turned away for a long time, forcing Lot to wait. When Abraham finally faced him and held up the fruit, Lot nodded again. Abraham tossed it over to him and said, "I forgot your name. What was it again?" That attempt was just insulting. Lot raised an eyebrow and took a bite out of his apple.

Abraham stroked his beard. "Mmm, now I'll have to wait a whole year just to find out what your name is... I should have asked you a few more questions first."

At camp that night, the forest chittering around them, Abraham lay down with his hands behind his head. "These bauran devils are everywhere from what I've been told. So, if you have any trouble tonight, just shout out my name and I'll try to help you. You'll have to shout a lot, though. I'm hard of hearing and difficult to wake."

Lot's nerves sprang and he looked around. The joy of being on crucible was starting to fade as he became more exhausted. And, being out in the wilderness had felt much safer before what had happened in Antioch.

The next morning, Abraham nudged him. "Boy. *Boooyeee.* Time to get up."

Lot didn't remember having fallen asleep. He shot up in a panic with his face and hands flared, astounding Abraham by not crying out. The old man was beyond impressed then - he was amused - and started planning a more creative way to trick a word out of the boy.

The crucible of resolve wasn't normally spent in the constant presence of the Circle's templar. Most initiates who had completed it had escaped with accidental speech at one time or another during the course of the year, in the haze of waking up or in the moment they found an insect crawling on their skin, simply because there hadn't been a paladin around to hear it. Lot's would be a difficult test.

That day Abraham was the one to incessantly converse.

"Things in their natural way work the way they're supposed to, boy. Men, beasts, plants, they all do what they're meant to do and the world works. It has an order to it. When things start doing otherwise, that's when you've got a problem. That's when a good, natural thing becomes a devil. For two hundred years, the church's mission has been to keep things the way they are. The way they're supposed to be. Sometimes that means stamping out a devil."

"Now, these bauran are aberrations, without a doubt, but they're strange examples to say the least. A better example of what I'm talking about would be oh, say... a gunder. Normally not a danger to people, but if he doesn't think the way he's supposed to, all of a sudden he becomes *terrifying*. You've never seen something so quick and so savage. Have you ever had a bad gunder where you're from? One that had to be hunted down?"

Lot shook his head. He'd never even heard the word "gunder" before. They used a different word for that creature in the north and none of Lot's people had ever seen one. The King's Men had destroyed all the northern gunders a long time ago. Lot didn't know of them as the half human crossbreeds they really were either. The stories he'd heard made them out to be a creepy kind of wood-geek.

Abraham made a raking motion over the scars on his face. "These are a gunder's."

Lot stared.

"Naturally, a gunder doesn't have a taste for man's flesh and is afraid of him. If they did, have a taste for us that is, there'd be no gunders or there'd be no men. That's the truth. But, they're meant to eat deer, and that's good, the way it's supposed to be. Every once in a while, however, one of them doesn't work the way he's supposed to... There are gunders in these woods, you know."

Lot was suspicious of Abraham's trickery by then, but stiffened up and glanced around regardless.

"There are outlaws in these mountains as well, evil men. When men do things they're not supposed to do, that makes them devils too. Did you know that? Rape, murder, heresy, these are the unforgivable evils of men, mortal sins. When men do them, they're devils too."

All that day through the forest, Abraham described different kinds of devils and the gruesome things they did to people. He mentioned gaffots and Lot recognized them by the description. In the north, they called those vampires. By the time they were at the campfire, Abraham had done his very best to convince Lot they were surrounded in the world by legions of evil.

The old man smacked on a salt-pork sandwich. "Mmm, once you've been ordained, you can never look back. To fight against the devils, you must become a devil yourself. That's why our vows are so important. Men aren't supposed to be this powerful. It's unnatural. By taking our vows, we agree to become devils on a leash - a leash of strict, inhibiting law. The other devils can see the evil in us too and often mark us as one of their own." He again made the raking gesture over his face.

Lot definitely knew what Abraham was trying to do and was frightened silly nonetheless.

Abraham yawned. "Oh, it must be late. I'll just turn in. Now remember, if you hear anything, you shout out my name. You've got to be vigilant, boy, and quick to shout. Some of the things I've told you about can gut a man before he can even scream. Especially if he's not wearing any armor. Mmm, I've just thought of something. Fifteen years from now, oh, most likely more than that, you're going to fail quite a few crucibles if you make it through any of them at all. Anyway, when you're middle-aged, we'll have to look into finding someone who can make you a sleeve like mine. It helps protect you from the *claws* and the *teeth*, you see. Alright, then. Goodnight."

Lot wasn't about to have a good night. He twitched at every noise he heard in the forest. Then, when he knew for sure something was actually approaching, he shivered and listened to it come, hoping it was only an investigating deer, or better yet, a rabbit. It was not.

Lot watched, petrified, as a silent, black-eyed stranger shuffled out of the dark into their campfire's light. He knew what it was right away - a murdering gunder rapist. The bauran was upon him before he could react. It pushed him down and seemed to be trying to rip off his clothes. Lot tried to get away but it was too strong. He remembered that he could shout for Abraham. He kept his mouth clamped and fought.

As he kicked and flailed against the monster above him, its smoke fell down into his eyes and rode his breath into his lungs. Lot coughed. He tried as hard as he could to stay quiet, but he couldn't keep from coughing.

The bauran's weight suddenly lifted away and there was a sound - *whock*.

Lot didn't see what had happened. He was grinding his palms into his eye-sockets from the pain and trying to hold his breath, trying to force his lungs to obey. They wouldn't. With every cough, a spasm of remorse swept through his body, because he thought he was failing to remain silent. Each involuntary convulsion was quickly followed by a renewed determination to at least stop the next one.

Abraham had never witnessed such a raw display of willpower. He put Lot to sleep, eradicating the infection instantly. Lot wouldn't remember any of it. Abraham was sorry then for having tormented him and said, "Don't worry, boy. Coughing doesn't count."

* * *

They followed a path steadily upward into the mountains. The sawmill blades screamed from miles away. At first Lot thought it was the screech of some awful devil Abraham had told him about. But, it was too constant for that, too mechanical. Before long they walked their mounts in toward the wooden buildings of Sawmill Proper. They moved at a slower pace than the sailors would a year from then. It was near evening and it was cold outside.

Abraham surveyed the town contemptuously. "Mount Tabor Sawmill. I have never known a more lawless den of drunken lumberjacks. We must be cautious."

Lot smiled at him. Lumberjacks crossed the street, wearing red plaid shirts and big boots. Women made their way through town too, in dresses and pretty braids. The sounds of business being done came from all around. It was a welcome return to civilization.

Abraham said, "We'll stop here for the night and move on for Salem tomorrow. It's a longer way to there and harder than we've had so far. Also, there's a man here I want to see."

They tied Absinth and their cow to a post outside of Logan's Tavern. Some of the townsfolk recognized Abraham's habit from when Gabriel had come weeks before. They laughed, expecting soon to hear some more preaching in the street. Abraham lifted his caligan from the saddle and slung it around his waist, glaring at those townsfolk before going inside.

When they passed through the swinging doors, Abraham was severely disappointed. "This isn't a tavern. It's a *saloon!*" Lot peeked around from behind him. Logan's smelled like sawdust and something delicious. There was a big, warm fire in there too.

Carter, Miller and some of the gang were sharing a meal at the table by the fireplace. They were in the middle of a discussion about impending revolution. Miller said, "We do all the work and they take all the money. It isn't right. What we should do is stop paying our taxes. Hell, we should shut down the sawmill!" Some of them nodded and agreed.

Carter said, "Hold on, we'd have the law all over us if we did that. Let's keep our heads and pick our battles. No need to rush in to anything."

Miller said, "Let them come. We'll wait for them over the ravine. We'll drop an avalanche on them." There was more nodding and agreeing to that.

Logan ran the bar. He was a rough man who catered to rough customers. When he saw Abraham and Lot come in, he brought everyone's attention to them. "Looky here! Fancy britches, fella. What can I get for you and your little boyfriend?" The outlaws stopped talking to have a look.

Abraham went closer. "I don't have any money. I'll accept whatever you offer us for free."

Logan said, "You'll get what you pay for here, granddad."

"I'm a man of the church! Where is your honor?"

Logan looked around incredulously. "Same place as your money?" The tavern laughed.

"Fine. Tell me where I can find Samuel then. He'd be dressed as I am."

"You mean that big fella with the neck?" Logan motioned at his throat.

"No, no… shorter, missing teeth." Abraham motioned at his mouth.

Logan looked over Abraham's scars. "You fellas ought to buy some helmets."

Sawyer the drunk was at the bar. He said, slowly and seemingly about to fall asleep, "Logan, you… hodger. This here's one o' them preachers out a' Antioch. Don't you know nothin?"

Abraham did not like the Circle being referred to as *preachers.*

Sawyer said, "You'd better feed him…" And then he pointed at Logan with a wavering finger for a full three seconds before continuing, "cause if'n you don't, he'll spit on you somethin' fierce!"

Logan laughed. "Don't spit on me now, preacher."

Abraham was disgusted. "This drunken fool is referring to *hospital.* I'm a healer." It was his duty to offer it, whether hospitality was offered to him or not. He glared around the room as if he'd rather butcher them all than heal even one. "Does anyone in here require hospital?" None of those men wanted some strange witchdoctor laying hands on them anyway.

Sawyer said, "Oh yeah, that's the right, his spittle. It's magic!"

"No, no, you idiot! Hospital! Hospital!"

The tavern laughed.

Miller was gruff. "What's a healer need a sword like that for? Are you one of the king's men?"

"I don't serve a king."

Logan said, "Well, if you're not buying, you'd best be on your way, *healer.* I don't let just anyone loaf around in here, bothering my paying customers."

Abraham nodded. "Fine. Come, boy. We're not welcome." Lot's mouth fell open in silent dismay. It was cold outside and he wanted some of whatever those men at the table were eating. He was sick of salt-pork sandwiches. Lot pulled out a coin purse and showed it to his master. Abraham said, "Mmm, spend your money how you like. I'll wait for you by the fire."

As Abraham went to sit, and Logan went about trying to make a deal with a mute for food, Sawyer said, "Uh, oh, here he comes, Carter, clean your ears!" Some chortling and *ooh-woo*'ing followed.

Abraham stopped when he heard that name. He repeated it, "Carter?"

Carter was strong, confident and smiled where he sat. "That's right."

Abraham narrowed in on him. "What do you know about a gang of outlaws that's been causing trouble around here?"

Carter sighed. "You're not going to start up about God, are you? Your friend tried that already. Look around. It didn't work." Some of them chuckled about their godlessness.

"Mmrnmhrn… A man told me those outlaws raped his wife. What do you know about *that?*"

Carter shrugged. He couldn't control everything his men did. "Things happen in the world."

"So, do you confess to it then?"

"Sure, why not. What are you going to do about it, eh, you skinny old branch? Save my soul?"

Abraham opened the way like a floodgate as the lumberjacks laughed. Those men couldn't perceive the power washing over them. Abraham, however, could see riin better than what he could with his eyes. To him, the tavern was filled with ghosts.

Carter slumped over unconscious and hit the table with his face. Miller and the others looked at him, wondering what had happened.

While they were distracted, Abraham drew the caligan from behind his back. Holding it underhanded like a giant dagger, he reared up and then slammed it down through the reflection of Carter's heart, stapling him to the table with a violent - **KACHUNK!** Forks jumped and rattled on the plates. Everyone in the tavern leapt out of their chairs.

Miller roared and grabbed his axe. Then he collapsed. Another man drew a long knife from his belt. He collapsed. Abraham linked his hands, waiting to see if anyone else would try to avenge Carter. The rest of the ghosts swept away from him, collecting along the edges of the room.

Abraham took his caligan by the handle and pulled it out, leaving a three inch slot in Carter's body. Blood spurted from the wound and dotted their dinners, fried mountain catfish and potatoes. Abraham stood over Miller and said, "Any other rapists or murderers in here?"

The tavern emptied through its swinging doors. Logan ran out through the kitchen, leaving those men to die. Lot stood by the bar, stunned, holding his change purse by the strings.

The riin faded in Carter as his blood drained onto the floor, streaming from the hole in the table and over the sides. Abraham gestured at Miller. "What do you suppose this one's done, boy?" Lot couldn't say. Abraham wiped his blade on Miller's shirt and then put it away. "I guess it doesn't matter. Unless Samuel gets here soon, this whole town is doomed. Is that a *God* for you? What do you think?"

Lot didn't say a word.

William Harlan lives in Houston, Texas with his wife, Carrie, and son, Adrian. He's a pretty good Street Fighter player and a pretty loud singer.

Visit his website at www.WilliamEHarlan.com
Follow him at www.twitter.com/WilliamEHarlan
Like him at www.facebook.com/CircleOfSaints

Those sites will also have news about the next book of this series, *Golgotha - The Circle, Part Two.*

Made in the USA
Middletown, DE
05 January 2022

57649925R00195